THE COLLECTOR'S TREASURE

A SPELLBOUND CONSORTIUM
BOOK 1

A. Payne & N. D. Taylor

Names, characters, places, and incidents are the product of the author's imaginations or are used in a fictitious manner. Any resemblance to real persons, events, and locations are coincidental or used in a form of parody.

Payne
&
Taylor
Publishing

Cover by Mirella Santana

Edited by Lindsey Loucks

Proofread by Erica Cavazos

Glossary

Aisling: Pronounced Ashling or as Ashlin depending on the county in Ireland.

Avalon: Realm of the Faerie divided by two main factions, led by Queen Aeval of the Summer Court and Queen Morrigan of Winter.

bairn (Scottish): child

Bon après-midi (French): Good afternoon.

bonding: A pledge between two fae, tying their souls to one another. This is considered the closest thing the fae have to marriage.

brand: To bind an enchantment or magical spell to an object permanently or temporarily.

changeling: Offspring of a human and a Faerie. At the age of adolescence most are approached by their fae parent and offered a choice to join them in Avalon. The ones who remain in the mortal realm keep only a shadow of their powers.

Collector: Highly trained adventurers licensed to hunt down artifacts and to discover lost tombs. Men and women who become Collectors are paid well to risk their lives while exploring dangerous and legendary places.

Commandant: Chief of the Guardian forces. Serves one rank beneath a Vault's Marshal.

Diabolist: Magi who use dark magic gifted from pacts with demons.

Faerie/fae: magical denizens of Avalon. Fae are severely allergic to iron.

feytouched/feyblooded: A human with a fae in their lineage. Changelings who live mortal lives and bear children produce a feyblooded line.

Gaia: A magical realm that mirrors the mortal world, inhabited by the Sylvan nature spirits.

Gatekeeper: Magus employed by the Regency Board. They assist in covering up magical disturbances from the mundane public and often work in several media venues.

Guardian: The Vault's well-trained magical law enforcement operate as police officers of the magical society.

halfling: Offspring of a human and a Sylvan. Halfbreeds born from one of these unions can pass as human, but often bear the magical talents of their supernatural parent.

Healer: A magus who combines traditional medical training with magical spells. Typically nurses, doctors, and therapists adapt their skills to provide a service for the magical community.

High Council: A council of representatives from the magical community. Most members are wizards aspiring to become Regents and wealthy, high society mages.

Justiciar: Seven former Guardians chosen for their loyalty, integrity, and power. Each man or woman operates with the authority of a Regent with a worldwide jurisdiction. They are used to investigate claims of corruption and may overrule a Regent in his own Vault.

Magi (plural)/magus (singular): Any human born with the ability to harness magic.

malaka (Greek): a Greek insult akin to the English word asshole or wanker.

Marshal: Regent's second-in-command. Takes over during the absence or illness of the Regent.

mo chroí (Irish): Term of endearment.

mo stor (Irish): Term of endearment.

nagual: Shapeshifters of the Amazon rainforest able to take the form of a jaguar.

Otherkin: Supernatural beings who are not Faerie or Sylvan. Hags, vampires, and shifters are among their number.

Planeswalker: A magus with a rare talent to walk to any plane or realm of existence. Fewer than three or four live at any one time.

Prince of Hell: Seven high level demons who represent one of the seven sins.

Regent: Ruling official at the head of each major Vault. He or she is comparable to a politician, king, and even justice of the peace. Their rule is law.

Regency Board: Active Regents who convene twice a year to discuss magical law and changes affecting the entire mortal realm. Mundane humans and conspiracy theorists know them as the Illuminati.

Scribe: Researchers and administrative assistants employed at the Vault.

Seer: A magus with the ability to see the past, present, and future.

Shade: The corrupted mages or non-magical humans who bind their souls to a demon Prince to serve as his underling. In Catholic lore, this is known as Integration.

sidhe: Highborn fae of Avalon who resemble elves. They possess the strongest magic and rarely leave their homes in Avalon to venture to the human realm.

Sylvan: Nature spirits who dwell in Gaia. Many Greek myths stem from a time when the Sylvan walked more openly among men.

Vault: Very old magical organization and form of government for the wizards across the world. The Vault oversees all supernatural creatures in the mortal realm, from fae immigrating from Avalon to the vampires who require blood to survive.

Umbra: One of the seven realms, considered the glue that connects the other six worlds. The Umbra holds memories of the past, present, and future. Seers use it to gain visions.

ward: Spells cast to erect a magical barrier, usually in the shape of a circle. These may be used to keep something out or in, but their effects vary by the preferred magic of the spellcaster.

Prologue

Griffin summoned a witch light to hover over his palm as he and Aisling hurried along in the dark. They stepped by the edge of the lake, their camp nearly a mile behind them where their oblivious mentor and fellow students of magic slept. It was supposed to be an overnight field lesson to catalog Ireland's various magical creatures, which meant it was the ideal time for Griffin to get up to mischief.

It helped that Aisling had a wicked crush on him, and even if he didn't want to admit it to his friends, he had one on her too. Hell if he knew what to do about it. What to say half of the time.

"So... You'll turn away now, yes?" Aisling didn't look up at him when she released his hand to begin easing her sweater above her head, revealing a hint of tummy.

"Certainly." Griffin shuffled around with his back to her. Autumn, his familiar, kept him honest by snorting scalding steam when it appeared he might peek.

The small creature, no longer than Griffin's thumb, emitted a bold red glow and a surprising amount of warmth. The Faerie salamander preferred to appear as unintimidating as possible, and often took the form of a common red lizard with a slim tail.

"And you won't be taking my clothes either?"

He chuckled from behind her. "It crossed my mind," he confessed. Damn. Busted before the mischief even began.

Cloth rustled as she shed the rest of her clothing

"To the rock and back, then," she clarified.

"Aye, to the rock and back."

"All right, then..."

"Ash?"

"I'll not be dancing if that's what yer after," she called back, feet splashing into the cool water. "You can look now!"

"No, I..." He had a bad feeling about it suddenly. Something nestling in his gut told him to call the entire thing off. "It was a dumb dare, lass. It's too cold to be out there. I wouldn't want to get into it myself."

She continued into the lake until water swirled around her calves and then her knees. "You'll never be able to say I don't hold my end of a bargain, Griffin MacNeil."

It had all begun with a dare in the basement level of the Dublin Magus Archives. By day, the magical children of Ireland attended normal school like any other student, but in the evenings, they lived up to the expectations of their wizard parents by attending classes at the archives. They learned magic, charms, rhetoric, and the responsibility to harness their unique gifts.

Aisling may have been a year his junior, but he preferred her company over the students in his classes. She understood him, didn't discourage his mischief, and seemed to think him brilliant. And since she'd challenged him to a race with a friendly wager and lost, it was time to face her consequences.

She dove forward. For a long moment, she was nothing more than a pale shadow beneath the surface. A ripple preceded her head and shoulders as she came up for air.

"It's not so cold once you're inside," she called over.

Graceful strokes propelled her through the water, and he sighed in relief when she reached the rocky outcropping. Quartz gleamed upon its slick and mossy surface, tiny diamonds in the moonlit night.

"Y'did it. Now come back. That's good enough," Griffin called from the shore.

"Only a second," she called back. Her grasp slipped, and she plunged beneath the lake. She resurfaced sputtering.

"C'mon, sprite, swim back to me now."

Aisling started to make her way back with slower progress.

"Ash? This isn't the time to be proud. I'm comin' in myself to get you."

"Then we'll… We'll both be cold."

"I swam in colder conditions for the Collector Trials!" He shrugged out of his hooded sweatshirt. Autumn poked her crimson head from the pocket of the fallen garment and squealed.

"Griffin…"

"I'm comin' and there's nothin' you can say to change my mind about it. If somethin' happened to you, I'd never—"

He stared as spines emerged from the water behind Aisling, a trail of meter-high curved black lances glistening beneath the moon. He couldn't believe his eyes and stared at first before he found his voice.

"Ash, there's somethin' in there with you! Move faster! There's somethin' out there!" he called at the top of his lungs.

Autumn squealed in distress and terror.

The thing pursuing her gained rapidly. As it rose to the surface from beneath the once calm waters, the flicking of a thick tail writhed behind it like a boat's rudder. Its large maw opened.

"Griffin!" Aisling's frightened cry ended with a gurgle as she slipped beneath in her panic. She broke the surface seconds later, choking as she coughed up water.

What could he do against a monster as long as a school bus? Griffin kicked out of his shoes and sprinted toward the shore. He charged into the water and swam without a single plan.

The creature's mouth closed around Aisling. The last thing he saw were wide and terrified silver eyes in her pale, oval face.

"No!" Griffin screamed. Time stood still as he searched for signs of his friend or the beast who had claimed her. The murky depths revealed nothing, not even a single spine to be seen. Tears and lake water stung at his eyes, but Aisling was long gone.

For all of five seconds.

Five seconds were hours to Griffin who watched numbly as the monstrous beast broke the surface of the lake with a fountain spray that sent water in every direction. Its paddle-like appendages were short and stubby, designed to cut through the water. Each webbed arm was tipped in knife length claws and left gouges in the shoreline.

The saliva-covered girl appeared on the shoreline in a gush of water, unceremoniously deposited by the creature. She rolled across the grass and came to a motionless heap. It touched her pale, too-still body with its scaled snout as Griffin sped through the choppy waves.

The creature rounded on him as he stumbled onto the shore. Griffin staggered back and landed hard in the grass when it snapped at him.

"Get away from her!" Griffin snapped his fingers, calling a single flame imp. It bounded across the grass toward the lake monster.

Instead of fleeing, the reptilian beast lumbered forward to place itself between the fiery creation and Aisling. Sweeping its muscled tail through the water, it doused the baby imp and Griffin's hopes.

"Don't eat her... Please. You can eat me instead. It's my fault she's here. Just don't hurt her."

A quiet sob from Ash brought the creature's attention back to her. It nudged her shivering body again, and Griffin realized it was trying to protect her—from him.

They had met the spirit of the lake, a friendly beast trying to save a drowning girl. Only Aisling hadn't been drowning. But how could it know that?

"G-Griffin." Aisling's teeth chattered.

"I'm right here, dove. Right here," he called back to her while taking uncertain steps forward.

This time the creature didn't make any effort to warn Griffin back. Water slid up over the dull, slate blue scales as the reptilian behemoth retreated. Sinking into the lake, soon only the top of its snout and large, dark eyes were visible.

"Thank you," he said to the beast.

Then he grabbed his discarded sweatshirt and hurried over

"M'sorry, Ash. So, so sorry." Tears streamed down his cheeks as he wrapped both the sweatshirt and his arms around her.

Autumn scampered over and glowed with the intensity of a fully warmed hearth.

"N-not your fault," Ash chattered. The trail of tears trickling down her cheeks seemed to have no end. "I couldn't... I couldn't swim any faster and m'leg was cramping..."

His larger hand chafed against her bare leg. He couldn't pull her close enough and wished he could warm her with a mere wave of his hand.

"Was a stupid dare, just stupid. Oh God." he sobbed again, crying harder than the friend he held. "Don't know what I woulda done if…" The thought of a world without Aisling was inconceivable.

"You came after me…" She gazed up at him. "Griffin, you jumped in after me."

"Course I did. I couldn't… Christ, I won't ever dare you to do anythin' again. I swear it."

"Don't you dare let me win things."

"I almost lost m'best friend in the whole world, Ash. I don't care about winnin'. I'm just so damned glad to have you back."

With her out of the water and immediate danger, it all seemed less frightening. His gaze turned towards the lake in time to see the strange creature swimming away. The monster disappeared beneath the surface.

For a long time, the two held each other, quaking limbs stilling and silent tears ebbing. Griffin didn't dare let her go.

"Griffin?"

"Yeah?"

"Thank you for coming after me."

"I'll always come when you need me."

"M-maybe one day, I can come for you."

THE COLLECTOR'S TREASURE

Chapter 1

6 YEARS LATER

Serene notes of Celtic harp music filled Aisling's ears, gradually increasing in volume to stir her from sleep. She slapped at the machine clumsily until it silenced and lay five more minutes on the edge of sleep.

A rough tongue rasped her face.

"All right, Breda, all right. I'm up." On the pillow, a sleek feline with silvery-blue fur stretched out languidly with a wide yawn, earning an eye roll from Aisling who rose to her feet. "Oh, rub it in will ya? Horrible beast, you are."

The automatic tea machine greeted her with a fresh pot when she emerged from the shower. Before the hour ended, she had dressed for the day in dull office attire and braided back her long hair.

It took nearly thirty-five minutes on foot to reach the Dublin Vault, even with a stop for breakfast along the way at her favorite cafe. She enjoyed it on the run and was whisked into a flurry of activity from the moment she stepped into her place of employment. She quickly shrugged into her silver-trimmed white coat and rushed to help the influx of wounded wizards.

"What happened?" She swept her fingers over the brow of a ginger-haired man wheeled in on a gurney.

"Redcaps and a hag, Aisling," another mage replied. "'Fraid Kev caught the wrong end of a hex, though God only knows what she did to him. He won't wake up."

"Go let the Commandant know I'll look."

The next hours seemed to pass in a surreal haze. Guardian Sergeant Kevin Delaney was the unfortunate victim of a sleeping curse with a kick. He grimaced during his sleep and moaned between labored breaths.

Aisling sang in Gaelic as she worked. She had a talent for seeing even the most obscure threads of Faerie magic thanks to her heritage, and although she'd never met the sidhe lord who abandoned her grandmother, she'd inherited her gifts from him.

Soft light bathed her hands as she smoothed them over Kevin's forehead, her own eyes closed. With patience, Aisling unraveled the glistening threads of magic visible only to her. She plucked them as she would the strings of a harp, changing the discordant notes to pleasant tones that harmonized with her own song.

When she was done, the hex was gone. Kevin rested in an easy sleep with his breaths deep and even. Aisling's eyes fluttered open, and she swayed on her feet.

A pair of hands beneath her elbows kept her from falling. "You've been at that for hours, little cousin. C'mon, have a seat."

"What time is it?" Aisling found herself guided by her favorite cousin to a chair where a mug of warm tea awaited her. Fragrant notes of jasmine and peach wafted from the cup to her nose.

"Well past a proper lunch, which is exactly where I'm taking you once you can stand on your own," Krystine replied.

Between Aisling's fair porcelain skin and Krys's natural golden tan, no one would have guessed they were related. But they both carried the O'Brien blood in their veins, inheriting prestigious wizard ancestry.

"You will not be taking me from my work."

"I will so take you if I want. Commandant Whelan came by and watched for a time so I've been authorized to steal you away for a meal."

Despite Aisling's protest, the other sorceress prevailed and whisked her away from the building. It didn't take long for her to appreciate the gesture, however, once the cool whisper of the autumn breeze kissed her hair and restored her energy. The girls enjoyed a walk to a nearby cafe where they were seated at a shaded patio table to enjoy the mild weather.

"How are things at the *Magister's Almanac*?" Aisling asked, referring to the private paper that served the magical community.

Her cousin shrugged. "I'm off the bothersome gossip circuit finally. They're letting me cover real stories now."

"You almost got yourself killed to earn that promotion," Ash said in a disapproving tone.

Krys reached over to squeeze her hand. "We do what we have to do in my line of work."

Aisling sighed. "And how's Addison? I heard he was finally promoted to London's Lead Sergeant."

"He was, and he's already studying for the Lieutenant exams. Maddie and I baked a cake for him." Krys picked up a fry and munched on it. "Now, what about you? Ceara told me you missed another date."

Aisling grimaced. "Gran didn't waste any time, did she?"

"She worries, is all. Ever since that *malaka*—"

It wasn't the worst among the terrible insults her cousin had labeled to Griffin, but it bothered Aisling just as much. "Krys."

"You're *still* defending him?"

"I told you, I won't hear any more words against him. It's over and done. Let it rest."

Her cousin gave in and said no more. They finished lunch with lighter conversation, focused primarily on how Krys felt about dating a single father with a small toddler. After sharing dessert, they returned to the Vault arm in arm.

"Ceara has decided on a family dinner," Krys said as they reached Aisling's personal office. "You're expected to—" Her eyes glazed over as she stilled, going into a trance.

Knowing the look, Aisling waited until her cousin emerged from the vision.

Krys's maternal family line traced their ancestry to the Delphic Oracles. She was the youngest of seven daughters and the first in three generations to exhibit the gift of a seer. She saw the past, the future, and even events taking place over vast distances—a beneficial talent in her line of work.

Krys blinked the fog from her eyes. "I should get to the Regent now, Ash. I'll see you for dinner."

Then she left, hurrying out the office door and leaving Aisling to dread a family dinner with her grandmother. And whatever bachelor the old woman had convinced to court her this time.

"Jean-Luc?"

"*Bon après-midi*," the handsome Frenchman replied. "Is this still a good time for you, Mademoiselle Kavanagh?"

"It's fine, but how many times have I asked you to call me Aisling?" She pronounced it slow for him, otherwise he'd butcher it in his French accent. Ashling. Few people outside of Ireland ever got it right.

Jean-Luc visited her from the Parisian Vault, and she'd met never him with anything less than high spirits and impeccable manners. He'd quickly become one of her favorite patients, even if there was little she could do for his ailment. She'd tried all manner of curse removal, but nothing worked.

"At least one time more." He flashed her a dimpled grin. "Is everything all right? The young woman left in a rush."

"Oh, yes. My cousin took me out for lunch, but then she had to run off for work."

He gazed down the hall at Krys's retreating shape before she vanished around the corner.

"She's taken," Aisling said. "Dating a Guardian from Wales."

"Damn. You know me so well. So, are you going to invite me inside, or shall we discuss it in the corridor?"

Aisling blinked up at the lieutenant's smug face, realized he was teasing her, and then swatted his arm. "I would have remembered to invite you in if you weren't lecherously eyeballing my relative, I'll have you know."

Once Jean-Luc was seated at the desk, she prepared cups of floral-laced green tea for both of them and joined him in the adjacent chair. "I'm sorry for making you wait. The time always gets away from us whenever Krys visits me."

"It is no trouble. I came with plenty of time to spare and enjoy the time in your country. Such a beautiful place."

Beautiful was also an apt description for the young lieutenant. His dark hair nearly swept the open collar of his silk shirt, and he looked more like a model than an officer of the law with his flawless skin and perfectly straight nose.

Of course, she'd also grown numb to his good looks, first concealing her attraction to him beneath the veneer of professionalism, then coming to know him as a friend or a handsome older brother who enjoyed teasing her.

Jean-Luc stirred his tea absently and glanced out the window. To the human eye, nothing about him seemed strange or unusual. But when Aisling gazed at him with her magical senses, she felt the ripples of immense power, strange and alien to anything a normal mage possessed. Abnormal.

"You're quiet and you have tea for me," he said in a low voice. "That is never good."

"I wouldn't say it's bad either. More like nothing." She spread her hands and sighed. "I'm sorry, Jean-Luc, I haven't been able to find anything. Your case is unique."

He chewed his lower lip and glanced down at his porcelain cup. "I feared you would say as much when you phoned me to make this appointment. It is strange, you know? I imagine most people would be thrilled to have a second chance at life. After all, how many can claim to have died and come to life again? But this…"

Aisling studied him closer, hunting for signs of malevolence in his aura. Instead, she saw health and vitality. The strange power never appeared to cause him harm. "Perhaps it isn't a curse, after all."

He leaned toward her, aquamarine gaze trained on her face. "Are you certain? How can we know for sure?"

"Well, curses are usually meant to harm. To cause pain. They don't usually initiate miraculous resurrections."

"What else could it be?"

"I don't know," she admitted. "It's magic well beyond anything I know, but I wonder if we've spent these months looking at this the wrong way. What if it isn't a Faerie curse as I suspected before? What if it's…a blessing instead?"

Jean-Luc snorted. "If it is a blessing, I would like to know who bestowed it."

Aisling wondered the same. The power of life and death was beyond the means of any normal mage. Beyond even the Faeries of Avalon.

But if it wasn't a mage or a fae, who did that leave?

Chapter 2

For explorers like Griffin MacNeil, Egypt was a prosperous land of priceless treasure and deadly magic. He had always dreamed of conquering the desert's cursed tombs.

And maybe today he would.

"It's this way, fellas. We've already explored every alternate path, and this one's the final corridor," Jerry said.

"It had better be, otherwise you're doing a shit job as a cartographer," Liam grumped from the rear.

Griffin chuckled at the impatient Irishman.

Each corridor was lit by a cluster of ornate brass fixtures filled with enchanted stones. Without them, they would have had to rely on their own magical lighting.

Desiring one, Griffin studied it and wondered how the hell to unfasten it from the wall.

Jerry lurked behind him. "Interested in that little bauble, are you, mate?"

Griffin sighed. "I want to pry one of those lanterns from the wall for my daughter... I think she'd like it."

"Then you should've said so. You don't have the kind of tools for it, you know." Jerry folded up the map and tucked it away into his front shirt pocket. Suddenly, he had a knife in his hand. It gleamed like a diamond, sparkling in the gentle light.

The thrice-enchanted blade had been forged by the dwarves of Gaia. Jerry never sharpened it, but the edge could score and carve stone. The story of how he'd gotten it changed from telling to telling.

"Cut it down, then," Griffin said.

Jerry wedged the blade between the chain links and snapped them like dry twigs. "A second for your wifey?"

"No. Only getting one for Mara."

"No?" Jerry glanced over his shoulder. He was an average looking, dark-haired fellow just beneath six foot. His features were neither remarkable nor memorable, which had aided him greatly in his former occupation as a thief. "Mate, if I had a wife like yours waiting at home, I'd strip the entire ruin clean and leave nothing but dusty, barren bones."

"His wife's too petty for that," Liam chipped in. "If it's not from a high-end shop, it's trash."

Griffin grumbled. A year ago, he would have told Liam off for insulting his wife, but every word rang with truth.

"She never appreciates anything he brings home," Liam continued. "You ought to have heard him cryin' about the golden bangles she tossed aside without so much as a single glance—"

A rumbling noise overhead preceded a fine cloud of sand, ceiling debris, and dust speckling the shoulders of each man in the passage. Griffin shook out the tiny bits of rock littering his hair.

"What was that?" Liam asked.

Bertram shushed them. The tall Egyptian's face creased with a combination of age and sun damage. "Have we triggered a trap?"

"If we triggered something, Bert, you'd know it." Jerry sighed impatiently while Liam and Griffin exchanged glances.

More Collectors died in Egypt, Greece, South America, and Japan than any other place in the world. For those reasons, freelancers like Griffin's group made good money in the field.

Griffin couldn't blame Bertram for his panic, but this wasn't the time to freak out over a few creaks and groans in the ceiling. "Relax, Bert. It's only the ruin settling."

"No. Something has happened. Forget the artifact. We must return to the surface—"

"To hell with that," Jerry protested. "We're too deep now to retrace our steps."

"We've got your map, Jerry. We'll find our way back easily enough. We ought to hear him out and check the surface crew," Liam spoke up.

"I am going back with or without you," Bertram said.

Their world rumbled and shook around them with a thunderous noise from above. A crack split across the rocky ceiling.

Griffin did the only thing possible under the circumstances, by shielding both men beside him beneath a dome of magic. It flowed outward from his fingers in bright, pulsing shades of light as a deluge of rocks and sand showered the magical shield.

Too much. The force battered his senses, pushing against the strength of his mind like a chisel chipping stone.

Gritting his teeth, Griffin endured and held on to the end, only to fall to a knee when his strength gave out.

As his barrier faltered and flickered away, he threw himself into a tight ball and shielded the back of his neck and head with his hands. Rocks buffeted his shoulders and back until it finally stopped. The smell of the musty air filled his nostrils with traces of sand and grit.

When the dust settled, he heard the coughs of another survivor. Along with those pained, wheezing breaths, there was also a distant rumble that sounded like thunder.

A hot trickle slid down Griffin's brow when he angled his head down toward his shirt pocket. "Autumn, are you all right?"

She glowed red in response.

"Come on, lass. I need your help."

Autumn scuttled out of the pocket, emitting pulses of condensed crimson light to gradually spread and sweep farther over the dusty cavern. She crawled to Griffin's shoulder once he sat with his weight propped on both palms.

"Say something if you're conscious," Griffin called out.

"Something," Liam replied.

Large pieces of the ceiling lay in chunks around the two men. A motionless brown hand peeked from beneath the rubble near the path to their rear.

"Poor Bertram. What a crappy way to go." Griffin frowned. He and the other Collector may have butted heads often, but he'd respected Bertram's dedication to keeping their dig's safe. A sense of sorrow overwhelmed his exhausted body and drooped his shoulders even more. "Any sign of Jerry?"

"No, nothing."

Liam approached with a limp, favoring his right leg. Although blood matted his gritty red hair, he used his training as a field Healer to bandage Griffin first.

"What should we do now? Protocol states we wait for rescue, right?" Liam asked.

"Normally. We've got one man dead, and Jerry could have escaped by traveling further into the ruin. He might—"

"Griffin. No. If he escaped into the ruin, he'd be back to us by now."

"It's only a thought."

"I'd like to know where Jerry is as much as you, but if we're not present when rescuers arrive, they won't know where to find us."

Griffin hated to think about it, but he gestured toward the rocks. "Could be he's trapped beneath the rubble with Bertram." It was impossible to tell at a glance whether the debris concealed a second crushed corpse.

"Don't say that."

"Either he's under there, or he's in the ruin hiding, Liam. Take your pick. It wouldn't be the first time he ran like a rabbit and got himself lost."

So they both walked. They went side by side while they picked their way forward into the unexplored depths.

"That was a damned good shield, Griff." Liam's voice interrupted the silence between them as they carefully navigated the ruined tunnel by traveling farther into the unexplored pathway.

"It wasn't good enough," Griffin muttered. A better mage would have saved them all.

"It saved our skins. If you hadn't cast it…"

Neither of them wanted to consider the possible outcome. Griffin would have widowed his wife and left a child without a father. Liam was recently engaged.

Stairs carved in stone created a maddening descent for nearly half a mile, and sand spilled from the deep cracks in the ceiling. The deeper they searched, the more impatient Liam became. Griffin shook his head and sighed in defeat. Their map-maker was nowhere to be found.

"We've looked, Griff. Wherever Jerry is, he isn't injured or bleeding a puddle somewhere in these godforsaken ruins. Besides, he had no reason to run this far to escape that collapse."

Griffin squinted ahead. It would be a waste to turn around. "I don't like it. Try to send a wisp to the surface. I want to know what's happening."

"We know what happened. One of the tunnels was unstable from all of the digging and movement above, it collapsed, and we're trapped until they realize where to dig us out."

"Bullshit. It sounded like an explosion to me," Griffin said.

"The surface crew wouldn't blast while we were below the surface."

"What if it wasn't them?"

Liam summoned a wisp and silenced to concentrate on giving it a message. Seconds later, it faded through the rocky ceiling and disappeared.

It returned an hour later after the men had settled down to drink water and sort through their rations, preparing for the possibility of a prolonged stay.

"No response from above. It's scared. Now what do we do?"

Griffin shrugged. "We do what we set out to do, lad. We find the Crook of Osiris."

~*~

The unstable tunnels in the underground tomb didn't stop Griffin and Liam. Despite the danger from the rubble and loose sand raining down from above, they pressed forward.

They dug through a partially collapsed archway into an open room with two eternal torches framing an altar. Liam slid through with ease, but Griffin had to squeeze in sideways after scooping out a substantial amount of debris to fit his taller frame. The chamber's grit-covered floor ended in a growing slope in the corner where sand continued to spill in at an alarming rate. The room had no other exit.

"Hidden door, maybe?" Liam asked him.

"It's likely."

"So where the hell are we?"

"Beats me," Griffin replied with a shrug.

"A fine set of Collectors we are. Without our guide and trapped in an Egyptian tomb."

THE COLLECTOR'S TREASURE

Griffin kneaded his temple with one hand and dipped his head forward. The pulse seemed to pound right behind his left eye, the beginning of a brutal migraine. "Look. Jerry has the goddamned map, Liam. I can't remember it all offhand. I'll Xerox a copy next time. Satisfied? Does that make you happy?"

"I don't want to die down here, Griff. You've got that little girl waiting for you at home and I… Hell, Marjorie never wanted me to come along on this hunt, but I did it for *you*. I told her it'd be easy! An in-and-out snatch."

The payment from this job was generous enough to enjoy a year at home without working. Liam had joked he'd be lucky if the fortune lasted for a season with Mercedes blowing through their money as if it sprang from the sands. Griffin's wife had expensive tastes.

A blinking, dimly-glowing wisp descended from the ceiling after a desperate search to find them. It settled into Liam's upraised palm. The creature flashed orange. The two men exchanged looks with one another and waited anxiously for the fae to release its message.

A calm voice spoke in Arabic through the fae. *"Rescue attempts are underway. The dig site has been compromised and has taken substantial damage. Prepare to camp below ground for the night. Doctor O'Sullivan requests that you locate the Crook at all costs."*

"Brilliant. It's great to see where their hearts are in such a dangerous time," Liam seethed. "You're screwed by the way, so sit in the dirt for a night, and find our Crook whether you're dying of thirst or not."

"We're not dying of thirst," Griffin said.

"Yeah, well. They don't know that."

Liam used his talents as a conjurer to supply their canteens with fresh water easily. Water was always the least of their worries as long as he was at his best.

Faded murals decorated the wall behind the altar, which held four small statues. Three were grouped together on one end while a fourth statuette depicting Osiris stood apart. Liam moved up beside Griffin and crossed his arms over his chest.

"This one's yours. I hate puzzles."

"Appreciated," Griffin said dryly.

Griffin fiddled with the altar and was rewarded by a brilliant ball of flame. It came hurtling toward the back of his head. He swore as Liam redirected the flaming sphere into the pile of growing rubble in the corner. A streak of glass gleamed in its wake.

"Cutting it a little close, aren't you?" Griffin demanded. "Just because I'm flame retardant doesn't mean you've got to move like an old lad."

"My apologies. I expected that the professional puzzler wouldn't play with the dangerous altar without knowing what he's doing." Liam shook out his hands then scrutinized the blisters bubbling upon his fingers. He wasn't as fireproof as Griffin.

"Blow me, Liam."

"Mercedes would gut me if I moved in on her territory. What's it like anyway to be sleeping with a river succubus at night?" Liam asked.

Griffin didn't immediately reply while he was bent over the altar. He twisted the statues around with care this time. "The sex is amazing."

"She's a xana, Griff. Quarter, half, whatever it is, I'd be scared to death that she's going to swap a kid on me that isn't even mine."

"Mara resembles me more than her. Lass is like my female clone. Xana myth is a fairy tale. Mercedes is only a river nymph half-breed and nothin' more."

A rumbling noise preceded the slide of a hidden door. It stirred a cloud of dust.

"You want to play fast and dangerous with your piece, go ahead. I'm fine with my mortal girl. But tell me something, whatever happened with Aisling? I haven't seen you write her in months now. Not that she'll make mention of it."

"It's none of your goddamned business."

"Uh-huh."

Griffin grunted in reply and moved through the opening.

The clearing air revealed a cryptic line of hieroglyphics. Griffin was forced to tune Liam out to solve what appeared to be a rather routine and simple puzzle. Stone scraped against stone, revealing a hidden doorway.

THE COLLECTOR'S TREASURE

"See? Easy," Griffin said.

"So easy that you were nearly incinerated into a pile of foul-talking ash."

~*~

Days later, Griffin carried the fruit of their labors strapped across his back. The Crook of Osiris resembled a shepherd's staff with a curving, hooked end. After all they had been through, he had serious thoughts about asking for triple their original fee.

As time passed, they rationed out the remaining food and supplies between them. The humor of their Donner Party references gradually diminished until neither man remained in joking spirits.

"Wait!" Liam shouted.

Startled, Griffin nearly dropped his handful of crackers. "What is it?"

A week of traveling unrecognizable corridors and lantern lit paths had driven him mad with worry for his family. He missed his little girl, and his mother was likely beside herself with worry.

"We've been here! That's the seal of Anubis, and there's the juice stain Jerry left behind."

Griffin could have wept and kissed the ground in relief. The seal of Anubis was decorated with an accompanying mural depicting a small group of little human figures praising an obnoxiously large image of the god Osiris.

A statue nearby of a jackal-headed deity stood nearly as tall as Liam. The Egyptians liked to depict themselves as tiny compared to the all-powerful gods worshipped by their culture. Each human was only as large as Griffin's hand.

"I recognize the statue of Anubis too."

Liam used another precious pinch of Faerie dust and summoned a wisp to send to the surface. Eager for hot meals and soft beds, they rushed into a well-lit room where Liam stumbled over a jeweled scarab. He caught his balance by placing his hand on the shoulder of a jackal statue. Before his very eyes, stone rippled beneath his hand and became flesh.

Physical contact with the statue had activated an ancient magic, transforming it from stone to a living tomb guardian. After roaring its fury, the beast leveled its spear toward Liam.

Shit! Griffin hurled a bolt of frost at the creature. "Move your arse!" he shouted at Liam.

The effects of his elemental spell only angered the beast. It continued to snarl and snort steam from its nostrils, occasionally reaching over the distance with a slash of its well-sharpened spear. Neither of them dared to look behind them to receive more than a glimpse of its terrifying features.

"Kill it!"

"Even I can't kill an Outsider, you ginger galoot!"

They ran, but the monster pursued them with inhuman speed.

Autumn squealed, left the safety of Griffin's shirt pocket, and climbed to his shoulder. As she threw open her mouth, an intense jet of flame rushed out in a tight, compact line. She aimed for its eyes. The beast fell back with a roar and clutched a hand to its damaged face.

"Good girl, Autumn!" The fae deserved praise, even if Griffin suspected it was as much self-preservation as it was protecting him.

A mile or so of underground tunnel passed by before both men realized their pursuer had fallen behind. With his lungs burning for oxygen, Griffin leaned against the wall.

"Need to breathe," he rasped.

Liam wasn't much better off. "Thought you were...the one in shape? All of that...bloody running...and constant nagging...for me to get fit—"

"How often am I runnin' for my life?" Griffin asked.

"You're a Collector."

"Point made."

They took the climb to the surface at a jog, and eventually emerged from the tunnels on the other side of the collapse. Rocky boulders formed a slope down the middle passageway, but the dust was settled. Several lanterns lay on the ground. Some had spilled open to release their glowing contents on the floor, and others were smothered beneath the rocks.

Once or twice, it became necessary to twist and shuffle sideways through a narrow gap between a wall and a partial collapse, or to scurry over a slope of rocks. Griffin realized their path was mostly unhindered. If it wasn't the cave-in keeping their rescuers away for so long, then something else had.

When they went farther, they discovered signs of people recently occupying the area and evidence of an apparent rescue attempt. Abandoned gear. Blood on the ground.

"We're not out of it yet." Always Liam with the pessimism. Between the two of them, he looked the worst for wear. "Something happened here. This blood is fresh."

A blade came whistling out of the dark as an anubis rose from the stone of a statue positioned nearby. It ripped through Liam's flesh like a hot knife sliding through warmed butter, without resistance or even a tug. He went down without a fight, red soaking across his abdomen.

"Fuck!" Griffin jumped and threw up his hands defensively.

The next swing of the hooked blade met with a crackling shield of mana and energy. The anubis wrenched his weapon free and came after Griffin with renewed ferocity. It licked its muzzle and snarled while feinting left then right to get past his defenses.

Griffin wasn't the best elementalist, but he had spent a fair amount of time in study. Ice crystals glittered where patches of white frost spread out against the creature's powerful limbs, but that wasn't enough. Griffin couldn't maintain two complex spells at once.

Everything slowed for Griffin, and time itself seemed to stand still as he became aware of several things. He saw Liam on the ground, holding his gut with his hand. He saw the corpse of Jerry nearby in the shadowed corner, clutching his map with dead fingers. The mouth of their former cartographer was twisted open into a scream.

Griffin's last spell had to count. He charged his mana until it screamed to be released, the intensity burning his fingertips.

The curved blade ripped beneath Griffin's ear and caught into his neck. It opened his carotid artery. Hot blood spilled over his shirt.

Autumn screamed, but she was tapped out and useless to her human friend.

Griffin pounded it with everything he had, knowing he'd likely die for taking the offensive. He hated it for murdering poor Jerry, for what it did to Liam, and he hated it for letting them come so damned close to the exit before deciding to spring from the shadows of another conduit.

The anubis shrieked as its ears burned away in the white explosion of magical fire. Flesh melted under the assault of scorching heat, and it stumbled back blindly. Its weapon dropped to the sandy floor. Black and purple flames licked at its face and over its limbs, incinerating the flesh away down to the bone.

Griffin didn't realize he was on the ground until he felt Liam's hands on his gushing wound. He smelled his own blood, the stink of sulfur, and even brimstone as Liam poured magic into him.

"I've got you. Won't let you go."

"You... y..." Blood gurgled into his airway and bubbled beneath the hands that worked so quickly to save him.

"Don't try to speak. Help's on the way, Griff. Just hang on." Liam's gore-slicked hands kept Griffin alive, as his own life trickled away.

Chapter 3

About a month after the most devastating near-death experience of his life, Griffin stood in the office of Doctor Cameron O'Sullivan, Dublin's eccentric Regent. He couldn't remember much of what happened after Liam had healed him, the early days in Cairo's hospital a blur of agony and grief.

But he'd lived. He lived when so many others died. No amount of money would ever replace what he'd lost when the creature stole Liam from him, and each day since had been a struggle to endure.

Griffin stole a glance at his pocket watch and plastered a polite smile on his face. He should have been on his way five minutes ago for the Portal, but the old coot in front of him hadn't picked up the hint.

The Regent sported a wild mane of silver, white-streaked hair, a beard braided in dwarven style, and gold-framed rectangular spectacles perpetually falling down his nose. If his suit were red and if his belly greater, he could have passed for Santa Claus.

In the opinion of many people, he'd served too long as the protector and representative of Ireland. Was that why he wanted the Crook of Osiris? Did he plan to try to turn back time? Legend claimed the artifact could be used to outrun death himself.

"I'll gladly acquire the Goblets of the Sun for you, sir."

"Always a good lad. My assistant will contact you once we're ready to go ahead with the plan. It's a shame about Liam. One of the best field Healers the Regency ever had..." O'Sullivan laid a gentle hand on Griffin's arm. "If you ever need anything, lad, you be sure to ask. I appreciate what you both did for me. It won't be forgotten."

"Of course, Doctor O'Sullivan. I should be on my way. I've got a Portal scheduled to Barcelona."

"Well, please reconsider my offer, Griffin. It would be a pleasure to bring your talent to Ireland where it belongs. Full time work and all. None of this freelancing on the side. We'll pay you what you're worth."

"I'll keep it in mind. I really should go, or I'll miss my departure."

"Are you sure you wouldn't like to stay for t—"

"No thank you, sir. Take care."

Griffin left the office and stepped into the hall. Each Vault served as a hub for the world's magical seat of government, ruled by a nobleman known as the Regent. Doctor O'Sullivan was one such figure, and he had held his throne for over a century.

Beyond the storefront, there were over a dozen departments and offices dedicated to the different aspects of their magical culture. Most importantly, it protected their way of life and maintained secrecy from the mundane humans.

Griffin took the steps two at a time, and in his haste to leave, a young woman slammed into him at the stairs. Yelping in surprise, she clutched his suit jacket, her heel still slightly over the edge of the last step. The way his arm folded around her petite body crushed her against him so close he felt every curve outlining her body, but he couldn't see more than the top of her black mane of hair.

"Oh! I'm so sorry. Completely my fault," she said. As she leaned back, her gaze swept upwards and paused briefly on his scarred neck, then finally up to his face.

Silver eyes. Griffin recognized the mercurial color without delay. It was the rest of her he failed to recognize, finding it hard to equate the professionally dressed woman with the colorful girl he had known during his teens.

What the hell kind of growth spurt had she gone through?

"Aisling?" He had enough of his wits about him to wrap his other arm around her. "It's so good to see you again." After five years of separation... He hadn't seen her since months after his graduation from school when he'd tentatively returned to escort her to the Winter Gala in Dublin.

Less than two years ago, they tentatively began to write as pen-pals, a secret he had only shared with his best friend Liam.

Of course, Liam had been the one to convince him it was the right thing to do in the first place.

The changes to her physical attributes overwhelmed him when he saw how much she'd filled out since their teenage years. Her fair cheeks blushed rose as Griffin held her closely against him. She still smelled like lavender. Seeing her face-to-face brought back a rush of memories.

For a moment, he forgot how to speak, overwhelmed by the sight of her and tongue-tied.

How long had it been since he'd last held Ash? All he wanted was to continue holding her, and he'd be content to never let go.

"Griffin? You're here," she blurted, silver eyes welling up with moisture. "Oh my God, you're okay! I thought—I heard—" She blinked, tears spilling over as she threw her arms around his waist and hugged him tightly. Her fingers curled into his jacket, and her face buried against his chest.

"Of course I'm doing fine. Complete recovery," he reassured her, smoothing a hand down her dark hair. "They're callin' it a miracle." It felt so good to hug Aisling again that he reluctantly released her after he maneuvered them onto the landing of the stairs.

Things had been touch and go those first two days while the Healers fought to keep the wound closed. Against all odds, it began to heal into an angry red, hideous scar overtaking the entirety of his throat. It wasn't until days later that some mystery ointment arrived, and it began to show vast improvement.

"I'm sorry, it's been so busy at work lately, and I'm a mess." She inhaled shakily and swiped at her damp eyes. With the next breath, she fired questions about his health and when he had arrived in Ireland. How much longer would he be there?

"Slow down, slow down. Give me a moment to answer, lass. Mum brought me here a week ago, when they discharged me from the hospital, but I'm leavin' soon. Why didn't you answer my post?"

"Post? I didn't see any letters. I've got a huge pile at home. As I said, it's been a busy few days."

"I'll be sure to send the next one in an envelope of your favorite color so you won't ignore it too."

"Surely you don't recall something as silly as my favorite color."

"Green. Do you have the time to join an old friend for dinner? The letter is probably waiting for you since I sent the thing over a week ago."

Giving her no opportunity to refuse, he swept her out to the Dublin streets and to a cozy establishment off the main road. Griffin once worked as a waiter at The Dandy Lion during their school days, and he was welcomed back with all the perks of a VIP.

"Come this way, Mr. MacNeil and Miss Kavanagh. We've got a table for ye," the Irish lass said. She took menus and led them to the upper level to a table on the quiet balcony. A decorative heater stood nearby to keep them both comfortable.

Conversation flourished between them once they were seated and made their orders. Griffin regaled her with tales of treasure-seeking as the cheerful red-haired waitress brought expensive glasses of wine. Aisling spoke briefly of her own work with the Healers, and modestly admitted she still volunteered at the nursing center by their old school. That brought their conversation back to old times, revisiting school-year memories.

It wasn't until the conversation finally began to settle and silence fell between them that Griffin cleared his throat.

"Is something the matter, Aisling? It's... Perhaps it's none of my damned business, but you don't seem to be takin' proper care of yourself."

The Aisling of his memories wore pastels and bold jewel-toned colors. He remembered flowers and ribbons in her intricately braided hair. The woman sitting across from him in her dull and dark hues bore her no resemblance.

"I told you, I'm well enough. Truly. Breda and I have a place of our own, though I still visit Gran at the estate often. I even went to Greece this summer for a week." She sipped wine, shifting her advertent gaze back towards him. "But what of you? Griffin, I know it's been said, but I am very sorry for what happened to Liam and the others." Her expression became solemn and sincere.

"It's...different. Thanks, Ash." He feigned interest in the rest of his steak and potatoes. "He wanted to meet you, you know. We spoke of comin' this way for the holidays to pay visits."

"It would have been nice to meet him. His additions to your letters made me laugh. How is your family? I imagine you must be ready to return to them after so long in a hospital."

"Mara will be turnin' three in January. She's growin' so damned tall now, Ash."

"She was a beautiful baby in the picture you sent me."

"I'll have more photos next time," Griffin promised. "Looks more like me than her mum, I think. What of you, lass? Are all the men in Dublin blind now? Why's there no ring on your finger yet?"

"I've been on a few dates," she said. "I'm not a recluse with a hundred cats wandering about my flat if that's what has you frowning at me in such a way."

Griffin reached across the table and took her hand. "I wasn't frowning. Deep in thought, that's all... And glad to have this time to catch up with you, sprite. Lady Fortune must have been shinin' on us when we crossed paths."

For a moment, Griffin wondered if it was luck or a curse at play. Seeing Aisling was both a pleasure and pain, stirring up forgotten feelings.

"Perhaps she was," she agreed. She set her wine down so she could lean across and touch his scar. "I knew you were hurt, enough to send what I did, but your ma never told me how it happened." Her fingers traced down the scar to the end curve along his throat. They lingered for a moment, and then dropped away.

Her touch brought a rush to his pulse, warmth to his face, and sadness that always surfaced whenever the fresh memories of his and Liam's last stand were stirred.

"You were the one to send the medicine? They never gave me a name."

Aisling nodded and averted her gaze to trace a finger through the condensation on her glass. He'd almost forgotten how shy and humble she could be. "You look well, Griff, you really do."

He saw right through her attempt to change the subject, so he gave her that and didn't cling to the topic of her aid to him.

"So… You really don't find it unattractive, then?" His mind was drawn to the way she touched his skin, how her finger traced the ugly line without disgust or fear. For a brief but terrible moment, he hated where his life had gone.

"No, Griff, I think you look as handsome as ever. Maybe a wee bit dangerous, too," she teased, easing back in her seat.

"You're only sayin' that since the rest of my scars are beneath my clothes. Mercedes hates them; she'll hate this one all the more. *Everyone* can see it."

Aisling set her fork down with a clink of silverware to china, staring at him. "Griffin, I know it means little, coming as it is from me, but you're still every inch the charismatic young man I knew. No scar could change that, and given more time, even the angry color will fade from it. She… I mean…" She bit her lip and glanced away.

Griffin's chest tightened. "Your words bring some comfort to me all the same. Thanks. Your words mean *plenty*."

The chatter ended between them and settled into companionable silence without a rush to fill the lulls with meaningless words.

After a time, Griffin finally spoke up. "Come with me sometime."

"You don't have to do that," she said.

"No, I mean it. The next time an easy freelance job comes across my desk, I'll send word in the post. Score you a bit of money too."

"I could care less for the extra money, but… really?"

"Come on, Ash… I'll be insulted if you won't come along. You can take your own photos then."

"You think I could actually be of some help?"

She appeared uncertain, teetering on the edge of acceptance and refusal. Griffin could read her as easily in adulthood as he could as a teen. He was familiar with the way her brow creased and her silver eyes seemed to peer through him into his soul. She'd always done that whenever she felt suspicious of him or thought he was up to one of his tricks.

"Say you'll do it… C'mon. Put those healin' talents to use if I'm sloppy enough to blow m'self the fuck up again sometime.

Please? I'll beg. It'll be the saddest sight you ever laid eyes upon."

"Maybe…"

Got her, he thought to himself, feeling smug. "If you can get away, I'll arrange the expedition around your schedule."

It was an impulsive idea, but exciting. He thought Liam would be proud.

"Well… I suppose if you give me early enough warning so I can arrange for the time, and are sure to tell me everything I'll need to bring, I may be able to do it."

"I'll write a list."

"I'd really like that. Thank you," she said.

After their meal, Griffin paid the bill and left a generous tip.

They were nearly out the door when the hostess hurried over to stop him. "Mr. MacNeil, ye have to stay a moment. Jack's wantin' to say hello."

"Tell Jack I'll see him next time. I've got to escort Miss Kavanagh home."

Aisling led him to her home, an attractive brick apartment building overlooking a city park. They stopped in front of the door and faced each other to make their goodbyes.

"It's been a pleasure to see you again, Ash. I'll be back once I've gotten this next bauble for O'Sullivan. The old git wants us out in the field again now that I'm on my feet, so I'll write before I come."

"Be safe, Griffin."

Impulsively, Griffin kissed her brow before they parted. He waited for her to step safely inside the front doors, and then he returned to Dublin's Vault for a series of jumps through their Portal system that would deliver him home to Spain. To finally see his little girl again.

And to deal with the wife who hadn't visited him once during his month of recovery.

Chapter 4

Someone took the liberty of forwarding Griffin's belongings ahead when he missed his pre-arranged jump out of Dublin to Barcelona. He returned to the fond greetings of his coworkers and an abundance of get-well cards fanned over his desk in the Collections Department.

A short flight in his personal Cessna brought him home more quickly than by car. With a brief cab ride from the airstrip, Griffin reached the estate a few hours before midnight. The Spanish-style villa on the outskirts of Paradiso had been a wedding gift from his bride's father.

But the best part about home wasn't the backyard pool, the city-wide view from above, or even the professionally landscaped gardens. It was the little girl who squealed out in enthusiasm the moment he stepped a single foot through the door. Mara ran to him, and Griffin met her on his knees with his arms opened wide. Her little fingers felt his face, touched his cheeks and searched, following his jaw until they discovered the raised line of scar tissue at his throat.

Mercedes had hoped for a child who would closely resemble her, but what she received was a blind child who was a blend of her and Griffin's best features. Their daughter had acquired her mother's natural warm olive tones paired with freckles over the bridge of the nose and beneath her eyes. During the summer, her mousy brown hair tended to reveal golden highlights his wife despised.

To Griffin, Mara was perfection.

"Papá!"

"I missed you every day," he told her sincerely. For a while, he simply held her and enjoyed the warm feeling of a snuggly little body pressing closely against him. How long he knelt there holding her, he didn't know, but one of the servants rounded the corner, fretful that Mara had gotten away.

"*¿Dónde está tu madre, mi hija?*" he asked her first, only to repeat and ask where the girl's mother was in English. A sly glance determined Mercedes wasn't within sight or earshot. He thought he should be able to speak his preferred language in his own home.

"I am so very sorry, sir. I will take Señorita Mara to return her to bed—"

"No, you won't need to do that. I'll tuck her in," he told the housekeeper.

She lingered and fidgeted with the hem of her blouse. An awkward moment of silence passed between them. "I am glad to see you recovered completely, Señor MacNeil. Many of us were worried for your health. It is a blessing to see you returned to us."

"Thank you. Please, I've got this. You take it easy tonight, Elsa."

Elsa was one of three common housekeepers Mercedes had yet to run off from their household. She stood a little below five foot four, plump, and ordinary. Mercedes liked all the staff to be ordinary.

Contrasting his wife, all Griffin wanted was for them to be good people, kind to Mara, and dedicated to their jobs.

Mara clung to him and curled her tiny fingers into his collar. She wouldn't have released him if he'd tried to pass her into the supportive arms of her caretaker.

Sometimes, he feared his long absences were affecting her poorly, or that she wouldn't remember him at all when he returned. He was wrong. Mara remembered him and seemed to wait eagerly. In fact, Elsa and Belen both reported that ever since she began to take her first steps, she had moments where she'd stand near the foyer as if expecting him. Within a day or two, he would show up, so the staff now trusted Mara's intuition to anticipate his arrivals.

"All right, all right. You're wantin' to know what I have in my bag, aye? Come on then. Up to my office."

The MacNeil home showed no signs of harboring a child at all within its walls. Pristine furnishings in dark woods with cream-colored upholstery with taupe accents held brown pillows upon their cushions. Matching curtains and heavy linen draperies in ivory flowed to meet the geometric patterns of cocoa-colored marble stretching endlessly from one room to the next. Everything was always flawless. Mercedes's tasteful, professionally decorated home was cookie cutter perfection.

Griffin and Mara were prohibited from enjoying the room intended for the guests and entertaining company. That was well and fine since he preferred to spend whatever time he had outside at the pool or holed inside his study to work. Usually, Mara occupied her father's lap while he read, researched, pored through one book after another. Most importantly, he stayed out of his wife's way.

They ascended the stairs to approach a hardwood door that opened at his touch. Griffin's man cave was organized chaos tailored to his personal preferences.

Rich and colorful tapestries on the wall told a story of Scottish history. Both educational and fictional books lined the shelves in a variety of bindings, all varying in their sizes. Heavy cream linen draperies were boring but practical for keeping out the harsh sunlight, but one had a child-sized ink blotch handprint in black. Griffin hadn't permitted the staff to clean or remove it.

Souvenirs of his journeys into the ancient ruins brought life to the shelves positioned too high to be within reach of child-sized hands. Carved idols mounted on displays, and dangerously sharp instruments gleamed beyond little Mara's reach. Griffin had a fondness for knives and weaponry, so he tended to collect what he could.

He searched one of the bags he'd had sent ahead to his office and produced the lantern from the ruin. It emitted a cool breeze with its light.

"Cold!" she cried out to him, reaching up with her small hands.

He chuckled with amusement. A furrow wrinkled her brow, and curious fingers resumed their exploration of each star point until finally she squealed and took the entire lantern between both eager hands. An hour later, she fell asleep cradling her gift, and Griffin delivered her to bed. He quietly left the room to go on the hunt for his wife who hadn't bothered to welcome him home.

Griffin braced himself for the encounter. The blood pulsing through his half-breed wife's veins was enough to make a man's cock harder than a pillar crafted by a dwarf's hammer and chisel.

Her mother's people were once known as las xanas by the superstitious locals, but the Magi of Spain knew them by another name. Nereids of the Mediterranean Sea. Sirens.

His father-in-law shared the story of how the beautiful woman met with him throughout the spring season only to disappear before summer. He discovered a woven reed basket outside of his home in late winter, and it contained nothing more than a naked infant. Domingo believed she had departed to her native body of seawater and returned only to birth their child and abandon her to the humans. She never came into his life again.

Mercedes was the apple of her father's eye, beloved for inheriting his magical blood as much as bringing such honor to his family name.

Griffin immediately fell under his wife's scrutiny when he stepped into their bedroom.

"Does something trouble you, Griffin?" she asked.

"No." *Nothing except losing my best friend and recovering without you there*, he thought spitefully to himself.

Mercedes rose from her seat at the vanity. Her silken robe fell open, revealing how little she wore beneath it.

"Tell me," she urged him as she approached. Her fingers ran over his shirt and the defined pectoral muscles beneath. She unfastened the buttons with a coy smile, her sea-blue eyes upon his face all the while, until her hands slipped beneath the material and smoothed over his bare chest.

For the first time in all their marriage, she made his skin crawl. He wanted to be away from her. Needed to have distance, and internally he struggled with the contrast of what he remembered prior to the dismal mission in Egypt. He'd been happy with her, hadn't he? "It's nothin'."

"Nothing?" Her breath feathered against his throat.

Griffin landed on his back on the bed with his arms at his sides. It was a familiar position that the Scot knew well whenever Mercedes was in a mood to have her way with him. "I'm not feelin' up for it."

Her head dipped down to nip and playfully scrape her teeth over one of his nipples.

Sex was the last thing he wanted. She took ahold of him anyway, stroking him through his slacks while she nibbled his throat and hungrily tasted his skin.

"Now tell me what's the matter, and I will do everything I can to make it better," she crooned. Her kisses continued in a pattern that avoided his scar.

"Bouncing on my cock isn't going to make it better, Mercy." He said the words plainly, though his shaft behaved contrary to his words. It pulsed hot and came to life quickly under her touch, but Griffin shoved her quite firmly from atop him. He rolled to his left side. "Just glad to be home again, is all. I'm goin' to sleep now. Great to see you too." *For the first time in over a month...*

"How dare you turn your back on me after all I've done for you."

He sat up to twist and look at her with his weight partially propped on one elbow. "Where were you when I was in the hospital wantin' you there?"

"And what purpose would I have served at your bedside when there were matters requiring my attention here? I took care of our home and our crying child. I saw to the guests and tended to this house."

"Wait, wait... Guests? What guests?" He rolled over to face her.

Her eyes narrowed. "Members of the community concerned about your condition. I saw to them and eased their worries."

"You know damned well that if anyone wanted to know about my condition, they could've come to see me. Mum did."

"I thought it better you remain undisturbed to recover in peace. Of course, your mother did not listen to me." Mercedes sniffed disdainfully. "She should have respected my wishes."

"Mum did the bloody right thing in comin' to see me. I *asked* for you too. What about my fuckin' wishes?"

"*I* wish to lie with my husband." She huffed, pushing at his shirt. "The only thing that you should want is to be inside of me after weeks apart. Why fight it? Let me make things better."

Mercedes nearly persuaded him. For a while, he tolerated the silken touch of her lips. They trailed low, tracing his abs, and he anticipated the pleasure her mouth would bring. A hazy, warm feeling enveloped him, and he pumped his hips, lost to the moment. Lost until the memory of bright and wide silver eyes chased the temptation away and seemed to bring light to the darkness. Griffin shook his head and jerked back. He pried her fingers loose from him right away.

He didn't want this.

"No, Mercedes. I know my own mind, I know what I want and don't want. Sex doesn't make everything better."

"*Por que?*" She smacked his hands. "You ask me to be a good wife, and yet you turn me away when I seek to serve you."

"No. It's nothin' to do with service. I just... I wanted you to be there." He wanted to be held, and he wanted her to show him love.

"Come with me to the room, Griffin... Let me treat you as a husband should be treated."

"No." He shoved her off and left the bed, taking his pillow with him.

"Did the jackal take your manhood too?"

Griffin froze and lost his balance when she shoved at him with both of her hands.

There was one thing about nymph halflings most people underestimated. They were strong. Mercedes could be as gentle as placid waters or as powerful as the churning currents at tide.

His back slammed against the wall. "Mercy! What's gotten into you?"

He suppressed the urge to strike her and walked away, showing the kind of restraint his stepfather never had. No matter how much he wanted to throttle her, no matter how much he burned to hit her, he would not do it.

Throughout his childhood, Griffin had witnessed what it was like when a husband beat his wife, and he'd promised he would never be that man.

Behind him, his wife gave a petulant scream of frustration before hurling the remaining pillow at him.

"Get out of my sight then. I don't want to even look at you," she hissed.

"Gladly."

Chapter 5

A cluster of Healers and nurse trainees collected within the cozy lounge of the Dublin Vault, participating in a conversation about an upcoming bridal shower. One of the young women had become distracted from their girlish chatter, gazing beyond Aisling to a point of interest behind her.

"What do you keep staring at, Deirdre?"

"That man with the scar. He's staring over at us. He looks familiar."

When Aisling turned, she gazed directly into the gold-flecked green eyes of Griffin, who stood several feet away smiling goofily at her from the open doorway.

"Afternoon, lassies. I've come to steal this one away from you," he called.

The surprised look in her eyes and the soft blush to her cheeks left several of her friends and co-workers either giggling or speculatively looking her way. Aisling smoothed a hand along her prim skirt and mumbled quiet goodbyes as she gathered up her belongings. Her friends peppered her with questions all at once.

"Who's that, Aisling? A boyfriend?"

"Isn't that Fiona's son? He used to be so scrawny."

"Mrs. MacNeil's boy? I heard he was nearly beheaded by Inquisitors."

"That's Griffin?" another woman asked before leaning in closer to the clustered group. "Pity about his scar, though. I remember him bein' cuter in my memories."

"You shut your mouth, Noreen." Aisling's uncharacteristic snap raised a few brows. "He's very handsome."

Aisling excused herself from the group and crossed the room where Griffin remained patiently waiting. She stopped only a step away and peered up into his face.

"Well, hello there. Fancy meetin' you here."

"I work here," she replied, unable to keep from smiling. "Meaning it's you who's a surprise to see."

"Someone has to make certain you're eatin' properly, and mum says it's your lunch break," he replied with a broad grin on his face. He offered her an arm and paid no further mind to the group of gossiping women.

A reservation awaited the pair at their favorite restaurant. The hostess smiled and led them to the same quiet table, and it was there that they laughed and talked away the lunch hour. His surprise visit was a pleasant one, improved by their easy conversation and his exciting stories.

This time Jack caught them before they could leave.

The short, rotund man stood even with Aisling, though nearly thrice as wide, with frizzy red hair peeking out from beneath a blue bowler hat. Somehow, he made it work with his ruby jacket, the gold buttons buffed to a gleaming luster.

"Tried to escape again without comin' to share a word or two with your old friend Jack?" the short man asked indignantly.

"You know Griffin. Always afraid you're one prank ahead of him," Aisling chimed in, falling into old bantering ways.

"It's true. You know how it is, Jack. Things to do and more important people to see," Griffin replied. A warm smile on his face belied his words. Griffin and Jack had been at one another's throats for years with the sort of loving relationship better suited to brothers.

The man huffed. "There's never anyone more important to see than me. I noticed my gift has served you well, Griffin. Now come on into my office, the both of you. Those busybodies at the Vault can have her back when we're done with our chat."

"You never change, Jack." Griffin sighed.

The little rotund man broke out his best bottle of Irish whiskey to soothe Griffin's hurry to leave. They fondly reminisced over drinks until Griffin noticed another hour had passed.

"I'd better get her back to work, Jack. You know Ash is a lightweight."

"So says you. I recall keeping up just fine when you took me up to The Brazen Head." Aisling's protest came with a shrug and a nudge to her glass, which had hardly been touched.

Griffin grinned. He remembered the night well. They ate greasy food and drank until they were both barely able to stand and walk. Until he had no choice but to phone his father to come get them. His birth father. Not the drunk who masqueraded as his father for fifteen years of his life.

Adam hadn't minded, but he had shoved a bucket into Ash's hands, claiming the smaller ones always had the most puke in them. Griffin had vomited instead and spent the entirety of his next afternoon scrubbing the carpeting of the rear seat.

"I'll save a story for the next time *you* come to see me, wee lassie. I seem to recall our friend here grew out of my tales a long time ago, and I'd hate to bore him," Jack said.

Griffin rolled his eyes.

The pair bid farewell after they exchanged hugs and kisses, and only after Jack wrangled a binding promise from each of them that they'd return the next time Griffin's path brought him back to Ireland.

The perpetual cover of gray clouds over Ireland broke once or twice over the course of their walk. They had a distance to travel, but Griffin refused the notion of taking a bus. He wanted to stretch his legs and enjoy the fresh air.

"I hope I haven't gotten you into trouble."

"No worries about that. I'm not on a normal shift in the clinic like the others. If they'd needed me, they would have sent word," Aisling reassured him.

They strolled in peace down the quiet one-way street. Griffin chatted absently, flitting from subject to subject like a hummingbird, and as always, Aisling listened with a smile on her face.

"Did you really pick up the snake?" she asked after he finished his latest tale.

"Course, I did. There's no point usin' magic on a wee cobra. The way the others were behavin', you'd think we'd found a goddamned dragon."

"I've read those Egyptian snakes are a venomous lot. And mean."

"Nae, they're not so bad. There's too much Charmer talent in our family, and Mercedes at least taught me to—"

Brick and mortar exploded from a building to their right, sending chips of red stone in every direction. Pain lanced across Griffin's cheek when a storefront window shattered, but it paled in comparison to the burning sensation along his left arm. Hot blood soaked into his overcoat. Without thinking, he shoved Aisling behind him and ducked into an alley.

They moved quickly, but it didn't help as shots rang out from the opposite end of the narrow, single-lane pathway between the two buildings. Everything surrounding the pair warped as Aisling twisted mana into a mystical shell of armor. Arcane essence encircled them in a semi-translucent, shimmering dome as bullets plinked noisily and clattered to the ground at their feet.

Two armed men in military-style fatigues approached from their so-called safe exit and penned them in with nowhere to run.

"Shit," Griffin said under his breath, holding Ash's hand tightly in his grip.

"Why are they shooting at us?"

"I recognize one of 'em, Ash, I'm sure of it. He must have been a spy on the dig I was on for O'Sullivan."

"Griff, I've never held up a shield against gunfire before," she whispered. "I don't know how long it'll hold."

"I don't even know why they're shootin' at me," he whispered back, instinctively flinching each time another bullet pock-marked the mana shield. "Autumn. We need you. Autumn, *please.*"

The cherry-red Faerie salamander appeared in a puff of flame, her bright orange eyes larger than ever in her smiling face. She vanished from sight, and moments later the screams of a man on fire filled the narrow alley. The fae had chosen to reappear atop the soldier's dark hair, peering down into his face to exhale a fiery breath. The man screamed, swinging and slapping at his hairline, thoroughly distracting the second shooter at his side.

"If I drop the shield, can you keep the two busy?"

"Fuckin' right, I can."

"Language."

Aisling released his hand and pulled away. Her small body tensed and she leaned forward, but instead of running, she vanished after a single step. Griffin stared. Barely a second later, she blinked behind an unsuspecting shooter as he tried to help extinguish his partner. The moment her hand touched his skin, the man froze in place.

Griffin retrieved a corked glass vial from his inner coat pocket, filled nearly to its top with grains of sand from Egypt. "I really hate havin' to do this." They didn't come cheap or easy to make. The translucent cylinder was decorated with odd patterns drawn by a silver Sharpie marker.

When Griffin hurled it to the ground, the fine grains scattered to swirl in the air. They multiplied in number, releasing the memory of Egyptian heat, the smell of scorched desert, and one hell of a brutal sandstorm.

His assailants spit sand and staggered, blinded by the enchanted windstorm. Griffin sprinted for Aisling as his little fae friend skittered along their attacker's scalp, igniting hair wherever her small feet touched. She leapt from the man to Griffin's shoulder when he arrived to take Aisling by the hand.

"How the bloody hell did you learn that trick?"

"Jack," she said.

Their path led them down a narrow street, which intersected with another lane between two walls of buildings.

A dark van was to their left, along with a young man in similar army fatigues smoking a cigarette. It fell from his fingers when he spied the two mages. He chased the pair with a hail of gunfire, forcing a tactical retreat.

"Where are we going?" Griffin asked.

"If we're lucky, we'll catch a taxi on Coombe, else we'll be needing to hop a wall to get to St. Luke's."

Rushing into the street, they hailed a taxi in the nick of time. Aisling gave her home address while the concerned driver watched them through the rearview mirror.

"Why aren't we going to the Vault to report what happened? Those were bloody Inquisitors."

"Because it's what they'd be expecting." Her words were soft, meant for his ears only and not for the curious cabbie. "If they knew where we were going enough to ambush us, who's to say other ways are safe? I'll call as soon as we get inside."

Autumn began to whine and fuss when they reached the threshold of Aisling's apartment building. The salamander poked her ruby snout from within his coat pocket and quieted once they were inside, shining as bright as a beacon and sending off sparks that shimmered to the ground.

"So, this is where I call home for now. Needed to get out on my own…"

"Certainly frigid," he muttered as he followed her to the upper level.

Aisling unlocked the door to the second unit. "It's no colder than outside, Griffin."

Four windows lit the open floor of the single room apartment, their panes overlooking St. Steven's Green. Gauzy, moss-colored draperies filtered thin beams of dwindling sunlight that highlighted the simplistic interior of the flat. A queen-sized bed occupied the area to the right of the entrance, neatly made with a thick white comforter and pillows. Two smaller pale green pillows added a subtle splash of color. The bedside table, matching armoire, and a dresser in pale golden wood and ivory-hued marble completed the bedroom area.

A dark brown couch provided seating, paired with a glass-topped coffee table and a shelf full of books. The wooden floors were bare of any rugs, and only a few decorations adorned her cream-colored walls.

The comfortable interior was sparse and lacked the feeling of home that had always clung to her grandmother's estate. Toy mice and other furry toys littered the floor near a carpeted cat tree beside the spacious window.

It wasn't what Griffin expected to find in Aisling's home. The cat toys were typical, but as a teen, her bedroom had an abundance of rainbow colors and flowers. Not that he was supposed to have known what the inside of her bedroom looked like back then.

"It's like you forgot colors exist. It's so bland."

As he stepped into the stark and plain little flat, he wondered if her fae ancestry was to blame or if she'd merely grown up into someone different after all.

~*~

Forgot colors existed? Aisling blinked, staring around the room. Looking at it through his eyes, she knew he was right.

"There's usually flowers." She kept vases for them, but the little brownies who cleaned her flat had emptied them while she worked long hours. Sometimes they were too scatterbrained to remember to replace them.

Aisling phoned the Vault to relay what happened while Griffin shrugged out of his coat and examined his injured arm.

"Don't meddle with it, and I'll fix you right up when I'm off."

A few minutes later, she had out her medical kit. He became a poor excuse for a patient while she cleaned the shallow groove where a bullet had grazed him.

"The Commandant would like to speak with us both once our Guardians have combed over the area."

"Fantastic. Just what I'd like to spend my afternoon doing."

Her hands touched lightly over his tanned flesh, noticing the faded scars he had mentioned once before. She could clearly recall the last time he'd been shirtless in her presence. They had been at the beach with friends, and he hadn't been cut so leanly back then. Aisling thought now that he looked as if he belonged on the cover of a Scottish Highlands romance novel. He was only missing the kilt.

All fine muscle, defined abs, and a chiseled chest she longed to caress. Aisling tried to wet her lips but her mouth had gone completely dry. Even her heart stammered in her chest, flying at speeds she didn't think possible without exercise.

He's completely off-limits because he's got a family of his own, Aisling chided herself.

"There you go. It should hardly scar, I think." She smoothed a thin layer of herbal ointment over the wound. Within seconds, only a thin film of dried cream remained, and the skin appeared to be fully healed.

"Thanks, Ash, though I've got so many I doubt I'd notice one more." His torso already bore an impressive collection of small marks from old injuries. A puckered mark against his right pectoral, a thin line over his ribs, and countless other small marks told the history of his job.

The phone rang seconds after she put her kit away, and after a cordial greeting, she found herself at the frantic end of a concerned mother calling.

"Slow down, Ms. MacNeil. We're fine. *He's* fine."

"Oh, thank God. Commandant Whelan left my office only moments ago, and I had to rummage through my desk for your number, dear."

Aisling took a moment to give Fiona the basics of their encounter. She reassured the woman of Griffin's health, that it was only a minor wound, and then passed the phone to the man himself.

"Mum, nothin' bad happened to me this time. Unless you count Ash trying to freeze me. Keeps her place on the cool side." He shot Aisling a playful wink. He spent the next few minutes setting his mother's nerves at ease and finally ended the call with a promise to see her soon for dinner.

"I should call Mercedes too. Let her know I won't be home as planned."

Aisling stepped away into the kitchen to grant him as much privacy as she could in the open-floor design of her studio flat. His shirt was ruined, but she used the sink to remove most of the blood.

A short distance away, conversational chatter began in Spanish and continued for several minutes while Griffin paced a groove in her floor. Aisling didn't become truly concerned until his despondent replies softened to an almost inaudible state. His expression drooped, and his shoulders sagged until he finally ended the call. Griffin didn't look at her.

He looks so defeated. Lonely, she thought sadly.

"I'd better find a hotel. If I go home to Mum, she'll fuss over me the whole night. Toss that shirt into the dryer for a wee bit?"

Aisling returned to the sofa with a glass of whiskey and set it on the coffee table. "You won't need a hotel, Griffin. I know it's not much, but you're welcome to stay here until this is sorted."

"I... Well, maybe I should, then. That's a fancy bit of ward-work you did downstairs, by the way. I'm fuckin' impressed. Who taught you to do it? Was that one Jack too?"

"Wards downstairs?" Her brow creased in confusion. "I've only warded my home, Griff. The door and windows is all."

Griffin leaned back and gazed at her, skeptical. "There's a barrier against violent intent surrounding every inch of this buildin', lass. If you didn't do it, who did?"

"I've no idea what you're on about. This place feels no different than the manor."

"You're right. It doesn't..." He fell silent, only to clap his hands a moment later and change the subject. Classic Griffin. "Right, then. I'm filthy and sweaty. What's your solution?"

"I've got a shower, and there's a shop not far where I can pick you up some clothes." Of the two of them, Aisling was cleanest. "Go ahead and get cleaned up, and I'll be back in a jiff."

She fetched him fresh clothes while he showered, returning to find him loitering in a towel while perusing her shelves.

"I can't believe you kept this bit of rubbish I sent from the ruin beneath Barcelona."

"It was the very first thing you sent me."

"And worthless."

He really needs to get dressed, she thought. Clearing her throat, she nudged him with the shopping bag until he took the hint.

Each item from Griffin was as precious as the last. When their friendship resumed, he began to send salvaged goodies from his magical excavations into the deep ruins of ancient Spain. His gifts were plain and simple but lovingly displayed where she could find enjoyment in their presence.

"I suppose Mum and Mara aren't alone, then," he called from her bathroom while he dressed. "They keep everything I give to them too."

"I expect your home must be full of amazing things..."

"I keep everything in my study mostly. Well, you know Mara is blind, aye? She's fond of the things that emit some sort of sound or sensation, so I search for trinkets she'd like."

She flicked a concerned glance his way when he emerged in jeans and a T-shirt. "I always thought you'd want to proudly display your various finds."

"Mercedes doesn't want it all over—this is a borin' change of subject, Ash."

"I'm not the one changing it, but…" Her teeth skated over her bottom lip, revealing a small chip in her otherwise even smile. "Griffin, is everything okay between you?" she asked quietly, cheeks immediately flushing when she realized how presumptuous the personal inquiry sounded to her own ears.

"Aye. Everything is… I suppose it's…" He turned his attention from the souvenir collection and shook his head. "No. It isn't so good, but it's nothin' to worry yourself over."

Somehow she thought she would feel a certain sense of smug satisfaction. An 'I told you so' feeling of righteousness. Instead, empathy constricted her chest and made her struggle for each breath, making her hurt for the man who had once been closer to her than anyone else. Who had once been hers.

"My ear is always yours, Griff."

"What do you want to hear, Aisling?" He turned away from the organized display of Roman relics to study her.

"Whatever you wish to share, and only that. Your choice, Griffin, and I won't take offense if you tell me to mind my own business."

"I know how you feel about things." His brittle smile broke her heart. "Brought it all on myself, didn't I?"

"Maybe," she said with quiet honesty. "But I'm still your friend. The offer to listen is open, that's all I'm saying."

He traveled to the sofa and claimed a seat. "Where's Breda?"

As if speaking her name had summoned her, the sleek gray feline came leaping down from her perch on a shelf, immediately moving to twine around his legs. He reached down and gave the cat a long-due stroke along her spine, followed by a scratch right below her tiny chin once she accepted the invitation to his lap.

"She's missed you," Aisling murmured, lowering herself onto a seat at the other end of the couch.

"Glad that someone does."

THE COLLECTOR'S TREASURE

"Don't say that. You have people who love you and miss you." She included herself in the sentiment as well. "You seem…unhappy, Griffin. You've never been able to lie well to me, so please don't start now."

He'd come close to death, lost a friend who was a brother to him, and now admitted things were not so happy at home. Aisling was rightfully concerned.

"Mercedes didn't visit me once while I was ill. Not a single time," he finally confided. His attention remained on the gray feline in his lap, fingers scratching the itches Breda directed him to relieve.

"What? Why the feckin' hell not?" Her hands lifted to clap over her mouth once the angry question left her lips.

"Guests to attend to. You know. The variety of guests who visits cock first."

She stared long and hard at his profile while her anger boiled fast. Fury wouldn't do either of them any good, so she remained silent while she took in deep and even breaths to calm down.

"What did you do?" she finally asked.

"I asked for a divorce this mornin' after I had a while to think it over. Seemed like the thing to do, only she's not so agreeable to it."

"Griffin…" She had no idea what to say and offering apologies seemed so trite. So meaningless.

"I made my bed."

"You loved her." It was hard to say the words out loud, but they were true enough. They still hurt though.

"Damned right I did. Do… She's the mother of my child. I thought…" He trailed and gazed toward the window. Breda stood upon his lap on her hind legs, forepaws against his chest. The feline head butted him several times until his attention returned to her. "Part of me still does. She gave me Mara."

"She's beautiful, Griffin. When I heard… I thought you would make a wonderful dad. She's a lucky girl to have you." She glanced away a moment, wishing she had brought a whiskey for herself. "Why is she against the divorce so badly?"

"My name. The last time we had troubles…" He stared down at his hands. "I wanted to leave once, but she put up an argument against it. You know how I am about religion, but she's Catholic. Said her da' gave me my career and can take it away again if I shame her family. She's…become a stranger now. I don't understand why everythin' is goin' so wrong."

"What about counseling?" Her throat felt dry. She found bitter irony in the fact that she was trying to help him patch his relationship with the girl who had stolen him away. He'd been her Griffin once.

"Don't you think I asked already?" he snapped.

"I seem to recall a man who didn't like asking for help. But Griffin…you know Regent O'Sullivan and Director Moore would snatch you up in a minute."

"She won't let me take Mara with me," he told her in a hushed, broken tone.

"What about your grandfa—"

"No." His spine straightened and his shoulders tensed. "Not going to that bastard for help, grandfather or not."

The subject was closed, and Aisling knew better than to press. They gabbed long into the night about the dig Griffin planned for her, the topic bringing the liveliness and enthusiasm back to his features. The last thing she recalled before dozing off against the cushions was the sight of his smile.

~*~

Griffin awoke on the couch to the smell of sizzling bacon snuggled beneath his chin. He cracked open his bleary eyes, stroked the cat snuggled beside him, and debated whether to go back to sleep. Breakfast won, so he moved the cat and sat up.

"Good morning. How did you sleep?" Aisling smiled at him from the kitchen. Her sleep-rumpled braid hung over one shoulder.

"Like a wee bairn with this one protecting me throughout the night."

"First time in a long while I haven't had her purring on my pillow, but I suppose I can forgive her. She and Autumn decided to trade places, I guess."

Autumn peeked out from beneath her dark hair.

"She's missed you."

"And I her," she replied with a fond smile. "I've never been able to call another like her out, you know. I guess we were lucky that night."

So many years had passed since the evening when Aisling and Griffin came across the smoldering remains of an abandoned campfire. The smoking cinders had been inhabited by a creature of Avalon, newly born and afraid of her surroundings. Against all odds, she'd thrived with their attentive care to become a loving familiar.

The fire salamander raised her velvety soft nose for a rub against Aisling's cheek. She had matured over the years since the two friends grew apart and now resembled a blend between a common pet store gecko and miniature dragon. Retractable claws tipped each of her functional fingers and toes. Erratic curls of gray smoke escaped her slit nostrils when Aisling tickled a finger along her side. Autumn was like a child in many ways.

Their child. The closest they might ever come to having one.

"Are you going to be serving me my breakfast anytime soon? It smells goddamned amazin' from over here."

Aisling scoffed. She took a seat with her tea and gestured with a sweeping hand toward the kitchen. "I'm no maid to be serving you here, Griffin MacNeil. Fetch your own plate."

So he did. They enjoyed the meal together in good company, and for a time, they were able to ignore everything else gone wrong.

Chapter 6

The Vault had no answers for what had occurred on the city streets, but Griffin and Aisling were advised to be cautious until the investigation was complete. He returned to Spain in the afternoon after a lengthy report at the Dublin Vault and promised to send news in preparation of their upcoming adventure.

One of Aisling's friends, Deirdre, teased and poked fun relentlessly the next day. She had witnessed their parting hug.

"Was that a ring on his finger?" Deidre asked.

"Your eyes saw true." Aisling kept her gaze fixed on the release paperwork she signed for Kevin. The sergeant had fully recovered from his altercation with the hag and was ready to return to duty.

"What happened to the sweet lad who came calling for you only this last month? Michael, was it? The Scribe working with Collections. I never took you for the sort to tangle with becoming someone's mistress."

Aisling swallowed back the bile rising in her throat. "Ugh, no. Firstly, Michael is not so sweet, and I won't forget his years of bullying me in school. Second, I'm not tangling with anyone. Griffin is a friend only."

"Friends don't look at one another that way."

"Then you're seeing things, Deirdre. He made his choice long ago." She tossed the papers in the outbox then reached for the nearest chart, nearly knocking over a planter full of peppermint.

The sunny, pale yellow paint on the walls generated a feeling of warmth always coupled by the Healers' friendly personas. It was difficult to enter the Healers' station of the Dublin Vault without feeling loved and sheltered. Even harder to escape without smelling fragrant.

"So is he really Regent Rhydderch's *younger* grandson?"

Aisling glanced up, startled. "Where did you hear that?"

"Gossip spreads. You know how it is. Someone speculated and put it all together when Sergeant Rhydderch personally led a squad of constables through the Portal to assist with the investigation. Now *there's* a damned sexy man. He can arrest me any day he pleases." Deirdre suggestively raised one thin brow.

Aisling chuckled as she looked at Deirdre's dreamy expression. The plump woman's hazel eyes gazed far off while she twirled a dark auburn strand of hair around her finger. Her heavy bosom sometimes inspired shameless stares from her male patients.

Addison would arrest her plenty if he weren't already dating Krys, Aisling thought with a grin.

"Addison is a fine looking man, it's true enough. I've always seen him as an older brother though," she said.

"Well, if that cousin of yours lets him go, you be sure to let me know about it," Deirdre told her, jovial as always.

The two women exchanged charts and discussed the treatment of their most recent admission until a courier in a Vault uniform arrived bearing a sealed envelope. It was postmarked from Barcelona.

"Thank you," Aisling said as she tipped him in exchange for the letter. She eagerly broke the seal to pull out the contents inside. Her lips twitched when she saw the envelope inside was green. As promised.

Sprite,

I hope this letter finds you well and in timely fashion. As promised, I have included a list of equipment you will find handy while away on your first adventure. A friend in Cairo assures me that this site has been picked apart with a fine tooth comb, but I have a feeling there's more.

The paper smelled like him and had smudges over the otherwise perfect text, a casualty of his left-handed scrawl. The remainder of the letter was brief, yet personal. He asked her to RSVP at her earliest convenience and signed off with his initials.

Excitement washed over Aisling.

"A trip to Egypt, eh?" Deirdre peeked over her shoulder and playfully snatched away the second sheet of paper. "Canteens, hiking boots, a full field-healing kit…"

"I've been asked to help on a Collection dig, exactly as it looks."

"With your married friend?"

"Yes," Aisling murmured as she took back the list. "With my friend."

~*~

The sunbaked sand stretched for miles in every direction, laying a blanket of cream-colored landscape devoid of any life. Griffin knew better. Some of the greatest treasures of Egypt remained beneath the sands, deep below ground.

"This is rather unprecedented, isn't it?" the mercenary beside Griffin asked in a crisp, upper crust British accent.

Griffin glanced at the older wizard and nodded. "Aye, it is. I suppose the whole lot of you will be eating well for as long as Inquisitors are sabotaging our dig sites and camps. It isn't safe to go below ground or to enter forbidden temples while these bastards are so free with the dynamite. So? What do you think?"

"What do I think about all of this?"

"Aye. Can you do the job, Mr. Fitz?"

"It would certainly be to your benefit to hire an additional sword or two, but I am confident in my abilities to uphold the safety of your excavation."

While Griffin was lean with an athletic runner's build, Alistair Fitz Jr. had the broad build of a boxer. And a reputation as a magical brawler able to defeat a troll single-handedly in combat.

If he could kill a troll, he could slaughter an Outsider. With such accomplishments under his belt, there was no doubt in Griffin's mind that the man could safeguard them from assault rifle-carrying psychos too.

His close friend, a French Collector named Helene, met them as they stepped into the camp. She had model perfect long legs and skin dark as obsidian, her eyes the color of chocolate. Laughing, she threw her arms around Griffin and hugged him like a sister. One embrace from her always filled him with warmth. "You worry too much of these Inquisitors, *mon ami*. They do not show their faces in France where *our* Guardians patrol."

"Aye, but you get werewolves harassing diners. I'll pass, Helene. What're you thinkin' about this one?" He cocked his thumb back towards Alistair.

Helene chuckled warmly and stepped away from him. Her arms crossed against a meager bosom. "I think he will do. Give him the job, Griffin. We will not find a more prudent guard to serve our purposes." She smiled at him with reassurance. "Besides, you have already dragged him out here."

An hour later, they finished introducing Fitz to the topside camp where he would be stationed to keep the peace. Two Scribes, a graying Healer, and one Guardian Sergeant from the Cairo Vault all had instructions to follow his orders.

Griffin then embarked on a nine-hour drive north to the city and arrived with time to spare.

Aisling would arrive the next morning, and he absolutely couldn't wait. Normally, he would be exhausted after enduring such a trip by automobile, but he practically thrummed with excitement from the moment he stepped from the Cairo Portal and into the familiar Spanish Vault.

That was dashed to ribbons when Griffin entered the office and discovered Mercedes and his supervisor awaiting him. He stepped into the corner cubicle containing his desk and workspace to see his wife on the edge of his seat, with her long, tanned legs crossed. As always, Mercedes dressed impeccably for the public eye. Her black, curve hugging skirt skimmed above her knees in a respectable length, but the slit along the side rose high upon her thigh.

It took Griffin's brain no more than three seconds to understand what was happening when the Director's assistant, who stood with his back to the entry, hastily fumbled below his waist.

No. Not in my goddamned office, he thought. An overwhelming flood of emotion hit him, a veritable whirlwind of feelings waging war in the pit of his gut. Fury, heartache, and finally a sense of helpless despair ran through him.

A little part of him had known all along about her cheating, but he had always hoped to never prove it true. For Mara's sake, he could have forgiven anything else—anything but infidelity in his own office. The sheer disrespect toward his job and reputation boiled his blood.

He loudly cleared his throat, and the man in his cubicle turned to face him.

"Ahh, Griffin, I was not told to expect your return so early. I merely came to bring these documents to your desk," the middle-aged Spaniard said.

Griffin's gaze darted to the unfamiliar, thick manila folder of paperwork beside his office computer. "I asked *my wife* to meet me at my office. I left somethin' behind at home." His fingers twitched to put the man on his ass, but he also didn't want to lose his job.

The jerk made a hasty getaway. Griffin watched his retreating back while a rage-induced migraine pounded behind his eyelids.

"In my office?" he hissed at her. "In my fuckin' office, Mercedes?"

"I brought your trinket. Of course I am in your office. Where else would I give this to you?"

The flippant attitude and tone did not help his anger. He stared at her as she set aside a white parcel box.

"You are making a scene."

"You were slobbin' his knob in front of me, and you think I'm behaving dramatically?"

"Stuff it, Griffin. What did you expect to happen when you failed to do what is necessary to please me?" She flipped her hair over her shoulder and smiled at him smugly. Her cool gray-blue eyes narrowed, seeming to twinkle in the fluorescent lighting.

"What's necessary?" He leaned closer to her and dropped his voice dangerously low. "You never consider sex unless it's to be a bribe."

"When are you ever in our bed?" she fired back.

"Then if I'm not there, and I'm not doin' for you what you need, let me out of this fuckin' marriage. Let me take Mara back to Scotland."

"I will not drag the name of the Rivera family through the mud to grant you some self-serving divorce," she spat back at him. "You know how it will look. Papá is held in high esteem. We have Mara to think of—"

"When have you ever given a damn about Mara?" he hissed. Did her father's high esteem stop her from blowing his boss?

The voices in the adjacent cubicles silenced. They had an audience.

"I care plenty for our daughter. I am the one home with her each day while you are gallivanting about."

Griffin stared. The audacity. The lies. "You knew from the start what marrying a Collector would be like."

She could do anything she wanted to him, but he wouldn't allow her to pretend to be an upstanding and perfect mother. "You're a rotten mum, and if I could take Mara to my own mother while I'm away, I'd do that. You don't even give the girl a hug when she asks for it. You don't tuck her in, dress her, brush her hair; you don't do anythin' for her. You behave as if bein' a mother is a chore instead of a priv—"

The slap came without warning, a crack of her palm against his face. Griffin blinked, too stunned to utter a word, and so was the rest of the quieted office floor.

His hands moved toward her throat, and for one heart-pounding second, he nearly gave in to the murderous intent to snap her neck like a twig.

Griffin had never struck a woman in all of his life, and he wouldn't compromise his morals to do it now. Years of watching his stepfather in the act had been enough to thoroughly cement his beliefs. Mercedes wasn't worth it.

I knew it. Fuckin' knew it all along, he thought bitterly. But he didn't. He hadn't truly known anything more than a vague suspicion and a queasy feeling of doubt. He thought of nights when he lay awake beside her, too wary of launching a baseless accusation but wondering who it could possibly be. It didn't ease the pain any to learn the identity of the man pleasing his wife in his absence.

"That it, then? Keepin' me around for convenience while you do as you please?"

"You were the one my father and stepmother chose for me, Griffin, and you came to me gladly enough. It has always been a marriage of convenience."

And he was a fool to believe it was anything more.

"Aye, you're right, then, Mercedes. You're completely fuckin' right. And since it's no longer convenient for me, it's only fair we end it. You'll hear from my solicitor soon, and you'll sign the goddamned papers, because if you don't, I'll air out every scrap of dirty Rivera family laundry I've got. You'll see my exclusive tell-all story in the paper by next week."

Like a fish out of water, her mouth opened and closed several times. Her hands dropped to her sides as the color bleached from her face. "You wouldn't."

"Oh, I would. I know someone at the *Almanac*. Someone with plenty of reason to dislike you."

Griffin dropped his gold wedding band on the floor and with a snap of his fingers, sparks of heat and fire reduced it to a molten pool of metal. As she sputtered out for him to wait, he took the box holding Jerry's knife and stepped from the office cubicle. He made his way out of the department with his chin raised.

~*~

At six in the morning, the Cairo Vault bustled with activity. Griffin waited nervously outside the high archway as people shuffled to and from the magical transportation circle.

A working Portal stood as a symbol of prestige and power for the Vault owning it. They allowed rapid, instantaneous transport to any other Portal within the hub as long as the two circular rings were attuned to create the same song.

The ring of twenty-one pristine crystalline pillars made a perfect circle on the cement floor, each gemstone spire sitting on a golden disc. Fae charged top dollar for the extraordinary prisms mined from the world of Avalon, but their currency wasn't always mortal money.

It was the job of the Operators to maintain these gemstones and to change them every scheduled shift for the next destination. An incorrect tune could be as catastrophic as a crashing plane. People could die. Or worse, be taken captive by the rogue fae greedily awaiting such a tragedy.

The chimes of the glowing crystal spires announced the beautiful notes of Ireland's song. The whiteboard indicated in purple marker that Dublin was slated for arrival. The silver circle gleamed, and after a soft glow of rainbow colors, a dozen Magi stood in the formerly empty space.

Griffin spotted Aisling immediately. He picked her petite figure out of the bunch and felt a renewed sense of excitement. Instead of her usual skirts and dresses, she wore khaki pants and a pale pink, long-sleeved shirt. The color suited her far better than the dull grays, blues, blacks, and whites she wore during their most recent visits.

The moment she was within reach, he enfolded her in a tight embrace that lifted her from her feet. "Glad you made it. You're the last one here."

She smiled up at him and adjusted the strap of her heavily loaded leather bag. Griffin relieved her of its burden then led her outside to a rented vehicle.

Despite his eager greeting, Griffin fell into a subdued silence for the start of their journey out of the city. He thought of his divorce, the chat over the long phone call with his lawyer, and how much freedom would cost him. Conflicting emotions twisted his stomach into knots. Occasionally, he stole a glance at Aisling to find her staring with wide and curious eyes out the window, soaking in every sight of Cairo's streets.

"How far out do we have to go, Griff?"

"It's a wee bit of a drive by automobile, but I remembered you weren't so fond of heights. Otherwise we might have flown."

"I can't believe you pilot your own plane."

"We traveled quite a bit. Liam and I…" Thinking of Liam stabbed him in the chest, a knife in his heart whenever he remembered the days of adventuring with his friend. He focused on the world beyond the windshield to distract him from the memories, but it didn't work. The sand-dusted road ahead of them seemed to stretch endlessly into the expanse of Egyptian desert. "Was his idea."

"Maybe one day you can take me up," she said. "I know I always said I'd never want wings, but maybe, if only once, it might be nice to see the world as a bird does."

"Guess that means you'll have to come on another job with me."

"We'll see how this one goes." Aisling laughed softly and turned her gaze to look out at the passing scenery.

The Nile River provided a belt of green and city sprawls, but beyond the borders of the water, endless desert stretched on. Silence fell between them as they drove through the arid landscape.

"You've been brooding again."

"I don't brood."

"Then you're not Griffin MacNeil," Aisling teased, peering at him. "Anything in particular on your mind? Mara is well?"

"Nothin' serious," he replied while gazing ahead at the road. "We're supposed to be havin' a good time here, and I don't want to trouble you with my problems."

And they couldn't have a good time if he continued to be her morose and silent driver. He apologized and made a genuine effort to be more engaging company. A few times he caught her looking at him in concern, and he was quick to point out interesting sights and landmarks.

What remained of the drive was longer than Griffin initially led Aisling to believe, but the duration teemed with idle chatter and sometimes laughter. She sang to the satellite radio, and he encouraged her despite familiar taunts and urgings for him to join her in song. His voice wasn't anything special though.

"Here it is. Home for the next week or two."

Off the roads and several miles beyond the famed Valley of the Kings, the Collector camp sprawled out around a small oasis of green and blue. It was hardly more than a pond with a pair of date palms.

The merciless sun baked down with the sort of force that tightened the skin and reddened it within seconds. The dry, parched soil and sandy dunes seemed to stretch as far as the eye could see.

"It's so hot!" Aisling stepped out of the jeep, and her fair complexion seemed to immediately flush in the dry heat.

Griffin chuckled, then rounded the vehicle and draped a colorful, silk scarf over her hair.

"A gift for my Irish dove so you don't return home fried to a crisp."

"It's beautiful, Griff," she said as he tucked the fabric around her neck to shade her face.

He took the lead by guiding her to each station—their Healer's station especially. A woman in a long-sleeved olive dress and matching hijab greeted them. Halima smiled and treated Aisling with courtesy as if she were one of them.

"I know it's sparse, but it's—"

"Perfect," Aisling said, tilting her head to smile up at him. "It will be fine as any campout, and I'm glad to be here."

For that moment, Griffin felt his worries pass him by. With a team and a job to occupy his mind, he could forget the frustrating series of phone calls with his solicitor the previous night. Could forget the divorce set in motion.

~*~

Griffin sat among the group of mages passing bottles of the local Stella beer and Glenlivet around the campfire.

The friendly banter and enjoyable conversation eventually dwindled to serious topics. Two mages of their topside crew had died in the most recent attack.

"They've got ballistic armor that repels most magical assaults. A pair of them came at us in Dublin months ago," Griffin said.

"It is purely a matter of cooking the bloody bastards in their shell," Alistair said, waving off the concern. "Which I thought you knew, given your history."

Griffin sighed. Most people naturally expected him to resort to fire magic due to his family line, and they would be right. It came naturally to him. He was only a few generations removed from the greatest wizard of all time—Merlin.

"Who are they, exactly? We have heard only whispers of the Inquisitors down in Brazil," Juliana said. She came to them from the Vault in Rio de Janeiro upon recommendation from Regent O'Sullivan.

"They're nothing more than thugs for hire bearing the sign of the cross as an excuse to commit murder." Alistair shook his head.

"It is all of the cult activity from the Diabolists," Marius explained. "I am told the Inquisitors have grown quite bold in the United States where the cult is most prominent."

"*Oui.* Those murderers believe this is a world merely for normal, God-fearing humans," Helene said. "No Faeries, no Sylvan, and no Magi. Thanks to the cultists and their demon-summoning, the bigots hate all of us."

"We haven't had issues with necromancers in Ireland, though some of the darker fae have been stirred up as of late," Aisling informed them.

"The Winter Court?" Griffin asked.

Aisling nodded. "Them and some of the Otherkin. We had a Guardian at the bad end of a hag's curse a few months back, and since then a few redcap attacks, increased vampire feedings, and others."

"If this is any indication of what is to come, then we should not expect the Inquisition to go quietly into the night any time soon," Juliana said with a sigh. She rose from the campfire and brushed the sandy grit from her pants. "I will retire to my bed, but you are welcome to share a tent with me, Aisling."

"I suppose we should all be heading to bed." Helene stretched and stood. One by one, their little party broke up for the night.

Aisling gave Griffin's shoulder a comforting squeeze once she rose to her feet. "Get some sleep. I need you bright-eyed if you're to be taking me down into your tombs."

"Aye. Soon, lass. I won't be long."

"And Griffin... thank you. I'm glad to be here."

Despite his words to her, Griffin retreated last to their shelter. He finished the bottle of Glenlivet and left the campfire to crawl into the bedroll awaiting him.

The morning would bring a new adventure, and a second chance to regain what was lost between him and Aisling.

Was it right to move on so quickly following the end of his marriage to Mercedes? Was it wrong to covet the affection of his first love while emerging from the ruins of his broken family?

Griffin didn't know. What he did know was that he'd missed her, and losing Ash had left an irreparable hole in his heart.

And this quest gave him one more chance to have her back.

Chapter 7

Just five minutes. Five minutes was all Jean-Luc needed to rest his eyes before returning to work. Despite the chaos of the busy office, many voices of his fellow Guardians blurring together, he thought he could refresh himself with a few winks.

Classical music filtered softly through the office speakers, gently lulling him to sleep. The third level of the riverfront building was completely dedicated to the Vault's Guardian forces. Clustered desks in groups of four occupied the floor, decorated by the personal belongings of each individual employee. Pictures, diagrams, and lists detailing the current supernatural threats covered the walls.

"I know you're not like the rest of us, Chevalier, but even you need sleep at some point," Sylvie said.

Jean-Luc raised his head to acknowledge his partner just as she affectionately tousled his hair and sat on the edge of the desk.

He dropped his pen and sighed. "I did sleep."

"An hour's nap in the breakroom doesn't count as sleep, my good friend."

"It was two hours," he told her. "You're worried for nothing, Sylvie."

"I worry for something, Jean-Luc. You were projecting your aura again."

He glanced at the clock then groaned into one hand. "I didn't realize." Five minutes ago, the investigation room had been bustling with activity. Everyone had deserted it. "I didn't mean to chase everyone away again. I'm sorry. I'll leave to get some rest. I didn't intend to—"

"They know that, Luc." Sylvie smiled at him. "We want for you to get a night of sleep because we care, not because of…"

Jean-Luc followed her line of sight to the far wall behind him where the shadows danced and converged, growing into an ominously spreading force that threatened to overtake the sunny interior of the room. He was doing it again.

Ever since the night of his miraculous resurrection, Jean-Luc had been able to do things that no other magus could do. In fact, he had been purely mortal and mundane before that fateful evening. There wasn't a spark of magic in his family tree, and his abilities were a complete mystery. Even Aisling had no insights to offer from a medical standpoint.

Sylvie offered him a ride and refused his attempts to wave her off.

"So. How was dinner with Anton?" Jean-Luc asked.

The elevator dinged at its destination, and the doors slid open. They moved into the vacant parking garage at a casual stroll, headed for the inexpensive green sedan that Sylvie enjoyed.

Whatever her answer, the squeal of tires cut Sylvie off and drew their attention towards the garage entrance. Two Ford Mondeos swerved inside, one in the local police design and the second sleek and black.

"Chevalier!"

The sharp voice belonged to a tall man with a pencil-thin mustache over a mouth that always seemed to be in a tight, pinched line. He stepped from the police vehicle and turned his dark eyes on the pair of Guardians.

"Captain Cloutier, how may I—"

The officer raised a hand to cut Jean-Luc off and turned his attention to the handcuffed man in the rear of their vehicle. Two other Guardians pulled the lanky fellow from the backseat and onto his feet, each one escorting him by an arm.

"I need you for an interrogation," the captain said crisply. He strode past to lead the way back to the elevators. "Now."

"So much for being off of the job for the evening," Jean-Luc murmured as they turned to head back inside.

~*~

An unusual sense of dread tightened Sylvie's chest as she led the Guardians to the detention center below their underground garage. Cement floor stretched down a single hallway, decorated by intricate symbols serving a unique purpose—protection against magic and evil. Cold iron bars sealed the entrances of six tiny cells, and a solid steel door gleamed from the end of the corridor.

At first glance, the interrogation room appeared to be typical of any local precinct, but the arcane inscriptions in the floors and walls took away from any illusion of normalcy. A mirror covered the expanse of one wall with additional mystic designs etched into the two-way glass.

Sylvie stepped in first, followed by Captain Cloutier and their leading sergeant, Raoul Girard. The two men guided the prisoner to a chair and snapped restraints over his wrists. The rest of the Guardians who had accompanied them were directed to remain outside and close the door.

"You sure you can get what we need, Chevalier?" The captain directed Sylvie and Raoul to step back and to remain at the ready.

"I can get it out of him," Jean-Luc assured them. He drew the black hood off their prisoner.

"I'm not telling you a goddamned thing," the Inquisitor uttered.

"You will tell us everything," Jean-Luc replied.

"You can't make me say a fucking word. We know how your kind work."

"You are greatly mistaken if you believe that I must make you speak to learn what I want from you," Jean-Luc said.

Sylvie watched from a short distance away with her arms folded beneath her breasts.

Everyone knew the routine. Usually, the militant religious fanatics chose to die in combat before they could be taken by law enforcement. Taking one alive was a rare feat indeed.

"Fuck you. You can't do a damn thing to me." The defiant Inquisitor lifted his chin to stare at them.

"That is where you are wrong. There are many things that I can do to you."

A chill traveled Sylvie's spine.

"I'll die first."

Luc seized the Inquisitor by the face with both hands to maintain eye contact. The man in the chair became pale, and he began to shudder in the seat. With a white-knuckled grip of the arms of the interrogation chair, his fingernails dug into the metal until they splintered away from the nail beds. He screamed in terror.

"Much, much better. I feel that I must apologize for my poor manners. My name is Jean-Luc Chevalier, Guardian Lieutenant of this Vault. Who might you be, Monsieur?" His thumbs pressed into the man's cheeks, and his nails left crescent indentations in the flesh of his jaw.

"Fuck you," the man's voice quavered.

Jean-Luc applied unyielding pressure to the joints of the man's jaw from both sides. "Do you not like what you see? Perhaps you want to see more."

"No, wait! Stop! I'll tell you anything! Don't hurt her anymore! I can't... I can't watch..."

Her? Sylvie's eyes darted from their prisoner back to Jean-Luc. She'd seen him working his ability to inspire hallucinations in the past.

Her partner smiled grimly, but he didn't break eye contact with the prisoner. Overhead, the fluorescent light strips buzzed noisily. They flickered and cast eerie, crawling shadows over the interrogation room. The man thrashed in the seat as if in the throes of a seizure. His head turned to the left and right but failed to escape eye contact with the lieutenant.

"We're gonna blow them all to hell! That's the plan, okay?"

"Blow who? What?" Jean-Luc demanded, his voice made of steel.

"The sites. They wanna blow up your grave robbers. I swear that's it! Stop, please! No! I can't... I can't see it again!" The man begged and writhed, but Luc continued to deal the psychic torture.

Sylvie moved in, her hand outstretched towards her fellow lieutenant's shoulder. "Jean-Luc—"

"Let him work," Captain Cloutier barked at her.

A whisper slithered past Sylvie's ear, and a cold sensation of dread knotted her belly. Beside her, Raoul began to tremble. Perspiration dotted his brow as his eyes grew increasingly larger.

The lights overhead sparked and popped, and then finally dimmed entirely. The room plunged into darkness. Faint gleams of ruddy light originated from the runes on the floors and walls, while cooler hues of violet shone against the glass.

"Sylvie." The voice whispered past her ear, a caress that twisted her stomach. *"Sylvie."* Raoul stood to her left, but the cool breath of a phantom kissed her right ear. She flinched.

Captain Cloutier gave her a stern look. It was her second time witnessing Jean-Luc's rather unorthodox use of his talents, but she had yet to determine if their Captain also fell prey to the collateral effect.

"You let them do this. You." The apparition touched her with icy fingertips. Its odorous breath held the sickly sweet smell of cooked flesh. Swallowing, Sylvie closed her eyes and tried to block it out. None of it was real. *"They'll come for you next. You and Francois."*

"No," she whispered with a tremulous voice.

"Mommy!" screamed the phantom voice of her son, her *living* child who, under no circumstances, would ever be in the lower level of the Parisian Vault.

Raoul clawed at the knob of the door and rushed into the corridor. When Sylvie turned her head to watch him flee, she saw the disfigured face of her deceased husband at her side.

None of it is real... It is only in my imagination, she told herself. Despite the inward reassurance, it made her heart jump and skip just the same.

"Egypt!" the man in the chair cried, weeping. He struggled against his restraints until the metal cut into his flesh. He sang like a bird while Cloutier noted locations and cities in the Inquisitor plan of attack.

"I believe we have everything, Captain," Jean-Luc said.

"There has to be more. They're onto something big, Chevalier. Press him," Cloutier said firmly. "There are lives at stake."

The darkness of the room deepened. Shadows threatened to dim even the glow of the warding runes as Jean-Luc brought the prisoner's face nose to nose with his own. Sylvie felt the temperature drop seconds before her breath huffed out in a white mist.

Nothing here is real. It's not real, Sylvie told herself quietly. She faced forward and refused to budge again.

THE COLLECTOR'S TREASURE

The man held by Jean-Luc's hands spoke in gibberish between his screams. Or so it sounded to her ears.

Runes meant to guard them from danger began to smoke, and then they flared with blue fire. Sylvie couldn't recall a single time they had ever been pushed so far. Not even when they had captured a servant sworn to the demon Prince Asmodeus. As frightening as that possession had been, it paled in comparison to the cold dread and knee-quaking terror she experienced now.

Screams and mocking laughter filled her ears while she suffered a dizzying sense of falling. Despite knowing the wall stood behind her, she couldn't feel it. All sensations faded away except for the cold and the ever-present sense of something sinister pressing within her mind.

Something dangerous.

"Chevalier, enough!" Cloutier shouted.

The choked scream came as if from far away, in a voice she barely recognized as their captain's. Her own cries joined them, praying for it all to end.

~*~

Sylvie found Jean-Luc as he exited the men's room drying his hands on his slacks. Droplets of water darkened his fine silver shirt and glistened on his face.

"It isn't your fault," she told him softly.

"I know."

"Then why do I feel as if you are blaming yourself, Luc? You only did as you were told."

She didn't blame him. The captain couldn't blame him either since Jean-Luc had only followed his orders to the letter.

"I should have had better control over it."

"Perhaps. But this is not something that you do every day, Luc... It isn't your fault."

Her friend took in a ragged breath and ran his fingers through his sweat-dampened black hair. Whatever he had shown the mercenary was tearing him apart on the inside, and Sylvie's heart broke for him. She had known Jean-Luc since his days as a liaison officer of the law with the mundane police. He was a gentle-hearted man.

"Will he…" Sylvie's green eyes drifted to the hall, and she lowered her voice. "Recover?"

"No. There was nothing left, Sylvie. It…it felt like an execution," he murmured. "His body was there, but inside, there was nothing left at all. I couldn't stop. It was like attempting to brake in the rain. No matter how hard I tried, it only continued to go forward. The Healers say he's soul-dead."

Goosebumps raised across her back and arms. As she swallowed the sour taste in her mouth, she wrapped both arms around Jean-Luc and hugged him.

The basic, primitive part of her brain wanted to be as afraid of Jean-Luc as she was of the power he commanded, but deep down, she told herself he was the same man she'd always known.

A gentle vegetarian, a sweet friend who was there for any of them in a jam, and a man who never even discharged his firearm unless necessary.

She suppressed her own discomfort and squeezed him tighter, pressing her cheek against his shoulder.

The Vault had acquired precious information, but it hadn't come without a price.

Chapter 8

Collectors came in two variants—the crew who cleansed away all traces of magic by reducing a site to a state of mundane normalcy, and the sort of Collectors like Griffin who went in hard and fast to track down a relic.

Some wealthy old coot would get a wild need for a magical item he had read about in lore, and that's when Griffin investigated, studied, and determined whether the item existed. And then he found it if the stars were right and luck was with him.

It usually was.

"We discovered that as many of these pyramids and tombs were built by normal humans as they were by wizard Egyptians wantin' a proper send off to the afterlife," Griffin said. "This particular one is fabled to hold the Dagger of Night, a blade once owned by a priestess of Isis. Legends claim it can kill a grown man with a single scrape."

Aisling glanced up at him as they walked, her pack slung over her shoulder. When they reached the truck where the others were gathering, she finally blurted out the question that had been gnawing at her. "Where *is* this site of yours? I've been looking around all morning, but I've not seen any tombs or the like within sight."

"You mean that Griffin did not tell you?" Helene and Juliana exchanged dubious gazes. Both women had made short work of organizing their belongings and equipment into watertight bags.

"Well…ahh…I thought we'd explain it with her present." He rubbed the nape of his neck and looked away.

"Explain what?" Aisling asked.

"We must dive to the bottom of the pond. It is fifty feet," Odion said grimly. He was the only one among the five who lacked an eager grin.

"C'mon, Ash, don't look so worried. You're a great swimmer."

She blinked once and stared, then sighed quietly as she lowered her bag to the ground. "In that case, let's be sure to double bag the healing kit, please. Won't do to have wet herbs and bandages."

There were no scuba tanks. Instead, one of the vehicles came equipped with diving hoses.

The water was warm at the surface, pristine and blue as the skies above. Faint hints of a mossy green bottom implied a shallow depth of no more than three to four feet.

Aisling discovered that looks weren't always what they appeared to be. The water swished and splashed against her knees, her thighs and her waist. She continued forward until it reached her chin and tilted her head back to look at Griffin. He gave her an encouraging nod and helped her place the breathing hose.

"I promise I'll be right beside you and nothing will happen to you."

The illusion of a shallow bottom in the spring was shattered with her next step. Aisling made a blind step forward, feeling with her toes. The sensation of vast nothingness beneath her feet warred with the visual of the pond floor. It caught her by surprise and down she went.

The world became a realm of blues in every shade, growing darker the farther down she sank. Griffin's hand touched her wrist when she hit the silt on the bottom, his face illuminated in the glow of a waterproof lamp. She sucked in a deep and final breath then pulled the hose from her mouth, trusting him to lead her through safely.

They swam into a narrow, square entrance carved in the wall. It was the secret gateway into the underground tomb. Aisling kept pace beside Griffin with practiced ease as if she had done it all before.

The water-safe lamps finally blinked out entirely as they broke the surface, gasping for breath.

The pair swam to the edge and climbed from the water where the others awaited them. Aisling sat there and wrung out her heavy braid, clothes plastered to her skin. Only the glow of a magical lantern remained, casting a pale blue aura over the immediate surroundings. It was barely enough to see as Helene began to haul the remaining gear from the water and unpack additional sources of light.

"The soakin' wet part is always the worst," Griffin complained as he pulled off his shirt and tossed it aside. "Never get dry enough."

Despite seeing him topless in her flat while tending to a bullet graze, Aisling admired the lean muscles of tanned back as well as the chiseled biceps always hidden beneath his clothing.

Then she wondered why in hell she'd begun staring in the first place.

With her thoughts dragged back to the task at hand, she noticed Griffin wasn't the only one undressing. She hastily spun around with burning cheeks, dust and loose rocks scattering beneath her feet.

"Everything okay, Aisling?" Helene asked while pulling off her own shirt.

"Ah…hold it, gentlemen," Juliana spoke up.

Aisling heard the rustling noises stop as wet clothing remained in place, dripping.

"Uh…shit." Griffin said. "Forgot about you, Ash. Odion, how about the two of us head deeper into the tunnel."

Odion opened his mouth to protest until Griffin clapped him on the shoulder and directed him up the path.

"So, Aisling, you and Griffin… You are…?" A pregnant pause hung in the air, filled with underlying meaning.

"Friends," she replied softly. "We're only friends."

They met the men at the top of the slope to find them fully dressed and stowing away their soaked duds. On the inside, she felt like a fool for lusting after her childhood sweetheart. Their time had come and gone. The sooner she made herself remember that, the better off things would be.

Ahead, carved stone pillars rose up to a height of nine feet. The granite keystone held a sigil of swirling gold, bronze, and silver. A matching line of embedded metal stretched across the floor of the entrance. Aisling didn't see a single speck of dust or sand marring the gleaming metal. A sure sign of magic.

She hesitated, an uneasy feeling in her gut. "What is it? Some sort of ward?"

"It is only a blood line. Nothing to fear," Helene assured her with a bright smile. Her dark hair, bound in dozens of small braids, still dripped against her shoulders.

"It is an archaic form of magic. What happens when a magus charges a leyline with a defensive curse. In this case, the enchantment is infused with the blood of a human, so only a human may safely pass," Juliana said.

"Nothing to worry about. We are all human here, yes?" Odion said with a grin.

"Oh…" Aisling took a small step backwards and dropped her gaze away from the archway. She wrung her hands together. "Maybe I should stay out here, then. Or go back up."

"Don't be ridiculous, Aisling. You came all this way." Helene smiled in encouragement.

Odion stood on the other side of the line with his arms crossed. "This is a waste of time. You cannot turn back now; it would set us all back."

"Let her be," Juliana said.

"I think you can pass, Ash. You're more human than anythin' else."

"I'm also fae," she whispered.

"Trust me." Griffin gave her an imploring look, his green eyes beseeching her to come closer. He stood on the other side of the blood line with his hand out, fingers extended toward her.

Aisling felt every ounce of trust for Griffin, more than she'd ever felt during their school days. As she inhaled a deep breath, she accepted his hand and moved across the glittering line.

A jolt of electricity shocked the sole of her foot. It traveled throughout her body, buzzing to the tips of her fingers and toes. Nothing else remarkable happened, and she moved to his side unharmed.

"You may be gifted, Ash, but you're as human as the rest of us," Griffin told her.

~*~

THE COLLECTOR'S TREASURE

On the first day of the group's exploration, Griffin led them through several small chambers, each one grander than the last. Aisling followed and listened, watching with attentive eyes.

As promised, few injuries occurred, but his chest swelled with pride when she removed a minor curse from Odion after the man stumbled into a trap embedded in the dusty, tile floor.

Griffin had always known she would develop into a fine Healer.

She was meant for more than stuffy Vault infirmaries. This was where she belonged, following in the adventuring footsteps of her mother. He watched her grow confident in the passing days, curious but eager to learn.

"Ready for another lesson?" Griffin asked. They'd been underground a few days, and there was no shortage of tricks to teach her. "I imagine that cousin of yours is a cinch with these, given Krys's love for lightning magic. Y'see, all you need for the most basic of traps is the correct rune, a good bonding material like blood or certain alchemical reagents, and a charge of your mana."

"Considering I have no talent whatsoever for electricity, maybe you could show me something else instead? Helene mentioned something about water conjuring this morning."

"Aye." Griffin demonstrated by making a weak water-summoning rune. "Liam was more experienced at makin' these. I can split earth and make chasms, capture the elements, but I'm shite at conjuring things from afar. He taught this one to me in case I was ever without him and in need of water. It's simple transmutation. Good thing to know when on an adventure."

Cool, fresh water sprang like a swirling vortex above the rune in a geyser without a visible source beneath it. He held his canteen at the perfect angle to capture the thinning stream.

"Sometimes, for the severely wounded, we draw healing circles, but nothing so instantaneous as this."

"You know, as often as I've been in those, I'm still not sure how they work." He grinned and offered the canteen.

"It's an amplification spell, meant to help boost the energy of the Healer as well as the patient. It's exhausting, pouring all our magic into another person to knit their flesh, so we draw our circles across a natural ley line."

"I used to think my job was a pain in the ass. Glad I'm not a Healer."

After he smudged the water rune, they delved deeper into a burial chamber with a gilded sarcophagus. Griffin explained that many of the items within were meant to join the deceased in the afterlife. That included servants.

And cats.

"I could never mummify Breda. It wouldn't be right." A wrinkle of her small, upturned nose reflected her thoughts on the matter.

"Breda would make a nice stuffed kitty. She'd always be with us then," he teased.

"As if you'd stuff Autumn."

"I've considered it from time to time when she's gotten into one of her moods."

The fire salamander poked her head out of his pocket and stared. She snorted twin plumes of curling steam to show her distaste before diving into her hiding place again.

The days passed easily as other sinister examples of ancient magic were deployed against the group of adventurers. Fortunately, Griffin was able to clear a room of pit vipers with a few flares of magical fire, saving Aisling from the strenuous task of removing venom from her patients. One moment, they were little more than sticks of inert wood on the dusty floor. In the next, the group of five was surrounded by hissing, menacing serpents.

Aisling had no shortage of things to learn from Griffin or the others. Juliana and Helene took great enjoyment in teaching her the delicate task of reading a room without setting off every trap with brute force. Helene excelled at feeling out traps, so she could devise a strategy to unravel them with little damage or loss. Griffin, on the other hand, went in like a jackhammer.

"I propose we take a break for now," Odion declared.

Juliana and Helene hastily agreed and began to break down their supplies into camp.

Griffin sighed. "C'mon, Ash. Let the rest of them sit here and stuff their gobs. I promised you adventure."

As if a near brush with venom-inflicted death weren't adventurous enough. Thirty minutes later, their walk brought them to a wide chamber marked by an official emblem of the Collection Department.

"That means they've deemed this room cleared and safe."

"This is beautiful." Aisling stepped in and swept the light from her lantern on the walls.

Inlays of gold and crushed gemstones sparkled under the aura of warm yellow cast from her handheld lamp. The colorful murals remained untouched after hundreds of years.

The artistic depictions once again drew Griffin's attention. He had seen it all before during a previous visit but it remained impressive. "Helene swore it was all clear but..." He folded his arms against his chest and seemed most intrigued by the marble columns spanning from floor to ceiling. "That's odd."

"What is odd?" She set her lantern down to twist her hair off her neck while taking in her surroundings.

A faint beam shone from above, but his sharp eyes easily picked up the barely visible pool of light no larger than a dinner plate. He moved his lantern away to thoroughly dim the area. "That. It wasn't there the last time I came here. I'm sure of it. I'd remember a random beam of light shinin' from the ceiling."

He craned his neck and stared upward to discover the source of light intensified by the second. Movement from the corner of his eye showed Aisling moving closer to the oddity he described. With each of her steps, the beam spread and widened farther until they stood within a radiant circle bright enough to fill the room.

That's when Griffin saw the carving nearby. A stone sigil stood out keenly beside a silver representation of Isis. His inquisitive nature won over caution, and he quickly crossed the room to examine and touch the symbol. The wall rumbled in protest. Dust and bits of crumbling rock fell away, but the opening refused to move.

"Fuck!" He jerked his hand away. It glowed hot as an ember in the night.

It was never a good idea to touch unidentified objects in a site of ancient magic.

"Griffin?" Hearing his cry wrenched her mesmerized gaze away from the light. Aisling moved swiftly to his side. "Hand, please. Now."

"Never mind me, we need to get that opened all the way. There's another room beyond that wall."

"Griffin MacNeil, you will give me your hand now."

"Look, you can baby me to your bosom as much as wanted after we've checked out this new corridor."

"I don't have much of a bosom, and we won't be opening any corridor while you're hurt." She grabbed his arm and took a look for herself. Then she drew a sharp intake of air.

The burn began at his palm and was initially no larger than a coin. In the time since their argument began, the bubbling blisters had begun to travel down past his thumb toward the back of his hand. It spread toward his wrist, consisting of angry burn blisters that peeled away to reveal the extent of the damage.

It hadn't felt nearly so bad until she touched him. Until her fingers pressed against nerves and sent unbearable, shooting sensations of pain up and down his arm.

Griffin swore under his breath and clenched his jaw against the excruciating agony. If it became any worse, he knew he'd be praying to be put out of his misery.

And if his injury continued to spread, maybe he'd get that wish.

~*~

"This is bad, Griffin. Cursed."

Slithering tendrils of magic wormed through his flesh, a burn with an insidiously slow spread.

"Everythin' was supposed to be cleared down here."

"Stay still and quiet," Aisling ordered him sternly without looking up. With every breath he took, his injury seemed to spread until she feared he would be without a hand at all.

Feared it might consume more than his hand.

Please, give me the strength to heal him… she prayed in silence.

She began with a hum, fingers glowing faintly as she seemed to pluck at the air above his arm. Her pale brow furrowed, and sweat glistened along the line of her dark hair.

No, you can't have him. The decisive thought firmed in her mind as she pitted her will and magic against the curse.

THE COLLECTOR'S TREASURE

Aisling reached for a vial in her kit without ever taking her gaze from his hand. She broke the seal with a fingernail and dribbled a pungent herbal concoction over his undamaged flesh first. The last few drops sizzled as she brought them over the magical burn. Her humming had been steadily growing louder, but now she opened her mouth and began to sing.

She halted the ascent of the curse while Griffin watched her in mute fascination. Like watching time reverse, cracked white tissue and destroyed flesh became baby pink and healthy. The fresh skin felt warm to the touch and soft, tender as a newborn infant.

The lilting and dulcet tones of her voice faded to silence, but the mysterious glimmering light continued to dance around them.

"You're amazin'," he said while Aisling rolled a linen bandage around his freshly healed hand. "I always loved hearing you sing. Almost forgot what it was like…"

"It helps me focus if there's no time or use for a healing circle. Helps me tune the discordant notes of dark magic back into lighter ones."

"I'm glad you came with me. You saved my hand, dove. I don't…"

Her brows raised, wondering what he planned to say.

Tales of his adventures and mishaps with Liam had led her to believe the deceased Irishman had been greatly talented as a Healer. Still, she thought he would have struggled to turn the tide against a curse laid by fae. Griffin might have lost a finger or two, or worse, his whole hand.

A lost limb meant a career-ending injury for a Collector.

The realization made tears sting behind her lids. She blinked rapidly to keep them at bay. "There we go. We'll just keep an eye on it now, make sure I actually stopped the spread."

"Was foolish of me, anyway. I'm sorry. I just…I saw the thing and got so excited to show you somethin' new. I broke one of the first rules we're taught. I feel like a twat."

"You always did get giddy over showing me anything. It's just… I mean, I see Collectors come in all the time. It's different seeing it up close. What if I hadn't been able—" She sucked in a shaky breath and let it out on a huff of air. "Sorry. You scared me, is all."

"I would have lost it."

The touch of his hand as he smoothed back an errant curl from her face set butterflies loose in her stomach. She found herself getting lost in his emerald eyes and unable to look away. Green had always been her favorite color since meeting him.

He had greeted her so courteously when a well-meaning teacher volunteered Aisling to give their newest student—Griffin—a tour of their school. Unlike most of the student body, he hadn't minded her shy ways.

From that moment, they became inseparable and were always at one another's side. She shielded him from the bullies who teased him for his delicate frame, and likewise, he made a friend of a young woman whom others viewed as an oddity. As being different. Then over one summer, he'd changed. Filled out. Grown muscles and shot up so many inches he wasn't her scrawny bookworm any longer.

Part of her wanted to ask if she could remain and work with him again. To stay at his side on every dig. Together, they could travel back and forth wherever they were needed, whether in Egypt or across the ocean waters in other countries.

It seemed such a hopeless dream and one destined only for heartache.

Griffin touched her cheek, and she wanted nothing more than to lean forward and kiss him. She could still remember their first and their very last. Her eyes lingered at his mouth and perfect lips, but eventually the moment passed and left only pulse-pounding desire in its place. He lowered his hand, and she dropped her gaze away, humbled by the knowledge of his marriage and the wife awaiting him at home.

"C'mon. We've got a new room to explore. If you still trust me, that is."

"Of course I do. You know you don't have to ask that. But, Griff, the door didn't open…"

"I've got a suspicion, and I need you to come near it."

"I can't heal myself if I'm screaming. I know you, remember? I know you were swallowing back the pain." Even with her gaze held to his hand, she'd noted the tension in his body and the way his every breath shook while she worked.

"No. It's not goin' to hurt you. I'd never let you touch it if I thought it would hurt you. I'm certain enough to put my life on it. Your ancestors built this tomb, and it'll take a fae to lift the spell."

"I've only got a wee bit of Faerie blood." She flashed him a nervous smile.

"You're both. The best of both worlds, sprite."

The carved sigil remained pale silver in color as her hand hovered above it. Aisling hesitated a moment but then pressed her palm flat upon it, trusting in Griffin's intuition. The scrape of stone on stone rumbled throughout the chamber, and a perfectly cut, recessed circle opened in the previously smooth surface of the wall.

Fluorescent blue-green lamps held glow stones crafted by Avalon's best artisans. They lit the downwards sloping corridor and picked out gleams of color in the walls.

The friends descended another twenty feet below the earth where the sound of running water greeted them. An archway inlaid with gems precious to both Earth and the fae realm of Avalon decorated the edges. Like the light above, the fae stones brightened as the pair drew near. The moment they stepped through, several fire pits flared to life, each one bracketed by polished sheets of silver to intensify their light.

Aisling smelled and felt the moisture in the air long before she heard the rushing water spilling into the basin below. A massive fountain rose from a long pool of water, topped by a majestic, black onyx statue of an unknown woman.

She stared in wide-eyed wonder at it all, absolutely speechless. The fountain was a treasure unlike anything she had ever seen.

Ornate adornments of prismatic opal and silver draped over the feminine figure, pieces of jewelry she had likely worn in life. And there in her hand glistened the silver blade of a sacrificial knife.

"I can't believe… It's like everythin' all around is reactin' to you."

Aisling pulled her gaze away from the fountain and looked towards Griffin. Only then did she notice the urns full of glimmering flowers. "Those are from Avalon."

Many fae must have had a hand in building the place. Sprigs of dark plant matter and naked stems suddenly elongated and twisted into swirls of living vegetation. Buds swelled and spread, their tips split open, and petals unraveled to reveal cobalt blossoms releasing sweet fragrances rivaling the most aromatic jasmine.

Aisling felt moisture pricking at her eyes as she took in her surroundings. Her gaze fell on Griffin and lingered in appreciative study. *He looks like he belongs,* she thought.

"Thank you for bringing me. For sharing all of this."

"There's no one I'd rather have here."

They both removed their boots to cool their feet in the water. She splashed him, and he threatened to toss her in like old times. After a few moments of play, Griffin moved over to have a look at their discovery.

"As far as I can tell, none of these are magical. I want you to choose one or two, Ash."

"To keep?"

He laughed and grinned down at her. "Rule of Collections is finders keepers. You keep what you find fair and square, unless it's part of the job."

"Maybe just one…"

"C'mon, I'll give you a boost. You can fetch that shiny dagger for me too. Use my gloves. They're lined with firedrake skin, and if I'd been thinking, I would have used them in the room up above." He sighed.

Once she wore the impenetrable material, Griffin plucked Aisling from the ground as if she weighed no more than a dry twig and set her feet on the pedestal base.

"See, now, this is where I'd be inclined to think the horrors would pop up to stop me from taking anything pretty," she said only halfway in jest as she smiled down at her friend.

"Nae, we're safe here. We'd have encountered trouble by now." A genuine smile reached his eyes.

The dagger was the first thing to come down and was placed into a velvet-lined case with a foam inlay.

THE COLLECTOR'S TREASURE

"They're beautiful, aren't they? Made in the forges of Avalon, I've read. Do you have anythin' Faerie made?" he asked and crouched down to store the dagger among the belongings in his bag. He removed several cushioned jewel sacks for the remaining treasure.

"Gram gave me a bracelet on my seventeenth birthday that belonged to Ma. Said it was a gift from, you know… *Him*."

"I remember the photos of Ceara in her youth. With beauty like that, it's no wonder your gran could sweep a sidhe off his feet." He stood alongside the statue and below Aisling with one hand against her calf.

"Gram almost cried when I put it on. She said I looked like Ma and everything. Her spitting image, she said."

"Do you ever wonder if he still watched after them? Over you?"

"If that's true, then I wish he'd step in now and again. She's lonely… I can only visit so often."

Silence fell between them, crushing and heavy enough for Griffin to avert his gaze. "I'll visit her sometime," he finally whispered. "If she doesn't bash me off of her stoop and into the mud." He craned his neck to gaze up at her. "Now, enough of sad things. We've got loot to collect, lass."

His hand remained warm against her leg, and she told herself it was a supportive gesture to show he had her if she lost her footing. Nothing else. Even if she wanted something more from Griffin MacNeil, she could never bring herself to pursue a man still bound by marriage.

"She wouldn't beat you, Griffin." Aisling carefully picked her way down the statue while he steadied her. They both crouched at the base to look at the handful of jewelry retrieved. Each trinket, every bangle, and finally the jeweled headdress previously atop the statue's head earned a moment of her attention.

"You keep eyeing this one."

Of the assorted jewels and ancient relics of the past, a single silver cuff fell under Aisling's repeated scrutiny. Hieroglyphics etched the edges of the delicate bracelet with filigreed depictions of a crane and a lotus flower filling the center.

"It's pretty…"

"It's yours. We wouldn't have found this room without you. Here, I'll wrap it."

For a moment, Aisling considered protesting. Then she smiled and let her gaze drift across the pool while he marveled over the dagger taken into their possession. Shadows seemed to ripple over the dark surface.

"Griff… I thought I saw…"

The lights in the room flickered and shifted through a spectrum of colors. The cool blues and mellow ambers flared bright orange.

Autumn poked her head from Griffin's pocket, trilling a noisy squeal and warble of alarm.

"Thought what—Ash!"

Like a long distant memory coming to life, Aisling twisted at the waist to see something rise up from the dark waters behind her. Only this time instead of spines and a long snout, she saw scales bigger than her hand and a pair of green glowing eyes.

It bumped against her legs and sent her toppling backwards into the pool.

~*~

The fountain and the once placid waters came alive with activity. Long and thick, sinuous coils of midnight blue breached the surface of the dark pool. Hundreds of tightly woven scales glimmered in the torchlight and submerged anew.

Aisling bobbed nearly twenty feet away, where she tread water and sputtered.

"Griffin!" she cried.

The serpent rose tall above her, its head revealing a maw filled with dozens of fanged teeth. A single flick of its tail sent it cutting through the water toward Ash.

Griffin sprang to his feet as Autumn bounced down to the poolside edge to scream and squeal in panic.

What was he going to kill it with? A bracelet? Bare hands? He didn't remember grabbing it, but he clutched the dagger in a white-knuckled grip, a dagger reputed to kill with a single cut. Without thinking, Griffin dove in.

THE COLLECTOR'S TREASURE

Aisling vanished, jerked beneath the water mid-scream. A magical discharge erupted below the surface, illuminating their surroundings with the prismatic colors of Aisling's power. It left stars in Griffin's eyes, both blinding and reassuring.

Fight it. Don't give up, he prayed frantically. Aisling's survival instinct was strong, but he feared the serpent was stronger. Another flare of brilliant light told him she lived and still fought. It gave him the advantage needed to see the snake's muscular body wrapped around her hips, legs, and waist. Through great fortune, both of her arms remained free of the heavy coils.

The water serpent disapproved of Griffin's decision to come to Aisling's aid. The Collector saw a pinprick of light, a row full of teeth coming his way, and sent a spiraling bolt of kinetic force toward the open mouth. The power of his spell kicked him backwards and away from Aisling—not the direction he wanted to travel, but it certainly gave him an idea.

Griffin used his magic to his advantage to become an aerodynamic projectile, cutting efficiently through the water like a spear. The serpent's tail whipped around to lash out when he rocketed closer. It missed but attained a partial success by knocking him off course.

Keep fighting. Keep fighting. With the next intuitive expulsion of mana, he was careened toward the serpent's throat where he barely evaded a lethal bite. He wrapped one arm around the compactly muscled neck. The tail whipped his side and expelled the breath from his lungs. He ignored the pain in his ribs and clung to the thing's body with one arm, stabbing with the other. It felt like striking rubber.

The serpent roared in anger at and took its two passengers on a wild ride toward the bottom of the pool. Aisling hit the sandy bottom with a dull thump, slammed near a deep fissure littered with bones. Their time was running desperately short.

What if it wasn't the fabled blade from lore, able to prick and kill with a single stab? What if the priestess of Isis was entombed with it and this was some carbon copy to decorate her statue? So many possibilities plagued his mind.

You give her back!

Something gave beneath his hands. The softer underbelly of the serpent lacked the same protection, covered in upraised scales. It permitted the perfect angled strike. Griffin wedged the dangerous blade beneath its armor and bore down on the hilt with his palm.

Black blood seeped into the water. The serpent writhed in spasms, then slowly sank to the bottom.

Griffin swam for Aisling. Down, down, down to where he freed her from the limp coils. The dagger became a forgotten casualty of their battle and remained implanted to the hilt within its victim. Aisling was all that mattered.

Griffin dragged her from the chilly water and onto the marble floor. "Ash? Shit, shit, shit."

She lay motionless on the tiled floor, pale and clammy with blue-tinged lips. Visible bruises darkened her ribs when he peeled up her shirt for a look.

"Come on, lass, come back to me. Please... Y'can't do this to me."

He began compressions hard and fast, counting out loud between pleas for her to come back to him. Each unresponsive second dimmed his hopes further. It had taken him too much time to kill it; she'd been under the water so long, inhaled too much.

A choked sob escaped Griffin's throat before he dipped down for a breath. "Please, no. I've only just gotten you back, sprite. If you go now, I can't...I can't lose you again... Y'have to come back to me... We've so many more places to see... and ruins to explore... It's not worth it if yer not there."

Frantic compressions continued to drive the water from her tiny body. He demanded her heart to beat again and forced oxygen into her starved lungs. It couldn't end like this. Not after years of separation and longing, regret and sorrow, only to lose her on a supposedly easy treasure hunt.

Whether from Griffin's physical exertions or the heartbreaking words that he sobbed, a sputtering cough sent another gush of water from her mouth. She turned her head and twisted to expel more, and then she lay there gasping for air with her pale silver eyes wide open.

"Get it out. There y'go, get it all out, Ash... Oh sweet mother of Hecate, breathe for me, dove."

He helped her sit up and rubbed her back while she trembled against him and coughed up the remaining water.

"Th-that's it... N-no v-visits to t-t-the Lo-loch for us-s-s. N-Nessie will be n-n-next."

A sob twined with a laugh shook his shoulders, and tears streamed down his cheeks as he squeezed her close. Her fingers curled tightly into his wet shirt as if she'd never let go.

Chapter 9

Despite Griffin's best efforts, Aisling wouldn't allow him or Helene to escort her to the surface for medical care. She assured him nothing was broken and that if it were anyone else, he wouldn't fuss. He left her bundled beside a fire with Odion and Juliana, and then led Helene back to the newly opened chamber.

"It's down there." He gestured with a sweep of his hand toward the pool.

"It is so difficult to believe you two fought a water serpent while we lazed away at the camp. I am sorry, *mon ami*."

"Wasn't your fault... Christ. I should have gone back to camp to get you. I wasn't thinkin'. I didn't expect the tomb to have a guardian. It's not in any of the texts."

"It could happen to any of us," Helene assured him. Her voice held no judgment. "You stay this time. I will dive for the dagger."

"Helene, you don't—"

"Oh no," she insisted with a quick shake of her head. "*You* have suffered enough." She shrugged out of her shirt and stepped to the marble edge of the fountain's deep basin. "You should be with her."

"She's safe with the other two."

Helene chuckled and shook her head before diving under. A minute later, she surfaced and stared at Griffin incredulously.

"*Mon Dieu!* I know you said it was large, but that thing was positively beastly. Like no snake I have seen. I also think it may have come from some other place. The bottom of the pool is cracked."

Griffin gave a solemn nod of his head in return. "She was holdin' her own until it smacked her against the bottom. It's a miracle she doesn't have a single broken bone."

"She is strong. You make a good match for her." Helene pulled herself from the water and returned the blade and cuff bracelet found during her swim.

Concern for Aisling had eclipsed any desire to collect treasure, but they planned to return as a group once she recovered.

"Do I have to repeat myself in French? We're not a match, Helene." He crouched alongside his pack without looking up at her.

"Tell me, then. How did you feel when she went under? The truth, Griffin."

He drew in a slow, deep breath. He almost didn't answer at all, but a heart-wrenching ache forced him to speak up. "Like part of me was goin' to die with her."

"You have had many bad times. Second chances like your Aisling do not come often."

"She'll never have me now. Not after what I've done and the tears I've caused her."

"Men. All of them are so blind, I swear." Helene huffed as she twisted out her wet hair. "Your wife... I can say nothing you don't already know. I know it is hard now, but divorce is best. I'm glad you took the initiative."

Griffin only gave a grunt.

"As for Aisling, I have seen how she looks at you and you at her. I would not be so, ah...pessimistic." She gave his shoulder a squeeze. "What I am saying is this: if you have a chance at happiness—*true* happiness—you would be a fool to let it pass you by. You deserve some love. Think about that, *oui?*"

"Hypocrite. Did you ask out that chick at the Vault you have the hots for?"

"This is not about me." She winked at him and sauntered past en route for the ascending stairs that would lead to their camp.

~*~

Alistair Fitz Jr. shaded his eyes from the Egyptian sun while he gazed over the waves of heat shimmering in the distance. The group was due to return at any moment, a belief confirmed by the arrival of a fae wisp bearing Juliana's message. Fifteen minutes had passed since the little orb of glowing light vanished to its home realm. Halima crouched beside the oasis waters and carefully lowered the breathing hoses in preparation. Loitering Scribes sat beneath the shade of a tent playing a round of poker.

Everything appeared normal, yet the Guardian felt on edge.

The setting sun cast beams of dark gold over the sands while the sky deepened into shades of dusky purple with streaks of rose. The scorching desert proved an improvement over the intolerable smog of London. Working for the Collectors had to be one of the best jobs Alistair had pulled in years. Adventure, travel, and an all-expense paid vacation to a new and foreign place away from the screaming cacophony of the city.

Alistair squinted at the sky. "Is that a plane?"

One of the Scribes looked up from his game and squinted at the dark speck far above. "It is only a bird, perhaps."

"A bloody large bird."

A series of concussive blasts exploded above their heads. The sands erupted, sending pillars of the gritty substance flying towards the sky. Defensive wards surrounding the camp blazed to life in a vibrant display of crackling crimson and citron flashing light. The same wards buckled and shattered in less than a minute, but it gave them time to find cover and protected them from the initial assault.

Alistair pulled Halima to safety behind one of their jeeps just in time before shrapnel ripped through the camp. Canvas tents were sliced. Metal pinged off their vehicles. An explosive hiss of air announced the loss of several tires.

The Inquisition had found them again. It was all out war, and the enemy had come prepared.

Rapid-fire shots flew past Alistair as two dune buggies charged over the nearest crest of high-piled sand. He couldn't count the number of assailants aboard the vehicles.

The first buggy launched high into the air, suddenly without gravity. It rose swiftly and then came crashing down. A couple of the armored men were able to roll free of the wreckage. They came to their feet with guns blazing.

Alistair charged across the sand and drew his sword from its scabbard. The short length of gleaming blue-black metal neatly sliced through the air and into the armored torso of the first gun-toting Inquisitor he reached. Blood sprayed hotly into the man's face with the next blow. Their ammunition may as well have been fake bullets from a child's toy. Nothing penetrated the mage's shields, but his gladius easily sliced through their ballistic armor.

Alistair twisted and spun behind his foe to use him as a shield. Bullets riddled the Inquisitor's body as the weight of gravity surrounding the opposing squad of three shifted. They were crushed into the sand, buried up to their necks in a single, brutally efficient stroke of magic.

"Secure the civilians!" he called over the sound of battle toward the tent where Guardian Karim maintained a magical barrier of mana. The translucent dome shuddered, and a network of fine cracks and fissures splintered over its surface. They couldn't hold it forever.

"Hurry!"

Another Collector unrolled a scroll and bared it to the sun to unleash a fiery tempest. The clouds split open, giving birth to spears of flame which came hurtling toward the ground. One of the aircraft responsible for the initial attack flew into a molten bolt and began to spiral out of control.

"Fall back!" an enemy soldier cried.

"Over my cold corpse," Alistair muttered to himself. *"Gravitate. Frangit!"* His voice resonated over the sand, imbued with magic.

The attackers tried to retreat, but their steps became weighted. Several of them yelled in dismay, caught within a cyclone of rising sand. Alistair concentrated and thrust one fist before him to direct his willpower to the growing crater.

One of the buggies beat a hasty retreat for the horizon, but the men who failed to reach their third vehicle were doomed. Thousands of pounds of sand came crashing down upon them in a choking cloud, effectively burying them beneath the camp.

~*~

"I can't believe all of this happened while we were down below. Christ. Anyone hurt?" Griffin asked.

"Negative. A few bumps and bruises, nothing more. I trust your endeavor had more success."

The group had surfaced from under the water barely minutes after the battle ended. They found their campsite overrun with Guardians searching for any survivors among the attackers. Most had been reduced to charred corpses and asphyxiated mercenaries with lungs full of sand.

"We've got it. Aye." Griffin turned to survey the war zone. "I guess you were worth the price, then. You're a one-man hurricane."

Alistair nodded. "The Parisians showing up helped."

"We were happy to assist," the dark-haired lieutenant said. "Jean-Luc Chevalier, at your service."

Jean-Luc went on to explain that their fortuitous arrival had come courtesy of a captured Inquisition agent in Paris. Thorough questioning resulted in enough information to determine the location of the next Egyptian site in their targets.

"You, Monsieur MacNeil, were the connecting element. You were at the last site, and I was also informed of the attack upon you in Dublin. They do not seem to like you much."

The understatement made Griffin grumble under his breath. Of all the unfortunate things to happen to him recently, being on the receiving end of an unhealthy infatuation from the Inquisitors had to top it all.

"What about the ones who got away?" Griffin asked.

"We encountered a dune buggy many miles to the east. Monsieur Fitz softened them up for us, and they were no challenge. But enough of them for now. Are you well, Aisling? You are quite bruised," Jean-Luc said. A deep furrow wrinkled his brow, drawing them close together.

Aisling joined them as she wiped a damp cloth across her brow. The blue and purple mottling on her skin showed easily thanks to her tank top. The contusions had faded to yellow along the edges.

Jean-Luc placed his hand on her shoulder. His touch boiled Griffin's blood with irrational jealousy, and he wanted to punch the French prick in his face without even knowing why.

"Had a wee bit of adventure on our own down below, but all's well. I had Griffin with me."

Her smile soothed the heat coiling in Griffin's chest. Aisling wasn't looking at the model perfect Guardian beside her. She was looking at him. Only him.

He caught Helene watching them from across camp, a smug, self-satisfied smile on her face.

Helene will be an insufferable arse after this. Despite the exasperated thought, Griffin grinned.

Chapter 10

Their adventure in Egypt ended two weeks after it had begun, and Griffin dreaded the return home.

Moments after stepping inside the Cairo Vault and leaving the blistering heat behind, a courier rushed up to him with a sealed envelope. "Mr. MacNeil?"

"Aye, that's me."

"I need you to sign for this, sir."

He signed with a flourish, tossed the kid a few bills, then squinched his brows together when he saw the address. From the law offices of Cayo and Rueda? He hadn't expected correspondence from his lawyer so quickly after serving Mercy with the papers.

He tucked it under his arm and continued alongside Ash. "I'll escort you back."

"Oh, you don't have to do that."

He grinned down at her. "Who else is going to cart all this stuff through for you?"

Their last day in Cairo had ended with many new purchases after he nudged her into spending her well-earned cash. He had nearly regretted the decision after two hours of watching her *oooh* and *ahh* over silk rugs while she tried to decide what she wanted to buy.

She ended up purchasing seven.

"How much time do we have before the next Portal?" Aisling asked.

"Half an hour. Long enough for you to take a pee and get some coffee. I'll sit with our things."

While she went to freshen up in the restroom, he tore open the seal on the envelope and shuffled its contents into his hands.

Divorced. Uncontested. As of yesterday.

The bitch. Not only had she gotten the upper hand over him, but she'd attempted to take full custody as well without him present to defend himself.

Thankfully, Griffin's amazing legal counsel had presented the paperwork he'd filled out previously requesting joint custody. Mercy may have fast-tracked their divorce, but the judge had only awarded her temporary custody, pending a hearing next month.

He smirked and folded the envelope into his bag.

A free man.

The reality hit him all at once, and Helene's words came back to him. He deserved someone better, and that someone better was walking toward him with a smile on her face.

"Coffee for you, tea for me." Aisling offered out a cup.

"Thanks."

Within the hour, they were shuffled through the Portal back to Dublin where he delivered the treasure to O'Sullivan. Aisling made a quick check-in at the Healers' desk. Afterwards, they hailed a cab and headed to her flat. Griffin carted up the various bags and parcels without complaint.

"Delivered home, safe and sound, as promised."

"So you did. Just set it all down over there, and I'll sort through it later." Aisling directed him to set her belongings by the couch and moved to place her heavy pack near the bed. "Can you stay a little while?"

"Oh, I'd say so." Mercy had probably set fire to all of his things.

"Can I get you anything? There's not much 'til I go shopping, but I always have tea."

"No, I'm good. Happy to be back?"

"Yes and no." She kicked off her shoes. "Ready for the rest, I suppose, but I wouldn't trade our trip for anything."

"Now you've had a taste of adventure and will be wanting to come along with us again soon, aye?"

Aisling's expression brightened, and she gave a swift nod. "Of course I would join you again if you wanted me to."

"Course I want you there." Griffin lingered near the sofa and rubbed his sweaty palms against his pants. Thinking back, he couldn't recall a single time in all of his marriage when

Mercedes had gazed upon him with as much affection as Aisling did now.

Two steps forward bridged the space between them. He took her by her arms and drew her close.

"Griff?"

Part of him feared she would immediately bolt the moment he released her from his hold. He ensnared her with a single arm around the waist while his free hand claimed a fistful of her blouse. Without thinking about the consequences of his actions, he kissed her. Hard.

He expected a slap but was rewarded by a sigh of surrender. By the clutch of her fingers at his shirt. By the parting of her lips beneath the hunger of his kiss.

Suddenly, he had no idea which of them was the one pressing closer, or if they had both moved at once. Her kisses tasted as sweet as he remembered and soothed the ache carried in his heart for too long.

"Griffin, no…" Breathless words left her in a rush when his lips traveled from her mouth to the curve of her cheek.

"Why not?"

"We…we can't. Shouldn't…"

The reluctance of her protest was confirmed when her head turned to capture his lips once more. Aisling's fingers still held tightly to his shirt.

His hands began to crawl everywhere at once, traversing soft curves that had bloomed in adulthood to more generous proportions.

"I want you, Ash."

"I know," she whispered. Her lips trailed with tenderness over the scar disfiguring his throat. "But… Tell me why… Do you only want me for a night because you have an itch?"

"No!" he breathed out, aghast. "I'd never… I could never hurt you like that." But he had. Once upon a time, Griffin had done exactly that.

Of all the many hardships Griffin had faced over the course of his life, the decision to leave Aisling in Ireland had been the worst of them. He still couldn't recall why he had backed out of his promise to return. They'd danced the night away at the Winter Formal Gala during her final year at school, and he'd arrived by surprise to be her escort to the event. They'd spoken, and she'd convinced him pursuing a career in Spain was the wrong choice. He'd kissed her beneath the stars on the chilly balcony and...

The rest of the evening became a blur. He recalled a hateful bully wandering in on them, a popular rich kid named Michael Stoddard who made both of their lives hell, but then Griffin had returned to Spain by morning to end his relationship with Mercedes.

Years after Griffin and Aisling's last meeting, Liam had caught him staring morosely at an old photograph over a bottle of expensive whiskey one night in camp and encouraged him to contact her again.

"I know... I know I've hurt you, Ash. I know I can't ever take it back. I was an idiot to let Mercedes convince me to remain in Spain, and every time I think about all the ways I've screwed up when it comes to you, I curse myself for being weak. But I'm not that boy anymore."

Aisling didn't push him away, but she didn't invite him closer either.

"It's not about what happened in the past, hurtful or not. I can't be a mistress. I refuse to have only half of you."

"It's over, Ash." He stroked his thumb across her soft cheek and looked straight into her eyes. "She went behind my back and tried to do it all while I was gone. Tried to get complete custody of my little girl."

"What are you saying?"

"That my marriage is officially over. It's done. All that's left is the custody hearing. And, if you'll have me—if you can forgive my stupidity—I want to give us another shot."

Her fingers curled into his shirt, and her breath hitched. For a moment, she looked torn. Griffin's heart plummeted, fear of her rejection punching a fist into his gut.

"Do you want me, Ash?"

"I want you, Griffin. I've never wanted anyone but you."

The sincerity in her whispered words brought relief to the building pressure in his chest. Had she denied him, he would have bitterly accepted it was time to lie in the bed he'd made.

"I sense a 'but.'"

"But you've been divorced for only days, and you need time to heal. It wouldn't be right to do this now."

"I know," he admitted. "Does this mean I'm gettin' a chance to make things right?"

A chance to atone for breaking her heart?

Aisling's chin raised, and she held eye contact with him, her gray eyes filled with compassion he didn't deserve.

"I'll make tea, and we'll figure it out."

"You and your tea." Griffin laughed and rubbed the back of his neck, but he didn't argue.

There was something soothing about watching her in the kitchen. It reminded him of days spent at her grandmother's estate when Ceara had chaperoned their study dates.

They settled at the table with tea and a box of fancy biscuits.

"I suppose we should start with... What do we want? What do you want from this, Griffin?"

"I know we can't pick up where we were years ago, Ash. I'll always feel foolish for that, breaking up with you and leaving." He spread his hands in defeat, lacking a good excuse. "But I'm not here before you now because my marriage went down the crapper." He sipped his tea to wet his sudden case of dry mouth.

"Running into you that day on the stairs... I'd never been so happy," she confessed. "I'd missed you. This, though, it seems more like a dream."

"I know. It's the same for me."

"What will you do now? Stay in Barcelona?"

"No, I don't want to stay there. I saw an opening or two on the Collector bulletin I wanted to apply for."

"Oh? Where might that be?"

"Rio. There are old temples in South America full of ancient magic, Ash. Even more beautiful than Egypt."

She smiled and poured more tea for the both of them. "So far away from home, but I suppose that's what you always wanted. Excitement and exotic travels."

"As if you weren't eager to be away from Ireland for a time yourself. You've lived here your entire life and only left once. Why? What if you could continue to heal and still have adventure?"

"Gram is here."

"Come with me," he urged while reaching across the table to seize her hand. Her fingers were so small in his grasp, delicate. "Ceara would understand. She'd kick you off the isle herself if it meant you were happy."

Her lips twisted. "And us? What are you hoping for?"

"To one day have your trust again. The way I did before."

"I trusted you enough to go to Egypt."

"Aye, you did, but I want you to trust me with your heart again. Can you give me that chance?"

Tears accompanied the soundless parting of her lips, a quiet stare in disbelief. None fell, but they glittered in the corners of her eyes. "Yes," she whispered, only to repeat herself in a firmer voice. "Yes, I'd like that. I would really, truly like that, Griffin. I... I trust you again."

For a moment, he'd thought she would laugh in his face. Maybe kick him out. Relief lifted the weight from his shoulders. Then his heart soared, the rhythm taking off like a race horse at the starting line. "In that case, would you allow me to escort you to dinner tomorrow? A proper date. I'll bribe Jack to give us a table."

She laughed and ducked her head. "As if he'd need a bribe."

Griffin reached over and tucked her hair behind her ear to better see her blushing cheeks. "All the better. We'll have a lovely time. Will you wear a dress for me?"

"I suppose I could."

His grin widened in victory, and after tipping back the remainder of his tea, he stood. "In that case, I'll excuse myself and pick you up tomorrow evening at five."

"What? Are you leaving so soon?"

"I think it'd be prudent of me to stay with Mum tonight, and you deserve a quiet evening to yourself after the past week." His mother would want to spoil him anyway.

Aisling walked him to the door where he dipped down and stole a second kiss. Breaking away took every ounce of willpower he possessed, but he was determined to do everything right.

"Goodnight, lass. I'll see you tomorrow."

And tomorrow would be the first day of a new life, a life he could create with Aisling and Mara in whatever way he chose.

Chapter 11

For their daughter's sake, Griffin and Mercedes had drafted an awkward but beneficial arrangement allowing him to remain in the home until he settled elsewhere. He removed any remaining personal effects from the bedroom to his study and slept on the couch each night. It brought Mara comfort to have her father two doors away.

Christmas had been a strained affair, but at least he'd been able to spend the day with his little girl. He remained the entire week after, devoting every moment to Mara.

Leaving her behind to resume his work had been tough, but he kissed her goodbye and promised to return soon.

Sitting outside the Portal bound for Rio with time to spare, he checked in with Aisling and then called up his cousin.

"What did you do?" Addison demanded right off.

Griffin rolled his eyes at the abrupt greeting. "Is that any way to say hello to your cousin?"

"You forget, I know you. I know you too well. So...how's Mara and the bint?" Addison asked slowly, carefully.

"Mara's been well. Gets around the house better and better each time I come home. Can't hardly tell she's blind at all these days."

"And your wife?"

"What wife? I caught her blowing my boss in my office space. So I filed for divorce. Had to threaten a little blackmail to get it, but that's another matter altogether." Griffin minced no words while catching him up on the rest of the story.

"That's a load of hogwash. She can't keep you from Mara. If you'd allow me to speak with Gramps for you, I—"

"The old bastard and his money can go to hell. No offense, but y'know he doesn't give a shit about anyone but *you* and Uncle Cedric. Treats Mum as if she's some whore outside of his family line. I can handle Mercedes myself. I've got a good lawyer who knows what he's doing. We'll win. She's never wanted Mara."

As London's Regent, Tristan Rhydderch placed unrealistic expectations upon his progeny. He had alienated Griffin's mother when he forced her into marriage while pregnant with another man's child. He'd claimed the true father had been unsuitable.

And then they had hidden her away for months to save face with the magical community. Once Fiona's dowry ran dry and Tristan refused to provide more money, her husband beat her until she eventually ran away. She returned carrying Griffin, although she had lied for his safety and never revealed the truth until he was a teen. Tristan's authoritarian leadership style suited his duties at the Vault, but they'd failed him when raising a family. Griffin loathed him.

"All right. Forget that I've said anything about him," Addison said. "So what's next, then? You mentioned the Amazon."

"I've got an interview in Rio in thirty minutes. When it all ends, I'll hopefully have the means to get Mara out of Spain and with me. She can play with Madeline again."

"Maddie would love it. Me too."

"Keep your fingers crossed for me, then. I better go. It looks like they're setting up for Rio now."

"Best of luck, Griff. I'm always here if you need me."

~*~

The woman sitting opposite Griffin must have been breathtaking in her youth, and as a woman of middle age, a striking quality remained in her sun-golden features. Strange magical plants from the heart of the Brazilian rainforest decorated her office near the windows, and dozens of weathered tomes with leather bindings spanned the shelves. Glass displays glittered with trinkets from archaeological digs, protected beneath powerful defensive enchantments. It reminded him of his own office and held the same comforting atmosphere.

"Your reputation precedes you, Mr. MacNeil."

"I'm honored you're takin' this time to meet me in person, Director Mendoza."

"Hm. Better Collectors have flattered me and failed to win the job." She perused the enormous stack of paperwork serving as Griffin's resume but didn't appear moved by the number of his accomplishments.

Griffin tried to control his expression. "It isn't flattery. Brazil's got one of the best bloody Vaults in the Regency, and I'm one of the best licensed Collectors in the league."

"Tell me. You have a career in Spain. Why leave it behind? I want the truth."

"Ambition," he said. It was only a partial omission of the truth.

"I asked for the truth, Mr. MacNeil."

"Spain's not hospitable to me anymore. My ex-wife got that job for me, and now I'm ready to move on and find my own way for me and my little lass."

"I see."

"Greece and Rio were always where I wanted to be, but your Collections Department never gave me the time of day."

"I am told you've brought a Healer recommendation, as well, for our opening."

"I did, and you won't find anyone more talented than Aisling Kavanagh to fill it. She has a natural gift, and since she's Feytouched, she's able to overturn their curses. She's worth more than entry-level salary. Ahead of her years in skill."

Director Mendoza's features softened, and the hint of a smile touched her face, defining the laugh lines at the corners of her mouth. Her matronly appearance made Griffin feel at ease, as if he were speaking with his own mother.

"I expect to see you here bright and early in six weeks once Barcelona releases you from your contract. I will hire you on a probationary basis of six months. If I'm pleased with your work, the job as my lead will remain yours. As for Miss Kavanagh, I will contact the Chief Healer of Dublin and consult their Regent. A decision will arrive by courier."

Less than two hours later, he returned home to spend time with Mara and celebrate his success.

Griffin found Belén, their maid, kneeling over a faded pink stain on the floor in their foyer with a rag and bucket of bleach water. The strong smell of chlorine burned his nose as he warily approached.

The silence in the home hardly compared to the distressing revelation of Mara's absence. Not once in the many months since his child began to walk had she ever missed meeting her father at the door. Dread knotted in Griffin's stomach, and he knew without a doubt something terrible had happened.

"Oh, Señor MacNeil, it was horrible." Belén pushed to her feet, wringing her gloved hands together. "The little one... I am so sorry..."

~*~

The days passed swiftly for Aisling, who received only a brief call from Griffin about the results of his job interview.

He had the job, but he'd told the Director they came as a packaged deal.

Why did that make her tummy do little flips of anxiety? She'd never left home until visiting him in Egypt, and now they were rushing headfirst into a future together on another continent.

He'd then ended the call, citing a family emergency and that he'd tell her more when he had the chance.

A week later, Krys dangled out an opportunity Aisling couldn't decline—a job in Greece at an ancient site Rhiannon Kavanagh had helped to discover before Ash's birth.

"I may as well, I suppose." An amused laugh accompanied the words. "Fine, then. Tell him I'll come as soon as I clear it through my boss."

"Already done. Hektor called O'Sullivan up himself, but I asked if I could tell you about it." Krys slid her cellphone away with a satisfied grin and rose to her feet. "You'll join my family for dinner, then we'll see you to your dig."

A trip was what she needed to get her mind off her worries. She gave Griffin a call and left a message on his voicemail.

Maybe, just maybe, he could join her on an adventure of her choosing this time.

THE COLLECTOR'S TREASURE

Chapter 12

Jean-Luc felt like a child waiting outside of the principal's office.

"Regent Durant will see you now, Lieutenant," the receptionist murmured.

He rose from his chair, rubbed his clammy palms against his slacks, and muttered thanks in passing. Within the office of Rosamund Durant, he found an elegant space filled with pristine ivory and gilded accents. A cream rug with a floral design of crimson and pink rosebuds covered most of the polished wood floor.

Rosamund, a short French-Creole woman with a wavy bob of chestnut hair, smiled courteously from behind a cream-colored desk. She carried herself with the poise of a giant despite her five-foot stature.

She crossed from behind the desk, took his hands, and kissed each cheek. "I am glad you were able to join me on such short notice, Lieutenant. Coffee?"

"No, thank you. I must admit I'm a little confused by your summons. Everything is in my report, Regent Durant."

"I know, Jean-Luc, but I would like to hear more of it from you."

The inviting atmosphere of the spacious loveseat could have put Jean-Luc to sleep under normal circumstances. Warm rays of sunlight heated his skin, and the aromatic scent of caramel coffee gave him hunger pains. He regretted declining her offer.

"The attack near the Valley of the Kings is the sixth assault in a four month period. It's safe to assume the Inquisitors have an inside source. They know when and where to attack, but they did not expect to find such skilled opposition this time. MacNeil and his crew were fortunate to have hired the services of a veteran Guardian."

"I see. How close are we to discovering the source of the leak?"

"No closer than we were before. It could be any Vault, or many of them. I have no access and no way to continue my investigation without assistance. The mages of Cairo weren't very hospitable either," he muttered.

"I'm aware." Her lips pressed into a thin line of discontent. "I should be honest with you. I called you to discuss an opportunity for advancement."

"I... Excuse me, Regent Durant, but there are many more qualified Guardians—"

"There are none as powerful with as large a heart as you. Of course, I could nominate Captain Cloutier, but why should I? He's an ass. The power to enact justice would go to his head." Disapproval knit her brows and deepened the fine lines drawn by age.

His thoughts raced back to the night in the interrogation room and the screams of his fellow Guardians. He hadn't slept for days afterward.

"What I need, what our Regency needs, is a man able to make the right decision when the lives of many are on the line. A man with discretion, a good heart, and a *conscience*."

"What would you like of me?"

"There is an opening among the Regency Board's Justiciars. I wish for you to fill it."

Excitement stole the breath and the words from him. No Guardian could achieve a position higher than Justiciar, unless they were to become a Regent tied to an office. As one of their number, his authority would become unchallenged.

He would never have to accept another order from Cloutier again. He could travel to any distant Vault away from France to investigate claims of wrongdoing and corruption.

"Will I no longer work for you, Regent?"

"You will remain here as one of our lieutenants for now, Jean-Luc. You will spend the next two years in training as an undercover agent for me and Chancellor Rhydderch. Think of it as a chance to prove that you are ready to undertake such a responsibility for the Regency. Of course, the utmost discretion will be required. Only you, Chancellor Rhydderch, the Justiciar you're replacing, and I will know of this." She raised the lid of a silver dish upon the low coffee table, revealing an array of frosted cookies.

He took one gratefully and chased it down with a second. "I am honored, Re–"

"Rosamund," she corrected him gently with a touch of her fingers to his elbow. "We're equals now, or I would not have nominated you."

"Rosamund." Jean-Luc smiled. "Do you have any suggestions on where to look next?"

"Perhaps. For now, I wish for you to visit Madame Calliope of the Sweet Dreams Home for Orphaned Tots. She'll be expecting you."

Jean-Luc stayed long enough to clear most of the cookies, and then she shooed him from the office to embark on his duties. After he bid her a goodbye, he rode the elevator to the parking garage.

The lengthy drive took him from the city. Eventually urban sprawl gave way to greenery, and the Forest of Sénart provided a pleasant view. It gave him time to wonder why Rosamund wanted him to go to an orphanage.

The exterior of a cozy home greeted him, exuding a sort of unique, motherly warmth, big windows with bold red shutters and a matching door. Leaves with purple and blue flowers crawled over the brick exterior.

The yard lay within a white picket fence. From beyond it, the giggles and laughter of children traveled from the rear playground.

He rapped on the door and waited. A teenage girl opened a privacy window to peer out at him.

"Hello? Who are you?" Her French sounded clumsy and awkward, the words of a non-native new to the language.

"Lieutenant Jean-Luc Chevalier—"

"You're a Guardian," she said before he could announce his cover as a member of the French National Police. "What do you want?" she bit out in English, radiating distrust.

"That's enough, Sherrilyn. Let him inside. The lieutenant hasn't come to do us any harm," an amused voice spoke up.

The privacy window shut, then the door opened to reveal a spacious lobby with an L-shaped sofa beside a bubbling five-foot long aquarium.

Sherrilyn had a body suited for a Renaissance painting. Full curves with a little baby fat, an attractive face, and wild mahogany ringlets spilling over her shoulders made it a challenge to accurately guess her age. The timeless beauty of a half-dryad. Once he entered, she secured the door again.

A woman of unmatched beauty stood framed within the open doorway of the administration office. Silver hair surrounded a heart-shaped face with bright, lavender eyes. Inhuman eyes. She crossed to meet him and brought the smell of wild meadow flowers and grass with her. She kissed his cheeks in greeting, and the gesture felt strangely familiar. Soothing.

It reminded him he needed to visit home during the upcoming weekend, and he made a mental note to take his mother out for dinner.

"I'm Calliope. Welcome to our home," she greeted him in French.

Although she stood an inch or two taller than him, a quick glance down revealed Calliope was barefoot. She couldn't have been anything less than six feet tall.

He followed her into an office as quaint and warm as the rest of the house.

"Would you like a cookie?"

"You're the second woman today to offer me a cookie. Do I look underfed?"

"No, but they're fresh, and Aurora says they're your favorite." She took a seat behind the desk and grinned at him.

"I'm sorry. Who?" He twisted around to look and see if he had missed anyone in the room. Instead, he spotted a pair of large eyes peeking over the windowsill from outside. A child with the same pale silver coloring waved shyly through the glass. She ducked down out of his sight.

They *were* his favorite. A platter of warm, cinnamon palmier cookies awaited him on a plate at her desk. Thanking her, he took one and bit into it.

"Why did my Regent send me to you?"

"Why do you desire to stop the Inquisitors?"

Her return question bewildered him, and yet he wasn't able to formulate a properly intelligent response. "They are murdering people. Isn't that reason enough to stop them?"

She wasn't human, whatever she was, and a niggling thought in the rear of his mind whispered a warning. She held the power now, and he had stepped within her domain.

"Yes, it is. But why? Why are you a Guardian? Why do you help people?"

"It's the right thing to do. If it is not me, then who should it be?" he demanded.

"Not for pay or money?" she pressed. "Tell me more of you, and I will decide if you are worth my words."

"Not for money. I always wanted—no, I wanted to be a doctor like my mother and father," he finally admitted to her. "It was part of our plan. Then, when I was nearly old enough to enter medical school, someone killed my little sister. This is why the life of a police officer became my calling. My mother and father argued. They wanted me to be a physician, but this was my choice."

"I know, but I wanted to hear it from you. You are a good person, Jean-Luc. However, I do not see the end of the Inquisitors at your hands." She held up a hand before he could protest. "Not directly. You are meant to end an even greater threat. It is as much your destiny as it was for you to burn and become what you are now. You were chosen for this."

"By *whom*?" he demanded. He clutched the arms of the chair and gave her a hard look.

"You'll never learn if you're given the answers. You're smart enough to understand soon. In the meantime, know this—these uprisings by the Inquisitors are a cover to conceal something much greater. They are designed to distract us from the greater threat. It's a smokescreen," she told him. The twinkle faded from her eyes, and all mirth dimmed.

"A smokescreen for what? Please. If you know so much, tell me what I can do to fix it."

"I can't tell you. It will change everything, and the future will darken even further. You can save many, but many will become lost, Jean-Luc. Many will suffer greatly and they are those closest to you. These things *must* happen. There's nothing more to tell you without upsetting what has already been set in motion."

"Nothing at all?"

"Return to your roots. You'll find your answers there."

~*~

"Can't you look at this shit in your fancy new office, Chevalier?"

"I could, but I'm more interested in what I can find in your database," Jean-Luc replied.

His former coworker, a non-magical human and French cop, sat behind his desk while Jean-Luc hunched over the keyboard to search through digital police files. When the Vault accepted Jean-Luc into their force, Louis took over the mantle of Liaison officer between their worlds.

Louis rolled his eyes. "The mages have their own criminal record system."

"They do," Jean-Luc agreed. "I was told to return here to conduct my search."

They spent another hour reviewing recent files and then proceeded to cold cases. In several of them, Jean-Luc began to notice a trend. There were fires with no clear source, fatal hypothermia in the middle of summer, pulverized bones, and unexplained comas.

"Most of those were before we knew to call your people in." Louis pointed to the date on the current file, marked seven years back.

The radio on the desk crackled with an incoming transmission. The report consisted of two corpses discovered in a north-side tenement building ten minutes outside of Paris. Foul play was suspected, and an investigator was needed on the scene.

"Damn, I should check the map. Sounds like a no-go zone," Louis said.

"It's within *my* jurisdiction, however. So allow me, Louis. Something about this… I think this is the case I was meant to discover."

Jean-Luc drove straight over. In a rough suburban area on the outskirts of Paris, he encountered run-down housing projects and a population of people too poor to dwell inside the city.

The building stank of cigarette smoke and despair, its unbroken windows encrusted with grime. He took the stairs, distrusting the filthy box elevator and the rancid stench emanating from it. A moment later, he reached his destination.

While the majority of France's civil law enforcement remained unaware of the magical world, one thing was known to each and every officer—there were things which happened in the city beyond the scope of their ability, and they had a special number to call.

Once Jean-Luc flashed his Vault badge, the two nervous cops standing at the front door of the run-down apartment cooled their jets and began to relax. He entered the crime scene, greeted by the sickening scent of cooked human flesh, scorched hair, and burned bed sheets.

Piles of old clothing littered the floor, requiring Jean-Luc to tread carefully. He barely had any room to walk. Trash, opened boxes of food, and dirtied pots littered the kitchen counters and peeling linoleum floor. An old roll of fly tape carpeted in dead bugs hung from the stained ceiling. The bathroom Jean-Luc passed on the way to the bedroom smelled of stale piss and worse.

Equally disgusting bodies made a morbid sight. The first victim may have been a large man while alive, but in death he was reduced to a charred lump. Beside him, the nude body of a dead woman lay upon her back, covered in third and fourth degree burns.

"Who are you?" the lone cop in the room asked.

Jean-Luc held up his badge a second time. The scent of fresh fear permeated the air upon his arrival, wafting toward him from the cop. Relief and recognition swept over the man's features.

"Tell me what you have, officer. Please," Jean-Luc said.

"Neighbor smelled the smoke and came over with an old CO_2 canister. Claims the only noises he heard were, and I quote, 'cries like a cat being strangled, same as any other day.'" The French cop offered him a pair of gloves.

Jean-Luc tugged them on and stepped lightly around the bed. Only the right side of the female victim's face suffered damage during the fire, the remaining half sported a purple shiner and swollen eye. Her mouth hung open, frozen into an agonized shriek in death.

"I haven't done much except secure the scene, but I was looking and didn't see anything that could have started the fire."

"I'd like to look a little deeper. Tell the other two you're dismissed and that my department will carry out the rest from here," Jean-Luc told him.

"Are you sure you wouldn't like us to wait outside? They're not so friendly around here."

"You know what I am?"

"I...uh..." The officer gave a quick nod. "Yes, sir."

"Then you know I'll be fine."

The man winced and made a hasty exit from the room.

With the room cleared, Jean-Luc used the opportunity to examine the scene. The taint of mana hung like a heavy blanket over the corpses, leaving a metallic taste in his mouth as he breathed it in. He released his powers, and the dormant emotions in the room rushed him like ghostly apparitions.

Fear. Anger. Helplessness. Terror. Pleasure...

His pulse raced, carrying him on an incredible high. The two corpses on the bed might have preferred heroin, but fear was his drug of choice. Every hit of it tasted better than the last, more intoxicating than the finest wine.

What had he become? Guilt chased quickly on the heels of his enjoyment at their misery. Like a hard slap or cold splash of water, it sharply returned his focus to the matter at hand.

He tried to manipulate the curtain of mana with his own power, but it barely budged and seemed to require a more delicate touch. He wasn't a mage trained to handle the arcane manifestations of power, and he didn't want to disturb the evidence.

He made a call to the Guardian Department right away. "'Sylvie? I'll need a magus here. There's been a murder with dark magic involved beyond my abilities."

Barely half an hour later, reinforcements from the Vault arrived, but neither woman belonged with the French Vault.

"Hannah Blouchard. I've been sent to get a report." An older woman entered the room speaking English in a cultured, Québécois-accented voice. She wore her hair styled in a sleek bob of platinum blonde hair with hints of gray at the roots. Impeccably dressed in pleated black slacks and a matching jacket, her bold red heels seemed inappropriate for the crime scene.

The young woman who accompanied her dressed in an equally professional manner, clothed in charcoal slacks and a turquoise silk blouse. Her brown hair swept upwards into a tidy twist. Although he had only glimpsed the woman once in passing, he recognized her as Aisling's cousin.

He never forgot a pair of spectacular legs.

Jean-Luc took the card Hannah offered and frowned at it. A Gatekeeper from the Regency. They were the masters of weaving magical accidents with fiction for the mortals.

"I see. It is a pleasure to meet the both of you. Guardian Lieutenant Jean-Luc Chevalier, at your service," he said in English. He dipped into a polite bow after tucking the card into the pocket of his slacks.

"My assistant, Krystine Iamides," Hannah introduced before she brushed past him into the room to take photos.

"Lieutenant." Krystine briefly met his gaze. "Two Guardians are outside." She stepped past him, careful to avoid the piles of debris.

"Tell me what you think happened here," Hannah demanded.

"A murder." He bit his tongue in favor of maintaining his professionalism. "Neither victim appears to have been restrained, yet they burned to death. The woman died of shock first."

"He's right," Krystine said in a low voice as she neared the bed. Her trembling hand hovered a few inches above the still-warm corpse of the man. "I feel the remnants of a holding spell."

Hannah brushed past Jean-Luc, practically bumping him aside in the process. She circled the bed and watched her assistant with impassive, unsympathetic eyes. "Tell me."

"They wanted him held down for something. Her, too, but they used a weaker spell. Barely a trace left. The residual energies on him are so strong that they must have had him there a long time. He didn't move at all as he burned alive and…" Krystine paled initially before a flush spread over her features. Perspiration beaded at her brow. "Excuse me," she said hastily before she hurried from the room.

Hannah shook her head and unraveled the spell over the corpse. "Gravity-based spells like these are brutish but effective," she said as if discussing the weather.

"*Oui*, they are," Jean-Luc agreed. He picked up the sounds of retching from the corridor.

"Are these the only drugs?" Hannah gestured towards the handful of syringes and small baggies of white powder on the bedside table.

"That I've seen."

"We'll call it an unfortunate drug deal gone wrong. They pumped him full of heroin and lit him up. Her too."

"I believe more was done to the woman. Call it a hunch, but I plan to call for a full postmortem examination."

Someone had wanted the scene to appear to be an accident, and Jean-Luc had a hunch cultists were involved.

Chapter 13

One week beneath the Grecian sun gave Aisling's skin a subtle, sun-kissed glow. The winter weather reminded her of home in many ways, though the temperature seemed considerably warmer.

"To think all the myths of the labyrinth likely stemmed from here." She sighed wistfully at the notion.

"Don't forget, some arrogant magus could have decided to build this in an attempt to outdo the legend. We haven't confirmed it's the true labyrinth," Hektor said.

Aisling found comfort in Hektor's grin. The assistant to the Greek Director was old enough to be her father, a distinguished man with the first traces of silver at the temples of his dark hair.

He took her under his wing from the moment she arrived and had told her at least three times that she resembled her mother.

Aisling traced her fingers over a tablet propped on her lap. It bore the image of Hades, god of the dead. "It's all very beautiful and so vast that I can see why Ma had journals devoted to it. Nothing to help with this latest puzzle though."

"Hopefully your friend will shed some light on the mystery. I received word back from him, and he's accepted my invitation *this* time. The chopper should be here in about an hour."

A break in the rain left the ground around them slick and sparkling beneath the emerging sun. Aisling stood with Hektor when the helicopter arrived and felt butterflies in her stomach. Strong downdrafts from the spinning blades whipped her hair around her face, and excitement coiled in her gut as she watched the side door open and Griffin's lean frame hop down. Seeing his jaw covered in a heavier golden-red scruff than usual made her want to giggle.

He used to worry he'd never grow a proper beard...

Despite her initial worry, a smile lit upon her features as he crossed the rocky ground to reach them. The helo lifted off, taking its noise and gusty winds with it. Then his strong arms were around her, squeezing her tight as if time had never parted them.

It felt so good. She savored the moment of their reunion, only to squeal when he tickled her with his cheek.

"Missed you, Ash."

Hektor cleared his throat.

Griffin straightened and tucked Aisling against his side, freeing his right hand to shake with Hektor. "Apologies, Mr. Argyrios. So we meet at last. It's my pleasure to finally have the opportunity to work with you."

"While I wish you'd accepted my job offer all those years ago, it would seem your time with Spain was good to you. I hear nothing but excellent things about your work, MacNeil."

A few creases wrinkled Griffin's brow. The polite smile curving his lips faded completely. "If I had received notice, I would have accepted it. Greece and Rio were always among my first choices."

An awkward pause hung heavily in the air, and Aisling wondered what had happened there. Hektor spoke first, inviting them to follow him back to camp while filling Griffin in on their latest discoveries.

"It is too late to go down today, but I assure you the wait will be worthwhile."

"I look forward to it, Hektor. To be honest, I'll be glad for the rest before we begin."

Hektor and his lead man, Petros, wanted to catch Griffin up to speed, so while they spoke, Aisling retired to her own tent. While she burned to know about the family emergency he had cited during their phone call, his haggard appearance and the dark circles beneath his eyes stopped her from tiptoeing into his tent to question him.

The next day after breakfast, Hektor, Petros, and Griffin discussed splitting into teams to explore the newly revealed junction in the tunnels. Scouting ahead revealed the way beyond the rooms was magically sealed and required the joint effort of many mages to open it.

While the men discussed strategy, Aisling read the notes her mother had left behind in journals.

"I'll go this way," Griffin volunteered. "I'll send a wisp once I've located this part of the puzzle, and we'll communicate that way, aye?"

Aisling struggled to keep the grin from her face. "I'll just follow him, then. He's rubbish with Greek and might need a hand."

Hektor seemed pleased with the idea, but Petros protested. She put the flirtatious man down kindly, but firmly. With a nod to the rest of the crew, she strolled away to trail after Griffin, but his longer stride forced her to jog to close the distance between them.

"Watch out for the stone there," she called out, bearing a brass lantern in one hand. Its glow revealed a carving in the depiction of a half-avian, half-woman figure. "Sirens were known for luring folk to their doom on the seas, and I imagine it's no different in here."

He chuckled. "Why don't you guide me along then since you know the way?"

With Aisling in the lead, the pair continued until they reached the third chamber. Chiseled depictions of ancient deities decorated the marble walls. A floor in the same glossy finish was black instead of creamy ivory with a ceiling of rough, natural stone above them.

"So strange, isn't it?" he mused. "Three tunnels, three rooms with three dead ends. Three reliefs."

"All the rooms are the same, save for the carvings," she explained.

The very moment they reached the center of the room, an audible click preceded the clockwise rotation of the walls. They shifted, and the archway soon faced a rough-hewn wall of rock instead of an open passage.

Distant, muffled cries and the sounds of more rumbling rock sounded like the others encountered the same problem.

"Well, we've done something." Griffin moved forward a few steps to tentatively touch the indentations and holes in the wall. A sigh passed from his lips, and his hand rose to his brow, kneading at one temple.

"We have. But what?" She couldn't spot any visible type of trigger mechanism. She set down the lantern and joined him at the wall. She studied his pensive features and wondered what thoughts troubled his mind. "Is everything all right?"

"There's been a lot happenin' at home." Griffin walked his lucky coin across his knuckles over and over, a sure sign of something troubling him. She'd seen him do it many times before to soothe his nerves.

She scuffed the toe of her boot across the floor. "If you ever want to talk, you know my ear is open. I...I worried. I thought perhaps you had...regrets."

"What?" His eyes widened, and he turned to look at her.

"About your marriage. Us..."

"Regrets about divorcing Mercedes? No. That was a long time coming, and reuniting with you had nothing to do with it. She's surprisingly civil recently."

"Mara is all right?"

"Mara is fine. It's...It's the day I went for my interview in Rio, I came home and found the housekeeper cleaning blood from the floors. A lot of blood, Ash. Mercedes miscarried while I was gone. Didn't even know she was pregnant, to be honest."

A bucket of ice water couldn't have made her any colder than his words. Her face drained of color, and she felt nauseated. Empathy for the woman warred with years of hurt and resentment.

"I'm so sorry, Griffin, she whispered. "I hope Mercedes recovers. No woman should suffer such a loss. You either."

"I just want you to know I haven't touched her in *months*. So it wasn't mine. Doesn't mean I feel any less sympathy, but I'm relieved it wasn't mine, you know?"

"Griff..."

"Anyway, I didn't want to dump all of this on you."

"I didn't think you did. I'm only sorry you felt like you had to deal with it alone."

"I was ashamed for feeling upset over it, okay? Not my child, but it's strange. How do you go from thinking you love someone so much you can't breathe without them to...barely having a kind word to say?"

Her heart ached for him and the struggles he endured on his own. He was still the Griffin she knew best in her youth, willing to bear the weight of the world on his shoulders. "How's Mara holding up?"

"Mara's the one who found her. She has nightmares now. She couldn't see the blood, but she could smell it…and feel it. Her nanny found her covered in it, and it scared her too. For days, Mara wouldn't speak at all. She just wanted to be with me from the time she woke to the time she fell asleep. I nearly declined Hektor's proposal, but she finally sleeps the nights again."

"When we get out of this chamber, you go back to her. No one would say a bad word about needing to be with your little girl."

He smiled wryly. "I intended to, lass. Missin' her now, but Mum told me I needed to get my arse out of the house for a few days and take time for me. She phoned the mornin' Hektor's invitation arrived. She's got Mara now. Mercedes didn't argue it, us taking her away for a short time. It's got me hopeful she'll agree to a good shared custody plan."

"Good. That's good. We should try to find a way out, then. Get you home on time to your little miss."

"Aye. Right. Good plan," he agreed.

"We should try and contact the others, too. You could send Autumn to Petros with a note and not waste the wisp dust."

Griffin grunted. He must have noticed Petros harboring a crush.

"What? You think it won't work?" His surly silence only confused her further until she could no longer stand the brooding quiet. "Speak your mind, Griffin, before the weight of your thoughts crushes us," she teased.

He shook his head. "Autumn? Can you cross the barrier to reach the other Collectors?"

Autumn wriggled out of his pocket to poke her snout around. While he hastily scribbled a message for her to carry, she licked one of her eyeballs and preened herself. Once she held the tiny letter safely in her jaws, she poofed in a sizzle of fire and smoke.

"I missed you. Felt like all of my life went to hell at once, but I swear the next time I see that git undressing you with his eyes, I'll blacken both of them."

She moved closer and hugged him, relieved once he drew her into his embrace. Nothing beat the feeling of Griffin's strong arms around her. His security. His love and affection rolling off of him in waves.

"I'm sorry." He kissed the crown of her head. "I'm an arse for worrying you."

"You are."

"I'm your arse, aren't I?"

"Always."

Griffin lifted her against him, and without warning, kissed her. Worry for the future of their relationship diminished as he thoroughly claimed her mouth, leaving only raw need and desperate hunger in its place. Their current predicament slipped her mind completely, as did their fellow explorers. In that moment, only she and Griffin existed.

His mouth lowered to her collarbone next, and a warm hand slid beneath the back of her shirt to press against bare skin.

Heat pooled in her center as anticipation flushed her body with raw need, a primal and urgent craving for the man she'd desired since childhood. Her booted feet touched back down to the floor, but Griffin kept her near.

Elsewhere, two pairs of irritable Collectors struggled to escape the puzzle chambers while he kissed her with no one to bear witness but lovely carvings on the walls.

"Missed you... There's no words to describe it."

"Then show me," she whispered.

Her back touched the wall. When he guided her legs around his waist and supported her with his body, she felt the hardness of him press between her thighs. Press in an intimate way she'd craved from him for years.

"Griffin," she breathed.

"Hm?" His distracted voice whispered across her throat. Tender kisses followed.

"I want..." Wanted him to be her first. She burned for it with an indescribable ache, filled with unquenched desire.

"Want what?" he breathed in a husky voice.

Wanted to be able to think clearly, but that wasn't going to happen for as long as he was kissing her. Aisling sighed and tilted her head, exposing more of her throat to him.

Using his body to pin her in place freed his hands. Warm, calloused digits crept beneath her tank top and crawled over her ribs. He teased the skin just beneath the edge of her sports bra.

She wriggled against him, frustrated with the skimming touch that danced away each time she thought he'd breach the elastic band.

He ground against her again, nudging the perfect place to grant her pleasure.

"I'm not going to take you right here. When I do, it's going to be perfect," Griffin murmured against her cheek. He cupped a handful of each breast and rolled his thumbs over the tips until they hardened to stiff peaks.

She gasped. "Any time with you would be perfect."

His warm chuckle feathered across her ear. "Trust me, sprite."

Autumn appeared in a sudden flare of smoke and sparks. She trilled, and Aisling found herself blushing at the little fae's report.

"Guess we should get back to work." He nipped her ear a final time before setting her back down.

Aisling sighed but couldn't dredge up a proper argument. Her skin still tingled, and her heart continued to race, pounding in her chest.

Griffin unfurled the rolled scrap of paper taken from Autumn's jaw and held it toward the light. He sighed and offered it to her. "Hektor says he doesn't have any idea what happened, and they're still workin' on it."

Beneath Hektor's scrawl, another line read in Petros's handwriting, *Please ask your pet to refrain from licking me, friend.*

Chortling, Griffin resumed his examination of the wall. "That's a good lass, Autumn. He's only playin' hard to get."

"Keep on with that, and she'll decide he's better than you and leave," Aisling teased. She invited the salamander up to her shoulder and then made a slow circle of the room.

"She'd never leave me."

"That's what you think." Aisling's fingers touched lightly along the marble wall as she made her rounds, studying each of the carvings. "Hektor asked you to come because you're the best when it comes to figuring puzzles out. Because *you* are one of the best Collectors out there."

"He seems fond of you. Not the way Petros is, but quite taken all the same."

"He knew my mother," she told him. "Interned with her on a few digs. Told me he thought he'd seen a ghost when I showed up."

"That explains quite a bit, then… Your mother must have been quite the bonnie lass for him to confuse the two of you."

"Ma was…radiant. Like how you thought you saw me in the moonlight, but all the time. At least that's how I remember her. She always glowed like an angel fallen from Heaven."

"I didn't *think* I saw you that way. I *did*. Anyway, I'm lacking in my Greek, so why don't you tell me what this all is. Looks like a face in a cloud, blowing wind."

"The Anemoi, Greek gods of the winds."

"Four winds, three rooms."

"The eastern wind was considered unlucky, I believe."

"So which is this, then?"

Aisling stepped closer to run her hands over the wall. Deeply carved designs cut through the thick marble to allow glimpses of the passage beyond. Most importantly, it allowed fresh air to filter into the space.

"These are horses that his wind is forming," she noted as she traced her fingers over the reliefs. "If so, it could be, um…Baria—no, Boreas. He's the north wind."

"You think it has something to do with the puzzle?"

"You're the expert. I'm only a Healer. But…it makes me wonder if there's another opening, the way the room turned."

Communication with the others was slow, but after a series of back and forth notes via Autumn, the group decided to use elemental magic tied to each featured Anemoi.

"Hektor is with Notus, the bringer of the storm winds. If this is Boreas, then a simple ice spell ought to do the trick. That means Petros and Andrew are in the room with the relief of

Zephyrus, god of the summer breeze. Am I right? Ice, lightning, and fire."

"You'd be right. Should I?"

"Aye, you go ahead. I hate casting ice spells, and you're better at it."

Aisling summoned a chilly touch of frost to her hands. Extending her fingertips toward the wall, she funneled cold magic toward the relief. Within seconds, the entire mural glistened beneath a sheet of ice.

Griffin shivered and rubbed his arms. "Was it necessary to bring about the next Ice Age?"

The contained blizzard soon spun into something larger, bringing a flurry of snow down upon them. Autumn squeaked and took refuge in Griffin's pocket. He scooped Aisling into his arms and held her close. For those moments, his body heat was a blessing as she buried her face in the hollow of his neck, her eyes shut against the thick scar.

When it was over, she felt chilled but not as cold as Griffin appeared. Snow and ice encrusted their hair and clung to their clothes, which Autumn gradually began to thaw with her Faerie magic.

"Colder than a hag's tit. Christ. I hope Hektor didn't fry." Griffin chafed his hands up and down Aisling's arms. "You don't even have goosebumps. I should have had you shield me, aye?"

Turning clockwise in a smooth rotation, the entire chamber shifted until the room was in its original state. The open archway revealed the path to freedom, and from down the tunnels, she heard excited whoops and hollers of joyous excitement.

They found the others gathered in the central chamber. Hektor, Petros, and the two Scribes in their company looked a sad sight. Hektor's hair stood on end as if he'd stuck his finger in a light socket, while Petros dripped with sweat. Blisters on his hands told a tale of his predicament in the other chamber.

Griffin snickered from behind her.

"Ah, MacNeil," Petros called out. "Well done. We have a doorway down now thanks to your thinking." He flashed Aisling a charming grin, as if to apologize for the time she had spent in Griffin's dour company.

She smiled back briefly and moved toward Hektor.

"I had help," Griffin replied.

"Griffin suggested all the rooms needed to be turned at the same time though…" she said.

"Well, the central room's floor opened, forming steps downwards," Hektor told them. The discovery had restored a sort of boyish youth to his features.

"What now, then?" Griffin asked.

"We can go down now or break bread for dinner and see what awaits us come morning. I think you will be intrigued, Mr. MacNeil. I ventured down a few steps, and your expertise will certainly be needed, given your recent experiences with Egypt."

"Always where I need to be. I'm glad to be of use."

"Then please, after you." Hektor gestured for Griffin to take the lead.

While the upper levels had been mainly Greek with references to the Egyptian mythos, the walls of the spiral stairwell showcased a multitude of hieroglyphics and artistic murals. It was as if the group crossed through a portal into a completely different ruin. Black walls of marble with hints of gold accent glittered in the light of their lamps.

The descending stairwell twisted and finally emptied into an expansive, square chamber filled with the light of many torches with undying flames. The beauty of it all stole Aisling's breath. She'd never seen so much wealth, even during their Egypt adventure.

Each corner had an altar with unique treasure; a golden cup, a silver dagger, a jeweled headpiece, and a curved sword. They glimmered from their respective positions. Between the sword and the chalice at the distant wall, a mural made from thousands of precious gemstones depicted a lion with a human head. A sphinx.

"This isn't right," Griffin said in a soft voice. He didn't proceed beyond the sword, staring at the mural beyond it.

Aisling joined him and set a reassuring hand against his elbow. Griffin glanced toward her and offered a weak, uncertain smile. Something had to be wrong.

"Don't touch the statues," he warned. "I don't advise traveling any farther, Hektor. There appears to be a sphinx somewhere in the vicinity...possibly the next room. I'll be damned if I fight a dangerous magical creature this even—"

A pained cry erupted from one of the Scribes. The man tumbled into the group, stomping his foot wildly at the ground. A hard object skittered across the ground, flung from his dusty leather boot.

A jeweled scarab.

The shiny insect smacked against the wall and shook its wings. A low hum began then grew in volume, louder by the second.

"The wall's alive!" More of the gemstones peeled down and away from the marble, revealed as scuttling scarab beetles.

The group backed away from the advancing swarm and raised their shields, but the sharp wings of the insects sliced through their magical armor.

"They're diamond-cutter scarabs! Y'need fire!" Griffin raised one arm to defend his face from the flurry of hard bodies. He swept the other in front of him, creating a wave of flames.

"What devilry is this?" Petros aimed a stream of fire towards the wall where more of the magical beetles stirred.

"It's a common trap in Egypt," Griffin said between his teeth. "Autumn, help them!"

With a squeak, the salamander poofed from his shoulder. She blinked to the wall, leapt into the flame of a nearby torch, blending seamlessly into the fire, and vanished.

The flame at the sconce expanded and grew to a reptilian shape and spilled down from the fixture. It formed a monstrous creature composed of living fire with Autumn at its core. Leaving the tip of her elongated tail at the base of the flames, the rest of her body became as large as a crocodile. She snapped several scarabs from the air, and their bodies sizzled in the heat of her jaws.

Aisling could only call on the weakest, most unimpressive embers. Dark strands drifted to the floor when a beetle flew too close to her face and caught her hair in passing. Many others joined it and became a tangle in the snarled curls. She yelped when she felt stinging bites on her scalp and jerking tugs.

"My hair! Get them out of my hair!" Aisling shrieked. Her hands bled from multiple bites as she tried to yank the insects out.

"Don't touch them, Ash!"

Griffin rushed to her, and within seconds, his hands appeared as if he'd squeezed a handful of razorblades. He burned the beetles out of the air, singeing her hair in the process.

Petros and Hektor, along with their Greek comrades, took Griffin's advice to heart. With Autumn on their side, Petros was able to form a wall of flame while Hektor used precisely aimed blasts of wind and force to blow the creatures away from the group to their fiery doom.

"Ash, I need to cut—"

"Do it!" she urged him.

Griffin slashed with the knife. He stabbed forward, swept the blade left and right in deft movements as Autumn breathed fire. Bits of Aisling's hair fell around her in uneven lengths, a cloud of black curls and lustrous waves tangled in moving bodies. A few moments seemed an eternity, and then silence fell over the chamber. Tears and blood dampened her cheeks, and ashen clumps of her hair lay scattered around her on the floor amid the charred remains of three scarabs.

"Make sure none of those damned things is hiding in the room," Hektor barked as he crouched down to see to his wounded man. He turned his gaze towards Griffin and Aisling next, concern mingled with anger on his features. "Are you two all right?"

They'd ripped out her hair! How could anyone think she'd be all right? Somehow Aisling kept the churlish thought to herself, knowing she was lucky to have her life. If Griffin hadn't been so handy and quick with a knife, she could have lost much, much more than a few feet of her hair.

Instead of voicing complaints over trivial matters, she nodded. "L-l-let me s-see to him." She traded spots with Hektor, freeing him to move over and discuss what happened with Griffin. For a moment, she was able to tune them out while she dragged over her small pack to get to her healing supplies.

The scarab had chewed through the man's shoe and into his foot. His pinky toe had been chewed off.

"They're a warning, a precursor to the magical beast that's beyond this room. The sphinx'll be protecting the best part of the dig. The crown jewel, so to speak." Griffin wrapped a handkerchief around his wounded hands.

"So since we lack a leprechaun to charm out such riddles, I say we leave the sphinx alone," Petros said.

Hektor nodded in agreement. No one wanted to deal with a hungry sphinx that had been trapped for centuries and was, most likely, quite eager to be free.

"Rhiannon always did say she had a special feeling about this place," Hektor murmured.

He had enough warmth and fondness in his voice to make Aisling wonder—how close had her mother and Hektor grown during their expeditions?

"I've only encountered one, but I'll give my honest advice. If you're to take it on, you'll need additional support from at least five to six more highly trained Collectors and a pair of Charmers too," Griffin said.

"Are so many needed for one beast?"

Griffin nodded. "More would be safer, but that'll be more fingers in the pot, too, eatin' away at your rewards."

Hektor swore under his breath.

"There's no need to do it now—the warning is gone and your secrets are protected. No one, save us, will know it's here. You can come back years from now, and it'll be waiting."

"We'll proceed from here with all caution, you can be assured. There are other passages and chambers for us to explore while we decide what to do about this."

"We need to get back to the camp." Aisling rose to her feet, cleaning her hands with a wipe. "I've staunched the bleeding, but he'll need stitches. I also need to see to Griffin's injuries."

"Yes, a sound plan. You are both, of course, welcome to remain or to join us again whenever you like."

Aisling stood and resisted the urge to check her hair. In the grand scope of things, her loss meant nothing. "I can stay a few more days, but then I need to return home as well."

"Excellent. I hope that means Mr. MacNeil will remain for a time. I'd like to learn more about these sphinxes from him."

"I imagine you'll have to search far and wide to find a Charmer experienced with them. I'll look around for a bit myself, refer someone to you if I can. My cousin Addison is a good Charmer, one of the best the UK has to offer, but I doubt even he's capable of handling the sort of trouble that comes with sphinxes."

Thanks to the many feet of cold marble and stone separating the rest of the dig from the beast, Hektor wouldn't have to rush. Without the scarabs serving as a warning, anyone trying to muzzle in on his dig would be in for a rude and horrifying surprise if he managed to penetrate the sphinx's lair.

"Had a colleague once who lost an arm to one as he fled an underground temple."

Aisling's nose crinkled. Griffin was full of horror stories he'd never shared with her.

The return trip to the surface took longer than their journey down. After the injured man was taken to the medical tent to rest, Aisling finally assessed the damage to her hair.

"Your hair. I am so sorry, Aisling." Hektor's touch to the ebony curls didn't make her pull away as Petros's had. All she saw was his concern.

"It'll grow back." She put on a brave smile and was immediately sure he saw through it.

While a woman by the name of Zoe cleaned Aisling's cut hands, Hektor carefully trimmed and smoothed her uneven hair until she no longer resembled a banshee. The result wasn't worthy of a French salon, but it was better than nothing at all.

Later in the night, when the camp quieted, Griffin stole his way into her tent. They spoke little and only held each other close. He ran his fingers through her cropped hair and pressed kisses to her brow in silent apologies and reassurances. It was the first night in Greece she slept well, and it was the first night she didn't want to. When she awakened, Griffin was gone, and only a picked wildflower next to her pillow proved he had been there at all.

Once the usual morning routine was through, Aisling emerged from her tent, and after she circled the camp, she caught a Scribe in passing. "Where is everyone?"

"Inside. The Collector they called in, he had an idea for getting past some barrier."

After scrubbing in the portable shower room with lukewarm water and donning fresh garments for the day, Aisling found Hektor, Petros, and Griffin in the chamber she had inwardly dubbed the Scarab Room. All three men fussed above a scorched length of parchment on the floor.

She recognized Griffin's best trick, the earth-splitting scroll he'd made as a teen to cleave a chasm beneath the Archives.

"Whoever built this cage held great power." Petros sounded impressed.

Griffin didn't mirror his enthusiasm. Visibly fuming, he crouched down and tried to salvage what he could of the ruined scroll. Very little of it appeared to have survived.

"It took me two hours to write that," Griffin complained. "Well, I tried. There's nothing more I can offer while defensive enchantments guard the way in. You'll have to do it the old-fashioned way, Hektor. My apologies."

"Thank you for the attempt, MacNeil. Knowledge has been gained, at the very least." Hektor wiped a hand down his face, looking disappointed.

Aisling spent the remainder of the day assisting the trio. While Griffin and Hektor translated the hieroglyphic texts on the walls, she and Petros handled the artifacts.

"Do not worry. Before we attempted to use his earth magic charms, we checked for any more traps. The room is clean," Petros reassured her after she eyed a burned scarab husk with trepidation.

The atmosphere felt lighter. The men joked, swapped stories, and coaxed her into sharing her own. When Hektor called an end to their day, they all returned to the surface and shared a meal around a blazing campfire. Despite his earlier failure with his spell, Griffin seemed in good spirits. He smiled, laughed, and appeared more like the man she knew and loved.

Once again, he snuck into her tent when the rest of the camp was still. It reminded her of old times at the Archives over summer tutorials with their fellow students of magic.

"You know, we're adults now. You don't have to sneak in like you're breaking curfew," she teased.

Griffin crawled into the cot beside her, the narrow space forcing her to slide one thigh over his hip and snuggle close.

"Old habit. You know how much I enjoy the illusion of breaking the rules."

"You never change. Not that I mind."

"I've changed plenty, dove."

"You have, I suppose. And I like that, too." She ran her fingers up his arm beneath the blanket, keeping the touch light. "Will we always be sneaking though?"

At first he chuckled, and she didn't expect anything to come of it, but then Griffin maneuvered her above him, serving as a better mattress than the thin cushion. "No. No, we won't. But I feel like Hektor might read me the riot act if he knew I was here. He's protective of you."

She laughed and closed her eyes. The steady beat of his heart comforted her and lulled her into a relaxed state.

When she drifted to sleep, she knew better than to expect to see him beside her in the morning. His chopper was due to come early, and they both agreed it would be for the best if she didn't see him off.

Parting from Griffin's side always hurt too much.

~*~

Aisling remained in Greece for three days following Griffin's departure.

When she returned to Dublin, she found her office empty. Every personal belonging had been stripped and tucked neatly into boxes labeled with forwarding addresses to Rio de Janeiro.

It all felt so surreal. The changes in her life over the past few months had happened so quickly that it left her dizzy.

"Why didn't you tell me you applied in Brazil and asked for a transfer?"

Deirdre stood in her doorway, hands on hips and voice full of feigned outrage.

"Surprise," Aisling said with a weak attempt at a smile. "Honestly, I had no idea when I left for Greece if it was going to happen or not. I hadn't expected to be packed up, though."

Her friend moved inside. "They came through three days ago and boxed it all up. Oh, Aisling, I'm going to miss you so much. And—you cut your hair!"

Aisling touched her fingers to her shortened bob. The layered strands barely brushed against her shoulders. "There was an accident, and we had to cut it," she mumbled.

"It's cute!" Deirdre assured her.

"My hair's never been so short. Not since I was a child."

"Well, I like it, and it will probably suit you better in the tropics. Ready to do a final round with me? Everyone will want to say goodbye."

The remainder of her day passed with the comfortable familiarity of routine. She went from patient to patient, ran paperwork, and spent time mixing herbal poultices.

"Rumor says you're leaving us."

She turned and found the dark gaze of Michael Stoddard on her. While he was popular among the female clerks of the Dublin Vault, Ash knew him only as her childhood bully and the boy who interfered with her and Griffin's relationship. The hulking man worked as a Scribe in the Collections Department, his scores too inadequate to pass the Guardian Exams.

The stringent requirements of the elite magical police force judged strength of character, magical prowess, and a number of other attributes to separate the wheat from the chaff. It was an aspect of their society for which Aisling was eternally grateful.

"So it would seem, Michael. My services have been requested in Brazil."

"I've been looking to get out of here m'self. Sent an application to New York. I might have been convinced to apply to Brazil if I knew you'd be going there."

Aisling forced a phony smile. "My answer in Rio would be the same as it is here. No. Now, a good day to you. I have to finish making preparations."

She brushed past the burly Irishman without another glance and left straightaway to dispense healing tonics to their patients.

Michael's appearance had revealed another silver lining in her relocation to Brazil—she'd never have to see him again.

The thought put a skip in her step.

Moments after she joined Deirdre for lunch, her phone chirped with an incoming text from Griffin. He promised to be in on the evening Portal from Barcelona with all the provisions to celebrate their impending move.

"You're glowing again. Good news from your beau?"

"What makes you think—"

"Please. Anytime Griffin's name is mentioned, you light up, and the rumors have been swirling since your Egypt expedition. Was he in Greece, too? Oh my God, is that why you're moving to Brazil? You're running away with Griffin MacNeil, aren't you?"

"It's hardly running."

Deirdre squealed and clapped her hands. "Has he proposed?"

"No, it's not like that." Not yet. They'd done little more than kiss, and it was getting harder and harder to break away.

Tonight. Maybe tonight. A flush of warmth coursed through her when she imagined Griffin above her, his strong hands against her bare skin. Their kiss in Greece had been the closest they'd come to something more physical.

"Oh Lord. Are you still a v—"

Aisling swatted her friend hard enough to leave a bruise. "Never you mind whether I am or not."

"Definitely are. Well then, good luck. He's a fit one for sure. He'll probably keep you up all of the night."

"Deirdre!" she hissed, face flushed and ears hot.

"What? Would you rather be left after five minutes? Go on, I say, and get yourself prettied up. Take a nice long bath, put on some silk, and open some bubbly. I know you have a bottle. I gave you one a few months back, remember? Probably gathering dust in your pantry."

Now that her friend had put the idea in her head, Aisling couldn't get it off her mind. The afternoon alternated, seeming

THE COLLECTOR'S TREASURE

to drag by at points and fly at others. Deirdre finally convinced her to leave a half-hour before the end of her shift.

They hugged, promising to keep in contact, then Aisling hurried home.

The other Healer must have been touched by the gift of Sight, because Aisling found the bottle of champagne exactly where Deirdre predicted it would be.

"Thanks, Deirdre," she murmured.

After dusting the bottle off, she put it in the freezer to chill and then prepped up a casserole for the oven. She checked the time, set the temperature to low, then went off to get cleaned up. A relaxing bath helped sooth her nerves.

"What do you think, Breda? Casual or nice?" She held up two dresses for the cat's inspection but received nothing more than a wide yawn. "Some help you are."

By the time Griffin arrived, she'd settled on a black skirt and an emerald top. She skipped over and answered the door, giddy and tingling from head to toe.

He greeted her with a bouquet filled with blue and purple wildflowers accented by pink rosebuds and yellow baby's breath.

"Griffin, they're beautiful."

"Not as much as you. If I'd known you were going to dress up for me, I'd have brought you red roses."

"No, these are perfect." She leaned up and kissed his cheek, but he turned his head at the last minute and captured her lips instead. A classic Griffin mischief move.

"Are we going to stand here all night, or are you going to let me in?"

The warm amusement in his voice made her blush. She tugged him inside by the lapels of his jacket and nudged the door shut with her foot.

"Smells good in here."

"I thought dinner in would be nicer than going out. Besides, I have champagne."

"Oh, do you now? Does this mean you're excited? No second thoughts?" he asked.

"No. None."

"I'm serious," he said in a quieter voice. "I don't want to take you away from close friends and people you care about, Ash. I hope you know that."

"I know that." She set her flowers in a vase and stepped over to rest her hands on his chest. "I'll miss Ireland, but you were right. I've wanted to get away. I need to."

"I'll understand if it's too big a step for you. If it's too early. I teased you before, but I mean it. If you decide you'd rather stay in Ireland, I'll respect it."

Too early? Too big a step? He was the one rebuilding his entire life and starting from scratch. The one taking all the risks.

Several moments of strained silence passed between them as she struggled to find a response. He didn't speak, his gaze on the window behind her head.

The last time Griffin had looked so serious, Michael had told her he saw Griffin kissing Mercedes in the Archives.

Their quarrel had been heard across the estate. He'd been upset she believed it, and she'd been hurt he put himself in a position for Michael to lie.

It had been the beginning of the end for them. He'd been so upset, he broke up with her and dated Mercedes out of spite. Let her father pull the strings to get him into the Collector's League.

That wouldn't happen again. Griffin belonged to her.

"I'm leaving with you to Rio, and you'll have to tie me down to my empty desk in Dublin to stop me."

Chapter 14

Tie her to a desk in Dublin?

Despite the lift of her chin and the flash of anger in her eyes, Griffin grinned. "I can think of better places to tie you down."

More than anything, he loved flustering her. It had been a favorite game in their youth and still held the same appeal. He leaned down to brush his lips against her cheek, but Ash took him by surprise when she stole his move and turned her head to catch it on her lips instead. He'd always been a bad influence on her, or in this case, a good one.

Griffin tugged her down to the couch with him, guiding her knees to the outside of his thighs until she straddled him. Her skirt pooled over his lap.

"Dinner?" he asked, despite losing the appetite for anything that didn't involve undressing her.

"It will survive," she whispered between kisses. Her fingers nudged his jacket until he leaned forward enough to shrug it off.

He didn't like his shirt enough to have the patience to let her undress him. Buttons rolled to parts unknown when he ripped it open, then he tossed the shirt aside. Her quiet gasp made the loss worth it.

"I'll fix it later," he muttered.

Both hands glided beneath her skirt. He felt the warmth of her, feminine heat between her thighs and the soft cheeks encased in lace-trimmed silk. Her panties tore easily, then it was only bare skin in his palms.

For weeks, he'd planned that if he ever had the blessing to take Aisling to bed, he'd be the patient and slow lover she deserved. Need warred within him, a conflict between the desire to taste her or sate his urges.

Aisling solved the dilemma for him when she broke away and pulled off her top. Shell pink silk cupped her modest breasts.

"You're beautiful," he told her.

He carried her to the bed and stretched her over the sumptuous comforter before removing her clothes one article at a time, delighting in every additional inch of skin he bared.

She leaned up to return the favor until he was as bare as she was, and the proof of his desire stood tall and proud between them.

Then he thought he would die the moment she touched him. Dainty fingers surrounded his aching length, only to jerk when arousal made it pulse in her hand.

"Don't be shy now, Ash. It's only me."

"I've always been shy around you. I thought…" Her gaze ducked away, and her teeth skated across her lower lip. "I used to think I could never compare to a nymph…"

"I hope you know better now."

She nodded.

"I don't want a nymph. I want *you*. I want you to touch me. Want you to scream my name until you're hoarse and your neighbors are jealous." Griffin watched her gaze fly back to his face, her lips parted in a shocked O.

He stretched alongside her with his weight upon one elbow, one hand free to descend her ticklish ribs and down the rounded curve of a hip. His agile fingers played across her thighs and gently coaxed her slim legs to part for a slick, moisture-gathering trace.

She was wetter than he had anticipated and utterly responsive to his touch. He developed a rhythm and writhed beneath his attentions.

A breathy sigh, whimpered plea, and a call of his name rewarded him. "Griffin, please…"

Griffin let emotion and years of longing guide him. His index finger parted her entrance to tease shallow, wet strokes, and his lips lowered to her flat tummy. The ascending path of his mouth came to a plump breast, and her inner walls shuddered around his fingers when he claimed one tender pink nipple between his lips.

A slow, torturous descent began next, filled with trailing kisses and gentle nibbles.

By the time his mouth reached her navel, Aisling practically sobbed for him. Her thighs quivered as her hips bucked upwards to grind her downy mound against his hand.

"Griffin... Griffin, please, *mo chroí*..."

He gave the most intimate kiss that could be shared, closing his lips eagerly over the tender center between her thighs.

Aisling's toes curled into the cool sheets. One hand clenched in his hair, and the other grasped the adjacent pillow.

When she collapsed back to the mattress, she went limp and still. He felt fine tremors in her limbs as his lips turned to press a sweet kiss to her inner thigh.

"Mmm..." She tasted as good as he'd imagined in dreams. Her inviting warmth made him ache to claim her.

"That was for you. And there's more t'come."

"I never knew it could be like that. The girls..." She blushed, the color tinting her glorious body pale pink from head to toe. "Their stories, I never really thought them so..."

Griffin grinned. "I promise to show you firsthand."

Once he kissed his way back up to her, Griffin stretched over her body with his weight supported on one arm. Her petite body felt delicate beneath him, but perfectly matched to his form. Two halves of a whole.

"I'm only beginnin'," he said against her cheek. "I want to make love to you the way I fantasized of doin' for years."

"Then love me now," she said breathlessly.

"I've always loved you, Ash. Always will."

Each explorative touch of her fingers found encouragement. Sometimes they came as kisses, and at other times with affectionate murmurs of reassurance. Griffin whispered in Gaelic against her ear, his affectionate brogue punctuated by the first thick press of his girth.

When his hips surged forward and joined them as one, Aisling's fingernails bore down into his back sharply. He soothed her with a kiss delivered to one delicate ear and exerted every ounce of willpower he had to remain motionless above her.

"'M'sorry, lass. Breathe..."

"I'm good," she whispered on a shaky exhale.

"I waited years for you. What's one minute more?" he murmured, turning his face to brush his lips against the edge of her jaw. "You tell me if I hurt you. I mean it."

"No, no... It passed and—Sweet Lord, Griffin, you feel amazing."

With confident hands, he guided her hips, urging her to rise into each subsequent thrust.

The inviting clench of her virginal channel made each backstroke an exercise in self-discipline until he ached to plunge forward anew. The blissful heat of her body scorched through him and brought his orgasm dangerously close.

He'd dreamed of this moment once during the boyish fantasies of his youth. Memories surfaced of lying awake at night in his bedroom, wondering if Aisling thought of him too. They should have both explored their first time together, but somehow Griffin had lost his way. Her forgiveness humbled him.

His Aisling. His after so long. A beautiful gift he didn't deserve.

And just when he thought he couldn't take anymore, one of her heels pressed into his rear, bringing him back to her again. He buried his face against the curve of her throat and surrendered to the moment and the sweet embrace her body offered.

Griffin didn't last much longer, but when he reached the pinnacle, Aisling was right there with him in a shared climax accented by guiding touches and fervent kisses.

And he knew there was no way he could ever leave her again.

~*~

Very little movement happened over the course of the night aside from Griffin stumbling once into the kitchen to raid Ash's fridge.

He didn't stir again until nearly noon when the sun finally rose overhead to mercilessly point its beams through the window, penetrating the fragile moss green curtains.

After hiding his face against her dark hair, he inhaled its sweet fragrance and then blinked awake from the fog of dreamland to realize his surroundings were different.

"Ash..." he breathed against her disheveled curls. "Wake up, woman." He laughed at her languid, kitten-like stretch. "You're beautiful when you're just awakened, you know. More beautiful when you're in the kitchen."

After she'd crawled from bed and stood alongside it, he swatted her bottom, then soothed it with his palm. Really, he'd just wanted an excuse to continue touching her.

"Fine. I'll feed you, I suppose."

He watched her shrug into a silk robe and eventually joined her in the kitchen nook once he'd checked his cell phone for messages. Nothing vital or pressing.

"Ash, I was wonderin' if...y'know, whether..." Griffin leaned against her kitchen counter with his arms folded against his chest.

"Cat got your tongue?" She brushed flour from her hands once the quiche was placed in the oven.

"We didn't use any protection last night," he blurted out at last.

"You don't need to worry," she reassured him. "I take these disgusting potions once a season."

"Oh. Well then, that's good." He looped an arm around her waist and drew her back against him while she scrubbed her hands at the sink.

Even though they'd showered before bed, he still marveled over how any woman could awaken in the morning smelling like fresh flowers.

"How long until the food is done?"

Aisling squeaked off the faucets and shook her hands over the sink. "Twenty minutes or so. Why?"

He nudged forward with his hips, the rigid length of him settling firm between her cheeks. Finally he could satisfy all of those fantasies he'd carried for her over the years. Uninhibited.

"Reason enough?"

"More than."

He scooped her up and carried her back to the bed where he kept her thoroughly occupied until the oven timer buzzed.

He grinned as she scrambled naked across the loft to save their breakfast from burning.

After a shared shower and a filling meal, Griffin forced himself to dress instead of chasing Aisling into bed again.

"Off somewhere?" she called from the couch. Breda had claimed her lap.

"I've got a brief errand to run then I'll be right back again. Promise. I've just got to see Lachlan."

"You'd better go see Jack then, too, else I'll never hear the end of it if you visit with your Faerie godfather and skip him."

Truer words couldn't be said to him. He kissed her again before he took off and caught a cab outside her building. He gave the driver the address to a shop near Smithfield Square and paid with a generous tip once he reached his destination.

A wooden sign flapped in the wind outside a stone brick storefront, bearing script carefully applied with a delicate brush and black paint.

Covets & Cravings Rare Antiquities

A chime rang to announce Griffin's entrance, drawing the owner's attention.

Lachlan stood behind the counter, a lean man with shaggy auburn hair and an angular jaw covered in golden red stubble. He wore his black T-shirt fitted over ripped jeans, displaying his well-defined biceps.

Books lined wooden shelves, ancient coins glittered from beds of black velvet, and old suits of armor stood against a far wall. Trinkets and treasures all sat out on display for a buyer's perusal. Griffin had no interest in any of the baubles on the main floor.

"Long time without seein' you. How're things?" Lachlan said, his grin broadening.

Griffin felt abashed for a brief moment. In the many times he visited Aisling, rarely did he visit either of his two old friends. Jack let him know about it and shamed him, but never Lachlan.

"Sorry. They're decent enough, I suppose. Your shop is lookin' a bit empty these days."

"It is. Was thinkin' of makin' a move now, so I began to pack. Gettin' out of this city. The people here… They're a kind lot, but they remember this is the same face I've had for fifteen years. Haven't aged, haven't changed. They're wise to me now." He shrugged, and the grin faded from his face entirely. "The fuck's wrong now, Griff? Your aura's strange."

Griffin caught him up on the upheavals and changes in his life, laying it out in details Lachlan couldn't see with his magical fae senses.

"About time you wizened up to leave her." Lachlan nodded in approval. "And your wee bairn?"

"We'll return to court over her. Won't let me have her, but has no desire to care for her either unless it's to her convenience."

"I could handle her, y'know."

"Nae, Lachlan. I want to do this the right way. The mortal way. Besides, your price is too steep for me."

"For you, lad, I'd do it for free. Nothin' could bring a brighter smile to my face than pulling her to pieces. I know a red cap who knows a troll. We could do it clean, the three of us. No one would ever know. Nothin' left of her to find. I like nereid bones."

"Uh, no. As tempting as you've made the offer, Mara would miss her, and I don't want you in trouble for killing a mortal."

The two old friends smiled at each other for a moment, and then Lachlan stepped into the rear of the shop and invited Griffin to join him. He brought out the good whiskey and poured two glasses while the conversation quickly began to flow.

Griffin laid it all out from where the relationship ended with Mercedes to the change in his relationship with Aisling and their budding romance. Lachlan stared at him by the end.

"Weeks ago, I felt her life dimming, but the distance was far and out of my hands," Lachlan confessed. "Another dog would have come for her. Rumor says the weepers were in an uproar. Of course, I avoid those wailin' hags all I can."

Griffin smiled grimly and held his empty glass out for a refill, which he gratefully knocked back. He'd literally ripped Aisling away from Death's clutches when in Egypt.

For the banshees of Avalon to have wept, it meant she had come perilously close to leaving him forever.

"You're not bound to her as you are to me, but you still look after her, Lachlan. I appreciate it." He rose from the chair and left the empty glass on the table. Drinks with his Faerie godfather were fantastic but not the motivation for his visit.

"I don't mind it. She's a joy to be around."

"Now I need one more thing from you."

"What's that?"

"Heartstones. The ones that'll sing the prettiest."

Lachlan cast him a sly glance then grinned. "Oh? I might have such lovelies on hand, but what are you offering in payment?"

"What happened to doing things for free?"

"I'm charged with saving your life, lad, and jewels aren't a life or death decision. I need somethin' valuable to part with them."

"Can't offer you my firstborn. Though at this rate, it's a temptation if it'll get her away from her mum."

Lachlan chuckled and shook his head. "Next offer, then." He led Griffin down a stairwell into the lower level of the store. The items behind his main door were treasures, but the objects beneath the store were wonders—fantastic oddities of the Faerie realm, trinkets from the Nether Faire, and dangerous magical relics kept away from the prying eyes of humans.

"I'll bring a gift from my office."

"*If* you remember to part from your bonnie Irish lass when next you pay a visit. Try again."

Most fae eagerly accepted items in trade, but Griffin had no immediate access to the items he thought were unique enough to gain his godfather's interest. Considering it, he crouched down to peer through the enchanted display at eye level, observing the twinkle of the gems behind the glass. Their radiant sparkle matched the notes filling the air whenever Lachlan traced his fingertips over the rare jewels.

Heartstones came from Avalon. The Vault Portals used the same stones, albeit larger growths, in their magic.

"A favor to be paid."

His godfather whistled. "Means that much to you, then? Enough to offer an open favor?"

"Nothing against my morals, no deeds to get me in prison, and no harm to women or children," Griffin said, laying out the terms.

"They're yours."

They shook on it and hugged. Lachlan had always been a better dad to him in poor times than the man who raised him for most of his life. It was the fae's intervention which had led to him finding his true father. Adam O'Grady and Griffin kept in touch, although their phone calls had become more infrequent in the recent year. He needed to remedy that.

Can't believe I neglected everyone I love like this. Mum. Lachlan. Even Dad. I haven't returned his calls since he visited me while I was in the hospital, Griffin thought, overcome with shame. So absorbed in his own struggles, he had forgotten the people who mattered. Even Lachlan had visited him in Fiona's home to wish him a speedy recovery while he recuperated after his hospital discharge.

"I promise to visit you in your new shop, too, wherever it is. You send me a note once you're settled."

"May be a while now. Only began to send in my applications. Regent Cassidy in Manhattan hates fae in his city. I'm lookin' at Los Angeles, so I'll probably head that way over to California and see how I like the weather. If it's too warm."

"I hear Sunny's hobby is breeding poodles," Griffin said. The Regent of Los Angeles was a perky blonde woman with a bright smile and a hippy's sense of adventure. He'd only had the opportunity to work for her once. "She'll love you. Sire her some special pups while you're there."

"You're a cock."

"I know. Love you too."

Griffin started for the door with his expensive gems stored safely within a soft velvet pouch tucked into his jean pocket. He could still hear the tranquil echo of their melodic song. Moving to the door, he paused when Lachlan appeared beside him again, touching his wrist.

"Wait, Griffin. I cannot allow you to go without warnin'. I'm troubled. The thread bindin' your life to the rest of your clan is thin, fraying many times, yet it carries on into darkness too murky for me to see. Tread carefully, lad. You may be my godson, but there's only so much I can do from afar. Now that you're older, our connection grows weak."

"I will. Tell me one thing before I go."

"Yeah?"

"Did you ward the buildin' where Aisling lives?"

Lachlan stared at him, but then he shook his head and glanced toward the window. "No. Wasn't me that time. I don't deal in that brand of magic, though it wouldn't hurt me to learn."

"Then who was it?"

"You already know the answer."

THE COLLECTOR'S TREASURE

Chapter 15

Jean-Luc glanced up as Sylvie set a steaming cup of coffee on the desk beside a bag of fast food. The aroma of many different meals wafted through the air as she and other Guardians returned with takeout from local establishments.

"Dinner is served, my friend. Since you wouldn't take a break from your work, I brought a break to you," she said.

The enticing scent of fried onion lured Jean-Luc to open the bag from their favorite a lá carte restaurant. He dug into the meal eagerly, pleased she remembered his preferences. He was the sole vegetarian among the Guardian force, and during social events, Sylvie always made sure to supply fresh vegetables and fruit salads for him. Onion rings were among his favorite comfort foods.

"I appreciate it, Sylvie. You're the only one who looks out for me."

"You would waste away without me," she replied with a grin.

"How is Francois—" Shrill rings of an incoming phone call interrupted him. Jean-Luc raised the receiver from the cradle and pressed it to his ear, holding it in place with his shoulder. "Chevalier."

"Lieutenant Chevalier, this is Jacques Bellard of the IML. We have your test results."

"Fantastic. I had begun to wonder whether or not I should pay a visit in person."

Jacques usually did everything within his power to keep Jean-Luc away from his office. Dealing with corpses while in the presence of a man able to inspire fear with his thoughts wasn't a priority for most people. Their contacts did whatever was necessary to get him in and out as swiftly as possible.

"No. Unnecessary, Lieutenant. My apologies for the length of time it's taken to return this call, but we wanted to be sure of the results. You won't like this."

Jean-Luc fell silent, anticipation settling in his gut with the weight of a lead ball.

From the corner of his eye, he saw Sylvie covering the remnants of her meal and closing the top of his salad. After storing their goodies in the employee fridge, she returned to the edge of her seat.

"Your suspicions about Mademoiselle Paget were correct. We discovered evidence of sexual assault, but given the circumstances, we chose to retest the DNA samples."

"What circumstances?" Jean-Luc asked.

"Your perpetrator is a member of your Vault."

He blinked a few times, at a loss for words. "Shit." He raked his fingers through his hair. "This is much worse than I thought. Go on."

"What's happening?" Sylvie hissed.

Jean-Luc gestured at her with a hand, signaling for her to be patient. She practically bounced on the edge of her seat, brimming with anticipation. He reached with his right hand for the notepad on the table and scrawled out a hasty note in his neat penmanship.

Lab results are back. Victim raped. DNA evidence found. I'm getting other details,' the note read.

Sylvie nodded and mouthed at him, "Any leads?"

"Get on with it then, Jacques. *Who* is it?"

Less than two minutes later, Jean-Luc ended the phone call with all of the information necessary to make his arrest. He rubbed his face with one hand, disgust and anger warring from within. "Yes, we have a lead. You are not going to like this one bit, Sylvie." He raised the phone to his ear again and dialed the receptionist at the ground floor.

"Has Scribe Dupont arrived today?"

"Dupont? Not yet, Lieutenant. He's due to arrive for the night shift today. Should be here in about half an hour. Got a problem?" she asked, her chilly voice a reminder not to date in the office anymore.

"No, no problem. Thank you. I will catch him when he arrives." He quickly ended the call before he drowned in the waves of passive aggression filtering through the line.

Jean-Luc rose and faced the other Guardians at their desks. "Bellard cross-referenced the results of the DNA evidence with our registry. We have a match, and he's due to arrive in the next thirty minutes. Lieutenant Proulx and I will meet him at the front. The rest of you will ensure if he makes a run for it, he doesn't get far. I want him alive to talk. Understood?"

"Who is it?" Sylvie asked.

"Scribe Marius Dupont of the Collections Department. Consider him dangerous."

Reactions from the other seven Guardians varied from startled gasps to quiet murmurs. Beside him, Sylvie pressed her lips to a thin line and grunted.

She'd never liked Dupont, fed up with him coming on to her more than once.

"Marc and Orianne, we need you standing ready at the east alley. Remi and Ghislain, the west," Sylvie ordered.

The group reassembled in the lobby and split to take their individual posts. Jean-Luc and Sylvie decided to act natural by heading outside for a smoke break. Everyone knew of his bad habit while working a particularly rough case. He puffed like a freight train while Sylvie leaned against the wall beside him and appeared occupied with her mobile device.

With winter covering Paris in a fine layer of snow, Scribe Dupont arrived by metro each evening with mere minutes to spare before the start of his nine o'clock night shift. In his black parka, the man looked like any other civilian on the street. A gallery farther down the block was hosting a showing, resulting in thick pedestrian traffic in and out.

"There he is," Sylvie muttered under her breath, barely glancing up from her phone screen.

Jean-Luc stubbed out his third cigarette and flicked the butt of it into a nearby trashcan on the sidewalk. His gaze focused on the approaching man while Sylvie powered down the screen of her phone and placed the device into her holster. The cool night made them breathe warm steam, misting the frosty winter air.

The buses had run slow, and Marius Dupont arrived with barely a minute to spare before his assigned clock-in time.

"Lieutenants, cold night, isn't it?" Marius flashed the pair a grin as he approached.

"Incredibly," Jean-Luc replied.

The approaching magus slowed his steps and raised the buzzing mobile device at his hip to one ear. He listened for a second and cut his narrowed eyes toward the pair of Guardians.

Before Jean-Luc could open his mouth to speak, Marius pitched the phone toward them. It shattered on the sidewalk in a spray of sparks. The chain of current sizzled and exploded into a dozen branching streams of lightning, all of which seemed to arc from one person to the next.

While they were caught by the storm, Marius ran and practically bulldozed through the three young Constables who moved to stand in his path. He obliterated their shields with a single, searing bolt of electricity that lit the darkened city street.

At Jean-Luc's rear, Sylvie swore and leapt over the Guardian stunned by Marius's attack. Jean-Luc's stomach twisted as he gave chase. He hated to leave one of his men behind, but Ghislain would be in good hands. Marc fell back while Orianne continued on foot.

Jean-Luc leapt over a pair of trash cans thrown into his path and touched one foot against the brick wall, running across it in a perfect horizontal sprint without losing momentum.

"He's getting away!" he called over his shoulder.

"No, he isn't!" Sylvie cried before throwing herself to her hands and knees, her palms planted to the concrete path.

Several yards of sidewalk tore from the ground in a rippling, cracking pattern of devastation. Marius stumbled forward onto an upraised, jagged layer of cement as a pillar of earth shot from the ground inches from his chin.

As a talented earth mage, Sylvie manipulated the ground beneath their feet to her advantage. Marius narrowly evaded by spinning in the air to kick off of the column. He crashed through a store window and vanished from Jean-Luc's sight.

Shrill alarms screamed a warning to the police.

Crystal and glass crunched beneath Jean-Luc's steps as he followed. Floral perfume hung heavy in the air, an

THE COLLECTOR'S TREASURE

overwhelming mix of rose and gardenia. Before he could make it far in pursuit of their suspect, colorful silk fluttered and caught aflame, spreading in fiery fingers of orange over rows of stylish garments.

Damned dark wizards.

As Jean-Luc sprinted through a veil of fire meant to slow him down, another crash drew him farther inside to a back exit with Sylvie hot on his heels. A broken door led to a side street where cool air rushed in from the winter night.

Hurtling from the darkness, a flaming Peugeot rushed toward Sylvie and Jean-Luc the very moment they appeared through the doorway. Pieces of twisted metal, hot automobile parts, and shattered glass flew with the bulk of the vehicle.

Jean-Luc shoved Sylvie from the path of danger with all his strength. He disappeared beneath the wreckage.

"Luc!" Sylvie screamed.

Darkness enfolded him, a shroud of dark gray shadows and black.

In one moment he was in the path of the fiery car, and in the next he had stepped out from the shadows beneath a burned out streetlamp.

Behind Marius.

His foot connected with Marius's head, sending a satisfying spray of bloodied spittle. Shrieking in terror, the black wizard shot black-laced, purple flames toward Jean-Luc's face, which he barely evaded in time.

It wasn't any normal fire. It was Hellfire, and the sulfurous stench of it brought tears to Jean-Luc's eyes.

Only the most depraved individuals commanded the fires of Hell, often making sordid deals and contracts with the demons of the nether realm to acquire the powerful ability.

And then there were a handful of wizards like Griffin MacNeil who acquired it on account of birth circumstances. Still, it was a heavily discouraged talent. The use of Hellfire upon a human being was a crime punishable by death.

It was the only magic in the world able to destroy a soul along with the body.

Marius wasn't one of those wizards born with an unfortunate ancestor. His spirit was awash with the dark aura of Hell.

Another spear of flame fired at Jean-Luc. He twisted aside through the air in an acrobatic leap.

"What are you!?" Marius shrieked.

"I am your worst fears."

Marius became little more than a bag for Jean-Luc to punch. With each contact of his fist against the man's face, he gleaned knowledge of some atrocity the man committed. Murder and rape only tipped the iceberg of his crimes.

"Jean-Luc, you'll kill him!"

"Maybe I want to," he hissed back at Sylvie.

He could have split Marius's head against the ground, shattering it like overripe fruit for his transgressions against mankind, against Madame Paget, against untold numbers of other victims who suffered his insidious desires.

"He needs to be brought to justice, Luc."

"He's only a filthy rapist, not fit to be taken alive. A demon worshipper," Jean-Luc spat back.

"Remember your job," Sylvie beseeched him, her voice against his ear. Pleading. "Your job, Luc. What you believe in! This isn't you!"

Jean-Luc gazed down at the battered features of the man beneath him, blood trickling profusely from a face resembling ground hamburger. In his heart, he knew she was right. In his soul, he knew the only thing to do would be to slap the cuffs onto Marius's wrists and haul him before the Regent for a trial.

So he did.

He dragged Marius to his feet without assistance and slapped the handcuffs on his wrists as backup arrived.

"You'll nev—" A choked gurgle escaped their prisoner's throat. Marius convulsed and nearly jerked out of Jean-Luc's restraining grip.

"His eyes are bleeding!" Remi called out, both disgusted and horrified.

"Luc—"

"It's not me, Sylvie."

Marius convulsed again, his body shook, and he ripped free from their hold. A fount of dark liquid poured thickly down his chin. Remi swore and backed away with his hands up while Jean-Luc and Sylvie watched in horror. Their prisoner fell to his knees in spasms and collapsed to his side. Before their very eyes, he asphyxiated on the fluid filling his lungs.

"Shit! Do something!" Sylvie shouted.

Orianne had medical training. Within seconds of dropping to her knees beside him and hovering a palm above Marius's chest, she shook her head.

"He's gone. There is nothing for me to do. His lungs are filled with blood, and all of his internal organs have ruptured. All of them," she repeated with a frown.

Sylvie loosed a barrage of swears. "This is a mess. We have witnesses!" she hissed under her breath. "And how in the hell did you do that, Luc? You vanished and reappeared yards away!"

"I—"

Sirens sounded in the air and lights flashed in the darkness as reinforcements arrived. Captain Cloutier exited the lead vehicle, and Hannah Blouchard slid out right behind him. Jean-Luc barely suppressed a groan.

There weren't too many ways for his night to become any worse.

~*~

Jean-Luc was wrong. Things could always become much worse. Six hours later, the two Gatekeepers finished handling the shit storm outside.

A team of Guardians dispatched to Marius's home residence discovered a basement room filled with enough horrors to tape a snuff film. In fact, photography equipment, a video camera, and boxes of digital equipment indicated he had. Evidence of years of predatory behavior pointed to a lifestyle dedicated to the demonic Prince of Lust. As a disciple of Asmodeus, Marius honored her with ritualistic rape and murder. They estimated he may have been responsible for a vast number of the unsolved sexual assaults in the city.

It was enough to sicken everyone involved, excluding Blouchard. The woman had a heart of coal and a stony expression to match while they debriefed her on the events. She directed her assistant to handle the home while she took care of the messy public debacle.

Because Marius kept the bodies of many preserved in lewd poses for his own sick satisfaction, family members of missing girls going back for years would need to be notified.

The collection included local girls of college age, prostitutes, and even tourists. Since Marius didn't dispose of their possessions, they felt confident about identifying most of his victims. Boxes of passports, wallets, and belongings would be pieced together.

"He seemed so normal." Sylvie sighed. "What do we do now?"

"We hope something among his belongings will send us in the next direction to catch any of his accomplices. He could not have worked alone," Jean-Luc determined.

"Precisely why you two will be reviewing these." Captain Cloutier set a large case down on a table and unsnapped the lid to reveal an assortment of video media ranging from SD cards to old VHS cassettes. "I want to know if anyone else was involved, and I want a face to each of these girls."

Jean-Luc felt his stomach twist. A glance at Sylvie was enough to determine she felt the same way—nauseated.

"Yes, Captain. As you wish."

"When you're done, give the results to Blouchard's assistant. Miss Ia-whatever."

"Iamides," Luc supplied. "Krystine Iamides."

Cloutier gave a dismissive wave. "Yes, her. She's running the clean-up so far as the girls are concerned."

With the disgusting circumstances surrounding their combined efforts, he couldn't even appreciate the view while working alongside the beautiful Greek woman.

Jean-Luc cursed his luck.

Chapter 16

As Aisling adjusted to the new routine of learning her way around the Brazilian Healers' ward, Griffin settled into his job as Luisa's assistant. Initially, he expected mistreatment from the local Collectors passed over when he received the job, but they welcomed him with warm, open arms.

With their first field expedition coming up in three weeks, they both worked hard to catch up on everything. Griffin's knowledge of the local language gave him an edge, so each night after their shifts, he tutored Aisling in Brazilian Portuguese.

Aisling poured hot water for tea. "You're bristling with energy this evening."

"I'm excited about the dig. We'll be legends if we succeed."

Griffin, Luisa, and their researchers took great pains to pin down a lead to their next destination. For years, Director Mendoza had dreamed of discovering a single mythical location—El Dorado, the lost city of gold.

Aisling smiled at him from across the room. "I know. I'm excited, too."

"How are you likin' it here?" He dropped down on the couch and patted the space beside him until Aisling abandoned her puttering in the kitchen and joined him.

She set their tea aside on the coffee table. "It's all so different," she said as she settled against him. "But I like it. They've made me feel very welcome."

"You're happy, then?"

He ran his fingers through her dark hair. In the weeks since Greece, her hair had grown barely an inch, too short for a comfortable ponytail. "I am, Griff. I still have lots to learn, but I'm content with our new life."

"Good. I'm glad. That makes some of us at least."

"What do you mean?"

"I spoke with Addison on the phone while you took a bath. Seems he and Krys finally called it quits. He says it was amicable, but I could tell he was upset."

"Really?" She turned to him with a frown. "Did they fight?"

"He wouldn't say. He mentioned they grew apart."

Aisling was silent a moment, then shook her head. "They've always been a good pair but never seemed a perfect match."

"I suppose so. Guess this means our tentative truce is over now that she doesn't have to be nice for Addison's sake. She's hated me ever since I pulled that dumb shite at the Winter Gala. I can't blame her either. I hated me, too, for a long time. I can honestly say I never regretted anything more than leaving you behind for Mercedes."

When he thought back to the formal dance, his fuzzy memories blurred together. Aisling had been beautiful that night, he recalled that much, and his arrival had surprised her. They danced, talked, and ended the night with a kiss beneath the stars.

Everything after that lost focus. He had gone back to Spain and remained there despite every intention to leave.

"You must have thought the worst of me."

She averted her gaze and worried her lip between her teeth. "I did... Krys brought me out of a dark place, Griffin. When I eventually forgave, she did not."

"That's why I'm doing now what I should have done then." If he didn't pass out from lack of oxygen first. Reminding himself to breathe, he eased out from behind her and knelt on the floor by her feet. On one knee, he fished beneath the cushions and removed a single black velvet box.

None of the carefully rehearsed words he'd practiced in the mirror seemed appropriate.

"Griffin?" Her voice hitched, and her gaze focused on his face.

"I love you, and I want to marry you. I want the life we ought to have been havin' all this time." He opened the box to reveal a ring on a bed of white silk. The three heartstones he'd acquired from Lachlan sparkled from a platinum band decorated with Celtic knot work.

"Griffin…" Her silver eyes shined bright with tears, and a smile lit up her features.

"Will you marry me, Ash?"

"Yes!"

The single word loosened the tightness in his chest. Before he could rise to embrace her, Aisling threw herself into his arms. Laughing, he caught her against his chest and tumbled back against the emerald rug stretched over their living room floor.

"Yes, yes, yes," she said between exuberant kisses.

Griffin rolled her beneath him and slipped the ring onto her finger. It fit perfectly in place. A jolt of elation shot through his body and left his limbs tingling. At last, he could breathe. "I can't promise not to drive you nuts at times."

"I wouldn't have you any other way, Griffin MacNeil. I love you, brooding and all."

He leaned down and kissed her, moved beyond words. Pride surged through him and left a foreign sensation in his body of floating, weightless and untroubled by any worries. Finally, after too many years, all aspects of his life had once again fallen into place.

He thought his mother and father would be proud to hear the news. That their respective families would be thrilled to know they'd finally set their lives right again.

One kiss ended and another began, but eventually her lips trailed to his ear.

"We'll have to call everyone," he said.

She trapped his lobe between her teeth and nibbled. "Tomorrow. I've other things in mind for you tonight."

"I think I've been a bad influence on you."

Aisling laughed, her breath warm against his scarred throat. "Only in the best of ways."

Which she revealed with countless activities throughout the night, both startling and amazing him with her enthusiasm.

He awakened at the crack of dawn and spent a few moments watching Aisling sleep, admiring her serene features. The heartstones glittered on her finger, fair and flawless like the angel who wore them. His entire body hummed with excitement again, a rush of exquisite joy coursing through him each time he thought of the upcoming ceremony to be planned.

"Sprite," he whispered.

Aisling made a quiet groan and cracked her eyes open a fraction. "Is it time to go to work?"

He grinned down at her and shook his head. They weren't due to return to work for another two days. A weekend away from the usual occupational stress had been ideal for his proposal. "No, I just wanted to let you know I was going to be leaving soon."

"The hearing?" she asked in a drowsy mumble.

"Yeah. Phone our families together later, all right?"

"Okay. Call me if anything happens. It'll all go well, have faith in that."

He leaned over and kissed her brow. "Thanks, dove. Go back to sleep and I'll see you tomorrow."

And if everything went well, he'd bring Mara home to meet her future stepmother.

~*~

Hours after the end of Aisling's shift, the jubilant man who left their rental home returned in a somber mood. Griffin shut the door behind him without uttering a greeting and drifted toward the living room.

Despite having the day off, she'd received a call asking if she could spare a few hours to help with an unusual abundance of sick cases. With Griffin out of town, she'd stopped at the market on her way home and fetched the ingredients to make a humble meal for one. Worried, she abandoned her salad to follow him.

"What's wrong, Griffin? What happened?"

He didn't respond at first, busy pouring a healthy glass from a decanter of brandy.

"Griffin, talk to me. Please." She crossed over and touched his wrist, wise enough not to try pulling the liquor away. "You know that never makes anything better."

"I'm not a child," he snapped.

"Then stop acting as one. Drinking won't fix anything."

Griffin set the decanter aside with a hard *thunk* and leaned against the table on both of his palms. While his gaze remained averted toward the floor, he made an involuntary sound in his throat.

Aisling stepped close enough to guide him from the table and into her arms. He went to her without resistance, his soft sigh breezing against her hair despite the tension in his body.

Griffin would speak when he was ready. Some things never changed.

"My lawyer told me he was sure we could win it in a pinch. It's like the goddamned judge is in her family's pocket. I never had a chance, Ash. Not one. I'm away too often, he said. Not home for Mara. Doesn't care that I said I'll give up exploring and work desks if it means I'll have her with me. She's to remain with her mum, and there isn't anything I can do."

At first, she fumbled for words. None of them felt adequate in the face of Griffin's sorrow. Her stomach tightened into a cold, little leaden ball in the pit of her belly and her head swam with nausea.

It wasn't fair. He should have come home with his little girl. She'd even planned to welcome them both with a big dinner. Squeezing Griffin closer, she ran her palm up to the back of his head and stroked his blond hair. "Did they let you have time with Mara at all?"

"Two hours. It's all they gave me. All they were willin' to give me. Said I've got to notify 'em in writin' when I want to visit her again."

He swallowed again and swiped at his face with the back of his wrist. "M'sorry for yellin' at you. Not your fault."

"Better to yell at me a wee bit than sit alone and brood, I think. Your silence hurts worse." She turned her head and brushed a kiss against his chest. "I'm so sorry about Mara."

"I miss her so much, Ash. I know I'm not the best father, but… What am I supposed to do?"

"We'll figure it out. Together."

Chapter 17

Of all the expeditions he'd joined across the world, Griffin thought the Amazon would become his greatest adventure. He found a new sense of serenity beneath the thick canopy and a visceral satisfaction in forging his own path through the jungle foliage.

Luisa had put together an elite team, and their origins didn't matter to her—she cared only about having the best. Griffin had been both surprised and pleased to see Juliana among them. He was even more surprised to see other faces non-native to Brazil.

"Ash, look at the wee monkeys," Griffin said.

"Those are Golden Lion Tamarins," Justin said. The large Canadian gestured to a pair over their heads. "If you look close, you can see the baby on that one's back."

Griffin eyed him. "They just look like tiny monkeys to me, animal know-it-all. I swear, you're worse than my cousin Addison."

"Well, I think it's very fascinating," Aisling said when Justin's cheeks flared red. "They're adorable."

"Later on when we make camp, I'll see if I can lure some down," Justin told her.

Luisa chuckled. "Justin used to work as a safari tour guide at Disney's Animal Kingdom some years ago. Teaching us about the animals is a habit for him."

Juliana raised her brows. "Tour guide to jungle trekker?"

"It was a nice break," Justin said. "Took a mauling from a feral bear shifter when I was on a Russian dig, and I needed something relaxing for a while. No real danger. Just me, the animals, and a truckload of happy tourists."

"Shh, listen," Jorge said. Their guide crouched down beside one of the many waterways branching off from the Amazon River.

Griffin glanced at their map. "We should cross here. There are falls further down the river, and the current's strong."

Jorge shook his head. "No, there is something—"

Water splashed in a mighty font as an enormous river snake erupted from the river. Before anyone could react with a spell or even a shout, it wrapped around their guide and constricted around him. The sickening crunch of breaking bones filled the air then it tossed its victim aside.

Reflexes kicked in, placing Griffin in front of Ash, then he swung out with both hands to send a flash wave of fire over the snake. The ineffective spell fizzled out, although steam wafted from its slick scales. He blinked. "What the hell kind of snake is that?"

Aisling spread out her own arms, and within seconds, a defensive shield shimmered into place over their group. "Is it an anaconda?"

Juliana shook her head and drew a machete from its holster. "It's a *boiúna*. A water spirit. Fire will do nothing to it."

"Can we save Jorge?" Justin asked.

"He is already dead," Juliana replied.

Aisling flinched as the snake swayed left and right, watching her sphere as if searching for weaknesses. "Can we outrun it?"

Luisa crouched low and thrust her fingers into the black soil beneath their feet. "It will only follow us." With a few spoken words, pillars of rock and dirt speared from the ground between them and the serpent. Unfazed, it slithered between the pillars, undulating its liquid black coils each time a new spike broke through the ground.

"Then we kill it now," Griffin said. He adjusted his stance and drew Jerry's dwarven knife. The creature hissed. "Can you keep us shielded, Ash?"

Aisling nodded without taking her eyes from the water spirit. Sweat beaded across her brow. One of the trickiest lessons of any mage's education was creating a sustained shield. Even harder was juggling a barrier from one target to another.

Like Juliana, Justin pulled a machete from his pack. "Aim for its underbelly. The scales should be weaker there."

Drawing in a breath, Griffin smothered his anxiety and let the adrenaline pulse through his veins. Years ago, he used to love snakes.

Now every time he saw one of them, it was there to give him hell.

Trusting in Aisling to keep him safe, he broke ranks and lunged forward. As his blade sank into its belly, it struck at him and met a magical shield instead.

Justin's machete glanced off the creature's thicker scales then it twisted about in a move too quick for the human eye to follow. The snake hurled him against a tree with a strike of its tail and snapped its teeth at Juliana. When Luisa shouted a magical curse, the ground beneath the snake buckled and threw it off balance.

Strike by strike, slash by slash, the Collectors tried to fight off their enemy. Aisling shuffled her barrier shield each time its attention shifted.

A tidal wave of water rose from the river and swept them into the current. Griffin struggled to get his feet beneath him, but the river picked up speed and sent him tumbling.

"Griffin!" Aisling called.

Kicking his feet placed him within arm's reach to grab her. "Got you. I got you."

"It's going to try to drown us!" Juliana shouted.

"Then we better kill it before we reach the falls."

She clung to him as the snake rushed toward them, her eyes wild with fear. "I can't keep the barriers up forever. I'm trying."

Another shimmer layered over the magical shell Ash created, and the warmth of Luisa's magic encompassed them.

"I'll share the load and take over for now, Aisling. Can you freeze the river?"

"It's too warm."

"Try," Griffin urged her.

"Together we can do it," Juliana called over. She used her own magic to help Aisling ice over a section near the swampy bank. The floe expanded and rocketed across the water. After crawling onto the thick, temporary barrier, they hurried across the slippery surface and onto solid ground.

Undeterred, the *boiúna* followed.

"I've got a plan, but you're not going to like it," Justin huffed.

"Anything is better than running. It will outlast us," Luisa said.

"Then keep going about another fifty feet, and then be ready to turn and attack." Justin ducked aside and disappeared between two thick trees.

"Griffin, did you catch all that?"

"Sure did. Ash, be ready with that shield again."

The scaled wrecking ball continued after them, bursting through every obstacle one of the mages threw in its way, from Luisa's geomancy attacks to Juliana's walls of ice. They barely slowed it down enough to keep in the lead.

Griffin counted the steps in his head then skidded to a halt and spun around with fire blazing between his palms. Juliana took a stance beside him while Aisling and Luisa positioned themselves at the rear of the small group.

Glittering sparks exploded in the air when the river spirit collided with the magical barrier. The snake hissed and struck again, battering itself against the shield.

Justin slammed his machete down through the serpent's tail and into the ground beneath. He rolled out of the way as the beast thrashed and flailed.

As the serpent darted toward Ash, fury swept aside Griffin's common sense. He lunged in front of her and thrust up at its face. His blade sank into the soft flesh beneath its jaw, and he ripped it outward.

Juliana finished the beheading he began. The thick body thrashed across the ground, twitched and twisted around. No one dared to move until the last spasm ended.

"Well, that was fun." Griffin bent over, braced his hands against his knees, and tried to catch his breath.

"What a...lucky hit," Justin managed to get out between breaths. "Wow."

"Poor Jorge," Aisling murmured.

Luisa sighed. "He's the third guide we've lost since we began exploring this part of the Amazon. The creatures grow increasingly aggressive as we go."

"Christ," Griffin said. "Is there any chance of getting some local who lives out here and knows the dangers better?"

Luisa frowned. "The Wakani are the only tribe anywhere close, and they want nothing to do with us."

"Why's that?" Justin asked.

Luisa's jaw tightened. "It's their way," she said simply, leaving it at that. "Come. Let's retrieve Jorge. He doesn't deserve to be left here. I'll post a beacon for a chopper retrieval to get him back to civilization. As for us, we'll continue at dawn."

~*~

Despite the rocky beginning to their jungle exploration, Griffin enjoyed the rest of their time in the jungle. They met creatures frequently seen only in zoos, and fortunately, they were friendlier than the *boiúna*.

Aisling's delighted smiles each time she captured one on camera filled his heart with joy.

With Jorge gone, Luisa took over as their cartographer. She'd been over the rainforest enough times to once know most of it by heart, but enough years had passed for her confidence to waver.

"You've done a great job, Luisa. Honestly, we don't need a guide. If anything, we should probably have a Guardian with us, eh?" Griffin suggested.

"We have never required a Guardian in the past. This rainforest has always been a place of peace."

"I'd say those times are over. Jorge would probably be among the living if we'd had a professional spellchucker. Juliana and I are good—hell, even Justin knows his shit—but I'm not a combat mage."

"You could have fooled me," Luisa said.

Juliana glanced at him, dubious. "Me as well."

"Griffin is very humble," Ash said.

Luisa sighed and pushed forward ahead of them. Sensing something amiss, Griffin hurried through the thick growth behind her.

"Hey. I'm not trying to tell you how to run things. You've been out here decades longer than me. I'm only thinking maybe—"

"You are my assistant, Griffin. Your opinion is always valued. Otherwise, you wouldn't have the job."

"True."

"But there's a reason we've always brought the minimal amount of mages from the Vault into this rainforest."

"And what's that reason?"

"The Wakani. They distrust us, and our truce with the tribes is very fragile. There are at least a dozen clans spread throughout this rainforest, and each one dislikes us more than the last."

"I don't know much about them," he admitted.

"At last count, there were nine clans. There may be more now. They're aboriginals protected by a handful of were-jaguars called the nagual. Very powerful were-jaguars able to phase through magic spells. You thought that *boiúna* gave us a run for our money? You haven't met a pissed off nagual chieftain protecting his people from a trespassing mage."

"No shit?"

She flashed him a thin, mirthless smile. "No shit. Then there are the patasola—jungle vampires."

"Um, forgive me for saying so Luisa, but you're making it sound like you should already be bringing Guardians around."

"We keep our numbers as low as possible while here to avoid upsetting the balance. The more of us there are, the more attention we draw."

"We're already drawing attention. You've lost three guides."

She sighed. "Only recently. It was never like this before. Something is very wrong here and... You are right. We'll bring Guardians during our next excursion."

"One should be enough. No need to tromp through here with an army."

"All right. We'll try it your way," she agreed.

Chapter 18

The day after their return from the jungle, a courier brought Griffin an unexpected invitation from Mercedes to spend the week in Spain with Mara. Although he questioned her sudden change of heart, Aisling encouraged him to go and take advantage of the offer.

He wouldn't trade a single minute of their week together, even if Mara snuck into his bed each night and crowded him to the edge. As the days dwindled and rapidly approached the end of their promised time together, he began to fear the worst. How much longer would it be until the next visit?

"Is my hair pretty?" Mara asked, tilting her face toward him.

"The prettiest," Griffin assured his daughter as he combed his fingers through her mahogany waves. "And I'll make it pretty tomorrow too."

"Yay!"

Since becoming a father, he had become a master at braiding and other girlish hairstyles because Mercedes took no interest in doing it. At the end of their day together, Mara had wanted it down, making her brown hair a cloud of thick waves.

"Now get to bed. I'll be back in a bit."

She cheered and clapped her small hands together before scurrying away to do as told. He watched to make sure she made it to the guest room, then he turned down the hall and sought out his ex-wife.

"Mercedes?"

He knocked on the bedroom door. It swung open under his touch.

"In here."

With a frown on his face, Griffin pushed the door open all the way and took a single step forward, refusing to go farther than the doorway. Mercedes had already changed for bed, her silk clad back to him.

THE COLLECTOR'S TREASURE

"When do I get to see her again, Mercedes? I appreciate you doing this, but a week isn't enough. She's missed me too."

"Then you should be home where you belong." Mercedes watched him through her vanity mirror and ran a brush through her lustrous hair. "Perhaps you should stay with us a few weeks and consider your options."

"I don't need to consider it all. Did you forget how I found you in my office?"

Mercedes set the brush aside and coyly glanced at him over her shoulder. Her lower lip trembled, and tears glistened in her blue eyes. "I…did not know how much it would hurt to be without you. I miss you, Griffin. Our anniversary has passed, and you were not here to share it with me for the first time. Four years—does it mean so little?"

When she rose to her feet, the silk robe fell open to reveal a midnight blue, lace baby doll nightie. Griffin remembered purchasing it for her as a wedding gift, and it surprised him to discover she had kept it at all, after wearing it the one time.

The memory of their first night as husband and wife overwhelmed him. It had been the sweetest of them all.

Four years suddenly felt like decades. A long time to discard as if it were nothing.

"Come to bed with me, Griffin. I have made mistakes, but we can fix them," she said in placid tones. They lapped at his mind, gentle as waves. "We can start over. Remarry. A small wedding the way you always wanted."

"Merce—"

"I am sorry I lost our son."

Their son? Her spell over him broke, and he gave her an incredulous look, raising both of his brows before he mouthed the words in disbelief. She had to be insane if she thought for one hot second he'd believe that baby had been his.

"I'm not stupid, Mercedes. I know it wasn't my child. Unless you're the Virgin Mary herself and it was by immaculate conception. Which I certainly doubt given the way you can give a blowjob. You forget how long it's been since we've gone to bed together?"

"How dare you suggest I could have ever cheated on you."

Griffin smiled. "I saw you blowing my boss. I'm not blind, and I'm not dumb either." A cool sense of peace fell over him instead of the fury that should have sent him into a blind rage. That was over, part of his past. He thought of Aisling, the beautiful bride-to-be awaiting him at home and all those times with Mercedes became meaningless.

Her face tilted up to meet his gaze, the deep blue of her eyes hypnotic. As tranquil as the sea itself. "But to take another man inside my body. Never, Griffin." She raised her palm to his cheek and stroked his face.

And then he was hard as a steel pole, his erection surging to life with a mere thought. Conflicting emotions swam through his thoughts, fleeting but poignant. Strong. Within seconds, common sense returned, and he recognized the touch of her nymphly gift. He reminded himself of what she was while taking in shallow breaths through his nose, refusing to inhale the alluring scent of her perfume, the exotic smells of jasmine, cardamom, and rose oil.

It's magic. He convinced himself of it. Unnatural magic, and it was time to put his hatred of her to bed and move forward with his life.

Instinct took the helm and told him to leave. Swiftly. He brushed her hand aside, knocking her away from him. "No. It's time to move on. It's better for Mara this way."

All traces of tears and sorrow vanished as if they had never been there at all. "You are the one walking away, Griffin. Remember that," she hissed.

"We'll arrange my next visit tomorrow before I leave. Goodnight."

He returned to the guest bedchamber and crawled in beside the drooling young girl who was blissfully ignorant of the argument between her parents. Griffin pulled the blanket up over her and drew her close.

He'd do anything to get her away from Spain. Anything.

~*~

Due to no shortage of new friends at the Rio Vault and a visit from old pals, Aisling wasn't lonely during Griffin's week in

Spain. She played with Breda, went to dinner with Krys in Athens, spent time with her grandmother, and chatted with Jean-Luc over the phone.

A day after her fiancé's return, he swept her away to a private island getaway.

While he claimed to have snagged the hot vacation spot for an amazing deal, Aisling knew better. His eyes had danced with too much excitement, leading her to wonder why he'd fibbed over something so inconsequential as vacation plans.

He explained that the island belonged to Curator Lima, who had purchased it on a whim for a younger wife, now ex-wife. With no use for the romantic hot zone, he'd loaned it to Griffin.

They spent the first day becoming acquainted with the island home and its amenities. Later, they explored the tropical terrain surrounding the house and left to enjoy dinner on the mainland. On the second day, they swam and snorkeled together.

Earlier, Griffin had to run off for a brief meeting at the Vault among the heads of each department and their assistants, but he had promised to return in a timely manner. Aisling sat on the white curve of beach alone, watching the light of the full moon sparkling over the waters while a pod of dolphins played nearby. She wore a simple, gauzy white wrap tied around her, the filmy fabric ruffling in the slight breeze off the water.

She loved Ireland but enjoyed the tranquil, turquoise water stretching as far as her eyes could see.

"Aisling?"

She heard his call after the sound of the motorboat cut out, leaving only the lapping of the water against the sandy shore. She turned and spotted him as he came up the walkway from the pier, tie loosened and shirt untucked. His sandy hair took on a silvered sheen in the moonlight, and she thought he had never looked more handsome.

"Hey. I expected to come back to find you sleeping." His long strides brought him closer while he raked his green eyes over her slim legs and exposed shoulders, evidently pleased with the sight. It brought a thrilled flush of joy to her body every time Griffin looked at her that way.

"After all that swimming, I took a nap, so I'm quite awake. Besides, I can't talk to you or admire you if I'm asleep."

He grinned. "Well, I can't argue with that. Feel free to check me out as much as you want."

Before she had the chance to stand, he dipped down and swept her into his arms. She laughed and peppered kisses against his cheeks and brow.

"Did everything go well at your meeting?"

"Aye, it went well enough," he replied as he carried her toward the house nestled away from the shore. "But you tell me about your day instead. How're you liking it here? Be honest."

"It's beautiful. Lakes and ponds don't really compare." Aisling tilted her face up for a kiss and loosened his tie. "I love it. Just you and me, with no one else to bother us. I wish we had more than five days left to enjoy it."

Each kiss against her lips was playful and brief, none lingering until his mouth descended the curve of her jaw and reached her throat.

"I never tire of seein' you this way... but what's this thing in my way?" His warm breath heated her throat while his hand closed around a fistful of the ivory wrap.

"Far less than what you're wearing." Her eyes shut, and her head tilted back to bare more of her neck to his wandering lips. He nibbled a sensitive spot near her collarbone, earning a shiver of delight. Her nipples stiffened beneath the wrap, standing out as two hard peaks.

"I'm sure you'll fix that soon enough. You certainly undress me quicker than you shed your own clothes." He brushed his thumb against one sensitive tip then rolled it between his fingers. "How would you feel if I told you that we're welcome to return here whenever we have the desire?"

Damn him for turning her brain to jelly. Her attempt to voice an adequate response failed; a pleading moan escaped her instead.

"That's not an answer," he teased.

"I...yes, yes. This last week has been magical."

Magic touched their lives each and every day, but the time with him was special. Precious beyond compare.

The small beachfront home was comfortable in size with a delicate balance of colors that alluded to wealth. Each of the three bedrooms revealed a beautiful view of the sand and water, but only the master had a set of sliding doors leading directly to their personal beach. Carefully placed wards and enchantments ensured the house remained cool no matter the humidity and heat outside.

Griffin slid open the door to their room and brought them inside. For a moment, she was weightless, flying through the air. She hit the mattress and bounced; her laughter smothered as he joined her for a kiss.

"It's yours, Ash. Ours."

"What?" She could barely think when he was kissing and touching her like this.

His fingers crept along her inner thigh with playful intent and found no barrier to their explorations. "Y'know that poker game I stayed behind to play in Rio when we returned from the Amazon?"

When Aisling had returned from their jungle explorations with the Collectors, she had been eager to enjoy a week of bubble baths and hot tea. The next Portal to Barcelona wasn't scheduled until the morning, so he had sent her off with a kiss and lingered in the building for an evening game of poker with the Guardians on duty.

"What of it?"

"So, it turns out Curator Lima likes to indulge the Commandant, Luisa, and Regent Oliveira in high stakes poker. I sort of bluffed my way into their game a few nights ago."

"Oh my Lord, tell me everything."

So he did, weaving a colorful story for her about participating in their game. When he won the third game and amassed enough winnings from the group to make even the wealthy Curator gnash his teeth in suspicion, Griffin had begun to sweat and fear they would accuse him of cheating. He hadn't cheated. He had, in fact, forbidden Autumn from making an appearance, as she had a tendency of flitting about the room and peering at cards to warble words of warning.

"He wagered his island retreat?" She wasn't sure if her squeak had more to do with the thought of someone gambling something so large, or the fact that Griffin was kissing his way downwards from her bellybutton.

"Aye, he did. He wanted somethin' of mine badly enough to risk it. I owed you years of birthday presents, so I'm payin' it with interest." He coaxed her legs to part with ease, and then his mouth descended to the inside of her thigh. "Signed the papers today."

Concentration became increasingly difficult while Griffin lovingly kissed a trail toward the inner crease of her thigh. Aisling thought it was entirely unfair of him to speak of their new home while he had her head all fuzzy.

He divested her of the thin cover-up and allowed his fingers to do the rest of his talking. Her hips jerked from the silk-covered mattress in response to his devious tongue, and soft cries became the only sounds she uttered for the remainder of the night.

Chapter 19

Refreshed and ready to return to work, they left their little slice of paradise and decided to move their belongings in at their leisure. Absolute privacy was worth the price of a lengthy commute.

Their morning routines separated them until lunch, when Aisling slipped into his office with meals from a local cafe. Afterward, Griffin saw her to the door and playfully pinned her against its wooden pane to steal a kiss.

"You going so soon?"

"They're waiting for me. We'll finish this later," she promised.

After twisting the knob, she stepped backwards through the open door and nearly crashed into the man waiting on the other side. Griffin steadied her with a hand at her waist.

"*Bonjour, monsieur*," Jean-Luc greeted them. "*Mademoiselle.*"

Aisling lifted her gaze to a familiar face and bright, blue-green eyes. "Jean-Luc, what a surprise. I didn't expect to see you again so soon."

"Indeed. I...ahh, Unfortunately, this is not a social visit, Aisling. I have come to speak with Collector MacNeil."

"Uh oh. I swear, whatever it is, I didn't do it."

"Please, you misunderstand. I have come to speak with you regarding recent circumstances," Jean-Luc said.

Griffin's smile faded. "What circumstances? Is this related to the Inquisition?"

"Perhaps the two of us should take this talk into your office."

Aisling frowned. The mere mention of Inquisitors made her shudder as she recalled the shoot-out in Dublin months ago. They'd attempted to assassinate Griffin, and the Vault never uncovered any answers.

Griffin's embrace tightened around her. "Anything you have to say to me, you can say while Aisling is present."

Jean-Luc nodded. "As you wish."

After shuffling aside for the detective to enter, Griffin turned over the privacy sign on the door and shut it. His new office was a place of organized chaos, the spacious room filled with memories. He'd covered one wall with pictures of family and friends, another with images from sites. Behind his desk, a snapshot of Mara hung beside a photo of a gilded sarcophagus. Anywhere a visitor looked, physical relics from his jobs displayed his career achievements from bookshelves and his desk.

Griffin tugged her to sit with him behind his desk. Her fingers stroked along the nape of his neck in a reassuring manner then dropped away, both hands folding in her lap.

"All right. Hit me with it, Frenchie. What's going on?"

Jean-Luc scowled at him. "I suppose it is proper to begin with the good news. The Inquisitors have become suspiciously quiet, but that alone concerns me. As so much has happened in my home country, the Regency Board has personally assigned the case to me."

"Well, don't keep us in suspense," Griffin said.

Rolling his eyes, Jean-Luc continued despite the playful teasing. "In France, we face constant uprisings from the demonic cults. Two months ago, I intercepted a note found upon the corpse of a Diabolist who was in your employment."

"What?"

"Marius Dupont. You hired a French Scribe from our Vault. A good man, or so we all believed. The Regency chose to keep the truth out of the *Magister's Almanac* in hopes of discovering his contacts."

"I met him in Egypt." Aisling straightened. "He was there when the site was bombed."

"*Oui.*" Jean-Luc's expression looked grim. "It would seem the Diabolists have their eye upon Griffin. It took much time for us to identify their target, but all clues have led to you. Here. A copy. Read it and tell me your thoughts."

Jean-Luc passed a photocopied sheet of paper over the desk.

Griffin read the note in silence, features gradually changing from bewilderment to fury. Smoke curled up from the page and within seconds, the note became a handful of blackened ash.

"What did it say, Griff?"

"Nothin' for you to fret over."

"Griffin MacNeil—" The anger in his eyes gave her a reason to pause. Aisling knew when to press him for more and when to bite her tongue until his emotions cooled. This was the latter.

He'd be rational later, and probably tell her without coaxing since moments ago he'd boldly proclaimed the investigator could share anything with her.

Still. She didn't want to wait hours and decided she would get the information from Jean-Luc instead.

"Are you able to shed any light? If you can tell me anything at all, it could aid the investigation."

"Nae, I can't think of a thing."

"Monsieur MacNeil, there are demon-worshipping cultists on a mission to find you, and I cannot imagine anything good will come of it for you if they do. Please. If you remember anything able to help my investigation, do not hesitate to call at any hour." Jean-Luc rose from his seat and placed a card on the desk.

"I'll give Griffin your e-mail as well, if that's all right." Aisling offered a faint smile but made no move to leave Griffin's side immediately.

Jean-Luc left and Aisling turned to study Griffin's face a moment.

"Whatever it is they want, Griffin, I place my bets on you."

"It's nothin' for you to worry about, Ash. Same shite, different day. You know how those idiots feel about my grand…"

Aisling made an astute guess as to what he was about to say. Tristan Rhydderch, the great patriarch of their family, was a descendent of the greatest wizard to ever live. Also the greatest cambion to ever walk the earth. Merlin, child of an incubus, had sired a line known for their talent with the arcane arts and their strength.

While no such creatures lived in current times, cambion children were highly sought after. Typically, demon-tainted infants didn't come easy since they were rare and complicated to conceive, often resulting in either the death of the mother and child. Sometimes both.

Aisling raised to her tiptoes and kissed him. Jean-Luc would tell her everything. "I'll be going back to the clinic, then."

"I'll be here and ready to go when you're off."

As predicted, she found Jean-Luc standing by the Healers' station once she made it up to her level of the Vault. Painted murals of colorful sea creatures in an underwater paradise decorated the vibrant turquoise walls, and large windows spilled natural light into the healing ward.

He kissed Aisling's cheek, and she hugged him in return.

"I was hoping you would find me," he said with a faint smile.

"Of course I did. Something is the matter with Griffin, and you have answers."

She gestured for Jean-Luc to follow her behind the nurse station and into the room used as the staff lounge. The six Healers on staff appeared in overlapping shifts and often took their breaks inside. A television aired the daytime soap operas or evening television shows, and a small refrigerator kept their meals and snacks chilled.

Aisling took a seat and gestured for her friend to join her. "Now, what is he hiding?"

Jean-Luc sighed and for a moment, she thought he might not share with her at all.

"The cultists have orders to capture monsieur MacNeil alive and relatively unharmed. Anyone with him is…disposable. There is even a specific mention of dealing with any young woman in his company. Permanently." He fixed her with a look, one eyebrow raised.

"Oh…" Cold washed over her, his words more effective than a bucket of ice water. It wasn't enough to simply remove her from the picture. This time, more than a jealous and bitter teenage girl intended to steal Griffin away. Someone wanted him enough to kill her to have him.

"At the time, I did not realize you were the young woman mentioned in the letter since *this* development"—he pointed to her engagement ring—"was strangely absent from our recent conversations." The corner of his mouth rose in a wry smirk, dimpling his left cheek.

She wanted to punch him in his smug face. But that wasn't very Healer-like. "I'm sorry if our other topics are more interesting than discussing my relationship. Besides, it's not as if you tell me of *your* love life." Aisling sniffed.

"There is nothing to tell you, *mon amie*. I have no time for a love life, only for admiring the beautiful women who cross my path," he said with a wave of his hand. "Even if they are sometimes a pain in my ass and quite taken."

Grasping at any reason to throw the chill from her bones and recover from the terrifying news, Aisling smiled and dipped her face to hide her blush. "We're not even each other's types."

"I did not mean you, Aisling."

"Oh? Has someone caught your fancy, then? Who is she?"

Jean-Luc waved off her interest quickly. "No matter who. Though she is quite beautiful, it is not meant to be. Our schedules always too busy."

"Another Guardian?"

He shook his head. "It does not matter, and is a subject better left alone."

Damn. Not even a clue. Even though the mystery tickled her curiosity, she gave him his privacy and changed the subject. "At least I now know why you haven't e-mailed me recently."

"*Oui.* I intended to write once I returned home this evening. Funny that I should meet you here."

"You work too much. I'm sorry I haven't found much more about your situation."

"I would love to know anything about it… But you cannot be blamed for this, Aisling. It is a mystery no one seems able to solve."

"It's not fae, I've figured that much. I talked to my friend Jack, and he was tight-lipped about it. But he said it's beyond the powers of the Faeries to bring people back to life. Not like *this* thing you experienced. The fae charged with collecting souls and leading them onwards, like the cu sith, are pretty serious about their jobs."

"Cu sith?"

He mangled the word so badly with his French accent that Aisling had to laugh. She covered her mouth with one hand, giggling quietly. "Think of them as a variety of the Grim Reaper. Many fae have obligations in our world, and theirs is to collect the souls of humans with Celtic ancestry. Each culture has its own guide."

She went on to briefly explain that death attracted the spirit guides, but sometimes a particular fae would sometimes wait before collecting a soul. Those who could be saved, as she had in Egypt, received another chance.

"I was beyond saving, *cherie*. I was a coal briquette in the morgue. Why, then, was I not collected if they are so diligent in their duties?"

"I couldn't say. A force more powerful would be my only guess, but I can't think of many who would cross the sidhe."

"Another mystery to discover. I am not acquainted with the fae associated with my country."

And judging from the hardened expression of his features, Aisling thought he planned to expand his knowledge of the fae very soon.

Chapter 20

Spring melted away, and summer passed in Brazil before fading into the cooler climes of autumn. Another expedition in the dense outskirts of the rainforest led to more dead ends in their search for legendary treasure, but introduced them to the trials and tribulations of working in such a demanding location.

Griffin wouldn't have traded it for the world.

He watched proudly as Aisling grew in confidence and skill, reassured that he had done right by her in moving her job an ocean away.

Elsewhere in the world, things weren't so bright and happy. He received reports from his cousin Addison of an uprising from the Inquisitors. Their silence had been the calm before the storm, which eventually led to a series of bloody battles across the world. The worst of the murders occurred in France and the United Kingdom. Loved ones found several prominent Magi dead in their homes, slaughtered by violent methods of witch extermination.

And in the case of each murder, a single defining factor connected a majority of the killings—authorities discovered shrines within their homes dedicated to one of the seven demon Princes.

The situation was far from dangerous in Rio, but Aisling worried when a murder occurred near her grandmother's estate in Ireland.

Krys phoned her from the fiery scene of the crime to relay the news. Inquisitors had stormed the home and hung the three occupants, killing a wealthy employee of the Irish Vault, his wife, and their teenaged son. Setting fire to the home afterward hadn't concealed the crime committed by them.

Although Ceara rarely owned up to having fears, she admitted them then. Griffin and Ash voluntarily visited and spent the night in the manor, respectfully inhabiting different rooms while under her grandmother's roof. The next morning, he kissed her goodbye and set out for the early Portal to Spain. They planned to reunite by evening in the city at her flat. This time, he would have Mara with him for the first time in months.

He felt giddy when he emerged from the Portal and eager to enjoy the two weeks with his daughter. He bounced on his feet while waiting for the mechanic to service his plane. Would Aisling and Mara get along? Would they like one another?

Nervous anticipation rolled his stomach into knots until he arrived to find Mara awaiting him at the door. She flew toward him to leap into his arms, and he caught her gladly against him. Their hugs and kisses were interrupted by the subtle clearing of Mercedes's throat.

"I appreciate you lettin' us do this, Mercy. I really do. Is she packed?"

"No. I thought you would have a better idea of what would be appropriate, so I left it to you."

Mercy's docile and personable behavior set off alarms of caution, but she remained hospitable and even made him a steaming pot of coffee. Herself. That threw Griffin for a loop when she arrived at Mara's room with a mug. The aroma of a light roasted coffee with a dash of hazelnut put him in a chipper mood to talk.

"Bought a home, so I'll be forwardin' the rest of my things from here soon enough."

"There is no rush, Griffin. Take your time." She smiled and stepped back from the room.

Her sudden change put Griffin on edge, sending quivers to the pit of his stomach. Was his ex-wife bipolar? No. That was an insult to people suffering from the disorder.

Maybe she'd finally grown up. For Mara's sake, he hoped so.

He sipped coffee intermittently while packing his little girl's luggage. Clothes suitable for the cool Irish evenings went into her suitcase next to shorts and sundresses appropriate for the beach on the island.

He was surprised when Mercedes sent Mara off with a tight hug and a kiss to her head. It surprised him even more when she dipped in and quickly kissed his scruffy cheek.

"Take care, please. There are so many things happening now," she told him.

After a brief drive to the airfield, they were in flight for a return trip to Barcelona. Mara's blindness prevented her from enjoying the view, so she occupied herself with listening to a children's audiobook.

"Will Mommy be okay without me?" she asked him in Spanish.

"She'll be okay, lass. I bet she gets plenty of sleep while you're gone."

"But there's noises at night… What if something bad happens to Mommy?"

Griffin bit his lower lip and thoughtfully glanced back at her. Because of her blindness, Mara sometimes seemed to have more of an active imagination than most children. She dreamed up fantastic and amazing things, and she made him proud by never succumbing to her disability. Instead, she had made it into a great strength and advantage.

He'd allowed her to help him from time to time in his office while examining objects—she could hear the hum of magic and had told him each variety of spell had a different pitch or tone.

She was far too bright to immediately discredit her.

"What kind of sounds did you hear?"

"Scary noises. Thumps. Someone was crying, and I think Mommy was too."

He breathed a sigh of relief. So maybe Mercedes had a change of heart after all. It meant nothing to him, as it was too late to salvage their marriage, and he was content to move forward with his life plans… But he felt an inkling of pity for her.

"Your mama has a lot to cry over," he replied in English before regretting the remark. It wasn't nice to speak that way, even if it was true.

~*~

Aisling hummed along to a tune on the radio as she drove through the Irish countryside, hardly able to keep still in her seat. The day shined bright for a change, though the roads were damp after a typical soaking rain in the morning. Only an hour more and she would be with Griffin again, and she would be meeting the most important girl in his life. Mara.

God. She was sick with nerves. More than anything, she wanted his daughter to like her. To accept her in their life.

Those thoughts and wishes distracted her until she noticed a black SUV approaching in her rearview mirror, sunlight reflecting off its windshield in a bright flare. The automobile closed in fast enough for Aisling to maneuver to the right lane to let them pass.

The larger vehicle swerved into her passenger side.

She yelped and jerked on the wheel to stay on the road. Metal screeched and sparks flew up along her window with a second jarring collision. Her car hit the bank and careened off the road, rolling into a ditch. The airbag released with an explosive bang and left her stunned.

Dizzy, Aisling fumbled with her seatbelt and tried to open her door, but the mangled metal wouldn't budge. Her heart began to hammer when the SUV shut off. It had parked just a few yards away on the road. Frantic, she crawled across to the passenger door, where she tumbled out and down the embankment. Her fingers sank into an inch of mud.

"I'm sorry to be doing this, lass. You did me a good turn once, but I have instructions."

She recognized the voice and turned. Shocked, she stared up at the figure of Guardian Delaney and staggered up to her feet. "Kevin?"

Then Deirdre stepped into view beside him, and disbelief crashed over Aisling with the force of an icy wave. It wasn't possible. No. It shouldn't have been possible, but the woman she'd called friend for years ever since she'd taken her job at the Dublin Vault stood opposite her.

Deirdre's heartless smile constricted Aisling's heart into a painful knot. "Shut up already and kill the wee bitch. Talkin' to her isn't getting the job done."

Kevin ignored her. "Don't resist us, and I'll make it painless for you."

Aisling's feet made mushy imprints in the ground and began to sink. Geomancy. Swirling strands of mana seeped from

Kevin's hands into the ground, and with each step she took, she sank deeper, until the ground claimed one of her slippers.

"I'll suffocate her in the mud, Deirdre. It'll be a quick death and better than burning alive."

"Gone soft?" Deirdre sneered then her fingers lit ablaze with dark purple tongues of flame. Aisling recognized the spell—Griffin had once been fascinated with Hellfire in his teens.

"She was your feckin' friend, wasn't she? No need to be an absolute bastard while doing the Master's work."

Mud reached up to her knees as she sank deeper, and Aisling frantically tried to think of what she could do. Ice would only trap her in the ground. So she attacked instead. The first blast of frosty wind barely ruffled Deirdre's auburn hair.

She laughed. "You have to *mean* it, Aisling. You're too soft and sweet to cause anyone any real harm. You'd have never been anything more than a mediocre Healer. Relying on fae gifts to do what the rest of us accomplish with sheer talent and grit."

"You were my friend!" Aisling tried to pull herself out, but the ground all around her gave way into a sinking bog. It reached the undersides of her breasts while she endeavored to keep both hands out of the chilly muck.

"Was I?"

What appeared to be a black rabbit hopped along the roadside and approached them. Long ears pricked straight and tall as the creature moved closer to the group. As the rabbit shimmered and grew, it lurched forward in the shape of a tremendous ebon goat. Without warning, it hurtled into the back of Kevin's knees.

A puca. It wasn't a rabbit after all, but a shapeshifting creature from Avalon.

After throwing Kevin to the ground, the Faerie creature spun to evade Deirdre's Hellfire. The attack sailed over its horns, and then its head sank into her soft belly. With an oof, she teetered over.

Without wasting time, the fae bounded toward Aisling and bowed his head toward her.

Aisling grabbed the glossy horns of the puca and held tight until he pulled her free of the quagmire. The magical creature's hooves barely made a dent in the mushy earth as she stumbled to her feet with her sodden, mud-covered sundress clinging to her body.

Swearing, Deirdre climbed to her feet. Kevin threw out one hand toward them and tilted the earth. It raised and flowed upward in a curve, a great tidal wave of watery soil, roots, and silt.

Using her ice magic, Aisling froze the churning earth in its tracks. A perfect sculpture of frost-rimmed grass hung above them.

Down the road, a car flashed in the sunlight. The vehicle slowed, and a chipper-faced, elderly gentleman leaned his head out the window, squinting his eyes against the sun behind his spectacles. The heavily lined face of his wife peered out from beside him, while a little boy bounced in the back seat.

"Drive!" Aisling cried. "Get out of here!"

Deirdre's face twisted into a hideous mask of fury. She hurled a palmful of fire at the car as the concerned man tried to puzzle out the scene.

Blazing heat engulfed the vehicle and swallowed it whole within the inferno. The force of the fireball's collision rolled it a half dozen times until it lay on its hood without windows or a windshield.

Agony spread throughout Aisling's chest as a hoarse, inhuman scream tore from her lips. "No! How could you? How could you kill innocents for no reason at all? You're a Healer, Deirdre! You heal people, you help them!"

"Look at that. Ye can't do a bleedin' thing to save them. Can't even save yourself. They'd be alive by now if ye had just let us do our jobs."

"That feckin' hurt," Kevin complained.

He moved to his feet again but dipped to the side when Aisling loosed a cone of cold wind and ice, anger fueling her magic. Spells flew back and forth, fire meeting snow and causing bursts of sizzling steam. Kevin manipulated the ground around them, keeping the puca bouncing back and forth to keep its footing. Magic lit up the darkening sky, and heavy clouds rolled in to blot out the sun.

The puca breached Kevin's shields and slammed him into Dierdre with another headbutt. She held her ground, but yanked Kevin's gun from his holster.

A single steel-jacketed round pierced the goat's side. It screamed, its pained cry too human for Aisling's heart to bear. It collapsed to the ground while a generous amount of blood welled from the hole punched through its body. Steel. Iron. The bane of all Faeriekind. It thrashed and wept helplessly.

Fury unlike anything she had ever felt before swept through her when she saw Deirdre's gloating face. Aisling took a single step and vanished. She slipped between realms, skipping along their borders like a rock across water. In the span of a single heartbeat, she stepped out again and jerked Deirdre's head back by a handful of hair. Her hand curled around the woman's throat over the pulse of her beating heart, and she allowed her magic free reign.

"I've control of your every muscle, Deirdre. Every. Single. One," she whispered against the woman's ear. "You will *never* harm anyone again."

Deirdre's slack face paled, fading cyanotic blue at the corners of her lips. Aisling's magic pulsed hard and strong into the other Healer's body, holding her in a locked stasis.

She couldn't save the family in the little car, but she could save the puca.

A fist shaped from stone and dirt rose from the ground, but Aisling met Kevin's first attack with a rising wall of frost. The frozen barrier blocked even the boulders and waves of sludge hurtled by his geomancy prowess.

"She's suffocating!" Kevin yelled.

"She'll never take another breath. Consider her already dead," Aisling replied flatly. She released the line of mana connecting her to her former friend, and the blue-faced woman collapsed to the ground behind her.

Kevin's features hardened, eyes narrowing to thin slits.

He attempted to alter the terrain again, but discs of ice spread beneath each step of her feet, stabilizing the ground. Aisling's gaze never left him. More frost encrusted her dark hair in a fine layer of translucent slush.

Earth and snow collided as the two mages fought. Spears of razor sharp ice hurtled through the air and shattered against pillars of stone. The ground heaved and buckled. Thunder rumbled above them.

The first fall of rain became hailstones as Aisling's magic froze the air around them. The balls of deadly ice fell like comets from the sky.

Kevin hit a black patch of ice and slipped. He crashed down to the pavement hard with a sharp cry of pain as his elbow struck the concrete.

"You are a traitor."

A needle sharp spear of ice pierced upwards from the frozen road and tore through Kevin's left shoulder. The jagged spike kept him pinned, and Aisling turned away.

The wailing screech of Irish police sirens revealed another SUV en route.

Aisling ignored it and knelt by the mewling puca. It lay helpless on the road in its natural state, a small figure of dark and wrinkled flesh with gangly limbs. A smoking hole pierced his torso beneath the ribs.

She could see now that the fae was a he, with gracefully curving horns standing out like obsidian glass from long, ebon hair. Thin chains of living metal flowed back from the lank strands.

"You saved me. Now let me save you," she whispered. Frost melted away from her hands as she pressed them gently to the wound.

Praying the bullet hadn't ricocheted and bounced into his guts, she searched and found it lodged beneath his ribs. He thrashed and made a pitiful cry as she used magic to work it toward the surface and pluck it from the wound. Then she sang softly above him, each healing note of her song binding to him with mana.

When it was done, the little shifter reached up and touched her cheek to catch one of her falling tears. The droplet sparkled in rainbow colors, solidified, and became a perfectly rounded gemstone the size of a pearl.

Aisling accepted the gift with a trembling smile. It felt warm in her hands. Before her eyes, the puca shifted and shrunk. Once more a black rabbit, the fae hopped away and disappeared into the grass.

By the time the Guardians arrived to assess the scene, Aisling was ready to pass out from exhaustion.

"What's happened here? Where are they?" one wizard asked.

"Where's Delaney?" asked another.

"There he is. Got the bastard in my sights," someone muttered before they rushed away.

"Are you all right?" a familiar face asked.

They threw questions at her, some lingering for her protection, others spreading over the area, weaving spells and wards as they went.

For a time, she was left alone until a heavy blanket settled over the back of her shoulders. "Ash? Are you okay, love?"

"Addison?" She glanced up into his worried face, relieved to see him.

"Tried our bloody best to get here in time."

"How...?"

"Krys phoned from Greece. Grandfather stopped all traffic between the Portals and let us through straight away to Ireland after placing an emergency call to O'Sullivan. Turns out, they'd also received an anonymous tip from, get this, love—California of all places," Addison said.

She blinked up at him. "I don't know anyone in California."

The scene became a mix of Guardians from both Vaults, two squads of angry, burly men and a few keen-eyed women ready for a battle with the forces of evil. Their reactions to the aftermath of Aisling's handiwork ranged from disappointment to shock.

Apparently they had all been roused to the call of duty with promises of hurting cultists. They didn't expect to find their jobs completed for them when they arrived.

"Addison..." Aisling looked up at her friend. "I killed her."

"Ash—"

"She blew up that poor family, and she shot a puca. I killed her."

Without a single word of judgment, Addison hugged her close. She'd never killed anyone before, and the realization of it came crashing down all at once.

Addison had always been dependable and like a brother to her ever since she and Griffin first became friends. She curled in against him, more tired than she had ever known, sick at heart but still numbed. She couldn't dredge up a single tear for what she had done. Not yet.

"C'mon, I'll take you home. Then I'll make sure Griffin and Mara get there safely as well." He glanced toward the wreckage of the vehicle. "I'll have a word with the Commandant here about assigning someone to watch your apartment until we've gotten to the bottom of this."

Without a word of argument, Aisling clutched the puca's gift and allowed Addison to lead her away.

~*~

"Welcome back." Try as she might to sound upbeat and cheerful, the greeting sounded forced as Aisling opened the door upon Griffin's arrival. Weak and fragile.

After a lengthy shower and a change of clothes, she decided not to let the incident ruin Mara's trip.

"You must be Mara." She crouched down to put herself at eye level with the child who clutched at Griffin's pants and hid behind his leg. "I'm Aisling, and I'd like to welcome you to my home. Your father has told me many good things about you."

"*Hola, s—*"

"English, lass. Miss Ash doesn't know Spanish," Griffin coaxed her, gently urging his daughter from behind him.

Aisling reached out to touch Mara's hand, rewarded when the child traced her fingers over her bare wrists and up her arm. She followed Aisling's limb up to her shoulder and eventually found her curly hair.

"Hello, Miss Ash," the girl murmured. She had her father's green eyes, but a milky cloud hid her pupils.

The next few hours allowed Mara to learn the layout of the spacious flat. Aisling led her on a tour and answered the girl's curious questions with remarkable patience. They ordered dinner in, and eventually Mara fell asleep on the couch. Griffin tucked her into Aisling's bed, and then he joined his woman on the couch.

"Tell me about what happened, Ash. Addison told me it was all over by the time they arrived to help you." He cupped his hand against her cheek and studied her with concerned eyes.

"I was on my way to get you when I was run off the road," she began quietly. Her fingers twisted together in her lap until Griffin reached over and took them with his other hand. "I knew them, Griffin. I saved Kevin from a hag's curse back around the time you were hurt in Egypt. And Deirdre was my friend. For years we've talked and worked together, had lunches together during and away from work. She even planned a baby shower for one of the other Healers. I invited her to *our* wedding,"

"Christ. I had hoped the letter was bullshit, or something meant to scare me. I never in a million years would have thought it was true, Ash. I'm sorry. I can't..." He released a lungful of air and sank back against the couch, looking older than his twenty-four years.

"I killed today, Griffin." Her chest tightened, and her breath barely formed the words. "I saw what she had done, and I killed her."

He drew her closer and held her tight with his cheek against her black curls. "You did what you had to do to survive, Ash. What was necessary."

Despite the truth of his words, her heart and mind opposed his logic. The loss of a life by her hands was a painful act to bear, and her tears soaked his shirt while he stroked her hair and placed soft kisses to her brow. Patient as always, he waited until her silent sobs finally ebbed.

"I...never told you about this, but after Mercedes miscarried, I found a letter in my box. I'd stopped by to check on my mail, y'see, to make sure Luisa hadn't sent me anything I needed to know about the new job. Plain envelope, unfamiliar handwriting, but addressed to me and sealed with magic. Someone had gotten ahold of one of my hairs and enchanted the envelope to open only by my hands."

"What did it say?"

"They wanted me to consider serving the one true Master. It never said much, but I knew what they referred to. Told me where to meet them and when to go. Said to tell no one. I went to Greece instead to meet you. I wanted no part in their devil-worshipping business and still don't. And now I can't help but feel it's my fault they came after you."

"No, Griff. It's *their* fault." She sat up and met his gaze. "I won't have you shouldering this burden. But you should tell Jean-Luc. Do you still have the letter?" Of course he did. Her Griffin had always been a crafty, clever, and curious fellow, too inquisitive for his own good.

"Aye. Left it locked in my desk drawer in Mercedes's house. Wanted to study it."

"You should give it to him. Let him see if he can find anything about who sent it."

"I should," he agreed. Judging from the tone of his voice, there was no guarantee that 'I should' would actually become 'I will.'

"Please. I can't lose you to them. Mara can't…"

"Y'won't lose me. I'll notify him tomorrow, then, all right? No more worries over it."

Her hold on him tightened. "I'm scared, Griffin. How are we to know who they are? They could be anyone. Friends…"

"Aye, they could be anyone. But we know for sure who they aren't. Kevin always seemed like a cocksucker anyway, so it surprises me none. I'll be havin' a word with Addison about it, and, well, he can tell that old bastard about it and take it from there. I won't… I can't lose you," he finally finished in a pain-stricken voice.

He kissed her lips and together, they remained on her couch for a while longer, whispering in the dark as Mara slept on.

Chapter 21

Griffin frowned as he watched his cousin twist the screwdriver and tighten the hinges on the doll house. "You're goin' to break the goddamned thing if you screw it in so hard. Sweet mother of Hecate, give it here."

"Griffin Arthur MacNeil, mind your tongue!" his mother hissed at him. She gave him a stern look before heading into the next room.

"They can't hear me over that racket in the other room. Bunch of howler monkeys is what they are. Why are those girls screaming so loud?"

Addison shrugged and handed over the screwdriver. The pink and purple eyesore arrived as a gift from their grandfather with instructions to have it built and waiting beside the Christmas tree in the morning.

"The old codger could have given this to her at his house," Addison grumbled.

"And you would have had to carry it back home," Aisling chimed in from across the room. She worked on decorating cookies for Santa while the children played in another room with their grandmothers.

"Ha, she's got you there," Griffin laughed. He ducked a flying bit of doll furniture his cousin tossed.

"So, when's the date? Why haven't I received an invitation yet?" Addison asked.

Griffin rolled his eyes. "Haven't set it yet."

"And why not?"

"Plannin' everything else is her job. The bill and standing there in my spiffy suit is my part. She can order the dozens of doves and cake and all that rubbish. Already done it big once. Whatever Ash wants is fine with me."

"Why don't you consider attending the Christmas feast with us tomorrow, Griffin? Grandfather doesn't hate you."

"After what he did to Mum and me? Nae, Addison, I've got nothin' to say to him."

"Give it some thought, all right? It won't kill you to consider it. It's over and done in the past. Fiona's gotten away from the knob end, and you're both in a better place. Grandfather is sorry, so why can't everyone bury the axe and be done?"

"Wouldn't mind buryin' the axe *in* him," Griffin grunted as he snapped together the final piece. He sat back to survey his work. "What're you doing with the rest of the holiday?"

"I've got a hot date with this bird I met in New York City. Bloody model with a pair of legs to die for. Doesn't have much of an arse, but I'm willing to make an exception this time. Her name's Paula."

"Bet she's as empty-headed as that last bint you brought around," Griffin grumbled as he collected scraps of plastic wrapping from the floor. "There. All done and ready for them to bust it to wee pieces again. As much as I love Maddie, she plays with her toys like she's a giantess. Well, I suppose she is. I expect by next year she'll be taller than Ash."

"It's true. She's got the genes that skipped you. Mara's a bit on the tall side, too, I've noticed."

Griffin glowered at him.

The night passed smoothly, and once the girls set out their plate of cookies and glass of milk for Santa Claus, the two exhausted fathers tucked them into Madeline's bed. Then they helped themselves to some of Santa's goodies as payment for all their hard work.

The sun barely began its ascent when both girls woke and hurried out to discover their gifts. Madeline held Mara's hand and led the younger girl through the house.

Christmas morning consisted of flying wrapping paper, girlish squeals, good food, and the warmth of family.

Later, they visited Ireland to accept Ceara's hospitality. The elderly woman seemed delighted to have people in her home and to fill its walls with the sound of childish laughter again.

At last, life had taken a change for the better.

~*~

The winter holiday went by swiftly, but thanks to their carefully managed plans, enough time remained of their vacation to spirit Mara off to their island home. They planned to soak up the Brazilian sun, eat delicious seafood, and snorkel along the beach.

They arrived at the Dublin Vault bright and early New Year's Day to discover the building abuzz with gossip and stories of a battle in New York City. Wall to wall pedestrian traffic congested the lower level of the building. The Portal was shut down.

"Griffin!" Fiona flagged them down.

"Mum? What's happenin'? Why's everyone in a fret?"

"It's Addison—he's… There was an attack in the colonies. I'm waiting my turn to be let onto the next Portal to New York."

Griffin's heart lurched in his chest. "How is he?"

"Coma, according to O'Sullivan. He's been in touch with Tristan." Fiona looked around and smoothed a hand back over her hair nervously. "They're saying a dragon was there."

"Addison's dragon?"

A voice over the PA announced the next call for Manhattan. All around them, disgruntled travelers complained about the continued delay in the Portal schedule.

His mother pushed a priority pass into his hands. "You leave Mara with me and go. Call me as soon as you've got some word of what's happening. Soon as you hear anything at all."

"Y'sure?"

"Aye. Besides, Aisling will be of more use to him than I will. Any Healer they can get."

Griffin crouched down in front of his daughter and drew the girl into a goodbye hug. "Change of plans, Mara. Granny is going to take you to her place for a day or two."

"Is cousin Addison going to be okay?" she asked.

"Aye, love, we hope so. You be good for Granny."

"I will," she promised.

He and Aisling left their big bags and took only what they could easily carry during the rush into the crowded Portal room.

Their arrival in New York met with a flurry of activity. Guardian forces from London, Greece, and Ireland stood out among the American crowd as they directed traffic in and out. Not a bag went unchecked or a single person spared a thorough search. Griffin moved about restlessly during the wait.

A tough-faced New York City Guardian greedily eyed the gold coin in Griffin's wallet, but upon removing it, the golden bauble quickly vanished and reappeared in Griffin's hand. He would have grinned if the situation wasn't so dire.

Once cleared to proceed, they hurried upstairs. A harried looking Healer directed them toward Addison's room after Griffin identified himself as a relative.

"Ash!" Krys sobbed from the chair at Addison's bedside. She lurched from the seat and into their arms, hugging them both.

It twisted a knot into Griffin's stomach once his eyes adjusted to the dim room with only a single light by the bedside. Addison lay in the bed with the thin white sheets pulled modestly to his chest.

His skin was mottled with streaks of dark color, and he appeared a decade older. Lined with heavily defined wrinkles, his cheeks looked hollow and malnourished.

The health had been sucked from him.

"Christ... What happened, Kryssie?"

"I found him lying in a smoking crater up at the cemetery, that's what happened," she replied while she swiped at her cheeks.

Aisling offered her cousin a handkerchief.

Griffin blinked his eyes rapidly to keep the tears at bay. Addison was as close as he'd ever come to having a brother. A better sibling than the older sister who took off and left the family. "Start from the beginning."

"I have no idea. It was a mess, Griff. There were graves burst open and corpses all over the place. Some of them had been reduced to *ashes*."

"So it's true, then? He really summoned a dragon?" Aisling moved past them to stand beside Addison's prone form. She laid one hand over his forehead and the other over his heart.

"He once told me he never felt as if he'd be ready to pull that one off... Even told me his mentor advised against it until he was older. Where are Gwen and Uncle Cedric?" Griffin asked.

"They're speaking with the doctor." Krys slumped down in a chair and pulled her knees up to her chest. "Some of the damage is from me too."

"What?"

"The burns. Some of them at least. I zapped him until his heart began to beat again."

Griffin stared at Krys and understood why the usually put together woman looked like such a blubbering mess. It seemed as if decades had passed since he pulled Aisling's motionless body from the water, but the total fear and despair he'd felt then remained branded in his memory.

His gaze shifted to Aisling then back to Krystine before he dipped down to kiss her wet cheek.

"You did good, Kryssie. Always were the stubborn one."

Chapter 22

Time flew too fast, January and February passing in a blink and March threatening to slip by in the same manner. Aisling took a moment to look over the empty flat that had been her home for so long and let out a quiet sigh. Everything was packed, the boxes behind her the last items left to move to Brazil other than her bed and couch.

The change excited her as much as it made her sad, but she looked forward to their new life together. The official move to Rio wasn't the only change, either.

Shortly after Addison awakened from his month-long coma, he'd been awarded rulership of Manhattan—whether he wanted the title or not. She and Griffin could hardly believe his humble cousin had become the youngest Regent in the magical world.

Apparently, his predecessor had stepped down when speculations drew him into the scandal.

She and Griffin decided to plan a summer wedding to allow his cousin time to make a complete recovery and adjust to his new duties. She couldn't wait, and her heart became all aflutter with butterflies each time she thought of their upcoming nuptials.

Aisling MacNeil. She'd considered whether to keep her name, and Griffin had even teased her about becoming Griffin Kavanagh to shed his stepfather's name. In the end, they'd made the choice to keep the surname attached to his famous career.

Sometime after lunch, Aisling settled on the couch and spent an hour alternating between games with Breda and reading. One of her favorite series about a time-traveling nurse had released its most recent novel. Her cat prowled around the floor batting a catnip toy.

Aisling found it hard to concentrate. Her gaze continuously drifted away from her book and to the clock to check the time.

The Portal from Spain had been scheduled nearly three hours ago, but no word had come from Griffin.

Texting him hadn't worked either. He didn't return it or answer her calls.

The anticipation ate at her, so much on her mind and so many conversations to be held regarding the week's discoveries.

Her new discovery.

By six in the evening, her concern bloomed into full blown worry. She set aside her book and looked out the windows, tempted to call Spain's Vault until thunder shook her front door, and she realized it was a man's fist pounding the wood.

"Aisling!" Griffin bellowed before beating the door again.

She jumped up and quickly crossed to unlock the door. Her smile faded when she focused on his black eye, split lip, and bruised cheek.

He looked like hell and smelled like a Scotch distillery. Her nose crinkled, but she stepped back and allowed him into the flat.

"About time." Drunk and slurring, he made his way to the couch and threw himself upon the cushions. Dried blood stained his shirt.

"Griffin, what happened? Where've you been?"

"None of your business where I went. Can't you see I need somethin' for m'face?"

Aisling stiffened but bit her tongue. Griffin rarely showed a temper and was more the sort to brood in silence.

"I do see, Griffin," she said in a measured tone. "Give me a moment to collect some things, and I'll see to it."

Most of her items were packed away, but she'd labeled each box neatly when she worked. Within five minutes, she'd found what she wanted and prepared her supplies while a kettle of water boiled on the stove.

"Will you tell me what happened?" She carefully dabbed a wet cloth against his lip to clean up the crusted blood.

"Some fuckin' welcome this is. Haven't had a damned thing to eat since yesterday, but y'prefer to interrogate me."

"Griffin MacNeil, you've no call to spea—"

The telephone rang. Aisling drew in a deep breath. She rose to her feet, gave him the damp cloth, and picked up the phone.

"Are you not concerned about me in the least?"

She ignored him, nerves twisted into a frayed mess. "Aisling Kavanagh."

"Hallo, Aisling. Is this a good moment?" Jean-Luc asked.

"Luc, what a surprise. Your timing is impeccable considering this line will be disconnected tomorrow."

"Perhaps I have the gift of Foresight. Truly, you must learn to carry a cellular phone." His teasing and jovial voice brightened her mood and brought the smile back to her features.

Behind her, Griffin voiced a complaint about Jean-Luc in his native Scots that made her cringe again. It wasn't a very nice word.

"I called to tell you the invitation arrived this afternoon. I will be there to wish you both a wonderful day."

"Good! I'm glad you'll be able to make it." Her gaze shot briefly towards Griffin where he lounged on her couch with a scowl on his face.

"I would not dream of missing it for the world. Good luck in your travels to Brazil. I am off to New York myself to lend a hand while your friend Addison makes some much needed employee changes. He will do an amazing job there, I think. Regent Durant is thrilled."

"Keep an eye on him for me."

"You have my word, *cherie*. Then I will stop by to see you in Rio. Goodbye for now, Aisling."

"I'd really like that. Goodbye, Luc."

"You don't laugh that way when I call."

Aisling jumped and turned to find Griffin behind her. She'd never heard a sound of his approach.

For the first time in their relationship, she was afraid of him.

Something wasn't right. This wasn't her Griffin.

~*~

White-hot anger broiled through him with every word. While he lay on the sofa, hurting, aching, and miserable with a swollen face and bruised knuckles, she spoke on the phone to some French asshole. Helene had told him tales of Jean-Luc Chevalier.

He didn't trust him one bit.

"He wants to fuck you."

"Griffin, don't be ridiculous. We're only friends."

"That fuckin' frog would be balls deep in you this second! Don't tell me when I'm bein' ridiculous. I can see. Undressed you with his eyes right in front of me in my own office," he hissed.

No, he didn't, Griffin's subconscious interjected. He balked, conflicted. Jean-Luc Chevalier had been a perfect professional down to the last moment of their conversation. The detective had even kept in contact with Griffin regarding their investigation into the cultists who harassed him and nearly killed Aisling.

"Griffin, you're frightening me. Please, let's go sit, and I'll finish patching you up. I have some cream that'll clear the bruising right up."

"Aye…good idea. I'll just have a seat over here… M'head hurts," he said.

"I'll get you some water, too, and an aspirin. There's not much left in my fridge, but I can order something if you like."

Anything would be amazing right now, he thought. "You think I came all the way to Ireland fer goddamned take-out. Feed me like a man." The words left his mouth in a snarl.

"What's gotten into you?" Her voice raised. "Griffin, love, this isn't like you."

"You'd think that maybe, just maybe you'd be be willin' to be prepared fer when I'm here. You knew I'd be here. How hard would it have been to have had a hot meal? I've already had one sorry excuse fer a wife without adding a second to my troubles." The anger swelled again until it became a tidal wave of rage, threatening to spill.

Aisling paled.

He tried to get ahold of himself, but his hands shook. He stood rigid before her.

"Perhaps you should go to your ma for the night, Griffin," she said quietly. She trembled with her arms wrapped around her middle and studied him with inquisitive but concerned eyes. "I'll call you a cab."

She's right. I need to go. There's something wrong here.

"The hell did ye just say t'me?!" He should have left. He should have walked away from the moment he'd begun swearing at her, and yet he almost felt like a casual observer to the events of his own life. "I didn't ask to marry you for sass and lip."

No no no. He wanted to go home. It wasn't too late to end the argument, let it die where it was, go to his mother's to sleep for the night, and return in the morning sober with a clear head. His pulse hammered and heart pounded, roaring within his skull.

"I said I want you to go—AH!"

Her pained cry accompanied the crack of his hand across her cheek. He had never hit her before.

In fact, Griffin had never struck a single woman in all of his life.

He'd seen enough domestic abuse as a child. He knew the damage it did.

He'd always promised he would never be that man.

Griffin's hands moved of their own volition despite his protesting mind. He grabbed up a handful of pink cotton and dragged her in close to him with enough force to pop a slim strap. So much fabric fisted in his hand, it seemed a wonder any remained on her at all.

"Leave? I've only just gotten here, and y'kick me out like I'm some random nobody? Oh no…no no no… Learn the goddamned place y'belong and serve me the way I deserve. Should've been on yer knees to welcome me."

With a free hand, his dextrous fingers unbuckled his belt and whipped the slim leather from its loops. It slipped double over his fist and cut against her exposed legs with a sharp snap.

Aisling screamed and struggled in his hold. The harder she fought, the stronger the sensation of rage took hold.

He felt like a helpless spectator observing her beating at the hands of some stranger.

Do something, Ash! Don't let me do this to you. Please. Don't take this from me, he pleaded internally. *Make me stop. I know you can make me stop. You're stronger than I am.*

"Griffin, stop!" Aisling screamed again.

One of her hands grabbed his arm, and a wave of paralysis spread through his nerves like fire. It flew to his fingertips, and the belt dropped from his slackened grip before he could do more than swat her twice across the legs.

"Y'get over on the bed and take off all of that bullshit." Her top ripped as he dragged her. A single hot tear slipped down his cheek.

She slapped him, imbuing cold magic into her palm. The stinging frost temporarily blinded him, and before he could go after her again, Breda hissed at him from the floor with her silver coat fluffed in a threatening display. The cat swiped at his jean-clad legs, and Griffin punted her away.

"Griffin, I think you've been poisoned!" Aisling scrambled to put the bed between them. "You've been poisoned!"

Poison? It all made a sort of perverse sense. He ran the events of the day back through his head, beginning with the bar, the fights there, the swagger and bravado in his attitude when he arrived, how pissed he'd felt about surrendering Mara again, and the visit to Spain before that to return her to her mother's care. He had happily kissed Mara goodbye after enjoying a cup of coffee.

The day had gone downhill from there.

The bitch had poisoned him.

The knowledge fueled his fury to new heights. He lunged across the bed, though he feared what would happen next more than anything. She fought and kicked as they tumbled to the floor.

"Don't... No, no, no...! Griffin, I don't want to hurt you while you're like this!"

But she would. He heard it in her tone and rejoiced.

A low growl filled the apartment and rose into a piercing snarl. Sharp claws raked across Griffin's back, and a large, silver blur leapt over his shoulder to place itself between him and his target. Breda shimmered with a frosty aura, three times her usual size with a mouth full of unnatural teeth. Sharp spears of ice tipped her tufted ears.

He jerked back his wrist too late to avoid the feline's razor sharp claws. Breda sliced open his wrist as Aisling's foot connected with his face in a blinding flash of pain.

A. Payne & N. D. Taylor

I have to go. Have to go. "Aisling... Ash, m'sorry. So sorry," he choked out.

Moving with the jerky motions of a marionette, he backed away and forced himself to flee through the door. He didn't stop. Not even to shut it behind him. The air thickened as protective wards snapped shut at his rear and sealed him out of the building. The wards recognized him as an enemy.

Three connecting Portal jumps later, he reached Barcelona in record time.

Since leaving Aisling's flat, the unnatural fury had faded, replaced with a deeper, genuine anger. He stormed up the front walk and knocked loudly until Mercedes greeted him at the door. He clenched his fists, entire body trembling.

"Griffin, I did not expect to see you back so soon. Did you forget something?" She smiled.

"I know what y'did, Mercedes." He stepped forward and forced her back into the foyer. "What the hell did you put in my coffee?"

"You're making no sense, Griffin. I only put in your usual one lump."

"Stop lying!" he roared.

She dropped her air of innocence in favor of eyeing him shrewdly. "I hope you killed her. It's about the least your homewrecker deserves."

Her words twisted the proverbial knife in his back, but she had miscalculated. Instead of enraging him, Griffin felt a chilling sense of calm and determination. "Aisling isn't dead. I'm taking Mara and we're leaving. You've gone too far, Mercedes."

She laughed. "And go where? You think your precious Faerie spawn will accept you back? No, Griffin. You'll stay right here with us, where you should be. I should have known you were too much of a coward to do what was necessary, even with my help."

He pushed aside her attempt to touch him. "I'm taking Mara."

"Oh? And where will you go? I am sure by now half of Ireland and London is on the streets searching for you. Do you really think your little lamb has not gone to report your misbehavior?" She tapped her index finger against her lower lip and glanced away, only for her smile to broaden. "I am sure those men at the bar have…"

He froze. Mercedes had planned everything right from the start. "Why?"

"How does it feel to be a wanted man, Griffin? To know just how badly you have fucked up everything you've worked to make—"

He brought both hands forward in front of him with a clap, simultaneously erecting and demolishing a shield of mana so strong the explosive snap tossed Mercedes backward into the wall. He lingered a few precious seconds to touch her pulse and feel the steady beat of her heart. The shimmering fragments of his shield had left shallow cuts upon her cheeks.

It was the first and only time he'd ever intentionally struck a woman. And it was damned satisfying.

After confirming he hadn't killed his former wife, Griffin dashed upstairs. He found Mara hiding beneath the bed and clutching her favorite stuffed animal. She'd heard the screaming and noise, became frightened, and done as Griffin had once taught her. Autumn trilled gently from the girl's dark hair. More often than not, he chose to leave his companion with his daughter between visits.

"You're goin' home with Daddy now, princess. C'mon."

Mara clung to him and rode his hip as he sprinted down the stairs and out of his old home.

"Buckle up, lass," he told her from the front seat.

They drove away swiftly, but his heart hammered like a thousand drumbeats in his chest. He could hear the rush of his blood in his ears, the pounding of adrenaline urging him to drive faster despite his fear of drawing attention from the authorities.

He planned to kidnap his own child, and it never felt better. In his head, he plotted out a pit stop in France to acquire the aid of Jean-Luc and Helene. Once he got Mara to England, he would set old resentments aside and ask for help from the one man he swore to always avoid. His grandfather.

Surely Tristan Rhydderch could grant him one act of assistance.

Along the way, he chatted idly with Mara and put on a brave face she couldn't see. The girl had a talent for picking up on emotions, and he didn't want her to experience his anxiety, anger, and the other damning emotions sure to overwhelm her.

Griffin rolled up to the gate of the small private airfield and flashed his ID. The road that ran along the backside of the hangars was dim and mostly empty. He spotted a couple of cars that had been there upon his arrival, but nothing looked out of place. The keys fell out of his hands twice as he tried to unlock the heavy metal door to his assigned hangar.

"Daddy, I'm scared," she whispered in Spanish. "I don't want to go in there."

"We're almost to the plane, Mara. I promise."

"No, Daddy. This is a bad place."

Inside, the dark and quiet atmosphere made his heart jump. He reached to flip the lights and immediately froze.

Half a dozen Guardians from the Spanish Vault waited for him with weapons in their hands.

"MacNeil. Place the girl down and step away from her. No one has to come to harm," a voice spoke up in Spanish.

His Cessna was only a short sprint away, but Guardians surrounded it. Among them, he saw his former father-in-law, Commandant Domingo Rivera, with a smug smile on his face.

"She's my daughter too. I've got a right to her as much as anyone else," he replied in English. He held Mara tighter, divided between following their orders and holding her close. They were armed with pistols, and he feared his magic wouldn't hold against gunfire. Would they shoot a man holding a child? He hoped not, but he wouldn't bet Mara's life on it.

"You sacrificed those rights when you assaulted *my* daughter. It seems there are many people in Ireland searching for a man of your description for similar crimes. How unfortunate. We will have to take you into custody for your own protection of course until such matters are resolved. Now put down the girl."

He'd been set up.

He set Mara down gently and crouched beside his little girl. Why hadn't he listened to her?

"Papá?"

He kissed her tear-streaked cheek. "I love you, lass. I love you so much. Promise I'll see you again soon. You know who will look after you. She's our secret, aye?"

The moment he stepped away from his daughter, a Guardian rushed forward and clubbed him against the skull with his gun.

And Griffin saw nothing else.

Chapter 23

How had it all gone so wrong?

Imprisonment in Spain's wizard prison had taught Griffin a thing or two about Guardians and instilled a healthy distrust of them. During the sentencing, the Regent had treated him as an abusive ex-husband, a kidnapper, and a raving drunk.

He'd been kept isolated in a warded cell, denied visitors and any form of communication with the outside world. Not even Autumn could reach him. Weeks blurred into months.

Then one day, they opened his cell door, dragged him to the exit, and passed him over into Justiciar hands to be escorted to the Portal and out of the country. Over a year had passed. He barely had a moment to glance at the calendar before they sent him through the Portal to Rio.

August. Seventeen months, lost.

Griffin set a wooden coin on the desk and stared at it again. Once gleaming gold with a carved relief of Dapper Jack's smiling visage, it was now nothing more than a dull, wooden disc. The mischievous leprechaun had given him the lucky coin after Griffin's eighteenth birthday, a gift for outsmarting him but far from free.

Aisling and Griffin had been sweethearts then and their affection had shaped the leprechaun's enchantment.

By striking her, he'd committed one of the worst crimes in all of Avalon, the unforgivable sin of harming a loved one of Faerie blood. Even though it had been against his will, he'd done it thrice, shattering the charm and reducing the coin to mere junk.

Faerie magic didn't care about technicalities.

He couldn't face Ash yet. Not after what he'd done while under the influence of magic. No amount of time would be enough to come to terms with what Mercedes made him do.

THE COLLECTOR'S TREASURE

Like a coward, he crawled back to Brazil and discovered most of her belongings gone.

Luisa had told him why, blunt as ever without holding back. Aisling had returned to Ireland and her family to give birth to their twins.

He had twins, and he was too ashamed to even meet them. Too afraid his bad luck would corrupt them the way he tainted everything else.

Maybe he was right to avoid her after all. If he couldn't forgive himself, what made him think she could? Instead of calling or showing up at Ceara's estate, he wrote a generous check and sent it by Vault courier.

Aisling phoned him the night she received it. The outdated cellular device had remained active during his imprisonment, payments drafted automatically from his account for two years.

"Griffin, why on Earth are you sending me money?"

"To help with the twins and their needs. I can send more if it isn't enough."

"I don't want money. I don't need it."

"I won't be a deadbeat who doesn't pay his share, Aisling. I..." He sucked in a deep breath and closed his eyes. He imagined her birthing alone, rearing their two children, working as a nurse on the side in the Irish Vault and at home while bearing all of the financial and emotional strain.

And he hadn't been there.

"Griff, come home."

"And endanger the three of you? No. I can't do that anymore. I can't..." He began to pour a shot of whiskey, but paused to take the bottle with him to the couch instead. "I can't forgive myself for what I did to you."

"You weren't yourself."

"I should have been stronger."

Aisling huffed into the line. "She's a master with potions. Always has been. You had no idea."

"I trusted her, Ash. I made the choice to trust her again."

Nothing was sweeter than the sound of her voice after nearly two years of separation. For a while, Aisling remained quiet, and they were two people thousands of miles away listening to each other breathe.

A. Payne & N. D. Taylor

208

"What did you name them?"

"Rhiain and Liam," she answered in a soft voice. "For my ma and your old partner."

Tears stung his eyes. Liam, for his best friend. For the magus who brought them together again in friendship. The Healer who saved his life at the cost of his own.

"Y'chose well. Anyway, you take that money and spend it well. Let me know when you need more."

"Griff—"

"I mean it, Ash. Anything you need—"

"We need *you*," she cut in again.

Griffin thought of the anonymous letter he received under his door in prison, one among many delivered by unseen servants of the cult. "I miss you so much I don't know what to do with myself, but that time in prison was a warning. It'll be worse next time. I can't do it again. I just can't. Your safety comes before my happiness."

"Griffin… I understand you need time, and I'll give you some, but please don't stay away long. I don't—I can't—" Her voice hitched and shook. "I miss you."

"Never doubt how much I love you, Ash. Kiss the wee ones for me."

He hung up, and on his third day as a free man, he returned to the Vault and pleaded with Luisa to rehire him.

She had no qualms about admitting she couldn't find anyone interested in taking his job, despite her attempts to fill the position. No one among her current crew wanted the responsibility. It waited for him, so he returned to work.

The first excursion into the rainforest was met with heavy storms and flooding. The dangerous conditions became non-conducive to ferreting out long lost clues tied to the legend of El Dorado. They hunkered down and took shelter until a chopper came for them.

A week later, the second expedition began in better spirits, only to end with a face-off against cultists posing as travelers.

Everywhere Griffin went, they waited for him, an inescapable force eager to hurt everyone he loved.

Back to the Vault, they went to regroup and plan.

THE COLLECTOR'S TREASURE

A knock at the door jerked his head up. He couldn't concentrate on his paperwork or the map spread over the desk.

"Come in."

The door opened, and a young courier stepped inside. "Two letters for you, MacNeil. One is from Athens."

Griffin handed him a tip and opened the unaddressed letter first. Anything from Athens could only be from one source, and he wasn't in the mood to see what Hektor had to say.

Brother,

Word reached me of your trying and difficult times. My heart goes out to you. If you should ever wish to rekindle our relationship, I would be most agreeable to a meeting at a time and place to your convenience. You are always on my mind.

Best wishes, Alicia

Griffin rolled his eyes. His only memories of Alicia MacNeil were of the day she stormed out of the household after her seventeenth birthday. She'd called their mother every dirty name in the book and fled with fresh bruises on her cheek, courtesy of their stepfather. She'd also hated her little brother, the circumstances surrounding Griffin's birth, and that Fiona seemed to protect her male toddler more than her only daughter.

After discovering he had another father, he'd tried to reach out to the sister he'd never had the chance to really know, but gave up after six unanswered attempts.

Funny she would seek him now.

Giving it no further thought, Griffin opened the next letter.

Collector MacNeil,

I request your expertise in the handling of the sphinx at our dig site. The beast has killed three men, including one of our best Charmers. They could not answer its riddle. Since you are one of the few alive to have bested such a monstrosity, it is our hope you could come by to assess the situation.

Respectfully, Hektor Argyrios

He wadded both messages and tossed them into the trash bin. Two days later, another letter from Hektor arrived. It met the same fate. The third reached Luisa's desk directly, and she called him before her, waving the parchment while telling him off succinctly in Portuguese.

When their sister Vaults requested help, it was to be given. No ifs, ands, or buts allowed.

Griffin swallowed his pride and let his head dip a little further with each chastising word. Of the many people who were once his friends, Luisa was among a small number to remain at his side. She hadn't turned her back on him yet, and he'd disappointed her.

"Aye, Luisa. I'll go right away. Next Portal," he uttered in defeat.

"See about a trim before you go, too. You're representing our Vault, and just because you spent a year in prison doesn't mean you have to *look* like it, too."

Three hours later after a proper haircut, Griffin reached the site near Athens. From the air, he saw unimpressive, crumbling pillars scattered across the ground, but he knew the real wonders lying under the surface. As they circled around, Griffin noticed the usually bustling camp seemed empty and surmised that non-essentials had been given leave in the event things should go wrong with the sphinx.

Griffin hopped from the cabin and moved away from the chopper with his head ducked down. The strong downdrafts from the rotating blades flattened the grass and wild flowers growing out of the rocky ground. Once clear, he looked up and caught a quick glimpse of Hektor's stern face.

And his fist.

The punch cracked Griffin square in the jaw. He staggered backwards onto his ass in the dirt.

"Nice seein' you too," he muttered under his breath.

"Come, let's get this dealt with," Hektor said as he turned away.

Griffin followed the senior Collector and ran things over in his head a few times. A sphinx. A Faerie creature notorious for crafting clever riddles to trap foolish victims into its servitude. A beast so powerful that no less than five *trained* Magi were required to slay it. A beast trapped for centuries with an appetite.

Contrary to Griffin's expectations, no one stared at him or whispered behind his back. He didn't see knowing glances or judgmental glares. The few workers at the site gave cordial, smiling welcomes at odds with Hektor's cool and disapproving countenance.

They traveled silently into the ruin's bowels and entered a brightly lit chamber where the rest of the team worked.

"Ah, Griffin, welcome back," Petros said. The dark-haired, handsome Greek man greeted him with a fond embrace.

A pit that hadn't been there before yawned open wide and dark at the base of the wall once decorated by the diamond cutter scarabs. Griffin followed the men down a metal ladder riveted into place. The thirty foot descent ended in a finished chamber lit by alchemical devices.

"It took us a time to determine which wall to break open. The writing, you see?" Petros pointed out a line of archaic glyphs carved into the stone around them. "They promised a certain death if the wrong wall was breached. Once ready to make our choice, we did not have to dig far."

Griffin barely saw beyond three feet down the opened wall, the darkness so thick the lantern lights barely pierced it.

"Lights don't keep in the hall. Magical or mundane. Not for long, anyway. We had someone capable of creating a lasting one, but they're…unavailable to join us for this." Hektor frowned. "It's about another hundred feet."

"Those are fae runes of darkness. It's no wonder," Griffin said. "Only another fae can counter that. C'mon, Autumn, I'm gonna need your light for this."

Autumn crawled onto his shoulder and glowed crimson. The little fae had returned to him shortly after his release.

"Don't go beyond the entry," Petros cautioned. "We'll be right behind you."

Griffin stalked ahead. The salamander's light shone bright and strong to reveal a single archway of stone covered with swirling runes at the distant end. Beyond lay a rounded chamber lit by glow stones, but from his vantage, he couldn't see the sphinx. Only the remnants of her meals. Bones littered the floor.

"We learned the hard way that this one does not believe in backing out. If you pass the arch, you answer or you die. We lost a good man because he thought their rules were different," Hektor whispered in a solemn voice.

"What do you think, Griffin?" Petros asked.

Griffin stepped through and ignored the angered cries behind him.

"Griffin, what are you doing?"

"Checking out your beast."

Cautiously, he edged along the circumference of the room, passing carved marble pillars as thick as trees, until his quarry came into view.

Curled up much like a housecat, the fae creature dozed in the center. Between its paws, he saw a freshly gnawed bone with bits of clinging flesh.

The shaggy mane of the sphinx surrounded a handsome face. Paws as large as hubcaps sported claws resembling scythes.

"A new seeker wakes me from slumber." The sphinx's voice rumbled low, rattling a vibration through Griffin's gut. "Searching not for gold or plunder. Disgraced, loathed, shying from the dark you hide. Hated by most, your luck is dried." It licked its chops and hungrily continued to stare. Another slow grin curved the creature's lips, and its insidious chuckle crept over Griffin's spine.

"I came to answer your riddle, sphinx. Let's not play games, aye? Get to the point. What's your goddamned question?"

Few Magi ever mastered the fae tongue. It took a special connection to a Faerie patron before the mortal brain could begin to unravel the complex and mystical language. Thanks to his bond to Lachlan, friendship with Autumn, and his love for Aisling, it came to him easily.

The sphinx rose up and sat back on its furry haunches. Its tail swished across the marble floor.

"Had by few, treasured by all, I'm inside, I'm outside, I make men fall. Sometimes found, sometimes stolen, I can be lost and off times broken. What...am...I?"

Griffin stood before the sphinx for a long while. Behind him, he heard the mumbled voices of the other Collectors speculating. No one spoke fae, but it didn't sound like the same riddle used to stump Griffin's predecessors. The creature had changed it, and Griffin knew why.

"*Fuck* you," he hissed at it.

The creature's mouth spread into a broad grin. "Is this your answer, mortal? Do you desire the honor of becoming my next delicious treat? Or shall I keep you as a slave? You are quite handsome."

"You want an answer?" Griffin demanded.

The torches flared with the intensity of a dozen suns. Blinded explorers cried out in surprise and raised their hands to shield their eyes.

"Griffin!"

He ignored Hektor's startled cry. He stormed forward, filled with indignant fury manifested by spiraling ribbons of flame. A controlled line of fire singed the whiskers on the sphinx, lit its mane aflame, and successfully pissed it off into a frothing frenzy.

An earth-shattering roar threw Griffin off balance. He abraded both palms on the hard ground and quickly leapt to his feet. Autumn screamed.

I'm sorry, lass, Griffin thought. He couldn't ask for her to fight his battle, so he did the only responsible thing. "Go home, Autumn! Go home to Mara!"

The tiny fire salamander stubbornly glowed without blinking out of sight. She would have once. Once upon a time, Autumn would have shimmered away like a comet streaking across the night sky.

"This isn't the time to show your loyalty! Go!" he urged her again.

Apparently heartfelt displays of devotion didn't move the sphinx. Ivory fangs came inches from taking off Griffin's head. The stench of its rancid breath slammed him in the face. From the corner of his eye, Griffin saw Petros banging desperately on the invisible barrier.

"Y'want me so bad, puss? Come and get me!"

He sidestepped and twisted once to avoid the worst of the deadly claws. One raked his skin with the efficiency of a new axe cleaving through a soft branch. A flood of hot blood soaked into Griffin's white shirt from the deep furrows left behind.

"Shit!" His pained bellow was matched by a victorious roar.

The sphinx tore into him again. It twisted and turned with an impressive show of feline agility. Sent flying, he landed in a groaning heap and lay writhing in pain, a bloody stain left on the ground.

If not for Autumn's plaintive warble of warning, the fight would have come to an abrupt end when the airborne sphinx pounced forward with every claw extended. Griffin lurched to his feet and threw his mana into the strongest shield he could muster.

Sparks flew and shimmering energy shattered in every direction, but the prismatic dome held. He skidded backwards across the ground as the shield wavered, giving in beneath the assault but saving his life from being crushed.

The shield would have dissipated with another attack, but he manipulated his energy into something better. Brilliant white fire spears became exploded fireworks into his opponent and made it eat sparks. The lightshow disguised the dagger Griff sank into its paw pad. Jerry's dagger. The sphinx buried its teeth to the bone of Griff's shoulder. His collarbone cracked beneath the force, and he nearly passed out from the pain.

Autumn sailed above the enraged beast and twisted in midair to execute a perfect landing upon its shaggy backside.

"Autumn?" he cried, startled. "Don't!"

Autumn tripled in size. Quadrupled. She grew even further, elongating a slim, whip-like tail longer than Griffin's arm. Her exultant roar created a blowtorch that blistered the sphinx's ears and seared its glorious mane. Her claws dug into the beast, and she stuck fast as if glued to the ancient fae thrashing to remove her.

"Christ. Autumn, you grew!"

He couldn't believe the reptilian beast battling the sphinx was once too small to fill a shirt pocket. The salamander ferociously sizzled and charred her opponent's back, her claws red hot embers against the sphinx's fur. The acrid odor reached Griffin's nose and made his eyes water.

In the wild attempt to dislodge Autumn from its back, the sphinx dealt a bone-shattering blow to Griffin. Two ribs cracked when the beast's powerful tail struck his torso, lifting him from his feet.

He blacked out briefly from the pain, awakened by screams from Autumn begging him to get up. Blood dripped into his eyes from a cut above his brow. His head swam and lungs ached. Despite his pain and clouded vision, nothing obscured the sight of the sphinx crowing over its victory.

Autumn lay unmoving on the ground. A single ruby foreleg was gnashed between the sphinx's sharp teeth. Autumn's leg.

Burn it… Make it pay… an insidious voice whispered.

Half-crazed and half-suicidal, Griffin pushed up to his feet with his uninjured arm. He rushed the creature, touched one foot against the base of its tail, and leapt forward onto its still smoking, charred back.

Burn it…

"Go to Hell!" he screamed.

He held on like a pyromaniac cowboy on a rodeo bull with plumes of twisting, purple flames radiating around his fingers. Hellfire engulfed Griffin and the sphinx in hot waves that penetrated the magical barrier.

Shrieking in agony, the sphinx shambled about in an effort to remove the magus from its back. Onlookers shielded their eyes from the blinding inferno and helplessly held their breath.

~*~

The combined efforts of three Healers stabilized Griffin's condition. He awakened groggy and calling for Autumn. It took the bedside nurse five minutes to calm him, and a threat to sedate him again.

"She's right here. See? We tended to her as well."

The little red salamander lay beside him in a small crib with a heating lamp from a neonatal care center. Griffin saw a single gauze scrap wrapped around her left foreleg, but he was instantly relieved to see no other damage. She was neither the pocket-sized pet of his youth nor the crimson dragon from the sphinx's lair; she resembled the world's most exotic monitor lizard instead.

The stubby stump ended at her elbow, longer than he recalled. It led him to wonder if he had imagined the limb ripped from the shoulder during the fight.

They released Griffin the next day. In that time, Griffin and the Healers discovered Autumn's uncanny knack for regenerating. Better than a common mortal gecko, she re-grew more than her tail. It brought him great relief to know his actions hadn't led to her permanent maiming.

"We'll be home in Rio tomorrow, but Mara's probably missing you by now, eh?" He'd rented an inn room in the local mage community. Magical healing was the best kind of healing, but he didn't want to push his luck.

An hour later, he crawled into bed to count the hours until the next Portal to Brazil. Sleep would have found him if not for the knock at his door.

Hektor awaited him with a bottle of ouzo in hand and forced his way inside. He promptly pulled two shot glasses from his pockets and topped each one off with Greek liquor.

"What in Zeus's name were you trying to do, MacNeil? Get yourself killed?" He pushed one of the glasses into Griffin's hand and clinked his own to it. Then he took his shot and poured a refill.

"Guess I should have tried harder, then. Seems I've failed," Griffin commented dryly. He took the shot from Hektor gratefully.

"You take your punches like a man at least. Didn't even ask why I'd done it."

"I earned it." He didn't even know if he should be drinking while taking magical remedies, but he wasn't one to turn down good alcohol when it was provided on another man's dime.

"You deserved worse," Hektor said gruffly.

Griffin remained silent. He became the older Collector's dour drinking partner. Shame silenced him, but Hektor obliviously carried on. The man made sure their glasses never stayed empty for long.

"I am no stranger to…tangled relationships." A bittersweet smile crossed Hektor's face. He tossed back the remainder of his drink and topped it off again. "So were you trying to prove something there or looking for an easy way out?"

"I knew the answer to the riddle, but it was toying with me. It's what fae do."

"You knew?" The man stared at him a moment, and then he shook his head. "What riddle was so upsetting that you decided answering wasn't worth your bother?"

"What's it matter to you? You have your treasure now, and you didn't need to hire five men to do it."

Hektor jabbed a finger at him. "You ask me why it matters to talk? Let me tell you a story, son. Perhaps you'll learn something. You think you're the only man who's made mistakes?"

Griffin said nothing, but Autumn lifted her head from his pillow on the bed and chirped.

"I loved a woman once, more than anything else in this world, but I was young and ambitious. Love alone didn't satisfy me. I lost her. Such is what happens when we let anger and fear rule us without forgiveness or compassion."

"I'm not without compassion, Hektor, but I do know when it's time to give up."

"Oh? So tell me, what keeps *you* from giving forgiveness?" he asked. "What drove you to face a sphinx when you had only to give an answer you knew?"

Because I don't deserve it, he thought.

"Doesn't matter," Griffin said quietly. He turned the empty glass between his hands, haunted by Aisling's terrified face as she desperately fought him off. It had taken every ounce of his will to withdraw from that fight. He couldn't forgive himself for what happened. The breath that he drew in was unsteady, a shudder of sound from his lungs.

"I miss her so damned much, and there's nothing to be done about it, Hektor."

"You don't know that. She misses you. Needs you."

"I know everything I touch turns to shit. I ruin everything I touch. Look." He removed his wallet and flipped it open to remove the wooden coin. "My luck's run dry. Maybe I'm a fool to keep a leprechaun's coin that's lost its magic, but it reminds me of what happens when a fool relies on the luck and fortune of others. I won't make that mistake again."

Hektor pensively studied the dull coin. Deep furrows creased his brow, and his lips pressed into a thin frown.

"You didn't hear this, and it's best you say nothing, Hektor. I don't want to endanger you. I spent close to two years in that jail, and...one of the Guardians shoved a letter beneath my cell door. Asking me to join with the Master. Another letter from the Diabolists. They tried to kill her once before, Hektor. I can't risk goin' near her again."

"So...you are a coward?" Disapproval hung heavily in Hektor's voice. "You've abandoned your family out of misguided fear?"

"I'm not a coward. You don't know what it was like, hurting her like that. You don't understand. Felt like a bloody wild animal was wearing my skin. All I wanted to do was hurt her. I almost... I almost..." A ragged sob left him.

"Hurting her like what?" Hektor's sharp voice joined an incredulous expression. "MacNeil, what in the name of the gods are you spluttering on about?"

"You...you don't know, then?"

"If I'd been aware of any abuse, I would have thrown you to the sphinx myself. Explain."

Griffin sighed quietly and held out his shot glass for a refill. He needed the alcohol to recount the tale of what had been the most painful, miserable day in his life.

"I'll start from the beginning. Back in my school days when we first met in Dublin's archives, my ex-wife was a genius with brewing potions. An alchemical savant. I learned to make such good scroll parchment with her help. Aisling was jealous of the time we spent together, but I was sure Mercedes was only there to help. One day, a lad tells Ash he caught us snogging in the library. We argued. Broke up." The memory tightened his chest. "I wasn't kissing her, but the accusation ruined our friendship. And because I was an asshole back then, I dated Mercedes to rub it in even after Ash apologized. The Collector program accepted me, so I moved and I broke her heart for the first time."

Hektor listened, arms crossed over his chest as he leaned back.

THE COLLECTOR'S TREASURE

"Months later, I returned to escort Ash to the Winter Gala. I wanted to be friends. Hell, I suppose I always hoped she'd convince me to stay, but I was afraid to be a jobless bum like m'stepfather since I'd turned Ireland down. When she promised to get in touch with you, I swore I'd return. Ran home in a jiff, got m'things packed, sat down with Mercedes, and told her I was done... I remember feeling so nervous. Like a right twat fer using her. We drank coffee and talked about sending my things to Ireland."

"She did write," Hektor said. "I remember it because I had your resume on my desk anyways, and I was considering it. Then Rhiannon's girl wrote to me about your hard work. Your brilliance. Said she believed in you so much she'd given you her mother's translations book. I sent you my offer that very night."

"Hektor, I never received a single letter from you. I wanted Greece more than anything, and I've got no reason to lie. Wherever your letter went, it wasn't to me."

"Your ex."

Griffin took another drink of his liquor and stared ahead at the silent television unit while it aired late night television programming. "All I know is I was dead set against Spain. When I went to bed that night, Mercedes joined me and started a night of hard fuckin'. I never left. We posted the engagement letter, and I broke Aisling's heart again. Didn't even have the balls to tell her I'd not be coming back."

"Nymphs have a way about them, yes, but the coincidences imply there was more to your change of heart," the older man said drily.

"Didn't take long to become unhappy, but then Mara was born. I loved her. She's my wee princess, Hektor. I couldn't leave, and Mercedes fer all her faults, she'd been good to me."

His grip tightened on the glass, and his tongue became loosened by the alcohol. It felt good to get it off his chest and to speak with another man. "An old friend convinced me to write Ash again. Hearing from her was... It was like seein' the sun after days of clouds and storm. I kept her every letter. I looked forward to work and receivin' her missives by courier."

Both sat in silence for a moment. Hektor waited with patience for Griffin to collect himself and continue.

"When my marriage ended, I wondered what led me to staying so long. Why I'd done it. Nothing made sense. She tried to take my little girl from me, and then she gave her back. We made plans to share custody. I took Mara back to her mother so we could prepare the island home for her."

"But something happened."

"Aye. Mercedes made me a cup of coffee and we had a chat about the upcoming months. We always do. Can't cook to save her life, but she can make a damned good cup of joe. I gave Mara a kiss and flew to Barcelona." He summarized the rest in a dead, listless voice.

Hektor blew out a breath and scrubbed his palm down his face. "I couldn't begin to imagine…"

"So there you have it, Hektor. All my failures. My ex-wife *poisoned* me, Hektor. They sentenced me to two years beneath Barcelona in a tiny cell for every charge they could pin to me. I'm only out now because a good friend vouched for me and forced their hand."

"Have you not reported her? Sounds like black magic to me, and you know the Vault frowns on that."

"I told them it was poison. It was out of my system, so they painted me as a raging drunk. An abusive ex who tried to kidnap his child. The Regent threw the book at me because I'm the grandson of another Regent. Said they were holding me accountable fer it all and no favors would be given."

"I had no idea things were so bad. But…throwing your life away… You went in that room to die. Deny it, I dare you."

Griffin looked away and uttered in a tiny voice, "I did. At least, I thought I did."

"Thank the gods you came to your senses."

"You're one to talk. When do you plan to tell Aisling you're her father?"

Hektor blinked. "So. You're a clever bastard as well as a foolish one," the man said gruffly. "What gave it away?"

"I have a daughter. I know how a man looks at his little girl when he loves her."

Hektor grunted. "My situation is different. I made many wrong choices in my youth, Griffin, and letting Rhiannon

O'Brien walk away was the worst of them. You don't have to make those same mistakes."

"And you don't have to keep making your mistake. Ash lived her life without parents. Lost a stepfather as a wee babe and then a mother she loved. We used to laugh and say we'd share mine after we discovered the truth. *She* sent me to find my real pa. She did that, Hektor. So don't you tell me that it's too late to fix it with her. And don't you judge me until you fix your own mistakes."

"Maybe you're right, and maybe one day soon I will have that talk with her. But not right now. Right now, take your own advice, and don't deny those babies a father the same way their mother was denied hers."

They finished the bottle in silence, and Griffin stared at it long after Hektor left.

Chapter 24

The jungle brought peace to Griffin during dark times. Perched upon a fallen log, he kicked aside a jagged branch tangling with his bootlaces. Damage from the past storms left a gaping hole in the high canopy and sunlight pierced through. The wilderness reclaimed the ground, and thick ferns spread out in verdant new growth.

Juliana struggled to light the wood for the evening campfire. Griffin snapped his fingers from afar and sent a bounding little flame construct leaping over the grass toward her. It landed with a satisfying sizzle amidst the rubbish she'd gathered. Her grateful smile surprised him.

Lately, Juliana had barely tolerated his presence, and he knew she blamed him for the Diabolists in the once peaceful rainforest. Their dark magic and insidious intentions left a malignancy wherever they went. It unsettled the Amazon's natural inhabitants and made the dryads nervous.

A few minutes later, she sat beside him. "You are in higher spirits, my friend. Tell me what's on your mind."

He didn't speak to her at first and remained leaned forward with his weight supported on his knees. "Autumn brought this from Spain," he finally said. He drew a small photo from his pocket with a precise burn marring one side. The remaining half featured Mara. At a glance, it was easy to see a woman had been in the photo originally, as her manicured fingers rested over the girl's shoulder. He turned it over to reveal the inscribed Braille dots tediously placed by his child's hand. The message was simple: *'Te amo, Papá.'* I love you, Daddy.

"How does it feel to fuck up your life so badly?"

His head snapped up. "What?"

Juliana raised her brows. "I said everything happens for a reason, Griffin. Have faith that this will pass."

No, you didn't, he thought, but the earnest and genuine expression on her face was at odds with the cruel jab. It lingered with him, and for a few seconds, he couldn't do anything more than stare her down with hate brewing in his heart.

"Are you okay, Griffin?"

"I…" He shook his head. "Guess I'm not. I swear I heard you say something else."

His fellow explorer touched his shoulder in reassurance. "Sometimes when a thing becomes faulted, it must be broken down to be rebuilt better. You will come from this stronger."

"I hope you're right." But he wasn't convinced.

The woman patted his knee and rose to her feet. "I'll go scavenge for some fruit and make sure Justin didn't get turned around. Our friends from the Wakani tribe should be here soon."

"I'll be ready," he assured her.

Left to his thoughts, Griffin ducked his head to consider her words. He caressed his little girl's image with his thumb, and he wished he could be there to smooth her sad smile away. It didn't look right, as if her mother had instructed her on what she considered a proper pose.

"Griffin, they're here!" Luisa's excited call drew him from his thoughts.

He tucked the photograph away and moved over to join the others.

In the short time since his return to work, he'd discovered Luisa had close, albeit strained, ties to a local tribe in the western Amazon. She also had a son who lived among them, a were-jaguar named Felipe.

By helping the tribe vanquish a nasty curse, they had earned the Wakani's trust. Her son vowed to help them search for their treasure, and Luisa had been beside herself with giddiness ever since.

As members of an aboriginal tribe, Felipe and his wife wore a small amount of clothing, mostly trinkets around their necks and scraps of orange cloth circling their hips. Griffin barely gave Dahlia's bared breasts a second glance, but he had to nudge Justin in the ribs to remind him to stop staring.

Their luck took a turn for the better two weeks after the pair joined them. Dahlia knew a place feared even by the evil spirits of the Amazon.

"I do not like the way this place smells," Felipe said while scanning the trees above them. A dense jungle canopy blotted out the sun, the branches thick with foliage and vines.

"Looks like any other bit of jungle," Justin said.

"I would trust Felipe's nose, if I were you," Dahlia cautioned them. "He can smell magic that I can't sense."

Griffin glanced at her. Although she wasn't a native member of the Wakani, Dahlia offered talents rivaling Felipe's were-jaguar abilities.

Like being a vampire.

He didn't trust her as far as he could throw her, but she was beginning to grow on him and had no shortage of stories to share when they made camp at night.

"What do you suggest we do, then?" Luisa asked.

"Keep your eyes open and aware of your surroundings," Dahlia suggested to her mother-in-law.

"We're doing that anyway," Griffin said.

"Then we'll keep them extra open," Justin said.

Griffin shook his head and strode forward onto the path, only for a cold, heavy weight to land around his shoulders. Several writhing bodies moved and hissed, while Justin gave a startled shout.

"Snakes!" Paola cried. The poor Healer shrank back from them and hid behind Justin.

Griffin froze. "Are they venomous?"

"No, they do not appear to be," Dahlia said.

A few of the serpents clung to him like tenacious burrs, refusing to let go. With help, Griffin unwound the pythons from his arms and torso. The snakes followed the group until Felipe them his afternoon snack.

Once they were rid of their scaly dilemma, they struck gold on a winding path overtaken by the flourishing growth.

Literally.

"This is the place you've been searching for?" Dahlia moved over to stand above Griffin and Luisa. They knelt beside a stone marker heavily crusted in jungle detritus. Between his knife and Luisa's scrub brush, they revealed a golden figure embedded against the dark, carved stone.

"Aye, this is certainly a good sign. Best we've found yet." Griffin grinned up at her.

Twenty feet away, they found a second marker, and then a third. Dahlia pointed out each in turn before gesturing toward a split in the rocky ground hidden between two trees. Their twisting roots camouflaged the fissure.

Dahlia, Justin, Luisa, and Griffin made the descent through the crack to a tunnel below while the others secured a camp above. Autumn provided light from Griffin's shoulder.

"As I said, I was only able to make it down perhaps fifty feet," Dahlia said in a hushed tone. Her voice echoed against the unnaturally smooth walls of the narrow passage. "I felt compelled to leave."

"That means we've got to keep goin'. We'll find the source of the ward soon enough. They're harmless. Usually," Griffin said.

The claustrophobic tunnel's narrow space carved through a mountain rise. A chiseled pathway of descending stairs led them on a march below the earth's surface.

Musty and dank air grew heavier around Griffin's limbs with each step until at last, he realized they were approaching the heart of the warding magic. The oppressive atmosphere scrambled his concentration, bringing with it an insidious force that sought to tear the air from their lungs.

"The hell is this?" Justin demanded, sucking in a breath as he leaned against the wall.

"Magic. One of the worst wards I've ever seen. Someone powerful wanted to keep explorers far away from this place. We must continue beyond it," Luisa told them. "Take in as much air as you need now. Hyperventilate and hold it until we pass beyond the bubble of sorcery."

"Others before us did not fare so well." Dahlia drew their attention to the dusty floor of the tunnel.

Griffin nearly stumbled over the bones of a corpse in adventuring gear. Bits of skin and flesh clung to the bones of the desiccated body, and a relatively new model of flashlight clutched in the skeletal hand implied a recent, failed incursion.

"My skin...feels like it's on fire," Justin muttered. He wheezed against the wall where he supported his weight with one arm. "Lungs burning."

Griffin placed one arm around the man's shoulders and urged him to continue. "Have to push through. We can make it. It's part of the ward."

A pins and needles sensation spread over Griffin's fingers. The tingle reached his hands and wrists and became a dull burn. Ahead of him, Luisa gasped for breath and pushed through the viscous environment as if she were underwater. It felt like the flesh had been peeled from his bones and every strand of sinew beneath was soon to follow. It felt as if someone showered boiling hot water upon him and every steaming drop invaded his pores.

Dahlia assisted Luisa with an arm around the older woman, but she grabbed at Griffin with her other hand to shove him and Justin forward. The vampire appeared least harmed, but even she struggled within the cursed air.

Desire to breathe and survive overrode the weakness swimming through his skull. Justin seemed closer to passing out, and for that reason alone, Griffin forced himself to continue forward with an arm around his friend.

They broke through the last barrier and stumbled forward into an open space scented of cool water and damp earth. He sucked in rapid gulps of air and collapsed to the ground alongside his fellow Collectors. Luisa and Dahlia sprawled somewhere behind him, but the former croaked his name for attention minutes later.

Griffin twisted slowly and flopped onto his back, and then with a greater effort, he heaved his body into a sitting position.

"Griffin. We found it. Look," Luisa said in a strained voice.

He raised his head to take in his surroundings for the first time. Beams of sunlight streamed down from openings above, highlighting the ancient architecture of a forgotten city. Their lost city of gold.

Luisa wiped the tears from her face. "It's...the most beautiful thing I've ever seen."

"It's fuckin' gorgeous, is what it is," Griffin rasped back to her. His chest continued to burn from the lack of oxygen. His throat was raw, but he sucked in deep and thirsty breaths to soothe the lingering ache. He stared in wonder at his surroundings and the gold shining from every corner of the waiting room.

Daylight filtered through rectangular windows chiseled into aurous walls beneath the high, vaulted ceilings. A waterfall spilled into the cavernous structure to feed a pool down below. A gilded bridge led to a set of wide steps before a heavy door. Spears of rock carved to resemble marble pillars flanked the stairs and alternated with metallic animal statuary.

"I did not think the stories would be so literal," Dahlia said as they all gazed around in awe.

"The others will want to see this." Justin grinned.

"*Everyone* will want to see this." Griffin laughed and smacked the man on the back of the shoulder. "But first, the wards need to go."

"How long will it take you to dispel them?" Luisa asked.

"Three days." He glanced toward Dahlia and winked. "Two if she helps."

~*~

Griffin, Luisa, and the rest of the group dedicated their every waking moment to discovering the secrets of El Dorado. Instead of taking their standard break, Luisa sent an urgent message to Rio asking for additional supplies and more hands to help catalog their discovery.

A week later, a chopper arrived with old and new faces, the latter handpicked by both Luisa and Griffin. With the cultists and Inquisition posing a threat, they wanted trustworthy people on the team.

And he couldn't think of anyone more trustworthy than Alistair and Helene.

"C'mon. The doors are this way," Griffin said as he led Helene to the entrance. He gestured to the mural engraved beside the doors. "There's some shit here to decipher, but as far as I know there's only one man with a golden touch. This has to refer to Midas."

"King Midas is a Greek myth," Helene uttered.

"I know that. I spoke with a Greek Collector or two while at the labyrinth... But there's evidence at their site as well, pictures of a man with gold hands. Even they have reason to believe Midas crossed the ocean to find a new kingdom to rule."

Helene ran her fingers through her sweat-dampened hair. "Why did he cross the ocean is what I want to know. He had his own kingdom, so why start over from scratch? But enough with the speculation, when do we get to step inside? You mentioned locked doors in your letter."

Griffin grinned. "All solved. While waiting for your arrival, Juliana located the clan who constructed this beautiful marvel of dwarven craftsmanship. In exchange for getting to explore the place for signs of their own ancestors, they've made a replacement key for us. They simply forgot the place existed."

Each time he stepped inside the city was like the first time. Griffin's entire body tingled. He wiped his moist palms against his pants legs and led Helene into the ghost town.

The occasional dusty corpse lay undisturbed as a skeletal memory of the past. Each one appeared to be lavishly decorated in unique golden trinkets of immense beauty, and most still gleamed beneath a layer of dust. The team faced no difficulty with differentiating the objects molded by dwarven hands from those fashioned by human artisans.

"So many dead people," Helene murmured.

"I know. We've been wondering what the hell happened here?" Griffin said.

Felipe padded out from the rear of the group and shifted forms. His velvet fur became coal black hair falling past his brown shoulders, and the deep scars crossing over the panther's flank transferred to his bare skin, revealing a heavy network of disfiguring lines down the young man's lean thighs. He lingered near Dahlia.

"How many lived here, do you think?" Paola asked as she crouched down to inspect a set of brittle bones. "One hundred? Two? Surely no more than that..."

"We'll know if we finish taking count," Justin remarked from the rear. He waited on the low step of a winding staircase leading up to another level of the underground palace. Another deceased city inhabitant lay upon the stairs at his feet. "Hard to tell now if they died fleeing from something or what, but I'd think that even then, someone would have taken away their dead and not left them lying in the middle of a stairwell."

"Just mark it all on the map, Justin. We'll do a body count from that once we've completed this."

"What makes you think that we can completely chart this city?" Helene asked.

Griffin snorted derisively. "This isn't the labyrinth. We'll have a good record in a year if nothing slows us down."

They discovered residences carved from the rock with gilded doors and strategically placed windows to the outside world. They found adults with tiny skeletal remains in their arms, the bones of a farmer in an overgrown garden, and laborers who seemed to die around their tools.

"Death came swiftly." Dahlia lingered near a dull mural on the wall with faded paints barely perceptible to the eye. "It echoes."

"Something or someone slaughtered these people. We will get to the bottom of it," Luisa determined softly.

Griffin glanced at the remains of an adult and child at Luisa's feet. He nodded in agreement.

A Collector had a duty to more than the discovery of lost treasure and magnificent relics. As historians, they also sought the truth of the magical past. Together, they would solve the mystery of El Dorado.

~*~

Nine days of cautious exploration led the adventurers deeper into uncharted territory. They created a makeshift camp near the center beneath the shade of an overgrown orchard, erecting their tents and setting out bedrolls once their Guardians deemed it safe. Sunlight shone from above through openings in the stone.

Not far from the orchard, Griffin found a ten-foot granite statue with immense, golden hands raised toward the underground city's ceiling. "He's here. I know this is where he'll be. Look at this place. He built a goddamned statue of himself."

"It's a little warm in this area, isn't it? Practically stifling," Alistair muttered as he tugged at the collar of his shirt.

Juliana's glance seemed to suggest she'd prefer him to lose the shirt.

Nearby, a thirty yard drop from a dwarven-made cliff revealed a tranquil river. It separated the greater city from the majestic temple, spanned by a pathway of rocky posts jutting from the pool at odd intervals. On the opposite shore, a grand staircase of polished white marble ascended to the central structure resembling a large Grecian mausoleum. Extravagant pillars of impressive stone rose from the floor to the top of an elegant temple fit for a god.

"Goddamned water…" Griffin moaned at the sight of it.

Helene grinned. "I doubt there is a beastie awaiting you this time. Do not be so quick to complain. Shall we all make our way over now? I see the mechanics for a bridge."

"No. Not yet. Something seems wrong about this water." Luisa stood at the edge of the pool, staring dubiously down at it. She raised one hand in a 180-degree arc before her and chanted low spoken words, revealing an illusion concealing a danger greater than a serpent-infested water source.

The clear-running river became a bubbling pool of lava.

"Well. Fuck that. I'm not going over there," Justin stated.

"I can cross," Felipe offered. "It is only short walk."

Griffin gave him a ruminative glance.

"There are traps, Felipe, and you aren't trained for this," Luisa said, her voice filled with maternal warmth.

"Many traps," Helene agreed. She walked along the ledge back and forth, a thoughtful expression on her face. "I recognize gnomish engineering when I see it."

Gnomes maintained popularity among the French for their ingenuity and brilliance. Guillotine traps, poison-laced darts, and a variety of other hazards protected the historical French ruins. The assortment of perils awaiting their explorers was nearly as dangerous as the youkai-infested temples of Japan. The Japanese kept a terrifying reputation for their eagerness to bind infernal creatures to their valuables and estates.

"All right, then. I'll do it," Griffin said while shrugging off his pack and gear.

THE COLLECTOR'S TREASURE

Helene clapped him on the shoulder. "We will both do it. We are the fastest, *mon ami*. I will race you to the other side," she said with a wink.

Griffin and Helene glanced toward Luisa for approval, which she readily gave.

I can do this. There's nothin' to it, Griffin told himself as he stood at the ledge with Helene beside him. He backtracked and took it at a run. He didn't want to think about the molten bath below, didn't want to think about the lack of remains to return to his family, and he most certainly didn't allow his mind to wonder how much it would hurt before he was flash-fried and cooked.

Maybe it wouldn't hurt at all. Maybe it would be like the old videogames where he'd fall off the ledge into red doom for a quick Game Over. Unlike a video game, he wouldn't regenerate at the ledge to try again with a second life.

Tile clicked beneath his foot, and the first dagger whistled past his ear. It came painfully close to finding a home in his skull but knifed through the air instead. It slid with a dull clinking noise into the mouth of a mounted snakehead statue mirroring the one responsible for launching it.

Stone shattered and fell beneath his feet, crumbling by design or due to age. His boot slipped against a stone pillar's edge, and another projectile whizzed past his ear.

"They're almost there!" Justin shouted from the group's position on stable ground.

The next statue belched a fireball on a trajectory destined to give Helene a bad day. Griffin's hand shot out and palmed the fiery sphere as he leapt through the air. He batted it downward and landed in a crouch to duck the next dagger ejected toward him from Helene's side. The clockwork machines alternated, shooting from one side to the other. Their pattern became too complex to predict, keeping the two explorers on their toes. Then it stopped.

Nearly drowned out by the sound of his heartbeat, the grinding sound of gears announced the statues had emptied.

"They are priming again! Run!" Helene screamed.

The pathway narrowed until the pedestals came one after another. Helene moved ahead of him, and he traveled at her heels. The stone crumbled beneath the quick beat of her feet, but a well-timed forward handspring landed her on the next rising obelisk.

Griffin decided gnomes were evil little bastards, and if he survived to see one again, he might try to punt it to the moon.

The tower of rock teetered and toppled. Off balance, Helene tucked and rolled to safety at the other side. Griffin wasn't as fortunate. He hit the ledge hard, the stone edge buried into his midsection. He scrambled forward and sought to find purchase against the rocks, ignoring the sweat stinging his eyes. Helene pulled him up onto solid ground beside her and together, they collapsed breathlessly to the stone. He didn't move for a while, listening to the frantic rhythm of his heart and their steaming exhales. They waited for the adrenaline rush to end.

"That was intense," Helene said at last.

"Fuckin' right it was. Now let's get that bridge down."

Fifteen minutes later, the rest of the group safely joined the two Collectors. Griffin grinned from ear to ear as the last person crossed.

"That's it, then. We found him. King Midas's tomb was at El Dorado all along, Luisa. We did it."

Luisa nearly crushed Griffin with a sudden, impulsive hug. The ferocity of her affection startled him initially, and then he relaxed into the maternal embrace.

"We did it," she repeated with tears in her voice. When they separated, she swiped at her face quickly with one wrist and turned to the other explorers.

"I do not like this feeling. It is bad place. Very bad place," Felipe muttered from where he lingered near the outskirts of the group near Dahlia.

Griffin still caught Helene sneaking glances at the female vampire from time to time. Fortunately, Dahlia never seemed to take offense. For a leech, she had the kind of bottom he would have eagerly squeezed and fantasized about if his heart wasn't permanently attached to a woman beyond his reach.

"You've been quiet, Dahlia. What's on your mind?" he asked.

"Felipe is right. This place is forbidden." She shook her head and refused to move forward towards the temple entrance.

"What are you talkin' about?"

Felipe shook his head over and over, refusing to budge. Seconds later, he abandoned his human skin and returned to the safety of his jaguar form. Dahlia adjusted her stance until she stood between the shifter and the double doors. Two massive frames stood between the Collectors and their prize. A pictorial mural decorated in the art of ancient Greece told a story they all knew well. The tale of King Midas and his greed. A tale of wealth and sorrow.

"Funny… There's some parts of the story I don't recognize here," Luisa said.

"I don't either," Griffin said uncertainly. "This bit's in Greek, but I'm not feelin' so confident about my translations now."

"And our Greek expert is no longer among us," Juliana said.

This time, Griffin didn't shoot her a dirty glance or utter words of anger. He simply sighed. The fault for losing Aisling belonged with him and no one else.

"We can contact Hektor Argyrios. I am certain he would appreciate the opportunity to participate in thi—"

"It speaks of his crime." Dahlia rested a hand against Felipe's head, her fingers smoothing over his flattened ears. "Of his punishment by the gods."

Griffin glanced back over his shoulder and found the vampire's dark eyes locked on the mural.

"Look at the pictures," Dahlia told them. Her hand swept out to indicate the story depicted in the carved motifs. "Once there lived seven men of power, each craving more. They spilled innocent blood, killing one beloved of the gods."

The first panel displayed seven shrouded figures gathered around a limp form. In the next, the figures cowered beneath a brilliant aurora, shielding their faces.

"The gods punished and cursed them to crave their greatest weakness. In their shame, only animal blood sustained them." She pointed to the stylistic drawings depicting small creatures at the bottom of the next panel.

"Are you saying what I think you're saying…?" Luisa asked.

Dahlia turned her solemn gaze towards her and dipped her chin in a single nod. "I am saying, your King Midas... He is a Revenant. Perhaps the strongest I have ever felt in all my life. One of the original seven vampire mages."

Griffin's stomach flip-flopped, and anticipation tingled through his fingers. "The first Revenant. We found the fuckin' tomb of the first Revenant. We made *history*." His pulse sprinted wildly at the thought.

"You...do not intend to awaken him, I hope?" Paola clutched her rosary and gazed at them through wide eyes set within ashen features.

"Better to let him be," Dahlia said.

Helene nodded. "I agree with Paola and Dahlia. It is an amazing discovery, but far too great a risk. This great city became a tomb for nearly two hundred people, and now we find a vampire among their number. There can be only one culprit. He lies beyond this door."

Griffin swung a betrayed look across the room to her. Helene met his gaze evenly without flinching. Of the many people there, he expected her to have his side. "We found...the father of all vampires, and you're all wantin' to leave him there?"

"The seven mages were dangerous men," Dahlia said quietly. "Our bloodline is a curse from a god. Who is to say this one has changed his ways?"

"If Romanian Collectors found Dracula's crypt, they wouldn't be leavin' him behind." Griffin folded his arms against his chest.

"They would be dead," Helene said frankly. "The Drakul are vicious and *enjoy* blood. Griffin, *mon ami*, think of what you are saying."

Griffin sighed in defeat when the others began to chip in.

Alistair spoke up from his position near the door. "A monster so dangerous should not be left unattended in a prison of his own choosing. He could awake at any moment. It is in the best interest of all to involve the Regency Justiciars. A skilled Healer among them may strip the soul from a Revenant with little to no effort. Confine and secure him."

Felipe's low growl rumbled through the cavern and drew a wary glance from the Guardian. The snarling jaguar placed himself between the mages and his flinching wife. Griffin edged away and tugged Helene with him.

Luisa shot Alistair a warning look. "No one will harm Dahlia, Felipe. You have my word on that."

Alistair frowned. "You cannot seriously consider leaving him as he is."

"Whatever his crimes in the past, he was punished for them." Dahlia lifted her chin. "To lock him away in a bottle makes you no better than the Diabolists who enslave us for their use."

"He's a murderer, Dahlia," Justin said. "Look, I don't know what's right, but I know we passed by several dozen bodies on our way here. They're only suggesting for us to take action now before he comes for us instead."

"There is no proof to say he killed these people. Are you saying you are better than a god to punish him for the past?"

"Were you there, young lady? Any manner of creature may have placed this curse, but they certainly were not *my* God," Alistair said dismissively. "He is a danger to all."

Dahlia turned her dark gaze on him. "As a mage, you know there are *many* powers out there. To dismiss one because they are not yours is a foolish mistake."

"As far as I am concerned, there are no other powers. Have we witnessed a recent appearance by Zeus? Shiva? No. The acts of some errant spirit are an insufficient punishment for an inexcusable crime. Nearly two hundred humans murdered by this monster, and you suggest we leave him here."

The argument continued and tempers flared until Luisa broke up the fight with a shrill whistle. "All of you forget one simple thing. We don't have a key and couldn't awaken or disturb him if we wanted to. In the interest of all involved, I have decided it is neither safe nor prudent to abandon him, and we most certainly will not interrupt his sleep. I suggest we continue to catalog and explore the rest of the city for now. I'm sorry, but his fate isn't for *any* of us to decide." She stared daggers at Alistair. "I must report this to the Board. Griffin, may I have Autumn's assistance to send a message to Regent Oliveira?"

"Aye." Griffin sighed in defeat.

Their team's discovery of the tomb marked a victorious accomplishment for Rio. For Griffin, it became another step toward attaining his lifelong dream of going down in history.

And he couldn't wait to tell Aisling. For the first time since his release from prison, he felt the call tugging him home.

~*~

As the days passed, Griffin witnessed a strain to the friendly dynamic between the members of their party. Dahlia and Felipe grew distrustful of Alistair, while Helene became increasingly anxious. Griffin found her pacing in front of the temple, twisting one of her dark braids around her fingers and eyeballing the statue.

"I do not know, Griffin. It is something about this place. A feeling I cannot describe. I feel as if we should leave and never come back," she told him as they huddled on the marble steps. "The statue troubles me."

Behind them, a golden statue of a man in a fighting stance stood as a grim reminder of the entity beyond the doors.

"I feel as if it watches. As if it sees. I cannot sleep at night for fear of what lurks behind this door."

"I don't know if I believe it's a victim of King Midas, Helene. I mean... Why'd he use the gold touch on that poor bastard and kill all of the others in this city? None of it adds up to me, but as Collectors, isn't it our job to unravel the mysteries of the past and discover the truth?"

Helene had no answer, but she avoided the statue and left Griffin to examine it.

Luisa called an end to their discussion by announcing lunch. The hungry group eagerly joined the rest of their growing team back in the main section of the ancient city. Griffin spotted Dahlia and Felipe napping beneath a tree in the orchard, where the vampire curled against the panther.

"Should we wake them to eat?"

Luisa chuckled and shook her head. "Who do you think provided our meat? Come, Justin grilled the gator."

"Anything's better than all the snake we've h—"

Thick smoke billowed in from the city doors, driven by an unnatural gust of biting wind. Balls of flame hurled out of the concealment and exploded against the nearby building.

"Get the Guardian first!" a male voice snarled.

Alistair froze to the spot. His hand rested upon the hilt of his sword, but it was far too late to put the weapon to any use while paralyzed. Waves of the devious magic filtered through the air on magical cords of mana.

Men and women filed into the room from the tunnel, each one adorned with a scarlet cloak. Griffin's blood ran cold when he recognized the preferred color of the Diabolists. Instincts kicked in, driving him to gather his willpower into one defensive spell. A semi-translucent bubble of mana saved the Collectors, although their widespread positions complicated the spell. Alistair stood at the fringe of the shield, just beyond its border. Across the entry chamber, Justin bent near the water spring with a pail of water still clutched in his hand. He'd been paralyzed too.

Luisa gestured with her hands and threw both arms open wide. Stalactites rained from above, and the ground erupted simultaneously beneath the assailants' feet. "Why are you here?"

At the forefront of the attacking group, a female cultist flashed a sinister smile. Golden ringlets danced like a halo around her slim facial features. She looked familiar. And like a horse.

"We've come for Midas. It was awfully kind of you to send us such a nice message. But finding *him* here… That's a bonus," she said, fixing her eyes on Griffin. Her catty smile chilled his blood. "Give MacNeil to us, and perhaps we will allow the rest of you to live."

"And if we don't?" Luisa asked.

She swept a hand at Alistair then Justin. "I will kill these two men. Eventually, your own shield will fail. We have you outnumbered." Her smile broadened to a grin.

Horse-faced bitch, he thought again.

"Don't do it, Luisa. She will kill all of us once she has what she wants," Juliana hissed. She held a cold spell at her fingertips, ready to launch an offensive. The cultist leader was right—their shield couldn't last forever against the fifteen of them.

"Wrong answer," Horse-Face said.

Justin's startled cry echoed over the rocky interior of the cavernous city. Blood stained his shirt in spreading dime-sized spots, and small wounds appeared over his hands and arms. He remained within the throes of the paralyzing spell, his jaw clenched tight.

The blonde woman smiled. "This one has seen many pains over the course of his life. Many scars."

"No, don't. I'll come out, don't do it—" Griffin protested.

She moved her hands like a macabre maestro conducting an orchestra of flesh. A lifetime of nicks, cuts, and minor injuries reversed before their eyes. Justin's body jerked multiple times, each wound inflicted in rapid succession until they were too numerous to count and the spreading red stain soaked his shirt.

Bellowing from pain, Justin collapsed to the ground, released from the spell. Paola shrieked, and Juliana held her back to prevent her from crossing the magical field of protection.

With a labored grunt, Alistair whipped his sword from the scabbard and sliced through the fragile threads of mana connecting the witch's sorcery to his person. He sucked in thirsty gulps of air and charged her with his weapon drawn. He moved too slowly.

A black shadow blurred from atop one of the stone structures and took the leading female to the ground. Her scream gurgled in her throat as Felipe's teeth crushed her windpipe. He moved again without allowing the other cultists a chance to pinpoint his location.

Dahlia whipped around the attacker closest to Luisa and drove his face straight into the ground. His body impacted with a sickening crunch and went limp. The vampire sprang swiftly to the next in an acrobatic display. She swept a pyromancer's feet out from beneath her and pinned her down long enough for Felipe to finish her off with a crushing bite of his jaws.

Griffin nearly flicked the cork from one of his sandstorm vials, but gave it a second consideration. Quickly tucking it back into his vest, he removed a polished, wood-grain sphere instead. Its surface glimmered and shone with an internal light, silver white sparks and purple streaks glittering from within.

Lightning-struck wood was the best conductor for electrical enchantments.

"Get down!" he cried to Juliana.

He pitched it toward the cultists. It exploded into a lightning storm of bolts at their feet, effectively clearing a path towards Justin. That allowed Paola to make a frantic dash for their downed friend.

Before he could follow the Healer and cover her rear, a sweltering globe of Hellfire hurtled toward Helene. Griffin cried out in anguish when the twisting black and purple flames engulfed his longtime friend. He raced toward the shrieking woman to help, only to catch a flicker of movement from the corner of his eye.

Helene's attacker clutched at his throat, a thin red line glittering from ear to ear where blood wept from the clean slice. The illusion decoy vanished, and the true Helene winked from behind the Diabolist, gripping a red-smeared straight razor. She vanished again without a trace. Illusion magic. He should have guessed.

Most the cultists' focus seemed to split between Alistair and Luisa. As the two strongest mages among them, they took heavy hits, pinned down from all sides.

Alistair broke through their shields with a mighty swing of his gladius. The enchanted metal parted the magical barrier like butter, sending fragments of magical essence in every direction. The two mages beyond it only lasted a moment longer as he sliced the arm from one and impaled the other in the belly. When he kicked the second enemy from his sword, the original attacker sank into the earth, appropriately restrained by hundreds of pounds of gravity.

Guttural chants buzzed around the edges of Griffin's hearing. Hidden behind the chaos of the fight, another Diabolist worked in the shadows near the entrance, and the newly dead began to rise once more, animated as demonic corpses filled with Hellish souls. The zombies were a distraction from the true danger, as ruddy light flared in a circle drawn upon the ground. Smoke swirled inside with bright embers, announcing the arrival of a materializing dark shape. The beast within the summoning circle raised its horned head and loosed a deafening roar. Raising a claw-tipped hand, it made a gesture of arcane power toward Luisa.

Griffin jumped in front of Luisa with expectations of shielding her from Hellfire, but the monster had another plan in mind. The curse cut effortlessly through the best shield Griffin had ever formed in all of his life. Better than the spell responsible for saving his life in Egypt.

It struck with a wet crack and split his leg from knee to thigh, sending bits of flesh and bone fragment exploding from the limb. Searing pain overwhelmed his senses. A gush from his artery painted the floor. He collapsed to the ground.

The last thing he heard was the sound of Luisa screaming his name.

Chapter 25

The initial sight of the golden city stole Jean-Luc's breath away. He stood in awe for a moment, his gaze sweeping across the bejeweled architecture, before the reason for his presence brought his attention back to the matters at hand.

"I never believed El Dorado to be a real place." *And I did not dress for the occasion,* Jean-Luc thought with exasperation. The rich black soil of the Amazon stained the leather toes of his expensive shoes.

"Believe me, neither did I," Alistair said.

"Do you have any idea how the cultists found out? I understand you all kept this discovery rather hush hush for the time being."

Alistair shook his head. "As you've discovered yourself, it's hard to know who to trust anymore."

"*Oui.* A sad truth in these troubling times."

"There's more," Alistair informed him. "Having the chance at MacNeil was a bonus, I believe. I wager once the rest of us were dead or incapacitated, they planned to release King Midas from his tomb."

Alistair led him to the main temple over the sweltering pool of lava. They found a native woman sitting cross-legged before the door with an immense panther sprawled beside her. She took one look at Jean-Luc and rose to her feet. Her pet followed closely behind her.

Jean-Luc barely noticed her near naked state of dress, distracted by the golden statue near the doors. It felt wrong, and the shadows seemed to dance around it from the corner of his eye. Something whispered at the edges of his hearing and hinted at the statue being more than some mere bauble.

"Dahlia and Felipe. The panther is a shapeshifter from a local tribe," Alistair said.

"A pleasure," Jean-Luc said. He bowed to both.

"If only it were under better circumstances," Dahlia replied. "You are the Justiciar sent to investigate the attack?"

"*Oui*. What can you tell me about this statue? There seems to be something amiss with it. I cannot quite place the source of the disturbance, but it is something," he said as he circled around it. His gaze slid over Dahlia again when he recognized the same feeling slithered over his back in her presence.

"It is another Revenant like me," she said. "He has been encased within a prison of gold for all eternity."

"Is anyone else aware of this?" Jean-Luc asked.

She shook her head. "I did not know until recently, but it is true. I sense two of my kind here, and this is the weaker one. The other is in the tomb."

"A problem for another time perhaps. He is of no danger to us now." He stepped away from the trapped vampire and moved forward to the doors. "My counterpart is securing the two prisoners you managed to capture, but I am more interested in your take on the attack. Monsieur Fitz?"

Each accounting of the events matched down to the minor details. Jean-Luc discovered the cultists took them by surprise after wiping out the entirety of the camped crew outside. The death of their friends and companions struck a hard blow, and everyone anxiously awaited news about Griffin.

Access to the temple became prohibited by threat of incarceration, and no one argued the edict. Jean-Luc and his team of Guardians, along with a fellow Justiciar, set about securing the site. He had a handful of hours before the chopper returned with support, and two detainees to guard until the inevitable arrival of a dozen more trusted wizards.

He moved off to walk the perimeter and marveled at the beauty of the lost city. His wandering path brought him to the towering gemstone statue of Midas where he paused to study the intricate piece of art.

"Did they send you to judge him again?" Dahlia stepped out of the shadows and approached him slowly.

"I—excuse me?" he asked. "Did who? The Board?"

Dahlia hung away at a distance, resembling an animal on the defensive. He wondered if it was for her comfort or his, then watched her shift with the lean muscles of her legs tightened to bolt.

"It's safe to come closer to speak to me. I can promise you will come to no harm by my hands. Some of my best friends are vampires." In fact, he had even gone on a date with one, spending his time on and off with a vampire elder named Corinna who had no shortage of free time to pursue him over the summer. Unfortunately, she wasn't the woman he truly wanted. He had his eye on another prize, a Grecian beauty with honey-colored hair and violet eyes like the sky at dusk.

Dahlia stopped a few feet away and studied his face with her piercing gaze from beside one of the polished columns. "Did the gods send you to pass judgment upon Midas again for his crimes? You are their harbinger, are you not?"

"I do not know what you mean."

She stepped forward at arm's length and leaned forward, her nostrils flaring as she drew in a deep breath. Her nose crinkled, and her nimble steps quickly carried her beyond his reach. "I smell it in you, their touch. It is a scent all Revenants know. Human blood has a mixture of appeal and revulsion. We want and crave it, but yours is simply…revolting."

He wasn't sure whether to be insulted of thankful. "What does that mean?"

"You are touched by a god," Dahlia said again. Her brows drew together. "You do not know this?"

He shook his head. "You gave me an answer I have searched to find for many years, mademoiselle. Which god?"

She edged closer again and leaned toward him. She inhaled, seeming to fill her lungs with his scent. "I could not tell you which, only that you are one of seven chosen to face the evils of man."

"Thank you, Mademoiselle Dahlia. You have given me a place to start. But, please, tell me why you asked if I would judge him."

She blinked. "The Revenants became as we are because of a punishment by your patrons," she replied, then turned to look back towards the temple behind them. "Midas is one of the original murderers."

Jean-Luc opened his mouth to ask more, but Felipe padded over to join them and bumped his head against Dahlia's leg. According to Alistair, the shifter chose to remain in his animal form due to the attack, serving as an extra set of ears and eyes to keep his companions safe. Instead of pleading for more answers, Jean-Luc bid the pair a good night and excused himself to resume his rounds.

He finally had an answer to his dilemma and a place to start in the search for more.

Chapter 27

Griffin awoke screaming during the emergency flight by chopper to the nearest Vault. Colombian Collectors had responded promptly to the SOS call from Luisa, and their chopper arrived from another site within an hour. Paola spent the entirety of the same hour exerting every ounce of her mana to keep more than a pint of blood in his body.

Physically and emotionally drained, Griffin drifted in and out of a state of consciousness where his warring thoughts pleaded for death and prayed for survival. Eventually, they placed him beneath the effects of magical sedation in lieu of modern drugs.

At one point, Griffin opened his eyes to the sight of a sterile clinical room and his cousin Addison in a nearby chair. The heavy fog of too many pharmaceuticals and mind-clouding magic made it impossible to do more than flutter his eyelids.

"Rest, mate. I'll be right here."

He tried to protest the assertions of his cousin and eventually gave in to oblivion. It surrounded him and dragged him deeper until only the void of unconscious dreams surrounded every fiber of his being. It was bliss and hell all at once, an unending cycle of mental torment, the hiss of snakes, the terror of seeing a friend die before him, and the knowledge that he could have done more.

When Griffin awakened, several hours had turned the hand of the clock on the wall. Addison slumped in the adjacent chair, his head thrown back and mouth open to emit rumbling snores. With a groan, Griffin wriggled the toes of his left foot. His foot didn't respond, but the attempt sparked an eruption of pain. It traveled like electric jolts up and down the leaden limb beneath the blanket.

"Griff?" Addison stirred and groggily eased forward. He rubbed at his eyes in exhaustion. "Thank the Goddess... You scared the shit out of me. Out of all of us. Your Director only left a moment ago."

"My leg—"

"Still there. I wouldn't allow them to take it," Addison told him swiftly.

Take it. The world seemed to stop, as did his ability to breathe properly. The news snatched the rug from beneath him, and yet he could only lie in his sickbed staring at the solemn expression of his cousin. "They…they want to take m'leg?"

"They do," Addison told him honestly. He leaned closer toward the bed and lowered his voice. "But I told them that's rubbish, and they'd better do everything within their power to save it and to put in overtime if they had to. It's been two days."

"I've…been out two days?"

"You have."

Griffin reached for the blanket, but Addison stilled his hand with a touch and shook his head.

"How bad is it?" Griffin asked.

"I won't lie to you. It's…it's bad, Griff. You saved Director Mendoza's life, that's for bloody certain."

"What about the others?"

Addison cleared his throat. "I'm sorry, mate. There were a number of losses, but the others drove them off. Justiciar Chevalier told me it's likely the Diabolists didn't expect your Wakani friends."

Griffin let his head fall back against the pillow, and he shut his eyes. "Justin?"

"Paola tried to save him, but it was too late for that. Alberto, too, and the small group with him. The rest of your teammates survived."

No matter how Griffin tried to assure himself it could have been worse, it did little to lift the guilt weighing upon his conscience. As far as he knew, Justin's children were all adults with their own lives and now without a father.

"He's awake?" Aisling rushed into the hospital room.

Griffin's heart leapt to his throat. In a matter of seconds, he noted every difference in her features down to the most minute change. How long her hair had grown, the fullness of her breasts, and the tired circles beneath her eyes.

Addison rubbed his neck and glanced aside. "I'll be outside. I smell coffee calling my name."

Griffin barely heard him. He couldn't look away from her. "You came here."

"Of course I came, as soon as Luisa sent me a wisp." She moved closer and smoothed her hand over his brow. "I've been here for hours."

"Why?" His voice cracked.

Aisling's features softened, her expression almost too tender for him to bear. "Because I love you, Griffin, and this is where I needed to be. Where I *wanted* to be. I know you asked for time. I know you felt as if you couldn't come home, but it's been long enough."

"I don't know if I deserve you anymore. Look what I brought on us. On everyone."

What if Aisling and their children had only been safe for all of this time because he'd been away from them?

What if what happened at the dig site happened to them next?

Cold washed through his veins. He tilted his head back against the pillow and closed his eyes. "I missed you so much. After we returned from El Dorado, I was going to come home to visit at the least. I swear it. I wanted to bring you back something gold and tell you about the city. Think more about what the hell we're going to do now."

"I don't care about the city," she said in a thick voice. "Only you. Griffin, I... We almost lost you."

"That's just the problem. If you had been there. If they had gone after you..." His pulse spiked, and a cold sweat beaded against his brow.

"Shh." She leaned down and kissed him.

"But—"

"Please come home," she whispered. "We need you, all of us. We're stronger together."

"Do they know me?" he asked after a few moments of silence. "Will I be a stranger to them?"

"Only if you stay away."

Their conversation lasted a few minutes until his pain became too much for her to bear. Unwilling to watch him suffer, Aisling leaned outside to call a nurse Healer. One hurried in to administer more drugs, and Griffin slipped into the oblivion of sleep.

Chapter 28

Candles in silver holders burned on the hotel dresser, scenting the air with beeswax. Soft music played, turned too low to be heard over the energetic pair on the bed. The luxurious comforter and extravagant bed sheets hung askew from the mattress beneath them.

"Is that the best you can do? You fucked me harder than that last time," Mercedes teased.

Her companion yanked a handful of her hair, wrapped it around his fist, and tugged until her body bent. Tears moistened the corners of her eyes.

It was the same story each time, whenever the two met. She taunted and belittled him, and in return, he gave her the sex she craved. He knew what she needed, and he never failed to please.

"Better than the sniveling quim you took for a husband, isn't it?" he practically snarled against her ear.

She whimpered and strained against his possessive grip to little avail. Inciting his anger was always the best part. "I do not know... Griffin had his moments as a husband. I still remember the taste of his co—"

Hair strands snapped with the next merciless yank of her head. Her cry became a low moan of pleasure as he mounted her again from behind.

"Nobody fucks you better than I do. Especially not some pissant Scot."

He went on to prove his assertion, and the room became filled with panted breaths and pained ecstasy. Welts from his favorite toy crisscrossed her body, gleaming angry red beneath the flickering candlelight.

"You're mine, Mercedes. Sworn in blood before the only Lord who counts. Don't ever fucking forget it," he rasped against her ear. He left her on the bed to recover in peace while he showered.

When he strode back into the room, Mercedes pushed onto her elbows to greet him with bright eyes and a sultry half smile. "Soon we'll be together at last. The fool is nearly ready to become a proper vessel." She sighed as her fingers crawled over the perfect body of the man to whom she belonged. Once he reclined beside her, she inched her fingers down his chiseled abdomen, and then curled them around the sleeping flesh of his manhood in an effort to rekindle its need.

"A shame I never had the chance to spoil his whore during our school days. A greater shame none of our attempts to kill the little bitch have gone to plan."

"I've tried to the best of my ability, Michael. There is no killing her. Not while the sidhe guard her so thoroughly."

Michael rolled to his back and pulled her atop him. "Doesn't matter. After what you had him do last year, there's no reuniting them. How is Griffin anyways?"

"Alive, but only barely. You need to tell your men to take better care. They could have killed him. Ruined all of our plans. Years of work down the drain if he had died."

"I can't control them from Manhattan, baby."

"You are a Planeswalker. You cross into Hell and the beyond. Put the fear of Lucifer and our Lord into them if you must. If Griffin died, our work will have been in vain. All my time apart from you would be for nothing." Fear of another long separation upset her most of all, and it was a very real possibility if they were forced to prepare another spineless lamb.

"Our Lord will have his host, have no doubt. But first, we have to get rid of that bastard, Rhydderch. None of us could have imagined he'd survive each encounter we've thrown at him."

"About that… I had time to perfect the formula. Griffin was the ideal test." Mercedes rolled to her side and reached for the bag on the floor. She offered a tightly corked bottle of pale amber liquid to her bed partner. "Diluted in wine, it should have an immediate effect. Once the girl has a few sips, she will kill whoever is nearest to her. They will know she was poisoned, but I think the immediate death of a Regent requires the sacrifice of all subtlety."

"You're brilliant, baby."

She smiled coquettishly at him and traced her fingers along his chest. He reciprocated by teasing his fingers over the slick cleft between her legs. Mercedes twisted and raised her hips into his touch, rewarded by the deep press of his fingers.

"We will succeed, Michael. We'll get all of them."

Chapter 29

Griffin remained in the hospital for weeks before they allowed him to go home. Aisling was there for most of it, leaving his side only to mother their children.

He couldn't wait to meet them, but a hospital made for a poor place to have their first impression of him. For their sake, he pleaded with her not to bring them to him.

He received the first spot of bad news while Aisling was away overnight in Ireland tending to the twins. A stoic-faced doctor entered, a Healer with traditional medical training as well. She spoke with a gentle voice, touching his hand when she sat beside him in the nearby chair.

"There's no easy way to say this, Mr. MacNeil, but we've done everything we can for you at this point. We know the esteemed Regent Rhydderch forbid us to remove the leg during your sedation, but it simply cannot be saved."

"What do you mean? When I came here, it resembled minced meat, and now it looks like a leg again to me. What's the problem?"

Griffin glanced under the sheets at the whole limb beneath it. A long, jagged scar ran from the middle of his left thigh to his knee, but the leg was functional.

The doctor gazed at him with compassionate eyes. "Although magic has mended the bones and healed your flesh, a curse lingers in your marrow, sir. For lack of a better way to describe it, I would call this a malignant, magical cancer."

"So this is the source of my pain now?"

The Healer nodded. "It is. And you'll always be in pain until the curse spreads and consumes the marrow in the rest of your bones. And you die. It's taken me many weeks and consults with other doctors to pinpoint what's happening, but according to your x-rays, this thing has grown. It will continue to grow until it runs its course."

The world dropped out from beneath Griffin. It hit him like a punch to the gut, taking the wind from his lungs. He couldn't speak, couldn't breathe. He stared at her and struggled with her diagnosis until his tongue finally cooperated. "I'm dying?" It left him in a hoarse whisper.

"Yes."

"How far will you have to remove?"

The doctor gestured to his hip. "As high as possible. There are small strands reaching toward the pelvis. Had we removed it weeks ago, perhaps we could have salvaged—"

"You want to take the entire thing?" he blurted.

She nodded.

"No."

"Mr. MacNeil, we ask you to consider—"

"Not until I've had a second opinion."

Even in their world of magic, the loss of a limb was an irreversible procedure.

When Aisling returned, he put on a smile for her and kept the news to himself, unwilling to spoil her mood.

"Are you ready to go home?" she asked, jubilant and rosy-cheeked.

"More than ready."

Enough that he didn't argue when they brought a wheelchair for him. The trip through the Portal to Ireland and the ride to the O'Brien Estate passed in a hazy blur thanks to a generous dose of medication. Griffin stirred awake when the hired car pulled into the drive.

"Don't wheel me in," he begged. "Let me greet them on my feet."

"Griff, there's no shame—"

"Please, dove. Give me this."

"All right. C'mon, then." She helped him from the van and gave him the crutches provided by the hospital.

The cool weather and the overcast sky implied a rainstorm would sweep through the evening.

Fiona met them at the door, and Griffin felt another rush of shame when his mother wrapped her arms around him. He'd pushed everyone away, terrified they'd be hurt because of him.

"Welcome home, son."

"Thanks, Mum. Love you."

She squeezed him tighter before letting him go. "Come on inside. I have tea ready, and Hektor went up to check on the twins."

"Hektor's here?" He swiveled his gaze toward Aisling and raised his brows.

"He is," Ash replied. "Seems you did more in Egypt than fight a sphinx." Her eyes misted over a little, and she sniffed. "You gave me back a father."

She deserved more, he thought. The manor was quiet and empty without Ceara's feisty presence. Her death had been another thing he missed while in prison.

Mercedes had taken so much from him. His firstborn, the birth of the twins, and even his chance to say goodbye to a woman he respected.

The short walk from the front door to the family room took every ounce of willpower and strength he possessed. Griffin sank down on the sofa and exhaled a pent breath.

Aisling gazed at him in concern.

"I'll be fine, I promise. Need to catch my breath, is all."

"You're sure?"

"Aye. Go fetch the little ones. I'm fine."

Aisling hesitated a moment, but his smile seemed to reassure her and she disappeared around the corner. Griffin shifted on the couch, rubbed his sweaty palms against his pants, and swallowed back the nervous lump forming in his throat.

"What if they don't like me, Mum?"

"They're babies, Griffin. They love everyone."

"But they don't know me. I'm a stranger to them."

Fiona moved closer and laid her hand over the knee of his uninjured leg. "Those babies have had a picture of you in their room since they were born, Griffin. Your face isn't unknown to them. Now wipe that worried look off your face. I hear them coming."

Childish giggles floated down the hallway. A blond-haired boy ran into the room, hands in the air and a grin on his plump face. He hit the carpet, tripped, and pushed right back to his feet again without a fuss. Aisling followed a few steps behind with their daughter in her arms and Hektor behind her.

"Liam, look who's here," she called down.

Their son stopped his precarious toddling race across the room and turned around.

Griffin couldn't stop staring at him. "Hello, Liam."

The toddler retreated toward his mother and grabbed a fistful of her skirt, peeking around her legs.

"It's all right," Ash encouraged with a smile. "Who is that with your grams? Do you know, Rhiain?"

They were both beautiful, each with a thick head of strawberry blond curls and pale green eyes. Griffin blinked away the burning behind his lids.

Liam wandered over first, but Rhiain clung when her mother tried to set her down. So Aisling compromised and took a seat near Griffin instead, settling the child in her lap.

"They're not talking yet, of course, beyond a few words," Aisling said.

Liam plucked at Griffin's pants and giggled. "Da."

The single word broke open the flood gates. Warm tears leaked down Griffin's cheeks, hastily wiped away as he smiled down at his son for the first time.

"You want to come here and sit with me, wee lad?"

Contrary to his sibling's shyness, Liam allowed Griffin to lift him onto his right knee. He remained for a time, babbling and chatting in nonsensical baby talk, then scooted away to bring his father a toy.

Breda slunk in and watched Griffin from across the room. Unlike Aisling, the silver feline exhibited no signs of forgiveness, but at least she hadn't growled at him.

"I'll go help Hektor in the kitchen," Fiona said. Before Griffin could respond, she hightailed it from the living room.

With some gentle coaxing and patience, Rhiain sat down beside Griffin on the couch and played with a pair of plush fairy dolls. By the end of the afternoon, she'd crawled into his lap and fallen asleep.

"Here, I'll take her so we can go eat." Aisling picked their slumbering daughter up with practiced ease and moved her to a nearby playpen where her brother was already snoring beside Breda.

"Look at them, so big now. I'm sorry I wasn't there, sprite."

"Not your fault," Aisling reminded him.

"Still, it was selfish of me to stay away so long afterward. I was afraid I'd make it all worse." In a quieter voice he added, "Still am afraid."

"They'll have to bring an army if they want to get you through these wards," Aisling replied.

Griffin had his doubts. He'd seen their army already up close and personal, and her assurance did little to soothe his concerns.

A sudden weakness overcame Griffin on the way to the dining room. He stumbled, but Hektor's reflexes put him in the right place to steady him.

"What happened?" Fiona asked, fretting. "Are you all right?"

"I'm fine, Mum. Just a little weak. Healers told me it'll be a while before I've got all the strength back," he lied.

They celebrated his return with a huge lunch thrown together by Hektor and Fiona, and when the twins awakened from their naps, Griffin took his first steps without the aid of his crutch. Aisling found one of Ceara's old canes for him to use instead, allowing Liam to lead his father around the garden outside. Ireland's autumn dusk arrived early, and before the sun set, Fiona and Hektor bid him a fond farewell.

His mother hugged him tightly and kissed his face. "I won't be far if either of you need anything."

Griffin hugged her back. "I know, Mum."

"And the same is true of me," Hektor added. "If either of you need anything, and I do mean anything, be sure to let me know."

Once his mother and Aisling's father left the premises, a sense of nostalgia swept over him. It wasn't quite the same without Ceara there to guide him to her foyer or serve tea and cookies.

And he hated the Rivera family even more for denying him the chance to say goodbye to her.

"Ash?"

"Yes?"

"I'm sorry I wasn't here for you when Ceara passed."

Aisling's smile wavered, and moisture gleamed in her eyes. "She never stopped believing in you, Griff. Should have seen all the letters she wrote to Regent Oliveira."

"I believe it."

"Would you like to help me tuck them in or go put your feet up?"

Griffin grunted. "I'm not an invalid. I can lift a child."

Aisling leaned over and kissed his cheek. "I never said you were."

"You've been shooing me toward that chair the entire evening."

Liam came to him readily with upraised arms, and Griffin lifted him from the floor. Together, he and Ash took the twins to their nursery and tucked them into bed.

Within moments, the twins slept peacefully, their angelic features a perfect blend of their fair-skinned mother and blond father. He kissed Rhiain's brow and then the little boy in the adjacent crib. A son. He never imagined having a son.

"Luisa had some of your things sent over. I've put them in the bedroom already."

"I can sleep on the co—"

"You'll do no such thing." Aisling turned around and faced him. "This is our home, Griffin. Ours. You'll sleep in a proper bed. So you can either come to the bedroom on your own two feet or be thrown into it by a spell. Your choice."

His brows shot up. "You're adorable when you get bossy. And a little sexy too. Mostly sexy."

She blinked, her stern expression melting away into a shy smile. "Please come to our room?"

"*We* don't have a room," he pointed out, trying not to grin. "Because last I remember, Ceara was adamant about me sleeping in the guest room."

Aisling scrunched her nose. "Well, we have one now, and as you can see, the guest room became the nursery."

He grinned. "Don't know if I trust it. To be honest I wouldn't put it past her to curse the house against premarital hanky panky."

Her fingers skimmed against his chest as she stepped in closer, the gesture more an act of comfort than flirtatious. She looked up at him with concern in her eyes. "Is that what you're worried about?"

Griffin shook his head. "Only slightly. I think it's safe to say I've faced worse things than a stern granny's anti-intercourse jinxes."

"Come to bed," she said again. "No pressure for anything else. Perhaps it's selfish of me, but I miss having you beside me."

"All right."

She led him down the hall to her old bedroom.

"You didn't take Ceara's room?"

Aisling shook her head. "It didn't feel right, and mine is big enough."

"Thank God. Don't need the spirit of your gran watching me sleep."

Aisling swatted him.

It spite of all that had gone wrong, it felt good to joke again. His smile faded slightly as they stepped into her old room, and he saw his travel bags nearby.

"Remember that time I snuck through the window, and Ceara's hex blew me back onto the grass?"

"She never did believe you were only there to tell me about something you'd read in one of your study books." She laughed and moved across the room to draw the curtains. "We started meeting in the garden after that."

He glanced around suspiciously. "I really was innocent that time. And you wonder why I don't trust this house." He poked the curtains then gingerly sat on the edge of the bed, prepared for the worst. When nothing happened, he relaxed.

"I've your ring on my finger this time, so I'm certain you're quite safe."

"I really messed up your wedding plans, didn't I?"

Aisling sat beside him and took his hand between her palms. "No. Mercedes messed up *our* wedding plans. And the great thing about plans, Griffin, is that they can be rescheduled again. We'll have our wedding, and nothing will stop us this time."

~*~

THE COLLECTOR'S TREASURE

Patience was a virtue Aisling kept in abundance, but Griffin put hers to the test with his trips to Vaults all over the world in search of new opinions on his leg. Each time he returned home, he wore the same dejected expression on his face.

He wasn't the same man she remembered. She'd hoped having him home would bring back his smile.

"No luck in China?" she asked as she welcomed him inside and took his coat.

Griffin shook his head.

Her stomach hardened, and somehow, she managed to hide her trembling hands from him. She'd made it her duty to be the optimistic one, the supportive fiancée who encouraged him to do what he felt was best. But her energy was waning, and she didn't know how much longer she could carry on without breaking down. "I've been exploring prosthetics," she ventured while guiding him to the living room. "You would still be able to do some field work…"

"Nae, it's not the same. I don't want to be the man who flies in after something's been found by others. I may as well work at a desk."

"I know it's not as exciting, but it's still related to the work you love."

Griffin leaned over and kissed her brow, and Aisling's heart knotted up. Something seemed off in the gesture, waves of melancholy and fear rolling off of him.

"That's not my concern now, Ash."

"Please tell me what's going on in that head of yours. Don't bottle it up."

"I didn't want to worry all of you until I had it confirmed, but the curse is spreading. There's no cure in this realm able to reverse a demonic curse. I scheduled the operation today with Chief Healer Snow in Manhattan. They'll be ridding me of this thing next week, but…"

"What?"

"It may be too late."

Icy fingers tracked down her spine. "What do you mean by that? How much has it spread?"

"It's spreading through the bone in my leg, and it's aggressive. To my hip now. Removing my leg may not save me at all. Maybe it will, maybe it won't. Won't know until they've tried."

The world around her spun in a dizzying blur that threatened to pitch her to the ground. She dropped to the couch before her knees could give out. "No, there has to be something. Every curse has a cure. We just have to keep looking. I'll go through all my books again. I'll petition the sidhe queens for help."

He shook his head. "Summer won't answer, and Queen Morrigan will ask for one of your firstborns. I wouldn't trade myself for the twins or you. My life isn't worth your bondage."

A horrible feeling of helplessness made her sick to her stomach. They'd lost too much time already, and now their future could end in an instant.

"There's one possibility," Griffin said in a quiet voice.

"But you said there was nothing."

"Nothing but this, and it's not an option I'll ever take." He reached into his jacket pocket to produce a square of folded parchment. "One of the nurses must have planted it on my bedside table in the hospital. I woke up to find it beneath my water glass."

Aisling unfolded the note.

MacNeil,

By this time, you've seen the power we wield and understand the Master is capable of all things. No one is beyond his reach. Join us or perish. Your time is short.

The clock is ticking. Choose wisely or die.

Choose wisely or die. The words echoed through her thoughts. "Why didn't you tell us about this?" Her voice shook, and her fingers trembled around the letter.

"It wouldn't have changed anything. You see what this means, don't you? They cursed me to force my hand."

"But why? Why do they want you so badly?"

Griffin snapped his fingers, sending up a harmless plume of black fire. "Because I can do this."

She pressed her lips together in a disapproving line. "So could Addison if he ever truly wished to."

"But he hasn't, not once in his entire life. Besides, he has a bloody dragon for a conscience, so they'd never be able to sway him and they know it. Why bother? Me on the other hand, I've been in trouble before."

"Trouble and evil don't go hand in hand," she said.

He shrugged. "I see it as another tool in my arsenal, but Addison thinks it's evil magic. And we both know I've studied more of the black arts than most mages."

"Out of curiosity."

"Out of curiosity," he agreed. "But I know them. I'd never use them, but I know them. I know how to turn a man inside out and how to summon a greater demon with a sheet of paper. Why shouldn't they want me?"

She wanted nothing more than to point out flaws in his logic, but she had no valid argument to make. No matter how much she wanted him to be wrong, she knew Griffin was correct about his knack for black magic.

"Then we go to New York together. I'm not going to let you go through surgery alone. I want to be there."

"All right. Then we can all go. Besides, it's time for the twins to meet Lachlan. I'm a wee bit old to have a Faerie godfather, and it's time to pass the torch to the twins. If you'll have him. Turns out he's in New York City now. He phoned to tell me he wasn't so fond of the weather in California. Addison let him open shop in Manhattan, and Maddie's there too."

"I'd love that," she said quietly. "It would bring me comfort to know they're protected."

He loosed a relieved sigh. "Thanks, Ash."

"No, Griff, thank *you*."

Chapter 30

The following evening, Griffin sat alone on the sofa with his leg propped upon a pillow, sweat beading at his brow. His condition had taken a turn for the worst overnight, and he'd been overcome by excruciating pain. It had ruled his day from start to finish until he'd begged off of playtime and retreated to the sitting room.

Within the hour, Aisling approached to offer him a mug of foul-smelling potion to help with his pain. Moisture glistened in the corners of her red-rimmed eyes, and he knew without a doubt she'd cried over her cauldron.

"Why do you have to be such a drain on everyone, Griffin? How am I to raise two babies and care for you at the same time?"

He stared up at her and took in several quick shallow breaths. "A drain? Is that what you really think of me? I'm a drain on you now?"

Her expression changed, fine wrinkles deepening between her dark brows. "What? No! I'd never say such a thing. You get that foul thought out of your head right this moment, Griffin MacNeil. You've never been a drain."

"I heard you. You said it right there to my face!"

Her lashes fluttered as moisture gleamed against her eyes. "I said I have an *idea*. A way to save your leg if you were willing to hear me out."

"I... really?"

He was losing his mind. That could be the only explanation for what he'd heard, what he knew she'd said to him moments ago. The pain had finally driven him completely crazy. "I'm sorry," he whispered. "I'm hearing things."

Aisling watched him for a moment, then the tension eased from her shoulders. She nodded. "You're in pain. Drink this, please."

He took the drought without complaint, grimacing at the taste but chasing it down with the water she offered next. "I know you're trying your best, but we've been over this. I've seen some of the best Healers. Even visited Kryssie's mum." The bone-deep pain resumed at a low throb, aching behind the kneecap and spreading upward. Sometimes the discomfort radiated as a muscular ache, and sometimes it became a merciless drilling sensation pounding throughout his entire thigh.

"I thought… Luisa has a son, y'know. Nearly as old as us. Seein' them together gave me hope one day I'd be reunited with Mara. Even if I live to see her next birthday, they wouldn't allow me to see her anyway."

"You'll see her again, Griffin. We'll find a way to appeal. But first we need to do something about your leg."

"We are doing something. Lopping it off."

"But if we can save it, or at the very least, more of it before your surgery date?"

He didn't think it was possible, but Aisling's fervent expression made him bite back his retort and sigh. "What do you want to try?"

Aisling leaned forward and peered at him with a solemn gaze. "I want to find a unicorn."

He threw his head back and laughed. She had always been his dreamer, but this idealistic plot seemed too whimsical for even her standards. "That's rich, lass. Now what's your real plan?"

"I mean it," she said with a wounded expression. "Jack spoke of them to me once when I was feeling poorly and fat as a whale."

"Oh? Was he planning to find a mystical unicorn midwife to deliver the twins?" Griffin snorted and shook his head in disbelief.

She waggled a finger in his face. "You've fought serpents and a sphinx. Why not believe in unicorns? Griff, if I could find one, I could save your leg."

"I don't think anyone so pure of heart exists anymore, Ash. The last unicorn sighting in this plane was over two centuries ago. The Greeks killed the last one for her horn and plucked the feathers from the last pegasus. There's no more."

"Jack thinks otherwise."

"Jack is a storyteller, and you're chasing a fairytale," Griffin said. "Don't get your hopes up over a fantasy."

"Don't you see? I have to try. I can't lose you. Not again."

When Griffin opened his mouth to speak, Aisling cut him off. Her lips molded over his, and a single breath-stealing kiss vanquished the niggling worries dominating his thoughts.

For one moment, it was as if nothing had ever changed. It was coming up for air after spending minutes beneath water, only to realize how close he'd come to drowning. He drew Aisling close against him and into his lap. The sweet taste of her mouth overwhelmed his senses.

For one moment, everything was exactly as it should have been. He loathed the thought of letting her go. So he didn't.

"Let's hunt for your unicorn, then."

"Thank you. I know it's a long shot, but I have this week to try, and who better to ask about unicorns than another fae? Maybe Lachlan knows something."

"All right, since we're headed there anyway. But like you said, we can't wait any longer. Surgery is at the end of the week."

Aisling nodded and leaned in to feather tender kisses across his jaw. "That's all I'm asking. I'm—"

The phone rang, Aisling stepped away with reluctance to answer it. Griffin leaned his head back against the cushions and closed his eyes. He didn't hold a single hope for a miracle, but he didn't have the heart to tell her to give up the idea. If it gave her some peace, then he would let her question every Faerie in New York, just to keep the light in her eyes.

"Griffin, that was Healer Snow."

"Did something change about the operation?"

"No, nothing like that. She called to let you know that you'd have company in the Healer's ward."

Only one person came to mind. Addison. One of the two cousins was always in the hospital, as if their family was cursed to spend more time recovering than living.

Griffin sighed. "What's the big git gone and gotten himself into this time? Didn't he cause enough ruckus in the city?"

"Apparently not. She says he was stabbed and rushed to the Vault."

"What?" He struggled to his feet, willing to embrace the pain for his favorite cousin.

Aisling nodded, expression solemn. "It was an assassination attempt."

Griffin swore and checked his watch. He had the Portal schedule memorized and their time was limited if they wanted to make the next round. "S'pose we better be on our way then. We've got forty minutes until the Portal to Manhattan."

~*~

Evening in Ireland became afternoon in New York once Griffin led his family through the Portal. An inquiry at the Healer's ward revealed Addison was in no condition for visitors. They'd be contacted as soon as he was stabilized and awake.

They headed out to Lachlan's shop and knocked on the door moments after the sidhe dog reopened from his lunch break.

He seemed genuinely surprised to see them but no less welcoming, and though they had never met him, Liam and Rhiain immediately became entranced by their new friend. The two children wanted to touch and play with everything in his shop.

"Come to transfer your bond, have you? About damned time," Lachlan said.

Griffin glanced from Aisling to the Faerie hound. "How'd you know?"

"Just a hunch."

"Will you do it?"

"Or miss out on a two-for-one deal? What kind of fae do you take me for?"

With the consent of both parents, Lachlan terminated his twenty-six year bond to Griffin and transferred his guardianship to the twins. When Aisling passed him the toddlers, he held a child in each arm and grinned as if she'd gifted him a million dollars.

The children giggled and reached up with grabby hands for Lachlan's face. Rhiain caught his nose and Liam tugged on his long, elflike ear, earning laughter from all the adults. The magic surrounding them mesmerized both children. They clapped their hands and babbled.

For Griffin, the loss of his bond to his Faerie godfather left an uncomfortable void, filled only by the pleasure of knowing Lachlan would give them the same guidance and protection.

"I'm going to be the envy of every fae in Avalon, having these two in my charge."

"I'll never understand the fascination your kind have with mortal children. What the hell do you get from it?"

"Remember, these two carry the blood of Merlin and my kind as well, you blond git. Soon as you get Mara back, I'll get to add nymph to that list as well. It's like stamp collecting."

"You had better not trade them."

"Pfft. I wouldn't do that to you. Besides, it'd have to be for something feckin' good. Like my own island…"

"Not giving you my island."

"Damn."

"I suppose you two are off to see your clumsy oaf of a cousin. Any chance you'd leave these wee ones with me for a bit?"

Aisling glanced at Griffin. He eyed Lachlan, feeling a surge of skepticism. "Why?"

"No big reason."

"What small reason?" Aisling asked.

Caught by his own inability to lie, Lachlan sighed. "The ladies love babies. I'll sell more trinkets with these two smiling at everyone who wanders in. Besides, they'll be bored to tears at the Vault."

Aisling's eyes glittered with interest. Griffin stepped back and let her continue their deal, aware of when mischief was on her mind.

"Fair enough," she said, "but only if you'll help me with something first."

"Oh, sure. What is it?"

"I'd like to know where I can find a unicorn."

Lachlan stared at her.

Griffin sighed. "Like I said before to you, they're all gone."

"Actually, no. They're not."

Aisling's entire body tensed, then she whipped around toward the hound. "You've seen one? Really?"

"Yeah. I was starved for a good meal, so I took a jaunt through Gaia a few days ago. Saw one then. Spooked her, and she charged me. Just funny you should ask now."

"I've a notion I can save Griffin's leg if I find one. His operation is in a few days. Can you help me?"

Lachlan studied the pair of them while he bounced the twins.

"I don't go through Gaia if I can help it. A little warm this time of year." He grinned wide, revealing too many of his sharp, canine teeth.

"Not even for Griffin?" she pressed. "You won't help him?"

"Never said I wouldn't help. Besides, I'm like a minotaur in a china shop when I'm on those paths, lass. On top of that, unicorns are a prey animal, and if she sees me again, she'll take off with her wee one."

Aisling's face fell.

"But I know someone who can take you through, and I'm fairly certain she'll say yes."

Lachlan passed Liam over to Griffin to free up one arm and scribbled an address down on a notepad. "Go here. It's a place called the Dryad's Arbor. A nice half-nymph named Saraia owns the place, and since she's rather close to your cousin, I'm sure she'll do you a good turn."

"Thank you!" Aisling leaned up and kissed Lachlan's scruffy cheek. "Thank you so much."

"Everything is falling together," Griffin murmured.

Aisling stood on her tiptoes and kissed him. "Visit your cousin and send him my love. I'm going to find Saraia."

Chapter 31

Fallen chairs littered the floor of the empty dining room. Both patrons and employees vacated the premises after the attack to wait until police arrived on scene.

With Addison rushed off for emergency surgery and his attacker secured, the crime scene had become a bustle of activity.

"What a mess," Jean-Luc said. "Who has dessert for breakfast?"

Shattered glass, broken plates, and clumps of cheesecake littered the floor beside a single overturned table. Blood stained the fine carpet in a discolored patch.

"Brunch," one of the Guardians clarified. "They have all sorts of fancy crap here, looking at the menu. Besides, don't you French eat sweets at all hours?"

Jean-Luc grunted. "Crepes are not desserts. Anyway, what happened here? Why did she attack?"

"The waitstaff said they only saw Miss Worthington leave once for the bathroom during dessert. Their waiter said they were very tense at the start. Then he comes back, and they're laughing like old friends." Georgia, a young New York City Guardian, said.

"And who was she to him? A date?" Jean-Luc asked.

Georgia shook her head. "No, he's still close to Saraia as far as the rest of us know. It was a business meeting regarding the treatment of the Sylvan in New England."

"I see. Then let us divide the work for efficiency. You and you," he said while pointing out two Guardians, "review the tapes, if you have not already. Georgia and I shall peruse the floor and kitchens. You are good at sensing magical disturbances, yes?"

"I am," she confirmed.

Once Georgia stepped away from the main floor, Jean-Luc took the opportunity to use his disturbing but unique skill set. He tuned out all distractions and let his senses spread out.

The scent of fear hung heavily in the air. Like a caress, it skimmed his senses and told him much about the atmosphere of the restaurant in the moments before their arrival. A woman and her husband of many years had occupied an adjacent table. The supernatural echo of her terrified screams rang in his ears. He inhaled and breathed it in like a child picking roses on a midsummer's day.

He couldn't see into the past, but he could feel the psychic impression left by the trauma. Rhydderch's near murder had gouged a wound so deep, it would take weeks before the Umbra—also known as the Otherworld or spiritual plane—settled again. It would remember the assault and the anger behind it, sending ripples of violence echoing across the restaurant and influencing diners and waitstaff alike.

Addison's fear remained the most potent in the room, laced with the bitter notes of rage left by the attacker. Jean-Luc closed his eyes and allowed his inhuman senses to spread without limit until he became enveloped in a shadowed plane and the remnants of past events.

He heard three dozen murmuring voices, the *tinks* of glasses, and felt the sharp tang of Claudia Worthington's fury. Beneath it, he tasted the most brilliant morsel of terror.

The darkest echoes centered over the bloody section of floor. Everywhere else, faded specters moved away from the disturbance and dispersed throughout the gloomy surroundings.

A startled feminine gasp and a colorful flicker from the corner of his eye interrupted his concentration. He turned to discover the startled gaze of Krystine Iamides upon him.

"How did you do that?" she asked in a hushed voice.

"Any word on the Regent?" Georgia called as she returned to the dining floor.

"He's alive," Krystine replied. Her violet eyes remained large and trained on his face. "Healer Snow is with him, and the only word I have so far is that she's optimistic."

"I'll let the others know." Georgia ducked out again.

"Are you all right?" Jean-Luc studied her anxious features and offered out a handkerchief.

"I needed to see…to look at it and make sure…"

He moved away from the table and put himself in her path, blocking her view of the mess behind him. "No, this was your friend, and you belong at his side. Let someone else do the work this time, *cherie*."

"It wasn't for work." She let out a shaky breath and closed her eyes. "I *saw* what would have happened if the attempt had succeeded. I can't get it out of my head. I thought if I came here and looked at the room…"

He placed his hands on her shoulders and gave a gentle squeeze. "That you could forget the vision and see the reality. I'm sorry. I didn't know you carried such a burden, Krystine."

She opened her eyes and offered him a flimsy smile, barely needing to tilt her head to meet his gaze. "Don't go all soft on me, Jean-Luc. I won't know what to do with myself."

"I'll get back to ordering you away next time, I promise." He steered her away from the mess and back toward the doors. "As for now, you should go to Addison and be strong for him. That is *your* job. This is our job."

His encouraging words returned the straight posture to her spine. He gave her arms another supportive squeeze and then reached up to carefully fix her smudged makeup with a subtle sweep of his thumb beneath her eye.

"Go on," he coaxed.

Jean-Luc couldn't pinpoint the exact time when their professional relationship transitioned to friendship. Was it the many times they crossed paths while he investigated the rise of the Diabolists in France? Or was it the multiple occasions spent in her company while at the O'Brien mansion to visit Aisling during Griffin's imprisonment in Spain? Their mutual attraction grew, but an awful series of events had discouraged him from seeking romantic involvement with her.

Either she wasn't single or his life had been turned upside down by a new development in his caseload. She'd gone from dating Regent Rhydderch to some smarmy, alcoholic lieutenant working at the Manhattan Vault.

He watched her walk away, certain she deserved better.

"Guys. I found something, and you're going to wanna see it," Georgia called from the narrow corridor leading to the public restroom.

The tiled bathroom wall revealed a magical tear only arcane vision could discern. They determined something, or someone, had come through by unnatural means. Jean-Luc's team rushed to the manager's office to review a different security feed with view of the restroom door. Roughly an hour into the date, a fellow dressed in the appropriate waiter's garb exited the restroom and casually ambled into kitchen. None of them could recall seeing a man of the same appearance enter the restroom, no matter how far they rewound the footage.

"You cannot see his face from this angle," Jean-Luc muttered.

"You think he knew that when he came through?" another Guardian asked while scratching his blond head.

"Hell yeah, he did, Frank," Georgia said. "Look. He has something in his hand—"

The footage distorted. Appropriate security video resumed after five minutes of cream-colored screen. Everything carried on as normal. They saw the Rhydderch table's waiter emerge from the kitchen bearing their chosen dessert, wine, and a steaming porcelain cup of tea.

"The hell... That's a digital video!" Frank exclaimed. He screwed up his face and stared at the screen in awe.

"So now we know the asshole responsible isn't working alone. That was a technomancy move," Georgia said. "We have one at the Vault, and he's good at that kind of thing. He's always in someone's store video deleting evidence of the supernatural, even if it's closed circuit."

"*Oui*, so it would appear."

"So do you think he did something to their food?" Georgia asked.

Frank shrugged his shoulders. "They both ate the cheesecake, and Regent Rhydderch didn't go psycho. That doesn't leave much else for her to have consumed that could have been corrupted with magic or a potion. Except the wine maybe."

The investigators looked at each other and hurried back to the fallen table to collect their evidence.

THE COLLECTOR'S TREASURE

Chapter 32

While Aisling hunted down Saraia, Griffin paid his favorite cousin a visit. Someone offered to fetch a wheelchair from the Healers' floor and shrank back from the dirty look Griffin gave in return.

He took the stairs with ease and ignored the elevators entirely. It made him feel like an invalid whenever pitying eyes turned his way.

Then he ran into Michael Stoddard, the school bully who had antagonized him throughout his magical education. He'd picked on Aisling mercilessly and even lied to her, claiming he'd seen Mercedes and Griffin kissing in the academy's garden. That had caused the first rift in their friendship when they had only begun to explore a romantic relationship. He was everything Griffin loathed, a dishonest creep and womanizer of the worst kind.

"Damn, MacNeil. I knew you had one leg in the grave, but I never thought it would be literal."

"Blow me."

"I suppose someone has to. Your little fey whore, Aisling, isn't doing it anymore, is she? Did they take your cock with the curse too?"

Griffin didn't know what came over him. One moment, they stood within arm's reach, and in the next, his anger welled hot and fast, expressed as a rapid burst of strength behind his fist. His right crutch clattered noisily to the ground.

"Stop, stop! Someone help! There's a fight!" A clerk scurried for safety away from the two tussling men, losing some of her paperwork. She screamed again for assistance.

Stoddard got off a single punch that split Griffin's lip. He felt the stinging pain but fell atop his old bully to violently slam him twice against the ground. Two successive strikes winded Stoddard.

"Quick, come quick! A man on crutches is beating Michael!" someone called in the background.

Griffin barely heard it. He saw only blind, red fury. "Don't you ever say her name again."

Stoddard punched him, but Griffin held a sure grip of his crutch and pressed it over the Scribe's throat.

"Ever. You're not worthy of sayin' her name. You're beneath her and not worth the spit from her mouth, you—"

"What's going on here? Man, you'll kill him! You gotta stop!" a masculine southern drawl called from the upper level. The thundering sound of rapid steps descended to the landing.

"Fuck him!" Griffin yelled over his shoulder without letting up his hold. He put his weight behind the crutch at Stoddard's throat and gritted out another swear between his teeth.

Two strong arms hoisted Griffin away as another magus wearing a black polo helped Stoddard to his feet.

Guardians. A cool sliver of fear raced through him. He didn't want to return to jail. He couldn't. Not again.

"Calm down, man. Hey, LT, you got Mike over there?"

"Yeah, he'll be fine once he gets over the shame," the lieutenant replied. "C'mon, Mike. We'll grab an ice pack."

"I'll get this one upstairs and figure out what happened," the other man said.

Griffin received a complimentary escort upstairs to the Healers' level from a friendly guy with a polite smile and a head of curly, dark hair. He didn't judge or threaten, emanating an amiable aura.

"So. You gonna tell me what happened down there? You're Regent Rhydderch's cousin, right? The famous Collector?" Although the Guardian's high cheek bones and piercing eyes alluded to Native American roots, he had a pleasant Southern accent, the kind Griffin only heard in movies about cowboys.

Griff morosely nodded while massaging his hip with two fingers, too stubborn to ask for pain relief. "Said some things which should've never crossed his lips, is all."

"Mike can be a douche, yeah. Look...we'll just pretend this didn't happen, okay? No lastin' harm done. And, uh." He cleared his throat and glanced down at the tiled floor. "I know this sorta isn't the time but...uh, you don't s'pose it'll be too much to ask for two autographs before you leave? I got a pal and a girl who'll hang me if I don't."

"A pal and your girl? Or your pal and you?"

The Guardian blushed.

It brought Griffin a small measure of happiness to learn his reputation wasn't in complete shambles after all. A single fan was a fan to be treasured.

They took a selfie together and printed it at the nurse's station computer, which prompted the white-robed Healer on duty to demand one of her own with the infamous Collector. Griffin autographed each, one to Noah and one to Carrie. The sour mood born from his run in with Michael vanished. He forgot his split lip, forgot the anger, and promised to mail back autographed photos for the rest of the nurses.

The recent discovery of El Dorado had made him exceptionally beloved by the mages who kept up with Collections. He was like Indiana Jones. It put a smile on his face to hear Michael Stoddard whining from an examination room for drugs.

"Any chance I can see Addison yet?"

"You're family, so yes. He's been in and out of consciousness for the past hour, so don't expect too much out of him yet."

"Happy to sit there and read until he's up," Griffin assured her.

Carrie led Griffin to a private hospital suite where Addison slept like a baby with only a handful of monitors and machines.

"Do you need anything, Mr. MacNeil?" she asked from the doorway.

Griffin shook his head and settled into the chair. He left his crutches against the wall beside him. "Nothin' else."

"We shouldn't have asked you to take those photos with us… You're in pain, sir. If you'd like, I can bring you something to help alleviate the discomfort."

Griffin reluctantly gave a quiet nod of consent. Ten minutes later, Carrie had medicated him enough to be pain-free for a week. Or so he told her once the pleasant feeling swam through his head and the unrelenting, stabbing pains disappeared.

"Don't worry about the autographs. If I didn't like it, I'd have let you know," he assured her. "Could you tell your Chief Healer I'd like to see her?"

"Of course."

Griffin spent the rest of the time quietly reading an abandoned copy of the *Magister's Almanac* left at Addison's bedside.

"Nnngh…" Addison groaned and opened his eyes before Griffin could delve into the mysterious theories surrounding a disgruntled kraken capsizing boats in the Mediterranean.

Griffin released a relieved sigh. "Well, good afternoon to you, too, sleepyhead. About damned time you awakened."

Addison turned his head toward the sound of Griffin's voice. "Griff?"

"Who else would I be? Thought I'd come chastise you for nearly dyin' *again*. That's my job. What, are you trying to keep the score even?"

"Screw you, Griff."

"Noooo. From this seat, I'm thinkin' you were the one who got screwed. In the chest. With a knife, of all things."

Addison's laughter ended with a pained grimace.

"Glad to see you're goin' to make it, cousin."

"Aren't we a bloody good match now?"

"Aye, that we are. So what happened? Why'd she stab you? I've gotten nothin' but secondhand information."

"No clue yet. We were making progress, and then she flipped her shit at me. Chevalier is going to figure it out. What's going on with your leg?"

"I'm going to let Snow take it," Griffin confessed. "It's spreading."

Addison frowned at him. "I'm sorry."

"It isn't your fault. You did what you thought was best when you declined their request to amputate it. I'm not blaming you. Besides, I'd have been pissed if I woke up with pieces missing off me."

Nurse Carrie arrived with a dinner tray, and Addison accepted it happily. He stuffed his face and taunted his cousin with the delicious aroma until Griffin finally succumbed to his

THE COLLECTOR'S TREASURE

pride. He pleaded with Carrie for a plate of his own only to discover she'd already prepared another serving.

"That was amazing."

"It was. Did you come alone? How are Aisling and the twins?"

"Well, all well. Lachlan has the wee ones."

"Then where's Ash?" Addison asked.

Griffin leaned back in his seat and grinned. "Funny story, that. She's actually with your girl. They're chasing unicorns."

Chapter 33

The Dryad's Arbor looked exactly as Aisling imagined it, based on the name. Amid the bustling streets and urban sprawl, the greenhouse stood out like an emerald jewel. Trees with colorful leaves lined the sidewalk, and late fall flowers bloomed in pots scattered across the lawn.

A bell over the door announced her arrival, then the sweet scent of flowers and essential oils greeted her.

"Hello? Saraia?"

"In the back!" a woman's voice called through the door behind the counter. Warm air flowed from the open greenhouse.

Aisling stepped into the humid space and immediately located Saraia. It was impossible to miss the woman's head of vibrant copper curls, even amid all the colorful plants. She stood by a worktable with her hands covered in moist soil transferring several flowers into a large pot decorated with 'Get Well Soon' in delicate, brush stroked script.

"Hello. I'm not sure if you remember me—"

"Of course I do." Saraia's smile warmed her brown eyes. "How are you and your babies?"

"Well, thank you, and having a ball with their godfather, Lachlan."

Saraia's brows rose. "Small world if you're talking about the same Lachlan I know."

"I am, yes. He's actually the one who suggested I come to see you. It's a rather long story, actually, but I've come to ask for your help. If you don't have to be getting back to Addison, that is."

"Not much for me to do there, to be honest." Saraia worried her lower lip between her teeth. "I was there after they brought him in and the first time he roused. He told me to go home and not fret. So here I am. Fretting anyway and getting very little done." She gestured toward her unfinished project on the table, piles of plants with bare roots beside empty decorative pots.

"Sounds like him. Except I think he and Griffin forget it's hard not to worry over them, as often as they land in trouble."

Saraia chuckled. "The men of the Rhydderch family wouldn't know what to do with themselves if they weren't in danger."

"Well put."

"So, I'm guessing more brings you here than just Addison's injury, or you'd be pacing the Vault hallways. What's up?"

Aisling stepped past a planter overflowing with sweet pea blossoms and rounded to the other side of the worktable. "I've a favor to ask. A huge one."

"Okay, what did you need? Not flowers, I take it."

"I need to try and find a unicorn before Healer Snow amputates Griffin's leg. Lachlan said he saw one in Gaia a few days ago," she said in a rush.

Saraia canted her head to the side, red curls sliding across her shoulders. "I think I know who he means, and it's possible she might still be around. Unicorns have particular spots they like, but they come by so rarely…"

Excitement and hope brought a skipping beat to Aisling's pulse. "Could you take me there now?" she blurted. Her cheeks warmed. "Please. This is his only chance."

"Absolutely." Saraia brushed her hands against her jeans and looked around in consideration. "Let me lock everything up, and we can head straight out."

"Really?"

"Really," Saraia replied. "Though how do you feel about going nude?"

Aisling tried to ignore the warmth spreading over her ears. She swallowed and fidgeted, shifting back and forth on her feet. "Oh, um, well…"

"One of the bashful ones, are you? Don't worry. I have something upstairs you can wear, if you don't mind. The simpler and closer to nature a fabric is, the easier it is to pass through into the other realm."

"It's a bit like going to Avalon, then. And respectful, I imagine."

"Exactly."

While Saraia locked up her shop, Aisling changed in the upstairs apartment into a cotton nightgown. The oversized garment fell to her shins, and the wide neckline slipped down her shoulder.

But it was better than nothing, and she voiced no complaints.

They met again in the greenhouse where Saraia kept a variety of trees. The half-nymph had shed her clothes and led the way to an orange tree nestled amid a few smaller specimens.

"So we just walk into the tree?" Aisling eyed the narrow trunk with both wonder and uncertainty.

"Yup. I'll be holding your hand the entire time. It will feel like you're walking through water or into a stiff breeze. That's how Addison describes it, at least."

"So he's done this, then?"

Saraia laughed. "A few times, yes. Ready?"

Aisling didn't think she'd ever be ready to walk willingly into something as solid and hard as a tree, but she steeled her nerves and nodded. "I am."

Saraia melded with the tree, there one moment and gone the next, and Aisling closed her eyes tight before she followed. Sound seemed to muffle, and a gentle resistance pushed against her limbs, followed by a strange sense of comfort as she moved forward. She opened her eyes in time to see a swirling world of brown and gold coalesce into a radiant garden more beautiful than anything she'd ever seen. Birdsong drifted down from the treetops, and a breeze untainted by mankind stirred through her hair.

Each leaf and blade of grass in the Sylvan realm stood out in vibrant, natural colors too unreal to exist in the mortal world.

"It's beautiful." Aisling's banal words felt insufficient. The immeasurable wonder of the Gaian plane spread about her in wondrous hues of emerald and cyan.

"I'll show you the glade where I've seen one before. It's a start at least, and we can ask along the way." Beneath the slanting sunlight beams, Saraia resembled a true dryad— complete with curling flowers and trailing leaves in her copper-red hair.

"Thank you for this, Saraia. Truly. Even if we don't find her, at least I can say I tried everything I could."

Saraia squeezed her hand. "Addison worries about him. Even if you hadn't asked me, I'm sure he would have if the idea had come to him."

"He's right to," Aisling admitted. She swiped a few tears from her eyes with trembling fingers. "I need to save him."

"We'll do everything we can."

Full-blooded dryads and other shy Sylvan peeked at them during the journey. Aisling spotted furry-legged satyrs ahead and edged nearer to Saraia when the horned males approached.

"Lovely ladies, lovely ladies. Care for a chase?"

"Or a shag?" queried the second.

"Only a bit of rumpy-pumpy. We won't take long."

"No thanks," Saraia replied breezily. She hooked her arm through Aisling's and kept her close. "We're just passing through."

"A chase!" The satyrs clapped happily. Their cloven hooves crunched the amber and maroon leaves blanketing the forest floor. "We'll give you a head start. More fun that way."

"Or I could take the sparkly one behind the maple now." The second satyr, a handsome creature with cream-hued fur, trotted closer to Aisling and reached out to stroke her hair.

She leaned away from the touch. The move earned her a confused frown from the creature.

"No chasing today, guys. Go see if Melly wants to play." Saraia pulled Aisling along with her and moved past.

They sulked. "Fine. But you're missing out on all the fun."

The two women continued forward and left the protesting goat-men behind to whine. Their travel along the road continued at odd intervals with Saraia consulting the inhabitant of a tree or some passing pixie. All shook their heads. No one had seen a unicorn today.

Using the tree paths, Aisling and Saraia covered miles within minutes, but they found no divine mare no matter whom they questioned. In the distance, the barren plains of New York City stretched in a dismal mirror to the mortal realm. While they saw no skyscrapers or steel buildings, they saw lifeless soil surrounding the perfectly emerald, geometric shape representing

Central Park. Green life stood out vibrantly against the desolate landscape, revealing random trees, smaller city parks, and tiny home gardens.

"It's so sad," Aisling whispered while staring across the blighted landscape.

"So long as those small spots live on, there's still hope." Saraia guided her away from the sight and led her back into the tree line. "There's another glade this way. Maybe we'll spot the unicorn the—"

Nearly a dozen sharp arrowheads pointed at Saraia and Aisling. A dozen glossy pony hides led by muscled, human upper torsos stepped from the untended brush. Resembling a draft horse with his broad shoulders and intimidating build, the leader edged nearer without lowering his arrow.

"Why do you trespass?"

Saraia stepped forward, hands held up in a placating gesture. "No harm meant, noble ones. We are merely on a search and have crossed no boundaries I'm aware of."

"Child of the trees, you bring a stranger among us."

"I bring a magus and a friend."

"Whelps from the land of Winter do not belong in this world. Go back to where you belong."

"I can't leave without trying," Aisling whispered to Saraia.

The nymph responded with a tiny nod of her head. Her gaze focused upon the centaurs at their forefront. She and Aisling acted at the same time.

A blizzard erupted from the clear skies above them, showering the verdant realm with hail and glittering snowflakes. The two girls ducked and ran forward hand in hand as the world behind them bloomed into a living thorn grid. Writhing green vines snapped into place, crisscrossed by whip-thin stems and pliant sturdy branches. Sharp burrs littered the pursuing beasts' hides, and they cried out in surprise and dismay to find their pathway obscured. As the two women fled, Aisling laid an icy sheet behind them. A centaur's hooves slipped against the slick ground, and all four legs went out from beneath him.

They sprinted as if their lives depended upon it, because for all they knew, it did. Outraged cries continued to the rear, punctuated by the whistle of an arrow past Aisling's ear.

THE COLLECTOR'S TREASURE

"Hold on to me!" the half-nymph cried.

Aisling didn't have the chance to feel embarrassed by their lack of clothing or close quarters. She threw her arms around Saraia as the nymph reached out for a vine and swung them down to a rolling meadow's hill. They careened through the wide open spaces, the wind's caress felt through Aisling's unruly black curls.

At the conclusion of the death-defying, acrobatic ride, Saraia jerked her into a tree on the path. Aisling instinctively closed her eyes and waited for the inevitable splat of hard bark against her face. They collided hard but painlessly.

She and Saraia disappeared into the murky essence of Gaia's mystical paths, a mode of travel accessible by the dryad-kin alone. When they emerged farther down the way onto the sturdy ground again, their bare feet hit the slippery, dew-covered grass, and they spilled downhill. They tumbled quite inelegantly to the bottom, screaming surprised yelps all the while until they landed in a heap, all bare limbs and knotted, sweat-soaked cotton.

Aisling was almost ready to strip from the ruined nightgown, but her modesty prevailed. Saraia helped her up as two small heads popped from small doors in the hill.

"Where are you going?" one asked.

"Who are you?" the other asked.

A window opened to reveal a third head, its blonde curls decorated by small posies and errant four-leaf clovers. The red-cheeked gnome girl peered up at them. "Why're you stomping on our home?"

"Look, look, look, Tansy! This one sparkles like a fae. Little snowflakes in her hair."

"I...do?" Aisling said.

Saraia gave her a startled glance and shrugged meekly. "Sorry, I thought you knew. Gaia brings out the true nature and magic in people. Addison's tattoos practically glow like fireworks."

The hill gnomes all blinked at Saraia. They bent their heads together to speak in hushed, high-pitched whispers. Aisling thought they sounded like a record on fast-forward. After a moment they separated.

"What brings you by our hill?" Tansy asked.

"I'm looking for a unicorn," Aisling admitted. "Someone very dear to me is sick, and I'm coming to plead for help."

"Oh. You're looking for Calliope, then? She's that way. Saw her early this morning," the female gnome replied. The two males grunted complaints about ignorant bigger people and shut their doors tight with a slam. "You'd better get a move on. She and that tike won't be there for long!"

Spirits lifted, Aisling thanked the small gnome profusely, and she eagerly grabbed Saraia's hand to tug the redhead in the direction indicated. The lightly wooded hills evened out and opened into a wide meadow bordered by forest on one side and a lake on the other. Warm sunlight bathed the open space in a golden radiance and shimmered off the ever-blooming flowers.

Aisling's gaze drifted to the frost-trimmed forest. She turned her face to the wind, cheek exposed to a chill breeze. The horizon bled from natural cloud-laced blue tones to the rainbow hues of a fairytale world. The trees shone in radiant colors, pink canopies resembling candy floss above a snow-dusted, emerald grass.

Avalon.

Of all the places to land during their frantic escape from the centaurs, Saraia and Aisling had discovered one of the seams where the Sylvan and fae realms overlapped. Gentle snow drifts blew across the plains and seemed to call to her. She took one step.

Griffin needs me... The thought slowed Aisling and helped her resist the lure of winter.

Across the meadow at a great distance, an ivory mare stood amidst the swaying grass blades. Her horn gleamed white-gold beneath the sunlight, and her tousled silver mane rustled in the breeze. She grazed peacefully beside a small alicorn colt with matching white fur and a pair of glorious wings.

The mare raised her head from the lush clover. She and her child froze, still statues of pristine marble with delicate faces and shining lavender eyes.

"Please, don't run! I won't hurt you!" Aisling cried, afraid they would bolt in the next second. She stumbled forward into the meadow and dropped to her knees. The floral scented breeze blew strands of hair into her face and the sunlight warmed her bare shoulders, but she only had eyes for the two equine creatures. The vigilant mother shifted forward until she stood between the two women and her colt.

Her gentle eyes seemed too human within her slender face.

"Please," Aisling whispered. "Please, I need your help to save someone I love."

~*~

After Addison passed out, Griffin received a text from Aisling bidding him to pick up their twins from Lachlan's and to meet her at Addison's penthouse. Saraia had offered them the hospitality of their home and a safe place to lay their heads for the night.

Lachlan sulked about relinquishing the babies and asked him to visit again soon with them.

"He's a good pup, that one. We'll have to visit often," Griffin said to Liam. "Won't we?"

"Lock'in," Liam agreed.

Griffin beamed proudly then limped from the elevator to Addison's penthouse door.

Aisling let him inside, and together, they stripped the twins from their winter clothes and laid them to bed while she relayed her tales of exploring the nature spirit realm.

"I can't believe I missed you running around Gaia in your underclothes. Shame I missed that."

"You'd have been in yours as well," Aisling pointed out.

"I'm not as shy as you. I'd have gone without."

With their kids asleep, they stood together at the window and looked out at the city skyline. While Griffin loved the privacy offered by both their Irish and Brazilian home, he couldn't argue with the fact that Addison had one hell of an amazing view. A wizard in a modern day tower.

"I'm proud of you, Ash, and I'm sorry for doubting you. Should have learned by now to believe in your crazy ideas." He wrapped his arm around her waist and drew her closer.

"At least you finally admitted it," she teased.

"Did she say when...?"

Aisling leaned her head against his shoulder. "Soon. That's all she said."

"Are unicorns fae or Sylvan? Because the fae have odd notions about time, and some of the Sylvan are not much better. Soon for her could mean years for us."

"Madeline, it's bedtime," Saraia called out.

The little girl frowned from the couch where she watched *My Little Pony* re-runs. "Awwwww. But I want to see the unicorn! What if she's like Twilight Sparkle?"

"You should listen to her, dear. Sleep is important for a growing child, even one as grown-up as you," a gentle voice spoke from behind them.

They all whirled, although Griffin's leg protested the sudden movement. Behind them, a beautiful woman in radiant silver stood, her glittering dress flowing around her ankles like starlight spun into silk.

Madeline slapped her hands over her mouth and bounced in place, eyes wide and bright. "Saraia, is she a unicorn? Is she, is she?"

"I, uh… Yes, Maddie. I do believe she is," Saraia whispered, equally as awestruck. "I didn't know they could take human forms."

"She's more beautiful than Princess Celestia!"

Griffin tried to make his voice work. It failed him at first, too dazzled to utter more than, "You're really a unicorn?"

"Really," Calliope answered, her serene smile brightening the room.

Griffin's astonished expression didn't waver when the semi-divine being moved closer. "I… We were told the last unicorn and pegasus died years ago. Feathers stripped to make the Wings of Icarus. Tail used to sew the threads."

"Some of us knew where best to hide. But we are fewer than ever before."

He was speaking to a unicorn—a true, honest unicorn. He would have had a thousand questions under better circumstances.

"Why don't we all have a seat? More cozy that way," Calliope suggested. She gestured toward the couch but then turned to look at Madeline. "Except for you. Do you think you could do me a big favor?"

Maddie's face lit up. "Uh-huh."

"I thought you could." Calliope beamed down at her. "My daughter, Aurora, is in your room looking at your pony collection. Do you think you could go play with her for a little bit? She loves those little toys, but she always gets their names mixed up."

She didn't have to ask twice. Madeline squealed and darted toward her room without further prompting.

"There, that's better now. Only us adults. Don't you think?"

Griffin and the others all agreed as they took their seats. Aisling sat beside him and placed her hands in her lap, but she wrung her fingers together nervously. Griffin tried to shoot her a brave smile despite the brisk pace of his pulse.

"Do you mind if I look?" Calliope asked as she approached.

He blinked up at her in surprise and gave a small nod.

Calliope slid to the floor upon her knees alongside the couch. The unicorn didn't blush as she helped him from his pants, but he did. Something about a creature of immense purity and love taking down his trousers brought heat to his cheeks.

"This is an evil and old magic—a latent killing curse. Whoever cared for you in the moments afterward showed remarkable talent to save your life," Calliope muttered as her fingers traced over the malignant scar tissue. "I have seen such a curse only once before in my lifetime."

"Who?" Griffin loathed the weakness crippling his body, but her touch alleviated the worst discomforts.

"Your forefather. Merlin." Musical laughter parted her lips when Griffin's eyes practically bugged from his head. Calliope's other hand came to his chest, light pressure urging him to lean back.

"You knew Merlin?" Aisling asked.

"I did. Those of his seed are immune to Hellfire, but little else from the plane of the damned. He was struck by such a curse many centuries ago. My own mother healed him. I was but a filly then, young as my little one. I remember him as a good man of integrity and virtue. My mother was honored to heal his pains."

Childish laughter filtered in through the partially closed bedroom door. The sound brought a smile to Griffin's face, bittersweet as it was. He blinked back tears. Mara would have been enchanted.

"Where is your mother now?" Saraia asked.

"Gone, like many of my kind. We were once plentiful and roamed free across the mortal plane until man's evil overcame us. Greed and desire for wealth," Calliope explained in her soft-spoken voice.

"I didn't think she'd find you." He cast his gaze to Aisling and found her watching him, her eyes shining with moisture.

"A loved one's safety can become the most powerful motivation," Calliope informed him with a placid smile.

Again, he felt soothed as if a sedative laced his blood.

She leaned back upon her heels with both arms extended forward, palms down, and she closed her eyes in concentration. When a deep furrow etched in her brow, Griffin opened his mouth to question her distress. She shushed him.

Unicorn magic was unlike anything Griffin had ever experienced in all of his life. Wizard Healers' methods varied from numbing to painful, oftentimes a bitter but beneficial pill. This experience was something wholly different and new.

It was warm, lively, and radiating love. It enveloped him within a cocoon of the most compassionate emotion he had ever felt in all his life, even from Aisling herself. Deep beneath the surface of his thigh, he felt the cursed presence squirming as if alive with its own senses. It itched from within, insidiously seeking to escape by burrowing deeper into his pelvis. Searing heat flared like an internal detonation between his thigh and groin, lighting fingers of agony toward his knee.

"No," Calliope said in a low voice. "You don't deserve to be here." She scooped with her right hand, fingers surrounded by a glowing nimbus of radiant power, and the gesture carried the fiery pain from his joint.

It seared down his limb toward the knee where both her hands lowered to cup him tightly. Before Griffin's eyes, her magic restored the life to the network of raised scars and dead flesh. His skin became a white canvas of unhealthy pallor, and then pink flooded the appendage as the blood flow returned.

Faint scarring remained at his mid to lower thigh and appeared to remain the worst beneath her hands. She breathed unevenly and bent before him with her eyes closed in concentration.

"Aisling?" The unicorn's voice seemed to come from everywhere.

"What can I do?" Ash perched on the very edge of her seat, fingers still twisting together.

"Don't let it escape."

Griffin's eyelids felt too heavy. He couldn't combat the exhausted sensation settling like anchors into his limbs, nor could he struggle against the excruciating heat emanating dead center in his thigh. It exploded outward, dragged by the swift gesture of Calliope's hand. A black mass of sickness, rot, and death splattered to the floor in a glob, and there it writhed while sending out sickly feelings of corruption.

Ice crackled and formed in a thick dome around the festering mass on the wooden floors. The malignant growth resisted Aisling's efforts to contain it and melted through her icy prison. It slithered, creating wet suctioning sounds and insidious slurps. The cancerous, living plague moved desperately to return to its host.

"You are not welcome here," Calliope declared in resonant tones as she rose to her feet.

Barely clinging to consciousness, Griffin wondered if he'd already begun to dream when the silver-haired woman shifted into a magnificent equine shape. Through blurry eyes, he watched her lunge forward with her golden hooves.

In the passage of seconds, the only thing left behind was an ominous black stain and pitted marks in the glossy wood.

The world above him spun and dimmed. A velvety soft nose touched his cheek, its scent like sweet grass.

I couldn't remove it all, but I have taken the worst. A small part will always remain with you... A quiet voice echoed within his mind, filled with warmth and assurance. *It lurks, but it will not spread.*

Will it hurt? he asked, half out of his wits and fearing he'd already passed out.

Yes, she answered honestly. *It won't threaten your life, but you'll suffer for as long as it remains. Your wizard Healers are right to say it must go, but I have salvaged more. As did she.*

He felt Aisling's familiar touch, her fingers smoothing back his hair. He wanted to reassure his worried dove, but his eyes refused to open.

Rest now. Sweet dreams, Calliope's voice echoed within his mind. *You will need it in the coming days. Difficult times approach for you, Griffin MacNeil. Difficult times for all.*

Chapter 34

Thanks to Calliope, Griffin walked better by the next morning and was able to take the twins to Central Park.

After a few days spent with Addison during his own recovery, they decided to spend the remainder of their winter in the warmth and sunshine of their island home.

He missed Mara. The twins didn't replace his little girl, but he loved them unconditionally and with the same intensity. He enjoyed watching them play on the beach where the surf lapped gently onto the sand. The kids gleefully shrieked as they ran from the water only to run right back when it receded. At last, the day of laughter ended with tired twins and an aching Griffin. He lounged on the couch, rubbing his knee.

"Go on and head to bed," Aisling suggested after she tucked the twins into the bed intended for Mara. The third bedroom lacked furnishings.

"For wee people with legs so very short, it's damned hard to keep up with them," he complained, but the grin on his face never faded.

"Wait until they're older."

"How old do they have to be before I can start jinxing them?"

Aisling rolled her eyes.

"No, seriously."

"You know damned well you won't be jinxing the twins, Griffin MacNeil. Rhiain has you wrapped around her little finger. As does Liam."

He grinned back at her. "So when they're teenagers, then?"

She tossed a throw pillow at him. "C'mon. Bedtime. They'll be up with the sun."

Since their reunion, his injury hadn't allowed for cuddling in bed or any form of intimacy beyond a few tender kisses. Staying with Addison hadn't afforded them any privacy either since they shared the bed with the twins.

Out of habit, he and Ash took their preferred sides of the bed and turned out the light. Silky sheets kept his bare skin cool, and naturally he gravitated toward warmth and comfort. A gentle lavender scent invaded his nose and eventually soothed him into a calmer slumber dominated by dreams of petal soft flesh beneath his touch.

He awakened to Aisling's head nestled beneath his chin, their bodies pressed close together. Her slow breaths fanned along his scarred throat. Griffin stroked an errant curl from her cheek and tucked the strand behind her ear. It felt good to have her against him again, he realized. A dream come true for which he felt both immensely grateful and utterly unworthy.

Aisling stirred, rubbing her cheek against his neck, her exhale a contented sigh. The whisper of his name made his chest tighten.

"Morning, sprite."

Aisling blinked drowsily in the morning light and raised her head. It seemed perfectly natural to lean up and claim her lips in a tender kiss.

He missed the feeling of her fingers over his skin, her mouth at his throat, and the caress of inquisitive hands as they traveled over his body. Her touch was a balm to his tortured soul.

Their kiss deepened as he tugged her atop him fully. Her breasts crushed against his chest, and the silk between her thighs cradled his arousal. Griffin fought the temptation to strip her bare.

What goddamned right do I have to be happy here as if Mara doesn't exist anymore... It's not right. A sense of disloyalty quelled his mounting desire, and guilt overwhelmed any physical need. He'd become the worst father—playing at house with Aisling while elsewhere, his oldest child waited for him. Forgotten.

Griffin rolled Aisling beneath him and left the bed. She deserved more than excuses, so he gave her none.

"Sorry, Ash... I need a moment, all right?" He couldn't bear her pained expression, so he entered the bathroom. The pelting shower spray failed to assuage his worried mind, but it did wonders for the aches of his body. While standing in the hot stream, his thoughts traveled to their future together.

Had he exchanged one family for another? Moving forward felt like betrayal. Most of all, he feared Mercedes and her heartless family would spend Mara's childhood years molding her in their image. Turning her against him.

Griffin needed to rescue her somehow. The right way. He planned to recover his daughter with a new lawyer, his grandfather's and cousin's Regency muscle, and any other help he could find. The time for self-pity was over. He cast it all behind him in hopes of building a new future with his loved ones.

Feeling more like the old Griffin, he turned off the shower and stepped from the luxurious marble and glass construction to embrace the day.

He found Aisling feeding the twins breakfast, her demeanor quiet. She set a plate covered in fried eggs, sausage, and toast down for him without a word and went to help Rhiain with her fruit.

Once he dumped his empty plate in the sink, he leaned down to kiss three different cheeks. "I'm going into town to handle some business," he told her with a reassuring smile. "Can't promise I'll be back in time for dinner, but I'll make it as quick as I can. May I have a moment with you though before I leave?"

"All right." She stepped away from the table toward the sink and busied herself with starting the dishes. Griffin turned the water off and took her hands.

"I'm sorry for ruining things this morning. Needed to apologize to you for that one first. My thoughts got away from me."

Her chin dipped down toward her chest, severing eye contact between them. "I shouldn't have tried to rush things."

"Hey. No. None of that. You're not to blame for the things I do. I want you, Ash, I do, but I can't move on and enjoy a proper life here without fixing my old mistakes."

"No, I understand. You're thinking about Mara."

"I am, and this time I'm going to set aside my pride and do what I should have done all along. I'm going to contact my grandfather."

~*~

Sitting across from Tristan Rhydderch's massive desk, Griffin tried to quell the churning in his stomach by drawing in deep breaths. He hadn't seen his grandfather since he was a teenager. Time hadn't changed the imposing man much. Addison resembled him closely, the two sharing blue eyes, impressive heights, and a need for glasses.

"I'm not going to lie or mislead you about why I'm here," Griffin said. "I need help fighting the Riveras. They've kept my daughter from me for months now and it's time to put an end to their bullshit."

"So, the Riveras are keeping my great-granddaughter hostage. It seems fate has decided I'm to be buried in girls. Except I hear you have a son now."

"I do, and he's a bright lad. His mother believes he takes after me since he's always getting into trouble at home."

"I'd like to meet them someday. All three of them. So let's see what we can do about getting Mara back, shall we? Mind if I put Addison on the line?"

"Mum, too. She deserves to be a part of this. And there's something you need to tell her after all this time. It doesn't have to be right this moment, but you need to own up to your assholery. I'm sick of our family being in tatters. Sick of all the pain."

Tristan didn't argue. Griffin rubbed his palms over his pants and waited while his grandfather phoned Dublin and held a brief conversation with his estranged daughter.

The press of a button placed Griffin's mother on speakerphone then Addison was added to the conference call. "Addison, I have your cousin here in my office and Fiona on the line. It's time we deal with the Rivera situation."

"Griffin is there?"

"Right here, in the flesh," Griffin called out.

"About bloody time," Addison grumbled. "Are you there to ask for help with Mara?"

"Aye. The Riveras have kept her from me long enough."

"Then maybe it's time to tell him the truth about his release, Gramps."

"What about my release?"

Tristan propped his elbows on his desk and leaned forward. "I sent Justiciar Chevalier to apply direct pressure on Regent Ortega to release you. As I didn't believe you would appreciate my meddling in your life, I asked the others to keep my involvement a secret."

"Thank you." Saying the words wasn't as hard as he'd imagined, lifting an indescribable weight from his shoulders. "I know I haven't been the best grandfather. Or father, for that matter.

"My actions were reprehensible then, and I have no excuses for my behavior. Just believe me when I say this old man is ashamed of his past mistakes. I should have cared more about Fiona's happiness rather than the respectability and worth of the MacNeil family name. All that prestige meant diddly squat," Tristan told them.

"Thank you, Father," Fiona conceded. "I don't know if I can forgive you—not right now—but I'm willing to put it all aside for Griffin until we can solve his dilemma."

"You don't know how relieved I am that you're all planning to put this behind you," Addison said to ease the natural silence on the line. "I love all of you, and your fighting has been hell on the rest of us."

"I'm only sorry time didn't bring me the wisdom to understand my mistakes sooner," Tristan admitted. "So let us try to fix this all up. I'd like to bounce my great-grandbabies on my knee one day soon."

Griffin breathed a sigh of relief. "What have you dug up?"

"I've had Chevalier investigating the matter in his spare time. Three men pressed assault charges against Griffin the day Barcelona took him into custody. One of the little shits has a connection to another unsolved case. This news should interest you boys especially."

Not accustomed to hearing such language from his grandfather, Griffin coughed. "What's that, then?"

"A corrupt Guardian by the name of Kevin Delaney slit his own throat while in holding several months ago, when he had been relieved of all possessions. He left a sibling, whom you bashed over the head with a chair during a bar brawl. They're brothers."

The familiar name elevated his pulse to a snare drum rhythm. He only wished he'd been in the car with Aisling to dispense justice of his own. "He's the bastard who ran Ash off the road and tried to kill her." He growled it out, voice raised higher than intended.

"Calm down, mate," Addison said. "That numpty is in the ground now. What matters is that we've got a connection. A flimsy one, but it's a start. I've had Jean-Luc looking into something for me, as well. When I was attacked, my dining companion turned into a sudden raving psychotic. Traces of a rage-inducing poison were found in her wine glass. Sound familiar?"

"Aye, it does," Griffin replied bitterly. "You thinking what Mercedes used on me, was used during your business meeting?"

"Potions as dark as that are a rarity and take a skilled alchemist to concoct. She has the talent to do it, if I recall your boasting, but it's a tenuous connection with no real evidence. I plan to send Jean-Luc into Spain to continue his investigation. He's a good man. He'll handle things as he sees fit there," Addison said.

Another hour easily passed, spent in strategic planning of an appeal. Griffin left Tristan's office feeling like a new man with renewed hope for the future and bringing his daughter back into his life.

He had a chance to prove his innocence and win Mara back.

The time spent waiting on the Portal from the London Vault to Rio gave him a while to rehearse his thoughts out loud. Griffin parked alongside the portside dock and took the boat back out onto the water nearly two hours after dark. He felt the usual tingle of the wards as he passed beyond their boundary into the chilly home. All was quiet.

After he tiptoed to the makeshift nursery and saw two sleeping blond heads, his light steps carried him next to the master bedroom. He expected to find Aisling asleep or curled up with a book, reading by her small lamp.

He discovered something else.

She lay on the bed, flesh luminous beneath the silver moonlight streaming through the open window. Her fingers traced a path over her own skin, one hand stroking from her collar to her breasts, while the other skimmed lower along her body.

Griffin's greeting died on his lips, replaced by a soundless exhale. It felt wrong to watch, but at the same time, he was unable to tear his eyes away. Feeling dirty, he ogled her in secrecy from behind the door through the narrow sliver of space between it and the frame.

He saw very little through the partially cracked door. The slim rectangle of space framed her lovely face, the curved slope of one porcelain breast, and the scant coral silk stretched over her hips. Coral. She'd worn his favorite color.

"Griffin...my Griffin."

Her moans twisted his gut and sparked his desires. He loved the way she writhed against the sheets, the way her breasts quivered atop her slender frame, and how her fragile silk panties clung to her full hips. He couldn't breathe, absolutely mesmerized by the sight.

It's wrong to watch her like this...but what do I say? What the hell should I do? he wondered.

Griffin decided to leave and grant her privacy—only for his knee to buckle as he tried to maneuver from the room. He staggered forward against the door and bumped it completely open.

That would never have happened if his lucky coin hadn't been reduced to a piece of worthless wood.

~*~

The noise and creak of the door damn near stopped her heart. Her eyes flew open wide as she bolted upright, breasts heaving with her uneven breaths. It was torture, so close to relief only to be startled at the very last moment.

Griffin.

He stood framed within the open door. Their eyes locked while the silence between them lasted for what seemed like forever. Relief for his return warred with the hurt and the depths of her longing for him.

Her gaze followed him as he stepped inside and closed the door behind him. He remained silent, but he pulled his shirt over his head. She drank in the sight, pulse racing. With every fiber of her being, she wanted to touch and hold him again. To know the taste of his lips and the bliss of their joined bodies. Yet she feared his rejection a second time.

He eased those fears in an instant. He rid himself of his cargo shorts and the boxers beneath in one smooth motion, revealing the arousal inspired by watching her.

She reached for him.

The mattress dipped beneath his weight, and the heat of his body enveloped her. Firm lips touched against her neck, his breath a caress across her skin.

His touch followed the path her fingers had traced but brought the heat and gratification her hands could never recreate. Cool sheets greeted her back, her fingers in his hair as he trailed warm kisses down her body. His lips parted, teeth nibbling along a hip to catch her coral panties by the hemline.

She didn't know which she found sexier—the very first time he'd ripped her panties from her as if they were tissue, or dragging them off by his teeth with the scruff of his jaw and warm cheek trailing down her leg. His face tickled her. She wiggled and drew him back upwards, then pushed him into a roll until he lay on his back and she leaned over him.

Her lips whispered down his throat to linger on the curve of his scar. Moving lower, she paused at each mark on his body, whether left by some beast he'd encountered or an injury earned in the line of duty. Griffin's scars didn't disfigure him; they told a story of his bravery.

Griffin's breath released on a shaky exhale, and it took only a turn of her head for his silent plea to be met. She placed a feather-light kiss on the rounded tip of his shaft while her fingers slid down the rock hard, sinewy length. Her tongue played in a delicate tease over the sensitive crown, leaving a moist sheen. She didn't linger long, aching too much to remain selfless, and moved upward again until she straddled his hips.

He'd stumbled in before she found the release from a day of torment, and the desire only intensified once he lay beneath her.

"Please." His green eyes lifted to hers with the plea.

Her memories failed to do him justice. Sheathing him within her heated embrace, she sobbed his name and rocked him to a hilted fit with a rhythm her body had never forgotten. Her breasts became victim to the press of his palm, his inquisitive fingers gliding over the swollen nipple at each tip.

It took only a few moments to realize her slow and sinuous pace wouldn't be enough. Their mutual need for each other demanded hot and fast, a bright burning of shared passions. She wrapped her arms around his shoulders, and she buried her face against his throat to muffle her frenzied cries. His hands molded to the curve of her bottom and supported her movements.

Their bodies moved together until she felt the world around her spin. Her orgasm came as a burst of exquisite sensation, riding high on joyful waves. She muffled her keening cry in a press to his sweaty skin, body still rocking in a desperate bid to bring him the same relief.

Achieving shared climax had become the ultimate joy, and she desired nothing more than to experience it with him again. With hot tears on her cheeks, his name became a voiceless mantra she mouthed against his scarred throat. She rode him wildly with reckless abandon.

The scorching rhythm of her body urged him to the finish with each repetitious climb and desperate descent. Griffin thrust up against her with jerky movements and buried his hands in her thick hair. Together, they collapsed in a pile of sweaty limbs with their legs entangled and his churning length teasing her sensitive walls. He'd barely gone soft at all.

"Don't...don't let this night stop."

"Nae, lass." His chest heaved beneath her cheek while he caught his breath. "I think we've got two long years to be makin' up for now."

A. Payne & N. D. Taylor

"Are you sure you have it in you?"

He nudged with his hips and sought with one hand, his fingers discovering the slick pearl between her thighs. At a stroke and a knead with his fingertips, he set off another reaction of clenching aftershocks.

Her toes curled and she gasped. "I'll take that as a yes."

Griffin rolled her beneath him and looked down at her with bright eyes.

"You were gone so long I started to worry. Everything went well on the mainland?"

"Aye, so worried your fingers couldn't behave."

"My fingers were behaving quite well, thank you very much," she replied. "You left me in a right bind this morning."

"I know, and I'm sorry about that. I couldn't... I was worried about my wee lass."

She softened her expression and framed his face between her hands. "There's no need to apologize. I worry about her, too."

"We may not need to worry for long. There's...a whole lot to talk about," he said. "And I promise... I swear to you, dove, it's all good news."

Chapter 35

Jean-Luc nurtured no love for the Vault in Barcelona. They argued with him and challenged his authority often, but once Commandant Rivera strode away from the building, Jean-Luc began his work. He arrested a Guardian in the man's absence for obstruction of justice, acquired the keys to Rivera's personal mailbox, and he swept through the entire building like a well-dressed hurricane.

He left no stone unturned and whittled away over an hour in Rivera's personal records until he determined they were squeaky clean. Too clean.

He didn't find an actual clue until he followed a paper trail in the records office. There were additional payments to a few select Guardians and money from unknown sources filtering into Rivera's department. He pulled the records, and not a single Scribe dared to stop him.

The French agent struck gold during the second day of investigation by discovering a conspiracy so thick, Regent Ortega became too ashamed to make eye contact with him. His personal secretary attempted to flee the scene when it became grossly apparent Regency money had been funneled to alternate accounts. Embezzling, crooked deals, and other illegal activities flooded to the surface.

But he found no connections to Mercedes or the rest of the Rivera family.

Ortega's secretary provided little useful information, but Jean-Luc was cunning enough to trace the substantial amount of money siphoned from the Vault. Joint efforts between wizards and mortal law enforcement contacts brought the entire operation to a head two days later. The concluding raid ended with five less Diabolists in the world.

The small suburban home hardly looked like a nest for demon worshippers. The white picket fence, lace-curtained windows, and neatly tended flower beds lent the house an air of normalcy to anyone looking from the outside.

Inside, demonic sigils painted on the walls shattered the perfect upper-class illusion, accompanied by upside down crucifixes and grisly trophies of human bone. They took down three sorcerers in the back bedroom who were participating in a drug-fueled orgy. Two warlocks in the garage put up a fight, yet they promptly succumbed to the determined Guardians.

Among them, the small task force of French and British Guardians discovered a single human with no magical ties to their world. He put a bullet in an unprepared Guardian's chest, but ultimately lost the fight when three different elemental spells sizzled and sparkled through the air. Electrical currents, the lick of magical flames, and stinging hail reduced the man to huddling in the fetal position on the floor. They took him alive.

The prisoner's personal record revealed military service and the means to contact mercenary groups for contract hire. In his home, they found maps detailing several Collection sites, addresses of prominent mages, and extensive notes regarding scheduled Regency movements.

It was enough to prove Jean-Luc's darkest fears and what he had begun to suspect all along. The Diabolists pulled the puppet strings of the Inquisitors, wielding the ignorant mercenary group as a weapon to kill their sloppiest members and strike fear into elite Magi. The assaults on high-ranking mages made perverse sense once it all fell together.

Whether or not the die-hard, loyal servants of the anti-magus faction knew the twisted truth behind their orders, it only served to prove one thing.

Both groups needed to be stopped, and it had to end soon.

Chapter 36

The weeks leading up to Christmas passed in familial bliss.

Hope kept Griffin's spirits high as he and his family undertook the tedious task of appealing to the Spanish court system and a supposedly unbiased Regent. His mother brought gifts for each of them and promised to stay until New Year's.

Which was perfect, because he'd made plans for the evening and needed an adult in their home. Grinning from ear to ear, Griffin produced two early presents to his future wife, giving her a rectangular garment box and a slim envelope.

"What's this?"

"Early gifts. Go on and open them," he urged. Nervous excitement left him too restless to sit beside her on the couch. "Big one first."

Aisling set the long box over her lap and unraveled the ribbon bow. The lid came away to reveal an expensive, one of a kind dress ordered from a French dressmaker recommended by Helene. He tried not to think about the exorbitant price, focusing instead on the stunned expression from his girl.

"Griffin, it's gorgeous!" Aisling held the gown against her petite frame and stared down at it. The shimmering silk pooled around her like liquid moonlight spun from the heavens.

"Not as gorgeous as it'll be when you put it on."

"Where would I even wear such a thing?"

His grin widened to cheshire proportions. "Open the second one and see."

Aisling folded the gown up first and then opened the envelope. Two gold and red tickets slid out into her waiting hands.

"Really?" Her voice squeaked. "The Winter Gala?"

"I messed up our last one in Dublin right and proper, and we've missed so many since. It's right here in Rio this year, too. We can go and be back in a wink if something comes up with the twins. Mum came to watch them for us."

Aisling squealed and threw herself into his arms.

They never strayed from each other's sides during their evening out, always within reach. Always touching. During the event, Addison and Saraia greeted them warmly. They caught up with old friends and even crossed paths with Jean-Luc since he'd attended as part of the elite security task force, putting his other investigations on hold for a single night.

The last thing they saw before heading out early was Krys spinning across the dance floor on Jean-Luc's arm to a sexy tango beat.

"I hope she gets laid. Maybe he'll pull the stick out of her arse before he does it," Griffin said as they walked through the door.

"Griffin!"

"What? Would do her some good. Him, too, I wager. The man works more than anyone else I know. Does he even sleep?"

"Not much, he admitted to me."

When they returned to the island, Fiona met them outside and hugged them in relief. "Oh, I'm so glad you two made it back."

"Did you think we were going to sneak away for the entire night and miss Christmas?"

Fiona smacked his hand. "No, of course not. I've just gotten off the phone with Addison. Inquisitors crashed the ball, and he wanted to make sure you two had made it home."

Griffin and Aisling both startled at the news.

"No. Everything was fine when we left. What happened? Is everyone okay?" Aisling asked.

"Addison is fine."

"Krys?"

"She made it out, as well. I don't have details, but he said not to worry about it and that the situation was handled. I'll just text him to let him know you're safe."

"Thanks, Mum. Kids were good?"

"Little angels, as always. They're asleep and my presents are put out under the tree, so you two should go do the same."

Fiona bid them goodnight and headed inside to the guest room. Still clothed in their ball attire, Griffin and Aisling ate cookies baked earlier in the day with help from the twins. The pastries resembled garden gnomes more than Santas. Some of the reindeer had visible fingerprints, but the ones easily discerned as Griffin's artwork had an additional "leg."

Aisling frowned at him.

"What?"

"You're hopeless."

"Aye, and what's that say about you for lovin' me?"

She leaned over and kissed him. "It means I'm hopelessly in love with you, Griffin MacNeil. Now stop stuffing your gob and help me lay out presents."

He tugged at the sash on her dress, loosening it. "The only present I wanna unwrap right now is you."

She swatted his hand and giggled. "Your ma is in the other room."

Undeterred, he eased the zipper down her back. "Aye, and she sleeps like a rock."

They made love under the twinkling lights of the tree and exchanged whispered promises for their new life to come. Once sated, they took time to set out the piles of presents they'd hidden out of sight. Despite not truly understanding what Christmas was about, both twins woke early and cried to be let out of their new room.

They let the kids have presents first. Dolls, clothes, and books all received wondrous exclamations, only to be promptly set aside so they could play with Breda and the tissue paper. Aisling snapped photos with a laugh then passed out the first round of adult presents, starting with Griffin.

From Hektor, he received a pouch and found his first treasures contained within. He opened the bag to spill four ivory fangs from the mouth of a sphinx upon his palm.

"Well, then, let these be a reminder that while I most certainly do love you, you don't have to kill a raging beastie to prove it's mutual." Aisling laughed.

"Where's the fun in that? If a member of the Rhydderch family's not dyin', then it's not a party." He and Addison held a little too much notoriety for their constant brushes with death. "Here. Found one for you from Mum."

Upon removing the golden foil and simple scarlet ribbon, she opened the box to reveal a silver chain and a heart-shaped silver pendant. The beautiful filigreed front opened up fully into four separate hearts, resembling a four-leaf clover. Each frame held a picture. Liam, Rhiain, Griffin, and Mara. The back held a simple inscription. *Mo Chlann, mo stòr.* My family, my treasure. She stared down at the faces she loved most in this world, and then carefully closed the locket to clasp it around her neck. Griffin left his seat to help her while she pulled her hair out of the way.

"Thank you, Fiona, it's beautiful."

"Dada…"

"What is it, sweetling?" Griffin asked as he drew Rhiain close. The little girl held out a cookie with the icing licked away and Rudolph's face nibbled as if he'd been given an unfortunate frontal lobotomy.

"Go on, Griffin. She's sharin' with you," Fiona said with a laugh.

He glared at his mother. Grimacing, he accepted the tiniest bite he could muster of the soggy cookie. His reward was a bright, toothy smile.

Aisling extended a package to Griffin shyly. "Here's my gift for you."

He ripped the snowflake paper off and tore open the box. A leather-bound scrapbook awaited him, filled with memories shaped by paper and ink. Photographs of Aisling in various stages of her pregnancy dominated the first few sheets. Each page that he turned tightened the knot forming in his chest.

There was a picture for every single day of the twins' life, every precious change and event, accompanied by notes in Aisling's graceful cursive script. Moisture welled up in his eyes at a snapshot of Liam taking his first steps chasing after Breda. The next displayed Rhiain and Aisling sitting in the garden with fae perched on their shoulders and hair.

The final page held a single picture. Its glossy square captured him sitting with the twins on their first birthday.

"Fiona helped me put it together. We knew Barcelona would have to release you one day, and you'd be home to us."

Griffin wiped his eyes and pulled Aisling into his arms. "It's perfect. Absolutely perfect."

Chapter 37

A single phone call awakened Griffin in the hours after midnight. Aisling stirred beside him and mumbled something against her pillow, so he clumsily batted the phone from the nightstand and powered it on. Fearing it was his mother calling from Dublin's time zone, he raised it to his ear and groggily uttered a greeting. Celebratory New Year's Eve fireworks had kept the family up late to enjoy the show.

"Papá?"

"Mara?" He snapped awake and jolted up in the bed. Mara's voice cleaved through the hazy fog of too little sleep.

Aisling sat up beside him. "Griffin, what is it?"

"It's Mara. What's wrong, lass?" The sniffling sound of her voice covered his skin in a cold sweat. And while he wasn't typically the praying sort of man, he struck an internal bargain with anyone willing to listen: please let Mara be okay.

Mercedes never allowed his daughter to call him. The sound of her voice after so many months brought tears to his eyes.

"Mama…" Her ragged sob broke his heart.

"Mara, baby, please. Tell me what's wrong. What happened?" he asked again in Spanish.

"Mama died."

Griffin's pulse missed a beat before it kicked into overdrive, hammering against his ribs. He bit back a swear. "I'll be right there. I promise. I'll be right there. Is Autumn with you?"

"Yes."

"Good, y'keep her there with you, lass. Who's with you now?"

"Griffin, what's going on?" Aisling sat up and set her hand against his arm. He shook his head at her and raised one finger, asking for a moment.

"Belen."

"Let me talk to her, lass, then I'm coming for you."

The housekeeper came on the line to explain in a timid, trembling voice that she was watching Mara while the Rivera's handled arrangements. She apologized profusely for bothering him, but his daughter had been distraught and crying.

"You did the right thing, letting her call me. Can you tell me what happened?"

"Elsa find her in the bathtub last night, señor, wrists slit. So horrible. She say home is cursed now and quit."

Griffin's stomach dropped. Suicide didn't sound like Mercedes at all. If anything, it made him wary of the circumstances and eager to reach their former home.

"You keep a close eye on my girl, Belen. I'll be there as soon as I'm able."

After a series of phone calls between Rio, Barcelona, and finally Ireland, Griffin sat numbly on the bedside with the phone cradled in his palm. He wanted to rejoice and find pleasure in Mercedes' death, but another part of him felt pity—most of it for their child who had only wanted to love and be loved by her mother. He couldn't take any joy.

"I'm… I'll be bringin' her home with me, Ash. Give me a few days to get everything in order. I'll call when I get there."

"Are you sure you don't want me to come?"

"No. I need you and the twins here where I know you're safe. I don't trust the Riveras to be anywhere near you."

"Okay, but you call me every night to check in. Promise me."

"I promise to call you every night. There's nothing standing in the way of bringing her home this time."

~*~

Griffin's plan was simple: get in, get Mara, and get out. No time for small talk except to determine the day and hour of his ex-wife's funeral. He wouldn't deny Mara the chance to say goodbye to her mother.

Regent Ortega's cordial ruling had surprised him. Temporary custody of the girl was to be relinquished and permanently granted to him. The paperwork had been signed prior to his arrival in Barcelona. In truth, the declaration shouldn't have been so shocking when Carmen had never struck him as the grandmotherly sort, and Domingo Rivera barely played much of a role in his own daughter's life. It had never been about protecting Mara from a raving, violent drunk. It had been about socking it to him for daring to leave.

Lacking a key to let himself in, he beat the metal and glass door until Belen answered.

"Señor MacNeil. So good to see you again," she said before hurrying away.

"I don't want to stay a moment longer than necessary in this damned house, so let's make this quick," Griffin announced as he entered. Addison had given him advice over the phone while on the plane and told him to go in hard with his orders prepared.

"Quick?" Carmen asked, her brows raising.

Her husband stood beside her, the middle-aged wizard dressed in black slacks and a long overcoat. He wore his features in a neutral mask but hardly appeared to be mourning.

The bastard. Framing Griffin for a list of offenses then locking him away in front of Mara.

"Yes, quick. I'll take Mara with me to a hotel for tonight, but we won't be leaving the city until after Mercedes is put to rest."

"How kind of you to show such respect the day after my daughter's death, MacNeil."

He aimed a brittle smile at Rivera and quickly pushed his way deeper into the home and upstairs to begin packing Mara's belongings. When the bedroom door opened, she ran to him and flung her arms around his waist. Her tears soaked his shirt, and he held her tenderly until the last sobs ended and her shoulders merely shook with silent, dry grief.

"We're going to pack everything, lass. Don't leave a thing behind you're wantin' to keep. We're never comin' back to this place."

"Never again?"

"Never again," Griffin assured her.

Autumn chirped from Mara's shoulder, and Griffin ran his finger gently over the salamander's back. The fae creature squeaked then resumed her hiding spot in Mara's thick hair.

They worked quickly. Mara grabbed her dollies and told Griffin the things she wanted. He dragged her luggage from the closet and began to stuff the expensive suitcase.

"Griffin." The caress of his name slipped over his senses until he jerked around to look at Mara and Autumn. His fae companion studied him warily.

He shook it off, blaming his imagination, and resumed rifling through his clothes. "What about those shoes, Mara? Y'want the pretty rain boots too?" he asked.

"Yes, Papá."

"Griffin," the voice of his ex-wife persisted, a whisper against his ear.

"Don't forget your art supplies, lass. Where do you keep those?"

"Here." She brought them to him, and he nestled them alongside her clothing and lace dresses. He left most of the dainty, elegant garments hanging in the closet and took the belongings an active little girl needed to enjoy her days on a stretch of hot beach.

"Griffin... Please." Mercedes called from the reaches of a space beyond his daughter's room.

Griffin shook his head and raised his fingers to one temple. His head hurt.

"Mara... Did you hear your mum?"

Her tear-streaked face turned up to him and filled with confusion. "No, Papá."

"I want you to stay here for a moment. Autumn, you stay with her no matter what. You hear me? Give me your word you won't leave her side."

The small fae nodded.

"But Papá—"

"You wait here, sweetheart."

He dropped the luggage and burst from the room to take the steps two at a time. The voice called again, increasing in volume until he realized the location of the source. The small family chapel awaited him beyond a door, and he stepped inside almost expecting to find Mercedes knelt before the altar in prayer. An empty room greeted him, and the silence beckoned him to investigate.

THE COLLECTOR'S TREASURE

This had better not be a sick joke... Griffin thought. The toe of his boot struck a loose board, which creaked and came ajar to reveal a hidden door. His inquisitive nature got the best of him and within moments, he crouched gingerly near the square entrance with his pocket light in hand. He shined it into the space below.

"Mercedes?"

No one responded, but his thigh ached with a burning intensity not felt since before the unicorn had worked her magic. It shot up and down the length of his leg until the merciless stabbing reached his heel. He rubbed the knot, wearing a deep grimace on his face. Distracted by the pain, he fell victim to an abrupt kick to the back and tumbled face first down the dark hole.

Griffin scuffed his palms against a rough stone floor and rolled in an effort to spare his leg further damage. The sudden flare of ruddy light blinded him, and spots danced in his vision which he quickly tried to blink away. Thin, spiked heels blurred into view, illuminated by the orange glow of two iron braziers.

"How kind of you to join us, son."

Carmen Rivera smiled thinly down at him. Behind her expensive shoes, Griffin made out the slack body of an elderly woman who lay sprawled in an unnatural angle on the floor. The waxy, dead features of Mara's nanny brought bile rising into his throat. Elsa hadn't quit after all.

He leapt to his feet despite the searing discomfort in his left leg.

"It wasn't suicide. You killed Mercedes, didn't you?"

The woman shrugged. "I knew it would bring you here. Her death, while painful, brought our plans to completion. Despite her many failures with you, the Master will reward her richly."

"What the fuck do you want from me?"

"Your body." With a swift flick of her wrist, Carmen sent filaments of caustic energy flying across the small space.

They lashed against Griffin's skin and left thin lines of blood. He jerked back, and the binds tightened, cutting deeply into his flesh. He responded with searing gouts of fire and funneled the attack towards Carmen. The swirling flames snuffed out with a hiss as Domingo joined the fray.

"Start the summoning and leave him to me," Carmen commanded.

Unbearable sensation traveled in a blistering wave throughout the cursed limb supporting Griffin's weight. He nearly crumpled to the floor again but regained his balance on the other foot just in time to duck another biting lash. Carmen's keen reflexes kept him on his toes, extinguishing each of his assaults with a snap of fire in return. He drew his dagger, but she kept him too far away to use it.

At the altar, Domingo's bass voice rang out. The harsh and guttural words became a siren's lure, a temptation beseeching him to remain longer. Griffin shook it off when he recognized the forbidden language of Hell.

He lunged toward Domingo to disrupt the ritual, but Carmen blocked him from reaching her husband. She wanted him alive. Or, at least, intact. His body, she'd said.

His perceptive mind fit the pieces of the puzzle together.

"Fuck you."

"Oh, I intend to. Many times." Her smile widened. "Get him for me, pet."

A dark shape moved in the shadows of the underground shrine. Ivory scales reflected the glare of the flickering flames, casting an orange gleam over the serpent's hide. He knew the monster for what it was the moment it slithered within his field of vision.

Griffin immediately snapped his gaze away from the basilisk, but his reflexes came too late. They made eye contact, then a chain reaction began from the tips of his toes and the ends of his fingers. Stiffening, hardening, and growing more of a challenge to control by the second. Carmen's laughter chilled him and sent a flutter of goosebumps down the back of his legs.

This wasn't the way he wanted to lose the fight against evil, cheated by a dark witch and her beastly minion. Griffin sucked in a deep breath, focused, and shoved through it. It was like moving through quicksand or swimming in concrete.

He only had one shot, and he had to make it count.

Every ounce of Griffin's determination to see another day, all of his strength, and the desire to see his three children grow up fueled the snap of his wrist. He hurled his knife through the air in a precise throw. It sank with a meaty tear into Carmen's throat, slicing cleanly through the carotid artery.

Griffin had learned one thing about Jerry's dagger in the years since it came into his possession. It cut effortlessly through mana shields. Nothing could withstand the might of the dwarven-forged weapon. Blood spurted and trickled around the wound while Carmen's fingers clawed in a futile gesture around the blade hilt.

The paralysis crept steadily over his limbs, his body too exhausted to continue the fight. Griffin collapsed to the floor, unable to push himself up or even turn. The serpent lurked beyond his peripheral vision, but he heard the whisper of scales gliding over the stone floors and a deep, inhuman voice.

"Griffin, I have longed for this moment. You have taken my servant, but the prize remains mine. My prize. Mine."

The late Carmen Rivera's basilisk wasn't merely an animal. It became a conduit for something far darker. The last thing Griffin saw in the dwindling light of the dying brazier flame was a single, glowing green eye set within a terrifying reptilian face. Its teeth glistened, and then it lunged.

Chapter 38

Three silent days passed. Aisling waited to receive word from Valencia about Mara's state, the funeral, and when Griffin planned to return with his daughter. At first, she was willing to grant him the time to see to his family business and to tie up loose ends left behind in Barcelona. By the second day, when he didn't call as promised, Aisling began to truly fret.

By day four, she knew something had happened. She also knew she'd never forgive herself if she stood idly by when Griffin needed her.

Leaving the twins in Fiona's care, she took the next Portal to Barcelona with every intention of bringing her man back home. A thirty minute flight by air taxi transported her to the coast for an even briefer travel by cab to his former address.

A frazzled woman opened the door to the Spanish villa.

"Señor MacNeil..." The woman wrung her hands together and shook her head, gesturing Aisling away with a warding press of her palms. "Ill," she said. "*No bueno.*"

"I'm a Healer," Aisling insisted. "*La enfermera.*"

"Miss Ash?"

The sound of Mara's voice came as a relief to Aisling. The rotund maid turned and exchanged a flurry of words with the girl. After another worried and fearful glance, she stepped aside and allowed Aisling into the home. She continued out the door with her own luggage and didn't stop until she reached her automobile parked in the drive.

Mara stepped forward and threw her arms around Aisling's legs. Warm tears soaked through the material of Aisling's pants.

"Where's your dad, sweetie? Why aren't you packed up?" She smoothed her hand down over Mara's hair and hugged her close. Autumn puffed into being on the girl's shoulder.

"Papá packed for me. But he left."

THE COLLECTOR'S TREASURE

Aisling looked past her, brows knit together and lip caught between her teeth. The eerily quiet house made the hairs on her nape stand on end. "But where did he go?"

"He said he heard someone calling his name. He said he heard Mamá."

Dread curled in Aisling's stomach, and she wondered if it could be true. She didn't want to believe Mercedes was still alive and the notice of her death had been an elaborate trick to lure Griffin back to Spain.

"Did you hear her, Mara?"

The girl shook her head and clung all the tighter to her. "Now Papá says we must stay. He… He…" Mara sobbed and shook. "There are noises at night. Papá yells."

The oppressive atmosphere of the house settled around Aisling and accompanied a strange, unfamiliar scent reminiscent of metal and rot.

"Listen to me, Mara. I'm going to take you and your daddy home, okay?"

Mara's head tilted up to her, revealing her tear-streaked face. A bruise bloomed across her cheek.

"Mara…" Aghast, Aisling gently stroked her fingers over the bruise and let her magical touch flow in a healing caress. "Does that feel better now?"

The girl swiped at her cheek with the back of her wrist and nodded her head. "*Si…*"

Aisling looked to the salamander on the girl's shoulder and touched Autumn's scaly nose. "You did good. Stay with Mara no matter what."

Autumn trilled a quiet warning. *Griffin is not our Griffin. Not anymore.*

The fae's soft-spoken words filled Ash's belly with dread.

"I'll see to him. Mara, you stay right here by the door and wait for me."

Directions from Autumn led her upstairs to Griffin's study. She knocked once then pushed open the door.

Griffin slouched in a chair behind the desk with his weight supported on his left elbow and a bottle gripped in his right hand. Curtains once decorated the bay window behind him, but those were torn from the rods, strewn across the floor.

"The fuck're you doin' here?"

"I came to help you bring Mara home." The strong smell of alcohol assaulted her nose. It set off warning bells in her head. Griffin may have been a Scotsman, but he rarely drank after the series of unfortunate events that had landed him in prison. "What are you still doing here?"

"Settin' things right. I don't want *you* anymore. I want back m'wife. Y'take yer little arse back to Ireland and care fer yer own wee brats."

Aisling stiffened. Autumn's warning echoed in her head, and she focused her gaze on the man behind the desk. "What have you done with Griffin?"

"I am Griffin. Have you gone fuckin' blind too?"

"You look like my Griffin, but this filth spewing from your mouth isn't him."

"I made changes, is all. I know what I want now. What needs t'be done." He rose from behind the seat with surprising balance for a man who had to be hammered out of his mind. Without a trip or a stagger, he approached her only to halt all at once. He paused as if his feet became glued, both arms down at his sides and a sneer on his face. "Get out of my house."

"Griffin—"

"What part of get the fuck out did y'not understand, Irish hoor?" He moved forward faster than she expected and grabbed her by the wrist, twisting it painfully.

"Let me go!"

"Won't be needin' this anymore either."

Upon making contact with her engagement ring, his fingers sizzled, and foul-smelling smoke wafted upward. He jerked back and emitted an inhuman snarl. The sound raised the hairs at the back of her neck and covered her arms with goosebumps.

For a brief moment, his tortured eyes met her gaze. "Dove, go while it'll still let you. *Please.*"

Aisling slammed out of the room and rushed down the stairs, grabbing Mara in the hallway. With the young girl against her hip, she fled the home and ran onto the street, her feet pounding the ground at a furious pace. She didn't stop until her sides hitched and her lungs burned. Autumn squeaked in worry, and Mara sobbed against her shoulder.

"Papá, mi Papá," Mara cried, trembling and cold in Aisling's arms.

Without a second thought, Aisling shrugged out of her coat and tucked the material around the girl's quaking limbs. With Autumn inside the woolen jacket, Mara would be kept warm.

"Shh, Mara, shhh. I'm going to help your dad. I'm going to call someone right now."

A small handful of Magi possessed the rare ability to summon wisps without dust as a magical component. Aisling was one. After closing her eyes, she spoke quietly in the lyrical language of Avalon, calling for the aid of any creature willing to listen.

When she looked down at her cupped palms, she found a golden-toned dew drop fae instead of the usual wisp, its tiny hands a fragile presence against her cheek. Aisling blinked, and for a moment she felt a surge of hope.

What aid do you need?

"I need a message sent to Regent Addison Rhydderch, straight away. It's an emergency."

The small creature hung on to Aisling's every word, and at the end of her plea for help, its soft lips touched the tip of her nose.

I will not let you down. The fae vanished in a mist of gold dust.

Aisling and Mara were left alone to comfort one another, but minutes later, the fae returned with Addison's promise to bring help and a request for her to sit tight and safe.

Nearly three hours later, a procession of vehicles arrived. Aisling flagged them down from a small corner cafe.

The rear passenger door of one car flew open. "Aisling!" Helene called.

"Helene?"

"Come, ride with me."

Aisling hurried into the backseat with Mara. She huddled between the adults, sniffling and clinging to them both. A man wearing the uniform of a French Vault official glanced at them from the front, a Guardian beside him in the passenger seat.

"Are you both okay?" Helene asked. "Jean-Luc and Regent Durant remained at the Vault, but I think given their goal, that may not be the safest place to be right now. I know a good hotel in the area. These two do not speak much English, but they are Guardians and one will stay with you."

"No, I need to go help Griffin. Can you take Mara? She doesn't need to be anywhere near that house."

"Of course, but you should stay away, as well."

"I can't, Helene. He wouldn't leave me behind. I won't do the same to him."

Helene reached over and gripped her hand. "As you wish." She fired off a rapid series of orders in French to the driver, and they pulled off after the other cars.

Aisling filled her in on what happened in a quiet voice during the short trip. They pulled in against the curb at the end of the drive a few minutes later.

"I promise I will keep Mara safe," Helene said.

"I know you will. Griffin trusts you, and so do I."

"Miss Ash? What is happening?" Mara asked.

"Helene is going to take you to a hotel and stay with you. You can order whatever you want to eat and call Grandma Fiona." Aisling hugged Mara and tenderly kissed the girl's dampened cheeks.

"What about Papá?"

"I promise I'll bring your father back." After another kiss to Mara's cheek, she shut the door and watched the car drive away.

The impressive collection of authority figures made an intimidating sight. The Regents representing Barcelona, London, New York, and Dublin approached the home wearing troubled expressions.

"Lord have mercy…" O'Sullivan whistled. He stroked the white beard trailing down his chest then squinted his eyes at the house. "Do you see it, Tristan?"

"I see it. The aura surrounding this home is rotted beyond repair. We'll have to send a team to scourge the entire area once we've fetched the boy." The Rhydderch patriarch shot a sour glance at the Spanish Regent. "Do you see now, Ortega? This wasn't about wanting to pull my kin out of the proverbial fire. He's in very real danger due to the negligence of *your* Vault."

Aisling turned her own magical perceptions toward the Spanish home. She hadn't looked before, too afraid to follow instinct. Apprehension knotted her stomach. She expended enough magical effort to satisfy her curiosity and immediately wished she hadn't.

The home resembled a horror movie set. Pestilent decay formed a lattice of putrid webbing over the stucco walls. The manicured lawn appeared as a barren waste crawling with pulsating, cancerous growths converging toward the home's foundation. The ground shifted and undulated, disturbed by a menacing presence below.

"Forgive me, all of you." Ortega bowed his head in apology.

"I don't see whatever the rest of you are looking at, but I can sense it beneath me. The air smells and tastes as foul as a crypt. Whatever it is, we've got to get Griffin out of there." Addison squeezed Aisling's shoulder gently. "I've seen this before, but you haven't Ash. You don't have to come inside with us."

"Yes, I do," she said. "He was upstairs in his office when we ran. He didn't come after us, but I could see some part of him was still there."

The oppressive air of the Spanish villa weighed heavily upon her skin, a blanket of malevolent presence with stifling qualities. Her skin tingled as she crossed the threshold, and the smell of blood assaulted her nose.

Tristan took the lead up the stairs, followed by Ortega then Addison, O'Sullivan, Aisling, and several Guardians. A man in cowboy boots caught Aisling's arm when her foot slipped on a step.

"Steady there, ma'am. Marble can be slick. Never did understand why people'd want it for their stairs, of all things."

"The whims of the rich, Noah," replied the woman behind him.

A moment later they reached the office and stepped inside. Aisling caught her breath and stared in silent horror.

The barren study resembled a trash heap. Smashed bookshelves cluttered the floor along with glass from broken liquor bottles. Wooden fragments from the overturned desk's broken leg littered the lavish rug. Only a single furnishing remained untouched, home to the man who slumped within it with fresh blood dribbling down his arms from ragged gouges.

"Why did you bring these fools here, Aisling? I told you I didn't want you anymore. I told you not to come back."

"You're right, Ash. This isn't Griffin. Not at the moment, anyways." Addison surveyed the room. "We've got a possession."

"I'm the same Griffin I've always been, I've just been sick and tired of you fuckin' meddlers interferin' with my life. I sure as fuck don't want to see this little troublemakin' hoor in my house again. Get her out of here, Addison. I'll sell her to you for a pittance of the bullshit she's cost me. How's that? You like exotics, don't you?"

Addison flinched. "I—"

"Don't bother, son. Don't even acknowledge it," Tristan cut in. "Did you bring the Crook, Cameron?"

O'Sullivan nodded. "Of course I did. Knew this would come in handy." The elderly Irish magus opened his briefcase and pulled out the ancient work of artistry.

Aisling vaguely recognized it from countless Egyptian murals and hieroglyphics seen during her days working with Griffin. Supposedly it held power over the spiritual realm.

O'Sullivan caught her worried glance and reached over to pat her hand. "Don't you worry, child. With this, we'll open a doorway to the other side of the veil, then we'll go find Griffin."

"Find him?"

"Sorry. We discussed it along the way in the other vehicle while you rode with Mara," Addison explained in a low tone. "A possession has three stages. First, the victim suffers poor sleep and nightmares."

"Griffin's always slept poorly since we were young. You know that."

"I know. It's no surprise we didn't notice anything. Sometimes there are also hearing or visual disturbances. It's a mindfuck from Hell, meant to break down your awareness and the soul's defenses. Like when you don't take care of your body, and your immune system becomes weak to sickness."

"Mara said he heard Mercedes when he came to pack her up."

"Had he heard anything before that?"

"Sometimes he'd ask if I'd called him from the other room, but I never thought anything of it."

Addison nodded. "The second sign is a little more insidious. He may not have noticed it to make complaints. He'll have trouble crossing wards. Especially wards against evil."

Aisling blanched. Sour acid churned in her stomach, threatening to force its way up her throat. "He always complained about the estate. Kept asking me why I kept it so cold. I thought he'd just become acclimated to Rio, is all. Teased him about it, even."

"Sounds about right. He said the penthouse was hot, too. I use a lot of fire magic wards there. That's two out of three signs. Here's the third—they can't abide the touch of an object imbued by faith and love. Your faith in his love for you is in that ring. The demon didn't realize it when Griffin reached for you. He won't allow it again."

"What can we do?" she whispered, aghast.

"A while back, I defeated a demon on my own, but he had a direct link to our world from Hell through an object. I don't believe that's the case this time. Whoever it is, it's a bloody blight on the Umbra itself, so I assume it's there. When a person is possessed, their soul is sometimes imprisoned, for lack of a better word, while the demon wears their skin. I don't think Griffin is there at all anymore. He went and pissed it off by warning you, so we've got to assume it's overpowered him completely now."

Demon-Griffin peered at them from his seat. He idly tore at the wrist of his right arm with the nails of his left, unflinching.

More than anything she wanted to go to him and heal the hurts inflicted on his body. She stepped toward him but was drawn back by a strong hand at her shoulder.

"No, lass. It's what it wants," O'Sullivan told her. "It will hurt him, but it won't kill him. Hold that thought close."

"I think she came here expectin' to have the chance to suck my cock again. Is that what you were wantin', Aisling? Will you be willin' to go if I take it out for you now?" He chuckled quietly to himself, amused with his own joke.

"I've had enough of this shit from it," Addison grunted. He stepped forward toward the desk. "I'm addressing the entity inside Griffin MacNeil. Who are you, and why are you here?"

The rounded pupils of Griffin's eyes elongated into dark slits. He laughed. "What fun would it be to tell you so soon, mageling?"

Aisling covered her mouth with her hands and fought back the moisture gathering beneath her eyelashes.

Addison removed a flask from the inside of his cloak, uncapped the bottle, and splashed liquid on Griffin. It sizzled upon contact, and odorous steam rose in the air with curls of black smoke.

Griffin bellowed in pain and jerked back, raising both hands to shield his face. "Ah, it burns! Sprite, help me. Don't let them do this to me. You said you'd never let me suffer in pain for as long as you're there."

"Stop it," she whispered.

"Don't let them do this, dove."

"Stop it!" she yelled. Hot tears spilled down over her cheeks. "You get out of Griffin right now!"

"But I am Griffin now." The creature grinned. "I've been with him for months, and let me tell you, wee lass, no treat will ever taste as good as your tits."

Ash had never wanted to puke more.

"Erica, get her back," Noah said.

Her knees weakened beneath her, and a low, tortured sob parted her lips as Erica pulled her away. When she did, Tristan and Noah stepped forward, the two men thrusting out crucifixes. Aisling recognized Latin, even if she didn't understand the words.

"They're going to cast the spirit out," Erica told her. "Stay over here with me."

Aisling couldn't turn her eyes away from the scene despite the uncontrollable trembles overtaking her body. The mages worked together, each of them completing one component of the ritual. Addison chanted in Latin along with his grandfather as Noah and O'Sullivan read from a Holy Bible. Regent Ortega began weaving a complex spell with his hands and chanting in an unfamiliar tongue.

"We cast you out, unclean spirit!" With Addison's shout, an invisible force struck Griffin and contorted his body, slamming him from the desk chair.

"Begone and leave this body," Tristan called.

A nimbus of silver radiance washed over Griffin and hung him suspended in the air. He snarled and snapped with his teeth, spitting at the group of mages.

Ash hadn't attended any kind of church service since her grandmother's funeral, but she prayed harder than she had in all of her life. Blinded by her tears, she watched the spectacle on the other side of the office.

An inhuman laugh rumbled through the room, nearly shaking all of them off balance.

Each flick of holy water from Addison's flask left a red welt against Griffin's face. "Leave this body, foul demon. I command thee, in the name of the Eternal Lady and Lord, leave this place."

The demon ignored it in favor of beaming a lecherous smile at Noah, lips spread wide. "Hey Noah, how did it feel to be Asmodeus's bitch? Why don't you tell them? Tell them all about what you did with Lust's servant. Did it feel good?"

Noah paled. The hand bearing his crucifix wavered.

"Don't listen to him, Noah," Addison said. "The demon can see our insecurities. It'll use them against us. Twist them to its own deranged needs."

The demon's attention jerked back to Addison. He grinned toothily, revealing sharp fangs in his mouth. "Insecurities? Are there any as great as yours? Ah, the great Addison Rhydderch, brought low because of his cock over and over."

Addison leaned forward, placing himself on the demon's level. "You can't get in my head, demon. I've been to Hell and back, and I've already defeated one of your kind. I've owned my mistakes."

"Can your tree slut say the same? Maybe we should bring her back for another visit." Griffin licked his teeth. "And maybe I'll taste her this time."

"Something isn't right," Ortega muttered. "The exorcism should have worked. The demon should be driven out."

"Aww. Are you all going to cry now?" Demon-Griffin mocked. "The great Tristan never cries. Not even when his daughter was beaten within an inch of her life by that cretin he made her marry. All for a prestigious name."

"Addison, can you consult Acacius?" Tristan asked, ignoring the demon's attempts to rile them.

"Already have. He's listening."

For as long as Aisling had known Addison, she'd also known of the dragon linked to his soul in another plane. Acacius sometimes deemed it necessary to share his wisdom, and in other times the aloof dragon chose to make the Welshman puzzle out his own troubles.

"He says it's no normal demon. It's one of the Princes."

"Which?" Ortega asked.

"He doesn't know."

"You better figure it out quick, boyo, as it's the only way to banish him." O'Sullivan turned the Crook of Osiris in his hands and cast his gaze toward Aisling and the woman beside her. "Erica, m'dear, I think now would be a good time."

Erica swung a shotgun from behind her back in the same instant Noah pulled Aisling away to the corner of the room. She twisted in the Guardian's grip to the deafening sound of gunfire. While Aisling shrieked in terror, Erica unloaded a shell at Griffin, pumped the fore-end, and fired again.

Snarling as he rose, his chest smoked with the acrid stench of sulfur. He lunged at the armed woman, but she blew him back again. O'Sullivan's shields repelled the demon while Erica circled around and fired a fourth time.

Addison snapped a gold-flaked stick of chalk in half, passed one to Ortega, and both crouched to draw on the floor. Gold dust glittered from the powdery line when he and Ortega met at the completion of a perfect circle. "Now!"

O'Sullivan called out binding words in the Faerie tongue. Tristan echoed them in Latin and sealed the circle with his own blood. The barrier drawn around Demon-Griffin flared with bright sparks of magical energies and trapped him inside.

The monster captive within hardly resembled the man she loved any longer. It wore his face, but it dropped to the ground on all fours and undulated like a serpent. Its tongue flicked between pointed teeth. "I will pull the flesh from that waifling's bones while fucking her with his cock," it hissed at them all. Once, twice, and a third time it attempted to reach them, and each time the barrier repelled the demon-possessed Collector.

"A nun's ashes and rock salt. Works every time." Erica reloaded the shotgun and glanced toward Ash.

"Listen to me, Aisling," Tristan moved to stand between her and Griffin. He took her face between his hands and turned her horrified, teary gaze to his. "Listen to me. You are the strongest link we have to my grandson right now."

"You're not seriously thinking—" Addison started.

"Yes, Addison, I am," Tristan snapped. "That thing is in deeper than we imagined, and the only way we're going to find Griffin is with someone who holds a lasting tie to him. A more powerful bond than even your love for him."

Aisling felt the gaze of everyone in the room on her. The task ahead fell heavily on her shoulders, and she made no attempt to push it away. A strange calm fell over her.

"Tell me what to do."

Tristan gave her shoulders a pat. "It's no easy thing I'm asking. We need you to send your physical body into the Umbra to find Griffin's spirit. You'll be where the demon dwells."

"I've never faced a demon before," she whispered.

"I know you haven't, but Addison has." Tristan looked at his grandson. "Go with her. Protect her. We'll keep Griffin secure."

"What do I do when I find him?"

"Lead him back," Ortega said. "He will need to fight for his body."

"And I'll try to banish the demon while he's distracting it. Whoever it is," Addison added.

The Regents didn't need to voice the sentiment she saw in their solemn gazes. If she failed, Griffin wouldn't be the only one not coming back. There was a very real chance they would all die. Aisling closed her eyes and thought of her family, swallowing back her terror.

"I'll do it."

"Brave lass." O'Sullivan kissed her brow and Tristan squeezed her hands.

A single stroke from the Crook of Osiris tore open a rift between the Mortal plane and the Umbra. A shadowy, dark realm lurked beyond the gateway, a mirrored grayscale image with minute dashes of spectral color.

"Always knew I'd be using this," O'Sullivan admitted with a faint smile.

Addison stepped closer and offered a hand out to her. "Hold on tight, love, and think of him."

Aisling darted her gaze to Griffin and forced herself to look past his twisted features. "I will find you," she vowed. "I will find you, Griffin, and I will bring you back." She turned to Addison, left hand pressed over her heart. Her eyes closed, and she pictured green-gold eyes full of laughter and mischief. She held on to Griffin's memory and let it guide her.

She stepped forward into the rift, and their world became a silent vacuum.

"I'll find you," Aisling whispered to herself over and over.

Sound and sensation returned in a dizzying whirl as Aisling opened her eyes and waited to acclimate to the strange place. Addison stood alongside her, but he looked as disoriented as she felt by the transition between realms.

Everything mirrored the mortal plane in a reverse image, portraying the study as a black and white photo in grayscale, the world beyond the window composed of mist and swirling vapor. The hypnotic play of light led Aisling to step closer to Addison's side.

"This is why no one travels the Umbra, love. No one but Planeswalkers, and they're a rare breed. It's bloody impossible to find your way through the mist of life that connects each world. Wizards have lost decades in that stuff."

Shadows coalesced into shapes and dancing figures, which receded one moment and advanced toward them in the next. The office shifted and brightened marginally. A dim specter stood by the window without acknowledging them. His thin frame appeared haggard, his eyes sunken. Occasionally, he brought a hand to his thigh and closed his eyes in pain.

"It's an echo," Addison murmured, only to flinch when Mara's voice loudly reverberated through the dismal space.

"*Papá?*" Mara stood framed by the doorway behind them, clothed in the same nightgown she wore in the morning hours. Her bare toes curled anxiously against the floor. "*Papá? I heard the noise again.*"

"An echo?" Aisling said.

Mara appeared small and fragile in the memory. Aisling wanted to call out a warning.

"The Umbra is the sum of all memories. Magical, emotional, and physical. Past, present, and future. It's the glue binding every physical and magical plane. Imprints are left behind wherever a large amount of energy is expended, and true Seers like Krys pull their visions from it."

The memory Griffin jerked around towards his daughter, flinched, and then limped from behind the desk in a way Aisling found oddly familiar. He lurched forward in a shuffle, his steps reminiscent of a marionette resisting the guidance of a puppeteer. "*There's nothin' to fear from that noise, Mara. Nothin' in this house will harm you. Go back to your room, sweetheart.*"

"*But the noise, Papá...*" Mara bridged the distance and clutched her fingers at his shirt, seeking a hug while Griffin stood so still the veins and muscles of his neck became prominent.

He didn't move to comfort her, but his body trembled. "*You need to leave, Mara. Go back to your room.*"

"*Papá, please, I want——*"

The sound of the crack echoed a dozen times over and filled the small but ethereal place with a thunderous noise. Mara reeled and fell to the floor in a sprawl, sobbing and holding her face.

"*You stay the fuck outta my goddamned office!*"

Aisling flinched away and raised her hand to her mouth. "Griffin would never hit Mara. *Ever.*"

After nodding in agreement, Addison swallowed and turned his head. "C'mon, Ash. We won't find him here. It'll be at the heart of a memory that's... It's going to find the one that's the most painful to him. This one is rotten, but it's going to attach to something life-altering. Something that'll break him. That's where we'll find the real Griffin."

"How is this not the worst, Addison? He would never have struck her. Look at him…"

The Griffin in the memory knelt with his head down, face twisted in anguish and grief long after Mara's ghostly imprint faded from the room. He mouthed the word 'please' over and over again, and for the briefest moment, Aisling heard a ghostly chuckle cruelly slide over her senses.

Addison pulled her away from the sight into the misty hall. A mirror showed a dim view of laughing toddlers playing amidst wrapping paper behind cracked and splintered glass. In another picture frame's reflection, Aisling saw herself in a silver dress twirling in Griffin's arms on the dance floor, though the image faded in and out. Smothered.

"Addison, I don't understand. If a demon has Griffin, why keep Mara here? Why let us live?"

"Demons can be similar to the fae. They thrive on bargains, but typically of a darker, more malevolent sort. You and Mara were bargaining chips. Tools for it to use to its own benefit. By hurting Mara, Griffin would do anything it asked to keep her safe a little longer. It had to fight him for the body."

"This is horrible."

"I know, I know. It's what a demon does. They hurt you, and they twist everything you love until the fight is over and you're ready to succumb to their will. We've just got to find him before the fight is over."

A door opened to their left to reveal a torture chamber's dim interior, complete with devices and attached restraints. The air looked oily and hung heavy with the scent of blood and sweat. The shadows within forged vague, disturbing shapes.

Every alarm inside Aisling rang shrill for her to leave. Addison froze with a hand raised to a glass charm hanging from a thin leather cord around his neck.

"What is it?" she whispered.

"Mercedes is summoning the demon. It's him. She's summoned him once before, at the very least. Made a Pact with him of some sort. We can't watch this, Ash. It's risky."

"I thought demons require sacrifices."

"They do." Addison guided her through the shifting hallways. Lights flickered and bounced all around them, growing dim and brightening only to ebb and spread moments later. "Did anyone die in this home in the last couple years?"

"Mercedes had a miscarriage."

"I'd bet my crown there was more to it."

The two mages carefully headed down the steps into the lavish living room.

A younger, fresh-faced Griffin occupied the opulent foyer of the upscale villa. He wore a dress shirt and fine slacks fit for a ball.

"This is when he promised to come back to Ireland," she whispered.

Griffin approached the phantom Mercedes with a grim expression on his face. *"Packin' my things and goin' home, Mercedes."*

"You can't mean that. Griffin, what of your work? Papá and I have done so much to secure your job with the department. Why would you leave it now when you have come so far?"

"I know. I'm sorry for that, Mercy. I feel like the world's biggest eejit for comin' here at all. I love Ash, and I'm goin' back to her. I never meant to hurt you, and I'm sorry for this."

Fragile tendrils as thin as floss seeped from Mercedes toward Griffin. She set aside her coffee and approached him.

"I love you, Griffin. What will I do here without you? Stay with me a night to think it over. Make your decision in the morning."

"I... No, Mercedes... I said I'd be back tomorrow. I plan to pack and leave in the wee hours."

"All right," she agreed too easily.

He resisted the lure, but as phantom Griffin settled at a seat, Aisling and Addison saw additional components splatter into the coffee Mercedes prepared while they discussed his plans to move.

"He slept with her after that and told me he couldn't face you again afterward... I even punched him on his wedding day. We knew she was a bloody brilliant alchemist, but never in a thousand years would I have guessed... I should have known," Addison said, grieved by his own mistakes. "Not once did I question why he acted out of character for so long. Not once."

"She's a monster, and you had no way to know. She can't hurt us anymore. She's dead now," Aisling said. "I won't allow her memory to hurt us anymore either. Let's find him and pull him from this horrid place."

The sight of the opulent front parlor faded away, replaced by an image of a barren cell with a single cot and toilet. Griffin knelt beside the bed and worked on tearing and twisting his thin sheet into a rope.

"I hate mirrors," Addison muttered in a low voice.

Aisling followed his gaze to the rectangle of glass hanging over the tiny sink and agreed with him.

The misty pane played one of her worst memories, a time which should have been full of love and smiles as she shared her greatest news with her fiancé. Instead of celebrating their pregnancy, angry words and threats led to verbal barbs. The Griffin on the floor ceased his work and ran his shaking hands through his hair.

The beating began while the man on the floor began to tie a noose. The sound of their fight filled the room, Griffin's angry voice the loudest while her entreaties for him to fight the poison were garbled and warped.

"You never told me it was so bad, Ash. I…" Addison stared at the scene playing out in the memory.

The sight of Griffin's planned suicide took her breath away. Mute, she stared at the noose and felt as if the ground had been yanked from beneath her. When her attention returned to the mirror—and the echo of the beating she'd endured—the steel returned to her spine.

"It wasn't him, and the demon is showing him the worst of it. Griffin stopped himself, Adds. He pulled away. He resisted it at the end."

"I know, but this is… When Claudia attacked me in the restaurant, she never spoke, only attacked. Poison did this?"

"That and this demon's influence. I remember now, he was mad about how cold it was in the loft. The demon must have been with him even then."

A heavy breath whooshed from Addison's lungs. "They've planned this for a long time. They needed to break him, and to do that, they needed you out of the picture."

"I never blamed him," she said, a note of determination in her voice. "I never blamed him!" Her challenging yell echoed across the room and dispersed the shadowy images with the force of her anger.

Addison eased his arm around her shoulder and drew her close. "We need to keep moving. Does this place have a basem—"

The shifting mists coalesced into a corporeal form. Like a serpent made of darkness, a tail lashed and struck the pair from the side. A scream caught in Aisling's throat as the beast's ominous hiss filled the room.

Addison jerked her away from it and urged her toward safety. "Run!" he cried.

Chapter 39

Jean-Luc stood with his arms folded over his chest in front of the Portal. As soon as he and the Regents had come through to Barcelona with their security detail of Guardians, he had ordered the operators to deactivate it. No one was to come in or out without his permission.

Across from him, Commandant Rivera made angry gestures with his hands.

"This is a farce. Our Vault is now clean, and you have no business here, Justiciar," Domingo said.

"Please, we all know this is not true." The embezzlement scandal had cast a shadow over Barcelona's reputation. "And we also know you are pulling the strings. A puppeteer of the worst sort."

"You found no proof to connect me to that crazy old moron. Whatever he did, I was not involved. I tire of your lies and slander. If you were not a Justiciar—"

"But I *am* a Justiciar, and I am arresting you, Commandant."

Rivera sneered at him. The man clenched his fist, and his knuckles popped within the thin leather glove. "My daughter has been dead less than a week, and I must suffer this indignity?"

The dramatic scene drew an audience. Men and women watched quietly from doorways and the corridors beyond them.

"Go quietly, Domingo. Your treachery is dishonor enough without adding to it by resisting," the Marshal spoke up from across the room. He approached with Regent Durant at his side.

Rosamund smiled. "So it seems the Marshal was not so difficult to pull from his holiday along the coast. How fortunate."

Jean-Luc knew the look of a cornered animal when he saw one. Sweat beaded on Rivera's brow, which he nervously swiped away with a wrist.

How far the mighty have fallen, Jean-Luc thought, taking no small amount of pleasure. The smug bastard had smiled at him too happily when Jean-Luc had arrived to release Griffin MacNeil from Spanish custody. Had Tristan Rhydderch not insisted for him to do nothing more than a simple exchange of custody, he would have placed the entire Vault under his scrutiny back then. Maybe more lives could have been saved if he'd found the corruption earlier.

He should have trusted the feeling in his gut. The mistake would haunt Jean-Luc for the rest of his life as the first and only time he'd ignored his instincts to simply follow an order.

The same instincts told him it was time to move.

"*Fuego,*" Domingo whispered.

Jean-Luc opened his mouth to shout a warning to Rosamund just as an explosion thundered somewhere above them. The ceiling cracked.

Domingo must have organized a contingency plan in the event of the cult's discovery. A single spoken word ignited a dozen magical explosions, each one erupting around the periphery of the Vault. The underground chamber shuddered, the ceiling roared as it came tumbling down, and Luc was surprised to remain standing by the end. Around him, the Portal room lay in ruin. The groans of the wounded filled Jean-Luc's ears, and the metallic scent of blood wafted in the air. Once the dust cloud began to settle, he gained a visual of the few dozen bodies strewn beneath rubble from the shattered ceiling.

"Go after him!" Rosamund cried. She'd protected him and a cluster of innocents within an immense shield. The travelers crouched down within it appeared safe, and so did she.

Giving chase, Jean-Luc raced down unfamiliar hallways, wishing every Vault used the same layout. With Guardians posted at every entrance and exit, he had no idea where the Spaniard hoped to flee.

He discovered Rivera's plan when the two Guardians posted at a side entrance opened fire. A bullet storm flew at Jean-Luc, proving how deeply the corruption tainted the Spanish Vault. Magical fire bolts and crackling lightning whizzed over his head.

A. Payne & N. D. Taylor

Jean-Luc flipped through the air while drawing his firearm. He landed atop the gun-wielding Guardian with the man's neck between his knees. As he took his opponent to the ground, a quick twist snapped the man's neck while he shot the other in the face.

He swore when he saw the messy splatter of blood on his nice suit jacket.

The pursuit led out onto a wide veranda overlooking a tree filled, gated lawn. Cold air slapped against his face, and frost-rimmed grass crunched beneath his feet.

He had his enemy within reach when a rift tore open the air, revealing the shadowy world of the Umbra. The in-between space separating one world from the next became increasingly visible once a broad-shouldered, hooded figure reached through for Rivera.

Cliche, Jean-Luc seethed. The nameless villain's decision to wear an ostentatious crimson cloak offended him as much as the man's immoral activities.

Rivera made a mad dash for his escape route, and Jean-Luc put on a burst of preternatural speed. He narrowly avoided a fiery projectile flung over Rivera's shoulder, receiving only a few scorch marks to his suit jacket.

No you don't, you miserable bastard.

Jean-Luc saw his chance and instinctively lunged. The sensation of diving into ice cold water surrounded his body. Air whooshed from his lungs, his body tingled, and he crossed the final distance in a blink. He pushed through the shadow's syrupy resistance with one outstretched hand, grabbed Domingo Rivera by his ponytail, and jerked him back from the shrinking rift.

A quick blade stroke slit the Commandant's throat from ear to ear, sending out a salty fount of hot blood. Jean-Luc barely had the chance to register what was happening, when the man within the portal rift pressed his palm against the chest of the shocked wizard. Rivera's torso twisted and tore open, shocking Jean-Luc into releasing his catch. When he did, the Portal snapped shut.

Jean-Luc was wrong. It wasn't a rescue; the Planeswalker had come to tie up a loose end.

Chapter 40

Addison pushed Aisling ahead, still holding her hand as they ran.

"Don't stop running, love, no matter wha—" Something coiled about his ankle and jerked. His grip on Aisling's hand tore free and he fell. Hard. With contact between them severed, she vanished and only the demon's raspy breathing remained.

"Fool magus... You have no place here." The entity descended and stared into his soul with a single, reptilian green eye. It stopped his heart cold in his chest, surrounding him with envy, vehemence, and unrivaled hatred. Emotions Addison hadn't experienced in so long.

"I know your name, demon. You have no power over me!"

"Yesss..." the demon hissed. "Perhaps you are unafraid... But the girl is mine!"

A jarring sensation overwhelmed Addison before he could stumble to his feet to perform the banishing ritual. The fog rapidly distorted as the demon thrust him from the Umbra. He struck the wall of the parlor and rattled knickknacks upon their displays.

With his head swimming and ears ringing, Addison pushed to his feet and returned upstairs. He staggered into Erica, but she caught him with one arm.

"You okay, Regent?"

"Don't worry about me. You've got to send me back. Oh Goddess, send me back in. I saw him, and she doesn't have a chance if she fights him alone."

"I will carve your names into her bones. She will die screaming, defiled, loathing you for abandoning her." Appearing less human by the second, demon-Griffin crouched and swayed to the left and right like a cobra confronting a mongoose. His narrow tongue flicked between his teeth as his spine bent, splitting his shirt across the shoulders. Mottled patches of dull scales spread like a virus down his bleeding forearms.

They were too late. Griffin's soul had been completely displaced from his body, and only the demon remained. It leaned back and snapped its head forward to belch a wave of foul-smelling, caustic fluid over the floor. Their circle collapsed as waves of Hellfire rose and swept over the devastated office room.

"You take that side, Addison!" Tristan called. "I'll get this one."

Addison hurried to the other side of the room and redirected the fire away from their allies. The flames writhed perilously close before the two Regents smothered them.

"Everyone back! He's free!"

The Magi quickly vacated the office, preferring a tactical retreat over the risk of succumbing to the rising heat.

"What now?" Noah called over the roaring noise.

"We do everything we can to keep him in this house!"

~*~

Aisling raced through the ominous mists. A cold lump of dread formed in her middle, worsened by her fear for Addison. Blind trust in his words drove her forward. She ran without looking back.

"Griff... I thought I saw..."

She slowed.

"Thought what—Ash!"

A splash and scream bounced around the fog and drew Aisling into another room. Two pews sat before a small family altar in a tiny chapel. Instead of a place of light, she encountered a defiled space. A flicker of orange light drew her gaze to a square cut into the floor.

Griffin's familiar and plaintive voice drew her down the moldy steps into the swirling unknown. She plowed forward through the haze, her ring a gleaming beacon of light as she followed the noise. Moments of silence interspersed between splashes and gasping breaths.

"Come on, lass, come back to me. Please... Y'cant do this to me."

Thick fog dispersed to reveal the memory of an ancient temple, its massive pool spread before her. Across the space, she saw Griffin in muted colors.

"Griffin! Griffin, I'm here!" she called out across the pool between them.

"Please no… I've only just gotten you back, sprite… If you go now… I can't…I can't lose you again… Y'have to come back to me… We've so many more places to see… and ruins to explore… It's not worth it if you're not there." A choked sob escaped Griffin's throat before he dipped down to breathe into the limp body and resume desperate CPR compressions.

Aisling's echo remained motionless despite his tireless efforts, a still and cold little corpse with blue-tinged white flesh.

He shook her and finally collapsed weeping to her chest. "No! No! No!"

"Griffin, no, I'm here!" she called and tried to fight against the restraining lines of dark magic.

Several moments passed of him lying with his face hidden from her view while his shoulders shook with grief. Eventually, the dead doppelganger faded away, and the scene played out anew. He gazed up at the Phantom Aisling, and their fingers touched as priceless treasures exchanged hands.

"I love you," he whispered suddenly to her memory, bowing his head to wait in silence afterward until the demented broken record began anew. *"I don't want to fight anymore. Don't…"*

"No. No, no, no. It didn't happen this way. He saved me. You saved me!" she screamed, struggling harder against the forces pushing against her. "No! I will not let you keep him here in this lie!"

Aisling slashed through the gloom with her left hand and ignited the stones of her ring with a focused explosion of arcane light. Its brilliance split the darkness with a radiant flare, laying frost wherever it touched.

A furious blast of frigid winds transformed the fountain pool into an icy plain. Aisling raced across it, but no matter how fast she ran, the distance never seemed to shrink.

"You win… I…I can't take anymore," he whispered in defeat.

"Griffin! Griffin, love, please don't give up!" Aisling steeled herself, touched her left hand over her heart, and pushed with all the strength she could muster. The room warped, resisted, and then she finally broke through the barrier parting her from the memory constructed for Griffin's torment.

Splitting ice and crackling noises from the rear drew her gaze back over her shoulder. A black fin speared through the glacial floe and sent jagged chunks flying through the air.

With a grunt, she threw herself over the ridge of the pool and hit the ground beside Griffin in the same moment the thick body of the serpent exploded out of the water. Thick, scaled coils dropped down around the broken man and kept her at bay.

Recognition dawned as she stared into the face of Griffin's jailor. The green eye of envy stared unblinking within the face of a serpent she had seen many times before in many bodies. The same beast had followed Griffin from one site to the next, whether in Egypt, Greece, or the Brazilian jungles.

"Griffin, love, please hear me. It's Aisling. *Your* Aisling. I'm here."

"I love you so much, Ash… I love all of you. Liam, Rhiain, Mara… I'm sorry. Promise if I let you have my body, you'll not be hurtin' my family. You let her go. You send her home."

"No!"

Aisling violently lashed out with her magic. An arctic flurry of spears hurtled at the serpentine body.

"You have been a thorn in my side for far too long, little fae spawn."

"You didn't kill me then, and you won't succeed now."

"Look at him. See what you fight for?"

The man Aisling loved resembled a motionless ragdoll, captive in the demon's crushing hold. It slithered closer, its carrion stench mingled with sulfur.

"I'm fighting for love. For *him*, and for a future you couldn't even conceive." *If you can't remember, then I'll remember for you.*

Addison said the Umbra was a place of memories imprinted on the nether. If bad memories left a lasting echo, then good ones had to do the same. The demon had twisted a memory of loss and pain, so Aisling fought to set it back to rights.

"I told a horrible joke when I woke up, Griffin. Do you remember?"

"Th-that's it... N-no v-v-visits to t-the Lo-loch for us-s-s-s. N-Nessie will be n-n-next." The faint echo of her chattering voice whispered through the darkness.

Aisling focused on Griffin's listless face and relived the beauty of a moment lost from his memory. She used it to push away the lie. "For a moment, I saw it, the beautiful light of whatever lies beyond. I knew I'd see my mother again. But you were here, Griffin, and you called me back."

The demon swung its massive horned head around sharply at the sound of the phantom voice of a perfect memory coming to the surface. The carefully spun illusion of the Egyptian temple began to disintegrate into pale smoke as Aisling pit her truths against the false recollection.

"He is mine, and I will not relinquish my hold. This one's soul belongs with us and so shall yours."

The demon flung Griffin aside to the floor and opened its tooth-filled maw to exhale a furious stream of fetid water. It struck with the intensity of a high pressure jet, and Aisling's shields barely managed to deflect the acidic blast.

"He didn't give up on me then, and I refuse to believe he'll give up on me now."

The enormous snake lunged and struck her shield. It twisted to feint, biting at her to finish the fight it began years ago. It took her on in an exhausting game of cat and mouse without demonic magic, each snap and strike forcing Aisling back another step. All the while, Griffin lay abandoned, a gray and quiet apparition against the otherwise vivid memory held dear to them both.

Her magic crackled in a spreading latticework of frost against the demon's scaled hide. As it came in again, light glinted from her engagement ring upon its snout, raising sulphur-scented smoke plumes and steam. She threw herself to the side upon the floor hard, rolling away as fanged jaws snapped above her head.

"You can't have him, and you can't have me either!" she screamed, whipping her hand through the air. Heavy hailstones pounded with merciless force against the serpent, but it seemed unbothered.

The demon led her on a dance of skill, darting in and out between the massive temple columns despite its greater size. He undulated from side to side and struck from the left, only to miss and smash head first into a pillar. The collision split the marble and sent fragments of the pillar flying. Furious words carried on rotten breath filled the air.

"I will drag him to Hell. I will gnaw the flesh of your loved ones. I will make you watch. I will devour your kin."

The next hiss carried forth on a bloom of black fire. Aisling shrieked out a defiant note and gestured her arms forward to block. The shimmering mana shield ignited in rainbow colors, and for a moment, it even seemed to hold the flames at bay, her fae magic against the power of Hell.

Another fiery exhale from the demon seared through her shield and scorched her palms. The protective shell burst, exposing her to a world of pain.

In one moment, she faced certain doom, and in the next, Griffin threw himself between them.

"You won't harm her."

Aisling took cover behind the spirit's back until the inferno fizzled out. When the last flicker of flame vanished, Griffin collapsed to the floor at her feet.

And it was up to her again to defend him. Furious, she rose to her feet.

"I am Aisling, daughter of Rhiannon, child of the Sidhe!" she declared loudly. "And I love him. I refuse to let you take him. I *deny* you!" Little sparks of color began to shine within the swirling mists, revealing fae drawn to her presence. They brought color to the otherwise grayscale realm.

The demon opened its mouth again, but the light from her ring forced it to recoil anew. For the first time in years of possessing the treasure crafted from love, given in devotion, and worn with dedication, she took it off and held the silver band tightly in her fist.

"I deny you him, Leviathan!" She took a risk by using its true name, but overwhelming confidence flooded her with absolute certainty. "I deny you thrice, Leviathan, and I command you to return to the depths from whence you came!

You will not have him. You will not have me. You will have *nothing!*"

Without jealousy in her heart, Leviathan, Prince of Envy, held no power over her. Aisling's last resentments had died with Mercedes, perishing with the only woman to ever have anything she coveted—Griffin.

Leviathan's single green eye became a bright red, furious pinprick. The desperate act brought the beast toward her in a lunge, wide open maw revealing the cavernous space beyond its fangs. A rotten stench breezed over her. Time seemed to slow.

"I love you, Griffin."

She threw her left hand out and sent her blood-smeared ring flying forward with a wintry burst of power. The reaction was instantaneous when the metal circle disappeared down its yawning maw. Brilliant emerald flames and silver burned the hellish entity from the inside, cracking through its scales and melting away its flesh.

Aisling screamed as the demon made a final lunge. Her shields buckled. She found herself hurled back in the same moment Leviathan burst into a thousand smoking pieces. Air rushed around her, mist swirled, and then she struck a rough wall.

Everything went black.

Chapter 41

When Aisling awakened from her ordeal, it was in the silence of a Healers' ward patient room in Barcelona. Sunlight illuminated a pristine room and an adjacent bed made with tidy ivory linens. Addison slumped in a chair opposite her with his head slowly descending toward his chest, eyes closed.

"Griffin!" Aisling bolted up, tossed back the blankets, and swung her legs from the bed. Her legs nearly crumpled beneath her.

Addison jumped to his feet and caught her by the upper arms. "You shouldn't be standing so soon."

"Where's Griffin? Tell me he's all right, please!"

"Lay back down, Ash."

She swatted his hands when he attempted to place her back onto the bed. "No, Addison. I want to see him. I *need* to see him."

"They're working on him. You don't need to see that. Just sit tight for a moment, all right?"

"What do you mean they're working on him? How long has it been?"

"About a day."

"The last thing I remember is hurling my ring down that abomination's gullet and watching him burn from the inside out." It hurt to let the symbol of their enduring love go.

"Well, it worked. You and Griffin are both free of demonic taint."

"Then please take me to him."

"We need to talk first. I don't—"

"*Now*, Addison. Please." A sensation of urgency flit around her senses, telling her she had to be at Griffin's side. Had to see him with her own eyes. Nothing else would banish those final memories of his exhausted soul.

THE COLLECTOR'S TREASURE

Addison sighed but offered no further argument. Aisling moved on unsteady legs, but her determination carried her even when her balance faltered.

He led her into an airy room with a single bed beside the window. Limp and motionless, Griffin lay on the hospital bed, the pallor of his skin nearly the same shade as the white sheets. A Healer at the bedside held a pen light above his eyes. When she received no reaction, she glanced up and shook her head.

"He's... They believe he's soul-dead, Ash," Addison said in a pained voice. "That his body hasn't caught up yet to realize his soul is gone. But I don't think that's the case. I think... I just don't think it's the case. He's too stubborn to go that way."

Aisling pulled away and brushed past the Healer assessing Griffin's pulse. "Please leave us," she whispered on a trembling breath. Tears leaked down her cheeks.

The nurse left without complaint.

Perched on the bedside, Aisling held Griffin's hand to her cheek while she fought back sobs. The pressure built and built in her chest.

No... No! I banished the demon. He should be awake. He should be fine...

"I said leave us!" she snapped out suddenly. Her fierce gaze focused on a seemingly empty corner.

Addison shut the door gently once he stepped inside and gave a pause as if wavering between proceeding forward or backing into the hallway again. "Aisling, you did everything for him that you could. I'm sorry... I... Griffin would be grateful."

The pregnant pause and his caution didn't soften the blow, nor did it lighten the ache in Aisling's heart.

"Sometimes it isn't possible to return from the Umbra once a soul has been trapped for so long of a time. We've had the best spiritual Healer from India here for hours. The very best we could find."

The Umbra's most unfortunate victims eventually lost their physical forms and became poltergeists, terrifying specters that haunted the in-between separating the Mortal realm from the Umbra.

"He's not gone!" she yelled.

"Ash—"

Again her gaze shifted to the corner of the room, away from Griffin, and her gaze narrowed. "I told you to leave! You can't have him!"

Addison swept his blue eyes over the corner and stared for a while. "There's no one there, Ash."

Whether by her fae blood or because she had once been dead herself, Aisling clearly perceived the cu sith lurking in the corner. The Faerie hound was easily as large as a young bull with a thick and shaggy coat of dark blue-green fur. He observed without interrupting, dark brown eyes focused on Griffin.

"He's not dead, Lachlan. He's breathing and his heart is beating. If his soul is out there, isn't it your job to shepherd it back home? You were his godfather!" she yelled at the giant hound. "I wouldn't let Hell have him, and I'll be damned if I let you!"

The dog rose onto all fours and waited patiently throughout the chastisement.

Understanding dawned on Addison's face. "If *he's* here, then trust me. He looked for Griff, too, on the other side."

Reality shimmered between them as Lachlan stepped from beneath his magical veil.

Addison sharply inhaled and darted his gaze toward Aisling. "I didn't even see him there."

The hound's claws made an audible tap over the tiled floor when he stepped toward Ash and touched his warm face to her shoulder. He passed her a moment later and laid his furry muzzle against the linens, not as a looming reaper waiting to collect the dead, but in the fashion of a loyal companion holding vigil at its master's bedside.

"I couldn't save him…"

Addison set his hand on her shoulder. "Ash, you did enough. All you could."

"No, I didn't! Enough would have been fighting for him when we were kids. Enough would have been realizing sooner Mercedes had tricked us, and enough would have been saving him! I have to tell Mara that I couldn't keep my promise. I have to look at the children and tell them their father is never going to come back."

Aisling threw herself upon Griffin's chest in a sobbing heap, face buried against his throat.

"Please," she whimpered brokenly. "Please, Griffin, please don't leave me. Please don't leave us."

Later, a doctor and a Healer attempted to coerce her from the room, but Lachlan's rumbling growl bid them to leave and earned her a little more time. Eventually, he touched her cheek with his warm nose and faded from sight, leaving her behind in a lonely and quiet room.

"I love you," Ash whispered. "I will always love you…"

Wherever Griffin's soul had gone, she prayed he could hear her.

Epilogue

In the days following the discovery in Barcelona, Regent Ortega offered to step down, although he had been cleared of any wrongdoing. A full inquiry occurred, but the Board refused to accept his resignation. He remained and devoted his new purpose to ferreting out any remaining sleeper sects in the Vault.

Tristan and the Board tasked Jean-Luc with ending the Diabolists and their hired hands.

The men in power kept the truth under wraps, unable to predict the outcome of revealing ties between each group. Would the revelation make the deceived Inquisitors even more bloodthirsty, or would the shamed mage-hunters slowly diminish on their own?

The identity of the Planeswalker who had arrived to kill Domingo Rivera remained a mystery. Thinking back on the encounter, Jean-Luc couldn't shake the sneaking feeling of familiarity around the cloaked assailant. He couldn't put his finger on the exact detail, but he felt as if he'd met him before. When they next crossed paths, he planned to be ready.

The Spanish home in Valencia was razed to the ground, sanitized, and blessed by multiple wizards. After that was done, Addison pleaded for Calliope to pay the area a visit to dispense her own unique magic.

In Brazil, many Magi opposed the release of the world's oldest Revenant. When news finally leaked to the vampire covens, it became impossible to conceal the identity of the tomb's single living inhabitant. They stationed additional Guardian forces at the site in El Dorado, armed with tools to safeguard the precious historical monument from vampires' meddling fingers. Or worse.

A close vote from the Regency Board eventually decided against awakening King Midas thanks to a compelling argument from Dahlia. The Board declared him to be unsafe, determining his secrets weren't worth the risk. He could become another generation's problem. The suspended activities slowly began to resume, but things weren't the same without Griffin MacNeil.

Luisa reluctantly placed his job on the open market and mourned his loss.

Thanks to their reforged ties with the Wakani, El Dorado gained additional protection from the nagual. Warriors from each village rotated in and out, most often found stalking through the jungles surrounding the site rather than within it. Felipe conveyed on his next visit that many of their women were pregnant, and thus it was all the more important to safeguard their home while lacking so many from their able ranks. The baby boom's rare occurrence put their warriors on edge, lessened their numbers, and made the rainforest unsafe for any menace intending to cause the Wakani or the Collectors harm. A new generation of were-jaguars would soon be born, increasing their numbers.

The joyous news was also unsettling... Had the tribe received a sudden blessing, or was it an omen alluding to the danger soon to come?

~*~

Aisling sat on the crescent curve of white sand and stared over turquoise waters with little appreciation. Three weeks without a change in Griffin's condition gave her reason to expect the worst outcome. Her last visit had ended with her in tears until Luisa had brought her back home. They celebrated Mara's sixth birthday as well as they could, but it wasn't the same. Not without him.

The children played quietly a few feet away with shovels and buckets. Liam gleefully brought every hermit crab he could find to the sandcastle his sisters built and clapped his hands when the small crustaceans burrowed inside.

Occasionally, Mara stared toward their personal dock, but the little girl always shook her head and resumed her silent play. Griffin's firstborn may not have been Aisling's daughter by blood, but she made a welcomed presence within their island home, and Aisling loved her as her own.

For her family, she had to be strong. She watched them with a quiet smile, only to turn her head to an approaching motorboat's noise. Their evening visitor came unexpected, so she rose and lifted a hand to shade her eyes from the setting sun. An unfamiliar green boat rocked against their dock while a masculine figure limped down the wooden path.

"Griffin…" Aisling whispered in disbelief. Her book fell from slack fingers and hit the beach with a soft thud. "Griffin!" She rushed across the sand and threw herself into his arms as the children's jubilant cries filled the evening air.

She didn't know how he'd come back to them, and she didn't care. He swept her into a tight embrace and buried his face against her dark hair as three sets of bare feet pounded the sand.

In the shade of a palm, two figures lurked and watched the overdue reunion. Lachlan leaned against the tree with a small, green-clothed figure perched upon his shoulder. The jolly, red-haired leprechaun puffed his pipe and chuckled.

"A fine sight to see the lot of them together again."

"Aye…it is. Told ye I'd find him. Plan to restore the charm to his coin?"

"Nae. He needs my luck no longer. He's made his own now. The only treasures needed by Griffin MacNeil are right there, lad."

Jack blinked from sight after the two fae exchanged knowing looks. Lachlan remained a moment longer, then he shimmered into his true guise and bounded away to let the family have their moment.

They had more than earned it.

About the Authors

VIENNE SAVAGE is a pseudonym for the spicier work of A. Payne and N.D. Taylor.

As a fantasy novel and horror movie enthusiast, NICOLE TAYLOR enjoys writing as an outlet for her creativity. The works of Tolkien have inspired her and remain some of her favorite novels. She is a video gamer by nature but also enjoys jogs outdoors, animals, and renaissance festivals. Nicole is currently a registered nurse in Texas and the mother of two beautiful children.

ALISHA PAYNE loves to read and has always had a fondness for creative writing. She loves reading a whole range of genres and authors from Tolkien to James Rollins, and blames her love for reading on her mother, who introduced her to the worlds of Pern and Xanth. Alisha is a former Petty Officer of the United States Navy, which is where she met her wonderful husband. She currently resides with her family in Virginia.